All of a sudden, Sam hauled her into his lap.

He held her there in the firm circle of his powerful arms. "Shh, Élise. It's going to be all right. I'm not going to allow anything to happen to you."

"How...how can...you promise that?" she gasped out. She couldn't take a deep breath, couldn't breathe at all...

"I promise it," he murmured. "I promise."

His big, blunt fingers pressed through the fabric of her dress and into the tight muscles of her back. He gathered her closer to him, and she curled up against the hardness of his chest. Just as her breaths began to calm, his hand cupped her cheek and tilted her face toward his. Then, his lips touched hers.

Her own reaction shocked her. She should have pulled away, slapped him. But she did none of that.

Instead she melted against him. His lips transferred calmness and strength into her. They glided over her mouth in a gentle caress, exploring, tasting, soothing. He tasted smooth and warm and sweet.

How could such a man, such a large masculine man, taste sweet? But he did. He was *delicious*. She gripped his coat in her hands and pulled herself even closer to him.

Praise for the Novels of Jennifer Haymore

THE ROGUE'S PROPOSAL

"4½ stars! Top pick! Haymore secures her reputation for crafting original, suspenseful, highly sensual love stories...Readers looking for solid writing and action/adventure with an edge of the erotic need look no further." **—RT Book Reviews**

"A must-read...Once again, Ms. Haymore has written a series that is sure to capture your heart and will linger in your soul long after you read the last page." **—MyBookAddictionandMore.com**

THE DUCHESS HUNT

"4½ stars! Top pick!...Emotional, sensual, and enchanting, this tale of forbidden love is a romance to savor. Appealing characters, a beautiful, unconventional love story and family dynamics—as well as deft plotting and depth of emotion—make this a keeper." **—RT Book Reviews**

"She grabs the reader from the first page to the last page and holds them in awe as the multifaceted plot comes together...I can hardly wait to see what the House of Trent has in store next." **—MyBookAddictionReviews.com**

PLEASURES OF A TEMPTED LADY

"4½ stars! Wonderfully realistic characters, adventure, passion, and unexpected plot twists...another delightful entry in the Donovan series." **—RT Book Reviews**

SECRETS OF AN ACCIDENTAL DUCHESS

"4½ stars! Haymore's characters leap off the pages...Written with gentleness and emotional strength, it's a creative romance readers will not soon forget." **—RT Book Reviews**

CONFESSIONS OF AN IMPROPER BRIDE

"Beautifully rendered characters, lush sensuality, and a riveting story line...gets Haymore's new series off to a delightful start."
—*Library Journal*

"4½ stars! Top pick! Haymore carefully crafts an original 'second chance at love' romance that showcases her creativity and understanding of what readers want. Her three-dimensional characters and their depth of emotion strengthen an already powerful plot. Those new to Haymore's work will be enchanted."
—*RT Book Reviews*

A SEASON OF SEDUCTION

"4½ stars! Haymore uses the Christmas season as an enhancing backdrop for a mystery/romance that is both original and fulfilling. Her fresh voice and ability to build sensual tension into lively love stories...make this tale shine."
—*RT Book Reviews*

A TOUCH OF SCANDAL

"Jennifer Haymore's books are sophisticated, deeply sensual, and emotionally complex. With a dead-sexy hero, a sweetly practical heroine, and a love story that draws together two people from vastly different backgrounds, *A Touch of Scandal* is positively captivating!"
—**Elizabeth Hoyt,** *New York Times* **bestselling author**

A HINT OF WICKED

"Sweep-you-off-your-feet historical romance! Jennifer Haymore sparkles!"   —**Liz Carlyle,** *New York Times* **bestselling author**

"A unique, heart-tugging story with sympathetic, larger-than-life characters, intriguing plot twists, and sensual love scenes."
—**Nicole Jordan,** *New York Times* **bestselling author**

Also by Jennifer Haymore

A Hint of Wicked
A Touch of Scandal
A Season of Seduction

Confessions of an Improper Bride
Once Upon a Wicked Night (ebook)
Secrets of an Accidental Duchess
Pleasures of a Tempted Lady

The Devil's Pearl (ebook)
The Duchess Hunt
His for Christmas (ebook)
The Rogue's Proposal
One Night with an Earl (ebook)

The Scoundrel's Seduction

A House of Trent Novel

BY

JENNIFER HAYMORE

FOREVER

NEW YORK   BOSTON

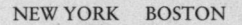

Copyright © 2014 by Jennifer Haymore
Excerpt from *The Duchess Hunt* © 2013 by Jennifer Haymore

Forever
Hachette Book Group
237 Park Avenue
New York, NY 10017
HachetteBookGroup.com

Printed in the United States of America

First Edition: May 2014
10 9 8 7 6 5 4 3 2 1

OPM

Forever is an imprint of Grand Central Publishing.
The Forever name and logo are trademarks of Hachette Book Group, Inc.

The Hachette Speakers Bureau provides a wide range of authors for speaking events. To find out more, go to www.hachettespeakersbureau.com or call (866) 376-6591.

The publisher is not responsible for websites (or their content) that are not owned by the publisher.

ATTENTION CORPORATIONS AND ORGANIZATIONS:

Most Hachette Book Group books are available at quantity discounts with bulk purchase for educational, business, or sales promotional use. For information, please call or write:

Special Markets Department, Hachette Book Group
237 Park Avenue, New York, NY 10017
Telephone: 1-800-222-6747 Fax: 1-800-477-5925

For my better half, Lawrence. It's been a rough couple of years, but you've been by my side, holding my hand, the whole time. I can't tell you how much that means to me.

Acknowledgments

A huge thank-you to my editor, Michele Bidelspach, for her brilliance and insight, and to Megha Parekh and everyone at Grand Central Publishing. You guys are the absolute best! Thanks to my beta readers, Kate McKinley and Cindy Benser. Without your advice and support, I'd be terrified to let my books out into the world. And to my loyal readers . . . thank you. You truly are my inspiration.

Chapter One

❧❦❧

$\mathcal{S}$amson Hawkins eyed the chamber of his pistol, then lowered it to his lap, glancing at the lad sitting beside him in the unmoving carriage. Laurent stared straight ahead, his forehead creased with worry and his eyes shining with some emotion Sam couldn't name. The boy was young— only fifteen—and new to being in the field.

Sam's lips firmed, and he looked away, thrusting aside the impulse to mutter something comforting. Laurent had chosen this life for himself. It wasn't a life for the weak but for the hard and pitiless. Sam never forgot that, and neither should Laurent, if he wished to survive.

Sam looked out the carriage window, scanning up the back wall of the opulent Mayfair town house until his gaze snagged on the second-story window. The window appeared innocuous enough, with the glow of the lamps inside the room casting golden light through the indigo silk curtains.

The Viscount Dunthorpe was in that room right now,

by himself. Perhaps reading, perhaps drinking. Perhaps engaged in more nefarious pursuits, such as treachery and treason. Waiting for Sam—or, more correctly, for Sam's alias.

Waiting for death, though he didn't know it yet.

Sam drew in a long breath, and his fingers tightened around the grip of his pistol.

"Watch for my signal," he told Laurent in a low voice. "It should come after the first shot. I'll be down thirty seconds after I give it. As soon as I am inside, double-check the streets and ensure everything's clear." He tucked his pistol into an inner pocket of his coat.

"Aye."

He met Laurent's gaze evenly. "When all's said and done, it shouldn't take more than five minutes. If a quarter of an hour passes and I haven't returned, you and Carter know what to do."

"I understand."

Sam's fingers curled over the door handle, but Laurent grabbed his forearm. "Hawk?"

He glanced back at the boy, arching his brows expectantly.

"Good luck."

Sam pressed his lips together and gave the boy a tight nod.

"We must do this. We must keep the Regent safe."

Laurent was trying to convince himself they were doing the right thing. "Yes, lad," Sam said quietly. It was true—this was the right thing to do. Dunthorpe required elimination. The man had brought about too much death and misery already, and if he remained alive, he would be the cause of much, much more.

Sam slipped out of the carriage. In measured, unhurried strides, he walked around the corner to the front of the town house. It was late, and the streets weren't as busy as at midday, but this was London—a city that never completely slept. He took thorough stock of the people who passed him—a woman flanked by two small children, the three of them huddled against the chill. A man hurrying down the street. A rubbish wagon, a closed carriage, and a handful of men on horseback. None of them paid him any heed.

He walked up the four stairs and stepped onto the town house's landing. Then, as if he were here on civilized business, he knocked on the door.

A manservant answered. The butler, Sam knew. Name was Richards.

"May I help you?"

"Denis Martin," Sam said, layering on a thick French accent. He'd learned the language as a child and had spent so many years on the Continent that he could speak the language fluently and as flawlessly as a native. "His lordship expects me."

"Of course, sir." Richards's expression didn't change, but there was a slight flicker of something in his eyes. The French weren't the most popular of people in England right now, and this man didn't particularly approve of a frog-eater visiting his master.

The butler stepped aside to allow Sam into the entry hall. Sam kept his hat low over his brow, his face turned away and in shadows.

"May I take your hat and coat, sir?"

"*Non.* It is not necessary. My message is a quick one." With a flick of his wrist, he gestured toward the interior of the house, then toward the front door. "I shall be in and out in a matter of moments."

"Very well. Right this way."

Sam followed the servant up a narrow set of stairs, then down a corridor lit sparsely with two gilded wall sconces set widely apart. They stopped at the elegant door at its end, and Richards knocked before opening the door to the gruff, "Yes?" from its other side.

Sam waited in a shadow between the sconces, his gaze lowered.

"Mr. Martin is here, sir."

There was a pause, long enough to make the hairs on the back of Sam's neck crawl.

"Enter, Martin."

Richards opened the door wider, moving aside to allow Sam to pass. Sam stepped into the drawing room.

Once inside, he raised his head. As always, he scanned his surroundings. He'd been in this room before, conducting preliminary information gathering. Nothing had changed—the furniture crowding the place bordered on ostentatious, with much carved oak and gilt and silk and velvet upholstering. The many-paned window hung on the opposite wall, large and square and covered by that indigo curtain. He pictured Laurent down there, anxiously awaiting him.

Laurent wouldn't need to wait long. In minutes, Sam would be back in the carriage and they'd be fading into the night.

His gaze moved to his target. Viscount Dunthorpe was in his late forties, with a full head of gray hair and dark, penetrating eyes that let nothing slip past. He was well known for his biting cynicism and cold wit and as one of the most brilliant debaters in parliament.

He was also a traitor.

"Lord Dunthorpe." Keeping his French accent firmly in place, Sam held out his hand. "It is an honor to finally make your acquaintance."

His face impassive, the viscount took Sam's hand. The handshake was terse and businesslike. Dunthorpe turned to his servant. "That will be all, Richards. You may retire for the evening."

After the butler left, Dunthorpe gazed at Sam, his expression cold and calculating. Sam schooled his own features to absolute flatness. He needed to delay for approximately sixty seconds. That would give Richards sufficient time to walk to his quarters in the attic.

"Do you have the schedule?" Dunthorpe asked.

"*Oui*, I do," Sam said gruffly.

Dunthorpe held out his hand, palm open. "Give it over," he commanded. He spoke as a man accustomed to authority.

Sam glanced meaningfully at the tea service he'd seen placed on a round table in the corner. "Will you invite me to tea, milord?"

Dunthorpe crossed his arms over his chest and gave Sam an arch look. "Indeed, I hadn't intended to do any such thing."

Sam rubbed his frigid hands together. He hadn't worn gloves for a reason. "It is very cold outside. Brandy, then?"

Dunthorpe narrowed his eyes. "*French* brandy? What do you take me for, a common smuggler?"

No, this man dealt in much more serious crimes. Sam shook his head. "*Mais non*," he said gravely. "Of course not, milord."

Dunthorpe sneered. "You haven't even removed your hat. You don't look at all like a man interested in settling down for a nice cup of tea or a nip of brandy. You look like a man prepared to do your duty and then scuttle away in the event I should decide you know too much."

Well, then. Already hurling threats. Sam supposed that one had been meant to infuse some kind of fear into him, but it hadn't worked. He had dealt with men of Dunthorpe's ilk too often.

He'd given Richards enough time. By now the man was entering his chamber, and in another few seconds, he would be donning his nightcap and preparing for bed.

"*Alors.* In that case, I shall hand over the plans, monsieur." Sam reached into his coat. His fingers slid against the cold metal barrel of his pistol before he clasped the edge of the folded pages. He drew them out and held them out to Dunthorpe.

The man snatched the pages and opened them greedily. Sam's lip would have curled in disgust if he'd allowed it. The bastard held such enthusiasm for destroying everything the British held dear.

In truth, these papers contained a plethora of false statements that made Sam grind his teeth. The powers that be had decided it would be "too traumatic" should the populace hear the truth about their national hero, who'd served as an officer of the British Navy for eighteen years. In fact, the only man Dunthorpe had ever served was himself. He cared only about his own gain. He'd been selling secrets to the French since he was a youth, and now he had organized this conspiracy, all for personal political and economic gain.

Deceiving the populace was something that ranked

low on Sam's list of preferred activities, but his superiors wanted to show Dunthorpe, this traitor, as a hero of the people. These documents would serve as "proof" that he had died defending the Regent, not embroiled in a profitable scheme to murder him.

It wasn't Sam's place to question his superiors. He never had, and he probably never would. He was here to follow orders, and he would do so, like he always did. This was his life, spent defending the greater good...despite the concessions that needed to be made in order to do so.

"What's this?"

Sam watched Dunthorpe skim the papers, his movements growing more frantic, his eyes widening at what he was reading—all the sordid details about the plot, with the slight twist eliminating Dunthorpe from the list of those at fault and instead pointing to him as the hero.

"You bastard. This isn't the schedule." He flung the papers away. They fluttered to the floor as Dunthorpe lifted dark, furious eyes at him. "Who are you?" he growled.

Sam raised a brow. His heart wasn't even beating hard. He might as well have been sitting in his desk chair reading the *Times*.

What did this say about him? If nothing else, it said that he was too far gone to ever feel truly human again.

He shrugged and said softly, using his own, English-accented voice, "I am a concerned citizen. For God, king, and country, my lord. We cannot let you destroy it."

He reached into his coat again, this time drawing out his weapon, cocking it at the same time. But Dunthorpe was faster than his aging appearance made him out to be. The man scrambled backward, hands fumbling with the desk drawer behind him. He jerked it open and yanked out his own pistol as Sam advanced on him, aiming.

Sam possessed the advantage. He had plenty of time. His heartbeat had still not increased in tempo. He was perfectly calm.

He squeezed the trigger while Dunthorpe's gun was still pointed at the floor.

The resulting *boom* of gunfire echoed through Sam's skull, loud enough to rouse every Londoner in a half-mile radius. Dunthorpe lurched backward and slammed into the desk, his body flailing as if he were a rag doll before crumpling to the carpeted floor.

For the first time, Sam's heart kicked against his ribs. *Now* he needed to hurry. Needed to vanish before the authorities were summoned, before Richards showed his face in this room. Sam didn't want to hurt the butler— there was no evidence that he had been privy to any of Dunthorpe's traitorous deeds.

Sam glanced at Dunthorpe's fallen body, saw that the shot had been clean, straight through the man's heart. He quickly bent down to check for a pulse. The viscount was already dead.

Rising, Sam strode to the window and shook the curtains to signal Laurent that he was on his way down. Then he turned and made for the door.

A noise stopped him in his tracks. A tiny, feminine whimper. One he wouldn't have heard had every one of his senses not been on high alert.

He homed in on the source of the noise, turning to that little round table tucked into the corner. It was covered with a silk tablecloth whose edges brushed the carpeted floor.

In two long strides, he was at the table. He ripped the tablecloth away, sending the china tea service that had lain upon it crashing to the floor. Hot tea splashed against his boots, steaming when it made contact with the cold leather.

It smelled damn good—strong and brisk. He wished Dunthorpe had offered him some.

A woman cowered beneath the table.

A small, blond, frail-looking woman dressed in white and curled up into a tight ball, as if she might be able to make herself so tiny he wouldn't be able to see her.

Goddammit. A *woman*. Sam ground his teeth.

She glanced up at him, her midnight-blue eyes shining with terror. "Please," she whispered. "Please."

Her slight French accent clicked everything into place. He knew who she was, of course. It was the surprise of seeing her so out of her element—cowering under a table—that had shocked him into not recognizing her immediately. He'd laid eyes on her once before, when he'd been watching Dunthorpe's movements. A month ago, she'd been on Dunthorpe's arm as they'd strolled into the Royal Opera House.

It was Lady Dunthorpe, Dunthorpe's beautiful, elegant, cultured *French* wife. She'd emigrated from France during the Revolution, after her entire family had suffered the wrath of the guillotine. She'd been rescued, sent to relatives who had found sanctuary in England, and had married Dunthorpe ten or eleven years ago. It was then that Dunthorpe's ties to the French had grown much stronger.

Because, of course, she was in league with him. She must be.

She wasn't supposed to be here tonight. She'd been at her residence in Brighton and wasn't due back in London for another week. Men had been watching the house for days, and no one had reported her entering or exiting the building.

Bloody hell.

"Get up," he told her brusquely.

Her eyes flicked toward Dunthorpe, who lay on the floor, blood seeping across his chest and turning his gray coat black. She drew in a terrified, stuttering breath. But she didn't get up.

Sam considered his options. Killing her with Dunthorpe's pistol was the first idea that came to mind. The odds were that she was as guilty as Dunthorpe was.

But Sam had drawn solid lines between those acts he would and would not commit. He would steal, lie, torture, and assassinate in the interests of king and country. He would not commit cold-blooded murder of an innocent British citizen, even to save his own hide. He would not perform any act that would put a member of his family in danger. And he would not kill a woman.

Those lines were all he had left—all he had to use as the threads by which he grasped on to the unraveling spool of his humanity.

Killing her was out of the question.

He could leave her here.

But she knew too much. Just from the short conversation he'd had with Dunthorpe, she would have learned enough to put everything at risk.

That left the only other option, one that was almost as unpalatable as the other two. He had to bring her with him.

"Get up," he repeated. His voice sounded harsh even to his own ears.

"I...don't...Please, I..." She moaned, appearing to make a valiant effort to follow his command but failing, her limbs trembling too violently to support her.

He jammed his pistol back into his coat pocket and crouched down beside her, aware that his time was already up. They needed to leave this place. *Now.*

"I'm not going to hurt you," he told her, and he prayed that it was true. "But I need you to come with me."

She made a little moaning sound of despair. With a sigh, Sam scooped her into his arms and rose. God, she was a little thing. Light as a feather. But she was stiff in his arms.

"I won't hurt you," he said again. Although he didn't blame her for not believing him. How could he? She'd just witnessed him kill her husband in cold blood.

He turned to the door, to the only escape from this room, and froze, tucking Lady Dunthorpe's rigid, shaking body tightly against him.

Running footsteps resounded on the wooden floor of the outside corridor, and then the door flew open.

Damn it. He'd run out of time.

* * *

The enormous man's hands, firm and unyielding, held Élise pressed against his body. No man had ever carried her before. She wouldn't have considered it unpleasant had it not been for the circumstances.

This man was dangerous. A killer. He'd killed Dunthorpe.

Dunthorpe. Her husband. She no longer had a husband. Dunthorpe was dead. She was…She was…a *widow*…

Her body folded in on itself, her arms tucked tightly into her chest. As if by making herself smaller, she could disappear right out of this terrible moment. Her breaths came in harsh pants, small whimpers erupting from her throat.

The man stopped short, and the strong arms around her squeezed her more tightly against him. She smelled fresh grasses underlying the pervading sharp tang of gunpowder.

The door burst open. Richards stood at the threshold, half dressed, pointing a pistol at the man who held her.

"What…? Lady…Lady Dunthorpe?" Richards blurted out.

The man holding her didn't move. "The lady is injured," he said calmly. "I must take her to safety."

Élise started to protest, but the man squeezed her tighter—a clear warning that made her freeze.

She needed to do something—to get away. But she didn't know what…or how. If she said anything, or tried to shimmy out of his grip, he would certainly hurt her. He might even kill her, like he'd killed Dunthorpe.

There was no escape from this man.

Not yet, anyhow. She hadn't endured so many years of hell by being a simpering fool. She'd wait for an opening and she'd take it. In the meantime, she could wallow in the very honest and real terror that washed unchecked through her body.

Richards's gaze moved frantically across the room, coming to a stop when it landed on Dunthorpe. She didn't look—she didn't want to lay eyes on his lifeless body again. She'd seen enough death to last multiple lifetimes already.

Allowing the fear to pulverize her, she squeezed her eyes shut.

"You killed him," Richards gasped. "You killed my master! You bitch!"

If it was possible, Élise's muscles tightened even more. Richards thought *she* had killed Dunthorpe. That she and this man were in league...No...*Dieu*, no. Bone-deep shudders racked her body.

"*Non*," the man said blandly. He bewildered her. First his accent was French, then English, now French again. "It was not the lady. It was a sharpshooter. The shot came through the window." An urgency edged into his tone with the next words. "We must leave this place. He might shoot into this room again."

"I don't see any broken glass." Richards's voice brimmed with doubt.

"*Alors.* Do you not understand when I tell you that we are in danger if we remain here?" The man pushed out an arm, and Élise opened her eyes in time to see him thrust Richards aside with no regard to the gun. Élise froze, expecting the butler to shoot, but he went stumbling back into the corridor and the shot never came. "Now. There is no hope for your master, but your mistress is in requirement of a doctor. You must fetch one. *Immédiatement.*"

"I...B-b-but..." Richards stuttered.

"Go now!" the man exclaimed, sounding exasperated. "Fetch the doctor. And give me that gun. If I see the shooter, I shall kill him myself." He wrenched the pistol from Richards's grip.

"*Allez!*" the man roared.

Richards stumbled down the corridor before them. The man held Élise tightly as he negotiated the stairs. At the bottom, he drew to a halt and watched Richards burst out the front door. It slammed behind him.

"Damn," the man muttered, sounding very English once again.

He just stood there, staring at the closed door, holding Élise against him. Seconds passed.

Élise peeked up at the man. He had a strong, solid face. Darkly handsome, with a square jaw and piercing dark eyes. He was staring down at her.

"I'm going to set you on your feet," he murmured. "Can you walk?"

"*Oui...*" She blinked, surprised by the French word emerging from her mouth. It had been a long time since she'd forgotten to speak English. "Yes."

Slowly, carefully, he slid her down his body until she wobbled on shaky legs. His fingers closed over her forearm, preventing her from running, as did the gun he still held in one hand. "Remain close to me. Do not say a word."

"Yes," she whispered.

She followed his order not to speak as he tugged her out onto the landing and down the steps that led to the street. Beyond the resident fear, a thousand questions simmered in her mind.

Why had he killed Dunthorpe? Why hadn't he killed her, too? Was he kidnapping her for a reason? For ransom? But if that were the case, how could he have known she was at home today? No one knew she was in London...

A black-lacquered, unmarked coach awaited them at the curb. The man glanced up at the driver, who tipped his cap low over his forehead and then looked away before Élise could discern any of his features. All she could tell was that he was an older man, with gray-streaked brown hair.

The man who'd shot Dunthorpe opened the door, lifted her by the waist, and thrust her inside the coach as if she were a slab of meat he'd just purchased from the butcher.

She stumbled in, her eyes unaccustomed to the darkness. Another figure sat inside the coach, shadowy in the darkness.

"For God's sake!" the shadowy figure exclaimed when she fell half on him. He took her shoulders and pushed her off him. *Dieu*, it was another of them. Maybe she had been unwise not to attempt escape earlier, when it was just one big, frightening man she'd had to deal with. Though this one, admittedly, was somewhat smaller.

"What's this, Hawk?" the shadowy man asked.

"Lady Dunthorpe." The big man's voice was completely flat as he said her name. He came up behind her and arranged her into the forward-facing seat opposite the smaller man. Then he sat beside her, his enormous body a threatening mass of muscle.

The carriage lurched into motion, and the man across from her studied her, his head tilted in fascination. She caught glimpses of his features from the shifting light that filtered in through the slim gaps in the curtains covering the windows. He was quite young—just a boy, really—with angular, handsome features. He looked rather... French.

She took a shuddering breath, then closed her eyes.

Dunthorpe is dead. Dunthorpe is dead.

If she were a good wife, she'd be weeping. Crying out, grieving, keening, mourning her dead husband. Trying to kill these men who had caused his death. But she knew, better than anyone, that Dunthorpe was undeserving of her tears. Or anyone's tears, for that matter, though no doubt his death would be considered a national tragedy.

The English could be such fools.

It was telling that, even though she was terrified to be a captive of these clearly dangerous men, this was less terrifying than being alone with Dunthorpe.

The big man—*Hawk*, the youth had called him—had promised not to hurt her. She looked at him now. Men would say anything to attain a woman's capitulation— she knew that. She couldn't trust him to hold to his word.

He met her eyes with his dark ones. His expression was flat—devoid of any emotion. That cool gaze sent shivers of trepidation skittering down her spine.

"Lady Dunthorpe," the youth mused, surprise evident in his young voice. "She wasn't supposed to be at home."

"No," Hawk said darkly, "she wasn't."

The youth drew in a breath. "Well, then. What do you intend to do with her?"

Élise glanced back and forth between the two as they talked about her as if she wasn't present. Neither of them spoke with a French accent now, so she assumed that Hawk had faked the accent earlier. But why?

And then the truth of it struck her. It was because he wished to make it appear as though Dunthorpe's assassin had been a Frenchman.

She understood completely. It was far easier to place

blame for the murder of such a well-loved man on an enemy than on a compatriot.

Hawk shook his head, and she saw the slightest tightening of his lips at the edges. This man didn't wear his emotions on his face. To read him, she'd have to watch him carefully, look out for the subtlest clues. If he didn't kill her before she had the opportunity to try to understand him.

Now that her mind was working properly, she realized she already understood a few things about him, and she collected those facts in her mind as the carriage rattled down a quiet London street. He was extremely large and extremely strong. He was ice-cold and impenetrable, but with chinks in that surface. He was a competent killer. He was not French. He knew something of Dunthorpe's nefarious deeds, and the latest scheme, whatever that might be, had been what had caused him to kill Dunthorpe.

And he probably thought she was in league with her husband.

She wrapped her arms over her chest and squeezed her body tight. She was cold—it was a chilly early-spring evening, and she had no coat.

Nevertheless, a kind of odd calmness flushed through her. She would accept her fate, whatever it might be. Dunthorpe was dead, and no matter what happened now, it would be all right. All that mattered was that he was dead.

A weight settled on her shoulders, and she glanced at the big man in surprise. He'd laid his own coat over her and now pulled at the front so she was tucked in tight, as if in a blanket.

A thoughtful kidnapper, this one.

"Keep her close," Hawk muttered to his friend as he

deemed her warm enough and turned away—a much-delayed and noncommittal answer to the youth's question about what he planned to do with her.

"Ah." The youth nodded, and then he glanced out the window. "We're almost there."

"Are we being followed?"

"I don't believe so."

"Did you see the butler?"

"Oh, I saw him, all right. He burst through the door and then set off running down the street like wolves were nipping at his arse." He cast Élise a guilty glance. "Beg pardon, my lady."

She didn't answer him, just stared at him blankly, and he raised a brow at his large friend. "I think you've gone and petrified her with fear, Hawk."

Hawk glanced down at her. Then he shrugged. "Easier this way."

She straightened her spine but tightened her arms around herself. As if her two spindly arms could protect her from men such as these. "Who are you?" she whispered. Her voice sounded rough—like she hadn't used it in a week.

"No one," Hawk said quietly. "Ghosts. Specters in the night. You've never seen us."

She frowned at the absurdity of this and opened her mouth to give a fitting retort, but just then the carriage came to an abrupt halt.

"And here we are!" the youth said cheerfully. "Home, sweet home."

Chapter Two

Sam entered the safe house, wrapping his arm firmly around Lady Dunthorpe's waist and pulling her small body against him. Laurent and Carter took care of the horses and carriage and ensured the outside was secure.

This house was located between the Covent Garden and Piccadilly—a very busy area of London. Sam had learned long ago that sometimes the best way to make oneself truly invisible was to make oneself as visible as possible.

He opened the door of the town house and stepped inside. The interior was dark, but he had prowled these corridors in the dead of night many times before. He led Lady Dunthorpe down a short set of stairs, guiding her carefully so she wouldn't stumble in the dark. He opened the first door to the right and led her inside.

The dungeon.

At least, that's what Laurent and Carter fondly called this particular room. In fact, it was a quite well-appointed bedchamber. Meant for prisoners, yes, but Sam's superiors liked to think of themselves as a highly civilized lot when they weren't arranging for people to be assassinated in cold blood. They didn't go for the chains and shackles or the dank cellars and rat-infested dungeons whose floors were ankle-deep in sewage. No, they kept their prisoners as they would a most esteemed guest. Many such "guests" never knew they were prisoners at all.

This one did, though, Sam thought grimly as the door closed behind them with a snap and her body went rigid.

He didn't comfort her. What could he say? If she was to be comforted, he certainly couldn't be the one to do it. Whenever she looked at him, she'd see only the man who'd killed her husband.

Instead he said, "Just a moment," and released her arm to go crouch at the hearth. In a few minutes, he had a fire going. Without looking at her, he lit the lamp on the small square walnut table beside the barred half window that looked over the surface of the street when its curtains were open. Iron bars were not considered odd for a window in London and certainly didn't rouse any suspicion. But unlike most barred windows, the purpose of this one was to keep people in, not to keep them out.

Finally, he glanced at her. She stood in the middle of the room, her body straight and tense, gazing at him with clear blue eyes. Tendrils of shining blond hair escaped from their coiffure and curled around her face, giving her a wild, ethereal look.

God, she was a beauty.

A traitorous, French beauty.

Yet she looked utterly fragile. Was she, though? Perhaps not. Perhaps that kitten-soft exterior hid ferocious claws.

Despite himself, he found her utterly intriguing.

"What are you going to do to me?" she asked sharply.

"To you?" he asked. "Nothing."

She stared at him, clearly not believing his words. Intelligent woman.

"You should go to bed. We'll talk more in the morning." He needed to send a message to Adams. This would be a complicated issue; there was no doubt about that. And he wanted out of it as soon as humanly possible. He'd accomplished his mission. Let someone else deal with Lady Dunthorpe.

Her eyes flickered to the large bed, which was covered in pillows and a rich silk counterpane embroidered in silver and gold.

"Bed," she repeated flatly. As if she couldn't quite understand what a bed was.

"Right." He strode over to the closet and opened the door. There were clothes of various sizes and uses hanging there, and he found a nightgown that would be far too large for her. It was the best he could do. As he withdrew it and laid it over the back of the chintz-covered armchair, his gaze snagged on her dress. It was a fashionable gown. One that required a maid's assistance to get into and out of.

Sam nearly groaned. But then he locked his composure firmly into place and took a step toward her.

She stumbled back, looking up at him with wide, terror-filled eyes. "You...killed Dunthorpe."

God, how he hated this. He'd been lucky to have few witnesses to his deeds over the years. "Yes. I did."

She nodded, as if confirming it to herself. "I—" She pressed her lips together, as if thinking better of what she'd been about to say; then she lowered her eyes. "Will you kill me, too?"

Damn and blast. "No," he told her firmly. "I won't. I told you I wouldn't hurt you."

"What is the word of a murderer?"

Not of much value, he had to admit. "Unfortunately, it is all I have."

She looked up again, and they locked eyes. "Will you rape me, then?"

"What?" For God's sake! "No!"

"Will they?" She gestured toward the door, presumably indicating Carter and Laurent.

"No. They won't touch you. You have my word on that as well. We aren't cretins, my lady." Though he really couldn't expect her to believe otherwise.

She took a shaky breath. She believed him, at least partially, because some of the tightness in her shoulders loosened.

"Why were you in London tonight?" he asked her gruffly. "You were supposed to be in Brighton."

Her eyes widened as he revealed that bit of knowledge about her supposed whereabouts, but she pressed her lips together, unwilling to answer him.

"Did Dunthorpe know you were there?"

She shook her head slightly. An answer to his question or a refusal to answer? He thought it might be an answer. So perhaps Dunthorpe hadn't been aware that his wife was in the room. Interesting.

He required answers, but he shouldn't be pushing her. Her husband had died and she was a lone woman facing his killer. It was a miracle she still stood, and indeed, that she could face him at all.

Sam ought to have some kind of sympathy for her situation. He dug about inside himself and found a small shard, long embedded and hidden within the coldhearted ruthlessness that he needed to hold close in order to maintain a semblance of sanity.

No more questions for her. Not tonight.

He cleared his throat. "I will send some wine and food. A washbasin and a brush for your hair—" Her hair was beautiful. Shining golden locks, deliciously disheveled. His hand had skimmed over it while he was holding her, and it had been soft as silk. His fingers itched to touch it again, to comb through the satin strands.

He pushed that thought away.

"And anything else you might require," he finished gruffly. He hesitated, then asked, "May I help you with your dress?"

She went rigid again. He sighed. She'd have to sleep in her dress and in her stays. She'd be uncomfortable. But her posture was so stiff, he feared she'd break if he touched her.

The bloody hell of it was, he wanted to touch her. And even more disconcerting, he didn't want her to break when he did so. He wanted to bring pleasure to those feminine curves, to soften those stiff muscles, to mold her body against his, to have her pliant and willing in his arms.

She's a traitor. She was French nobility, with high connections in the French government. And she'd been married to Dunthorpe.

He was tired. That must be it. Her pretty face, her

petite, curvaceous little body, the shimmering dress that hugged all those curves, that shining mass of blond curls. He hadn't slept in the two days leading up to this mission. He was tired, and exhaustion was bludgeoning his carefully constructed shields.

It had been a damn long time since he'd touched a woman. God, how he wanted to be touching this one.

She stood there. Waiting. As if she expected him to touch her. Almost as if she wanted him to.

No, that couldn't be right.

"I didn't mean it in a...an improper way," he told her. It was true—he hadn't. As much as his body seemed to reach out to her, to crave her...that could never happen. It was more than his professional duty and responsibility. More than the possibility that she was a traitor. More, even, than his resolve to keep all women at arm's length.

For God's sake—he'd just killed her husband. Jesus. He must be insane. He shook his head.

She saw the negative movement, and her brow furrowed.

"Sorry," he said softly. "You will require assistance with removing your dress. You'll be more comfortable tonight without it. I meant nothing untoward."

"I am to be your prisoner, then."

He nodded, keeping his expression flat. "For now."

"For how long?" she asked.

"Until we no longer have need of you." He tried not to flinch, but hell, that had sounded ominous. Calming overwrought ladies had seldom been part of his job, and he was definitely making a bungle of it. He needed to do better.

Her throat moved as she swallowed. Her blue eyes

studied him intently. "I am your prisoner," she said slowly, "yet you do not intend to hurt me."

"Just so."

"Then what *do* you intend to do with me?"

Not meeting her eyes, he shrugged. That was also quite ominous, but what else could he do? Adams would want to drag information from her, but that would be a duty for someone else. His specialty was eliminating threats, not pulling secrets from people's heads.

He'd probably be free of her by morning. Thank God. This woman...Some part of his shield had cracked, and she seemed to be insinuating herself in. He needed to get away from her. To fortify that crack so it couldn't be breached again.

She was staring at him, her blue eyes big in that lovely face. But suddenly, she turned her back to him.

"Please help with my buttons, Monsieur Hawk."

He stared at her for a moment. The soft curls tickling a neck. The row of buttons that traveled down her slender back, ending at the top of her buttocks. What would she look like naked? Beautiful. Perfect. Images of feminine curves and creamy skin assailed him.

He wanted to peel off her clothes and explore what lay beneath...

Taking a fortifying breath, he stepped forward and brushed the silky strands of hair away from her neck. She shuddered when his fingertips brushed over her soft, warm skin. His body went hard.

He gritted his teeth. *Focus, Hawkins.* But his body had no intention of listening to his mind, to all the reasons it shouldn't be aroused by this woman.

His gaze narrowed on the score or so of tiny pearl buttons that ran down her back. She wore a fine ivory silk gown, threaded through with gold embroidery and ribbons and embellished with pearls. Elegant and beautiful, and it fit her like a glove, highlighting all the feminine arcs and curves of that petite, lovely body...

Focus on the damned buttons.

He did. Starting from the top, he flicked them open one by one, revealing the soft white muslin of her petticoat beneath. And more of the pale flesh of her neck and upper back. Creamy and smooth, just like he'd known it would be.

Her shoulders rose and fell with his breaths, which made low, rasping sounds in the sudden quiet of the room. As his fingers traveled down her back, her breaths became ragged and uneven. And, God help him, but his body hardened further at the sound. It was almost, *almost* the sound of a woman in rapture.

He undid the last button and pulled the seams open so the dress gaped at her back. She turned quickly, clutching the bodice to her bosom so it didn't fall away.

It took all his skills to keep his expression emotionless, to not stare at her like a besotted schoolboy, to not allow his eyes to wander down that sweet, appealing body. To look at her with a gaze he knew was completely detached, completely impassive.

She was beautiful. The most beautiful woman he'd seen in a very, very long time. He'd thought so when he'd seen her on Dunthorpe's arm last month, and he thought so now.

Dunthorpe. The thought of the name alone was enough to throw a bucket of ice water over this errant attraction.

He stepped back from her and dragged his gaze from

where she clutched the bodice to her breasts. "Ah...do you require help with your stays?"

"*Non.*" The word was sharp and definitive, sounding very French. "I will manage."

"Very well. Laurent—he's the younger man, the one riding in the carriage with us—will bring you anything you require. Don't hesitate to ask him."

She stared at him, standing very still, still pressing her dress against her body. This was his cue to leave. But all of a sudden, he didn't want to. Even though he had missives to write, plans to make, orders to follow. Even though he *knew* he needed to clear his mind. And the only way to do that was to get the hell away from her.

"Don't fear Laurent," he said softly. The boy had a strong moral code when it came to women—perhaps stronger than his own. "He will be naught but a gentleman with you."

He watched her straighten her spine and square her shoulders. Her blue eyes sparked defiantly. "I do not fear him."

She was an enticing contradiction, this Frenchwoman, this English viscountess. A bundle of shivering fear one minute, then a stoic and stiff automaton, then an angry kitten.

He couldn't blame her for such hot-and-cold behavior. Her emotions must be rioting.

Still, he couldn't allow himself to feel sorry for her. She had brought this upon herself. Her and Dunthorpe.

"Will you be all right?" he asked her.

She gave him a brusque nod. He returned it, then gestured toward the bellpull beside the fireplace. "Ring if you need anything."

She raised an imperious brow, and anger snapped in those blue eyes. "If I need anything from the man who killed—who *murdered*—my husband? Who kidnapped me? Ah, yes. Very well, then." She flicked her fingers in the direction of the fireplace. "I shall ring your little bell if I need anything."

He narrowed his eyes. "I told you, we've no intention of harming you."

"Ah, Monsieur Hawk." Deep cynicism darkened her eyes, but they were clear and honest when they collided with his. "The whole world has intention of harming me. It always has. Always."

* * *

Dunthorpe is dead. Dunthorpe is dead.

Élise sat in the unfamiliar bed in an unfamiliar nightgown that dwarfed her, hugging her knees. The truth of it hammered inside her skull. Dunthorpe was dead, and her life would never be the same. His brother, Francis, would inherit not only the title but all of Dunthorpe's lands and possessions, and his fortune as well. She wasn't fool enough to hope he would have left her a single penny.

Not that it mattered. She had been born into money and had lost it for a while before coming into it again. It had taken her twenty-eight years to realize that some of the best days of her life had also been the poorest ones.

Dunthorpe is dead.

She was free.

Maybe not so very free. Francis would attempt to keep a tight rein on her. However, unlike Dunthorpe, Francis didn't have the legal right to control her. It'd be far easier to slip through his thick and clumsy fingers than it had been to escape Dunthorpe.

If she even had the opportunity to slip through Francis's fingers. First she had the problem of these three men.

Who were they? What did they want from her? Why had they killed Dunthorpe? The answers were not forthcoming. She knew well that Dunthorpe had many enemies. They could be working for themselves, for an outside individual, for one of any number of governments.

They were definitely British, though. Gentlemen spies? Because they were gentlemen—at least Hawk was. It was easy enough to discern that much from the cadence of his accent.

A soft knock sounded at the door, and she hugged her knees tighter and turned her head in the direction of the noise. The door opened, and Laurent, the youth, stood there carrying a tray that contained a plate of food and a glass of red liquid that must be wine.

He gave her a friendly smile, and she took in a measured breath, trying to control her trembling. It was so odd for a man to be walking into a room while she was in bed. She didn't think it had ever happened to her in her adult life, aside from those times Dunthorpe had entered her bedchamber to order her to perform her wifely duties. That had happened seldom in the past few years.

"Sorry." His voice was smooth, refined, and quite British, but Laurent was a French name. He was very young, so if his parents had been émigrés fleeing the Revolution, he had probably been born in England. "I didn't mean to disturb you, but I brought a bit of food—just some bread and cheese—and some wine."

She gazed at him as he set the tray on the table. She

struggled to find something to say. It was difficult to speak in normal tones with these men—how could one hold a pleasant, everyday conversation with the people who'd murdered one's husband?

"Right," Laurent said when she didn't answer. "Well, I'm heading off to bed now, but I wanted to let you know that if you need anything else, just ring the bell, and I'll come straightaway."

She kept herself in that tight curled-up ball seated upon the bed. She opened her mouth to speak, but what would she say? She wouldn't thank him. So she closed her mouth and simply nodded.

He bade her good night and closed the door, locking it behind him.

They might sleep, but she wouldn't. Not until she was far away from these dangerous Englishmen.

She'd go to Marie in Hampstead. Marie was her only true friend.

But Marie didn't have the resources to hide her from Francis. Marie didn't mean safety, and Élise had no desire to place her in danger. She couldn't stay with Marie for long. Just long enough to collect a few required items; then she'd leave. She'd disappear. Maybe go to France.

She scoffed out loud at that.

No, certainly *not* France. Somewhere no one would look for her. The Highlands of Scotland, maybe. Or Ireland. No one would think to hunt for her in Ireland.

A new start. A new life, where nobody knew her as Élisabeth de Longmont, and where no one knew her as Lady Dunthorpe. Freedom.

But first she needed to get free.

She waited for ten minutes. Then she straightened her

legs and swung them over the edge of the bed. She slid to standing, the floor planks cool under her still-stockinged feet. She went to the closet, which was packed with clothes for men and ladies of all sizes and shapes. She rifled through it until she found a shirt and a tattered pair of breeches, clearly for a youth of around Laurent's age.

Too large, but otherwise perfect.

Quickly, she slipped out of the ridiculous nightgown. She'd kept her stays on and her shift underneath, and she didn't remove them now. The stays flattened her breasts, and though she didn't harbor any illusions that she could truly look like a man, she had her size, this clothing, and the shadows of night to cloak her.

She pulled on the shirt, which hung past her knees over her stays, and tied it at the neck. She pulled on the breeches, but they wouldn't stay on. Her hips were too narrow, and she had no belt or braces with which to hold them up. Nor did the closet readily supply anything that could be of use.

Chewing her lip while holding the breeches on with one hand, she turned in a slow circle, perusing the room. It contained little besides the clothes, the bed and bedding, and a few other pieces of furniture. There was no adornment, no pictures on the walls or trinkets on the mantel. A thick blanket and silk counterpane covered the bed, and there were four pillows but no bed curtains. She went to the desk and pulled open the three drawers. All empty.

Her gaze moved to the dress she'd been wearing earlier this evening.

Letting the breeches fall, she stepped out of them. Ignoring the food and wine Laurent had placed on the desk, she lifted her dress off the chair and took it to the bed, laying it out with the seams of the skirt exposed.

With a firm yank, she tore the seams apart. She pulled on the thin gold ribbon that had been threaded through the hem of the dress, and it came out easily, weaving in and out of the ivory silk of the skirt.

When it was all the way out, she pulled the breeches back on and tied the gold ribbon about her waist. She looked down at herself. The waist of the breeches was bunched up over her shift and stays, tied by a silly, effeminate ribbon. More ridiculousness. But at least she wouldn't be running about on the streets of London naked.

She had found three coats in the closet. She took the smallest one and wrapped it around her, then took a single pin from her hair before setting a woolen cap at a jaunty angle on her head.

She approached the door with purpose, wielding the long hairpin like a weapon. When she reached it, she crouched down and inserted the pin into the lock.

It took several minutes of deep concentration, picturing the tumblers of the lock in her mind, probing with the pin. She was by no means a lock-picking expert, but eleven years as Dunthorpe's wife had forced her to learn a few things out of sheer self-preservation.

Click.

She froze. Then, belatedly realizing she'd been holding her breath, she let it out with a long, low whoosh.

Carefully, she withdrew the pin. Jamming it back into her hair beneath the cap, she rose. Then, ever so slowly, she opened the door.

Chapter Three

Carter clapped Sam on the back. "Here." He set a glass of port upon the desk in front of Sam. "It'll do you some good."

Sam's gaze flickered from the port up to Carter.

"You ought to sleep," Carter said.

Yes, he ought to. But Carter knew how elusive sleep could be for him. "Wish I could have Laurent's constitution," he said. "He just left her room, but he's probably already snoring into his pillow."

"No doubt." Carter gestured to the glass and spoke quietly. "It'll help. Drink up, lad."

Sam's lips quirked. The man was older than him, had been part of this game for longer. Nevertheless, Sam was no bumbling youth—he was thirty-two, but most days he felt far older. He was also Carter's superior, so it bemused him when the older man called him "lad." Carter knew this, and he grinned.

"Sleep," he said again, squeezing Sam's shoulder. "We'll work it all out in the morning."

"I'll go down in a minute." His room was adjacent to Lady Dunthorpe's. Close, so he could be near if his prisoner required anything—or attempted anything foolish, like escape—in the middle of the night.

Carter nodded, then slipped out the door, headed to his own bed in one of the upstairs chambers.

Alone for the first time tonight, Sam gazed down at the desk. To the left of the glass of port lay the single sheet of paper containing his current orders. Laurent had delivered his mission notes to Adams and within an hour had returned with the reply:

> *Keep the woman until you receive further instructions.*

Damn it.

He was stuck in London. Entertaining a woman who made his pulse pound every time he laid eyes on her.

A woman whose husband he'd killed. Whom she'd *seen* him kill.

He couldn't imagine anything he'd be less eager to do.

Searching for a distraction from thoughts of Lady Dunthorpe, he looked down again. To the right of his port glass lay a missive from Sam's younger half brother, the Duke of Trent.

The purpose of Trent's letter was to update Sam on the status of the search for their mother, who'd disappeared last spring. She'd been missing for almost a year now, and while they'd learned that she was most likely alive and in the company of a gypsy named Steven Lowell, they still possessed little evidence as to where she might be and no understanding of why she'd left her home in the dead of night last April.

He opened the letter and read it again.

Sam,

The search for Steven Lowell has finally yielded some information, though we still have not been able to pinpoint his location, nor that of our mother. I have discovered that the man is well known in certain circles in and outside of London. Evidently, he is the master of a troupe of traveling players.

Sam rubbed the bridge of his nose, shaking his head. *Traveling players.* He'd had to read that line ten times before fully absorbing it and the accompanying truth: His mother, the Dowager Duchess of Trent, had taken up with a motley band of jugglers, fortune-tellers, and God knew what else. He wondered if she performed with them. Knowing his mother, he didn't doubt it.

He continued reading.

The troupe met up with our mother in Wales before traveling into Lancashire. After that, however, their destination is unclear. They seem to flit from place to place with little plan or organization.

So their mother was probably still in England. She'd been in England this whole time, with half of the population of the country searching for her. Of course, no one would ever think to look for a dowager duchess within a band of traveling players led by a gypsy.

I am sending Theo and Mark to Lancashire in search of more information. You will hear promptly from one of us if we learn anything.

Theo and Mark were their two youngest brothers. Their other brother, Luke, had recently married and was busy with his new family. Trent wouldn't go himself—he had parliamentary duties here in London, not to mention that his wife had just given birth to their first child, a son, and he wouldn't want to leave them so soon.

Theo and Mark were competent. If there was any clue about their mother's whereabouts in Lancashire, they would find it.

Sam smiled a bit as he read the closing paragraph of Trent's letter.

All is well at Trent House. Young Lukas Samson is a strong, healthy boy, and the duchess has recovered from the ordeal of the birth. Luke and his wife have come for the baby's christening. I am pleased to report that we were correct—marriage suits our brother.

I hope I will see you at the christening; but if I do not, I understand why.

Please come dine with us when you have an evening free. You know you are welcome here anytime.

Trent

Sam folded the letter and replaced it to the right of his port glass. Not for the first time, he wished he could participate more actively in the search for his mother, but his duties with the Agency left him with no freedom or time to do so.

But the questions surrounding her disappearance ate at him. What had possessed her to run off with Steven Lowell? To leave her family with no word as to her whereabouts? To leave *him*?

Sam had alwa．s felt particularly close to his mother. As the illegitimate eldest son of the Duchess of Trent, he was shunned by the duke and by society as a whole. But his mother—she had given him confidence, taught him his value as a human being, had never allowed his siblings to treat him as anything but an equal, so that, as adults, they honestly believed he *was* their equal. She had been the pillar of strength in a childhood that would have drowned him in misery had she not been there to support him and love him at every turn.

How could she simply disappear—and they had recently learned she'd gone voluntarily—from his life like that? It chafed. It burned. It *hurt*.

He pressed his fingers to his temples, massaging lightly. Of course, he wouldn't be able to attend his new nephew's christening tomorrow. He would be busy entertaining a viscountess he'd made a widow.

Sighing, he rose and stretched. He needed to go to bed. He needed to sleep—or at least try to sleep. It was going to be a very long few days with Lady Dunthorpe. At least he hoped it would be a few days. Surely they'd decide what to do with the woman soon.

He made his way to the door, but right when his fingers curled over the handle, the softest sound broke the silence of the night—the slightest, lowest *click*.

It could be Laurent or Carter up and about for any number of reasons. But he knew it was not—he knew the subtle differences between the sounds of the front door to the house and the interior doors.

He'd been a fool to underestimate her.

He ran out of the drawing room and sprinted down the corridor, bellowing, "Laurent! Carter!"

He threw open the front door and looked down the street to the right and then to the left. There she was. A dark shadow at the end of the street. Dressed in breeches—*breeches*, for God's sake. The color of the hair peeking out from the dark cap gave her away. Moonlight shimmered over those golden tresses as she ran.

She disappeared from sight almost as soon as he'd seen her, turning down a narrow alleyway.

He took off at a dead run after her.

He'd never lost a prisoner before. He wasn't going to do so tonight.

*   *   *

Élise ran as fast as her legs would carry her. When she heard the shouting, she'd glanced back over her shoulder, and she'd seen the large, dark form at the threshold. *Hawk.*

Since then she hadn't looked back—to do so would only slow her down. She was fleet of foot, always had been, but it was questionable whether she could outrun such a mountain of a man.

Mountains didn't run, she told herself. Mountains were bulky, unwieldy things. Day or night, summer or winter, hot or cold, she could outrun a mountain.

So she ran, twisting and turning through the streets of

London, down cobbled streets and dark alleyways, until her breath came in harsh pants, and she reached a place she recognized. The Mall.

She knew where she was. She knew how to get to Hampstead Heath, to Marie's house. It wasn't close, maybe five miles at minimum, but she'd be there by dawn, which couldn't be much more than an hour away.

She flitted through the streets, envisioning herself as a wraith, a spirit, even though her lungs burned and her feet, clad in only the satin slippers she'd been wearing in her husband's drawing room, ached from all the pounding on the hard cobbles.

She didn't look back; she didn't dare. She hoped she'd lost him. She prayed he was far, far behind her, with no idea how to find her.

Her stride slowed to a jog. She couldn't sprint forever. Also, a "lad" running at top speed would draw attention. And while it was the deepest part of night, the occasional carriage still rattled by her, and she had passed half a dozen pedestrians.

He'd ask these pedestrians if they'd seen her. She imagined him questioning them, his imposing form and carriage so dominating.

They would tell him. Anyone would tell him anything.

Footsteps pounded on the pavement, some distance behind her. *Running* footsteps.

No!

She increased her pace to a sprint again and turned down an alley. But the footsteps grew louder, drew inexorably closer. There was nothing to do. Nothing left but to hope she could outrun him. But how could she when he'd pursued her this far?

He grabbed her elbow first, jerking her back. They both came to a screeching halt.

No. *No!*

A sob welled in her chest, but she managed to tamp it down and keep her expression stoic, despite the harsh breaths that sawed from her throat.

She flinched as he grabbed her around the waist and hauled her against him, her back against his front. Though she wasn't facing him and hadn't dared to look back while she'd been running, she knew it was Hawk. She had no idea how he'd found her. Her route had been so circuitous...

She squeezed her eyes shut, refusing to look at him.

"Lady Dunthorpe," he said softly. He wasn't even breathing hard, the bastard.

He kept one burly arm wrapped around her, holding her against him, her behind pressed against his hard thighs.

"Let me go!"

She pushed against his arm, but it was like iron about her body.

"Unhand me at once!"

He didn't budge.

"No," he murmured into her hair. His voice was almost gentle.

How to overcome a man such as this? *Bite him.* She twisted this way and that, but her mouth couldn't reach any part of him. *Kick him where it hurts the most.* She flailed, kicking her legs out, but none of her kicks connected where she wanted them to. He didn't react to them at all—they probably felt like gentle taps on his rock-hard legs.

Scream.

She opened her mouth to do just that, but as she drew in a preparatory breath, his hand clamped around her mouth.

"I don't think so, my lady."

There was no point in fighting it, no point in wasting precious energy attempting to overcome a man of steel who was twice her size.

He'd take her back to his elegant prison, and he'd keep her there until she told him all her secrets. Probably until she was dead. Because Englishmen like this one didn't care about one French *émigrée*, a woman, the wife of a traitor. No, they'd draw whatever information they could from her; then they'd dispose of her like so much rubbish.

Before she could stop it, a whimper emerged from her throat.

His grip instantly loosened. Not enough to allow her any movement whatsoever, though.

"Do you dislike our hospitality?" he asked her softly. But his voice was no longer gentle. It was low and dangerous, and it sent a shiver of trepidation skittering over her spine.

She shook her head.

"Good. Then we will return. Try not to make any loud noises. It will be uncomfortable for us both if you do."

Slowly, cautiously, he removed his hand from her mouth. When she didn't utter a sound, he grasped her arm and steered her in the direction from which she'd come.

A feeling of doom spread within her as she stumbled along at his side.

"There was no reason to run off like that, my lady. I told you I'm not going to hurt you," he said as a hackney rattled past them. "I don't hurt women."

Did he hurt spies for the French? Did he hurt traitors? Yes, he did. She'd seen that earlier tonight.

"You shall forgive me if I do not believe you."

His lips pressed together tightly, but he didn't respond. He directed her down Camden Street in silence for several minutes.

It was a clear night. If not for the coal haze of London, she imagined she'd see a billion stars overhead. Instead, only the brightest stars of the heavens had punctured through the gloom, and a sliver of a moon glimmered down at her, ambivalent to her second capture this evening.

* * *

Sam felt her surrender. It was different from when he'd first caught her and she'd made that valiant effort to escape from his grip. Then, he'd known her mind was alive and working, actively understanding. And her attempted escape from the safe house had shown an enormous amount of spirit. Despite his frustration, respect for her bloomed within him.

But now...there was nothing. A flatness. She moved as he directed her to, but there was no emotion in her expression, in her movements. She walked as a woman resigned to her own death.

He hated that. He hated that he was the one responsible for this. For sucking the spirit out of her.

"Are you well, my lady?" he asked her quietly.

Her lips were so pale as to be almost white. She nodded.

The way she was dressed—in those too-loose

breeches. Hell, if that wasn't one of the most erotic things he'd ever seen. The bulky wool couldn't hide the sinuous shape of her legs. It exposed the tiny circumference of her waist, the flare of her hips and the curve of her buttocks...

He took a breath and slipped his arm over her shoulder, dragging her close until her body was flush against his. They'd look like lovers if she were wearing a dress. Instead they'd look like two comrades reeling down the street after a night of drunken revelry.

"Come back to the house," he told her, "and sleep. Things will be better after some rest." He used Carter's words of comfort from earlier, because he couldn't invent any sufficient words on his own. But Carter had been right, after all.

She nodded. Then she glanced at him, and her blue eyes appeared tired and resigned. So much older than her twenty-eight years.

"There will never be freedom for me, I think."

He stiffened at that. "Traitors shouldn't expect freedom, should they?"

"Is that what you believe I am, monsieur? A traitor?" She made a small scoffing noise. "To which country? France or England?"

"I don't know. Why don't you tell me? Because if it is not one, won't it be the other?"

She didn't answer him.

"Then I must deduce that you are a traitor to England," he said finally, "like your husband."

"Ah. You make that assumption, then?" she asked, and if he wasn't mistaken, there was a renewed spark of life in her voice. "That I am a traitor to England? The country that has succored me and kept me safe since I was a child?"

"You married a traitor," he said.

"And that makes me a traitor by association?"

He shrugged. "You are also not English," he continued. "English blood does not flow through your veins."

"True," she agreed. "My veins are filled with French blood. The blood of my parents, who betrayed a generation. The blood of my countrymen, who murdered them. Such blood I have." Bitter venom resonated in her voice. "Who wouldn't remain loyal, after watching the head of her mother rolling upon the ground? Who wouldn't remain loyal, after gazing into the dead, blank face of her father?"

His arm tightened around her. "Things have changed since you were a child, my lady. Many of your aristocratic countrymen have been welcomed home with open arms."

"But have I?" she asked. "By the time Napoleon pardoned the *aristos*, I was married to an English viscount. Do you think he'd welcome me into his little fold?"

"Probably," Sam said dryly. "Especially when said viscount was passing secrets in his direction."

She made a low, scoffing noise. "Believe what you will, Monsieur Hawk."

"So you imply my beliefs are incorrect?"

They turned down a narrow alleyway, a shortcut to the safe house.

"Because if they *are* incorrect," he continued, "I wish you'd enlighten me."

But he didn't think he was incorrect. It was true, he'd no hard evidence proving her guilt, like he had her husband's. But Dunthorpe had done the most damage—they had all assumed that with him gone, the wife would be impotent. Now he realized that might have been a mistake. She was a wily, slippery one, tricking him with that tiny, feminine body and those innocent blue eyes.

He'd learned his lesson. He'd be more careful with her in the future.

She turned to look up at him. Fury simmered in her eyes. "*Non.* There is no point in it. You can believe what you wish of me, Monsieur Hawk, but you will not ever be made privy to my motivations." She paused, then added, "Until I am made privy to yours. And only then will I decide whether you are worthy of my confidences."

"Then we are at an impasse."

"We are."

They walked in silence. He mulled over why she insisted upon calling him "Monsieur." She'd been in this country since childhood. Surely she knew how to say "Mister."

She stumbled over a cobble. Once again, his arm firmed around her, steadying her. She stiffened under his grip.

"Are you all right?"

"Of course."

He drew in a slow breath. She'd had a long—an *extremely* long—night. Regardless of what was going on in that pretty head, she needed to go to bed. He would get nowhere with her tonight. This was not the first time he'd had that thought.

Usually, he was a patient man. But with her...She was a contradiction. He wanted—*needed*—to know what she was thinking, why she'd married Dunthorpe, what her motivations had been.

What her motivations were now.

They reached the door to the safe house, and she stopped abruptly, staring at it.

"We returned so fast," she murmured.

"I took a more direct route," he said, watching her carefully. Beyond the resignation in her eyes, he saw something else...but he couldn't define it.

She nodded, and they entered. Carter stood in the entry hall, and when he saw them, he raised a bushy brow. "Picked the lock, did you, my lady?"

"I did," she said shortly.

He nodded, impressed. "Right nice job of it, too." He met Sam's gaze, and Sam gave a small shake of his head. He'd deal with Lady Dunthorpe himself.

"Laurent should be back in a few minutes," Carter said.

Laurent had gone after Sam in the search for Lady Dunthorpe—had probably gone to Dunthorpe's town house, ensuring she hadn't gone there. He'd return when he didn't find her.

"Good. Wait up for him, will you? I'm putting Lady Dunthorpe to bed."

He didn't pause to see the look on Carter's face. Instead, with a firm grip on Lady Dunthorpe's arm, Sam dragged her to the end of the corridor and down the stairs. He returned her to her room and released her arm only after locking the door—what little good that would do. He got the fire going again, then turned back to her.

"You will sleep on the bed," he said mildly, pointing to it. He moved his finger to a spot on the carpet near the door. "And I'll sleep on the floor." If he slept at all.

She wrapped her arms over her slender body, defiance creeping back into her eyes.

"I gave you the opportunity for privacy," he told her.

"And I suppose you will say I took advantage," she bit out.

"You did."

Her lips pursed.

Using his chin, he gestured to the bed. "Go to sleep."

"Now?"

"Now."

Turning away from him, she vehemently kicked off her silver silk slippers and then crawled under the covers fully dressed. Not that he'd imagined she'd try to go to bed any other way. She lay in stony silence for a long moment, staring up at the plain white plaster ceiling.

He knelt to remove his boots, then set them tidily beside the table. He opened the closet and rummaged through it, finding a folded blanket on one of the shelves. Tucking the blanket under his arm, he went to the bed and laid his hand on one of the pillows.

"May I?" he asked.

"They are your pillows, are they not?"

Not exactly, but he wouldn't argue the point. He was as much of a guest as she was. Ultimately, as much of a prisoner, too, he supposed.

He plumped the pillow and set it on the floor, then lay on the carpet. He'd slept on harder surfaces in his life. He'd survive this night.

He pulled the blanket up over his body.

"Good night, Monsieur Hawk," she said, and he sensed that spirited edge back in her voice.

Despite himself, he smiled. "Good night, my lady."

Chapter Four

The next day dawned clear and bright but rather cold. Winter clung to London with a tenacious grip this year, and sun shone on the melting frost that edged the windowpanes, making it shimmer like a thousand tiny diamonds.

Sam stretched his body long, then twisted and turned, working out the kinks in his muscles. Shockingly, he'd actually snatched an hour or two of sleep. Perhaps he should sleep on floors more often.

All was silent in the room, and he stood, suddenly irrationally worried that Lady Dunthorpe had somehow found a way to escape again. That would have been impossible. He was a light sleeper. There was no way out but the door, and if she picked the lock again, she would have had to do it over his slumbering body.

He took two long strides to the edge of the bed.

She still slept, her face peaceful in slumber. Her features were lovely, her face a perfect ivory oval, her eyes closed in repose but when open, so large in her face and such a clear, dark shade of blue. Her nose was a small, sharp blade, narrow and triangular in profile—a very French nose, like a smaller, more feminine version of Laurent's. Her eyebrows were dark blond arches, her chin smooth, her cheekbones pronounced.

He shouldn't be admiring this woman's appearance, but...

She was lovely. He wished... Well, he wished circumstances were different.

Her eyelids fluttered and her eyes opened, then widened when she saw him gazing at her.

"Good morning," he said softly.

"Monsieur Hawk." Her voice was scratchy and low with sleep. "Have you been awake long?"

"No, in fact, I have not," he said.

"Mmm." She pulled the blankets up to her neck tight around her and rolled onto her back. "Here it is," she said softly. "My first day of widowhood." She smiled bitterly. "I thought he'd outlive me, you know. He was so... devious."

"He was overconfident." Sam sat on the edge of the bed. He studied her, knowing she'd run the gamut of emotions last night. Yet grief had not been prominent among them. "You didn't love him."

It was a statement, not a question, but she answered him. "Ah, no. Not at first, not ever."

"Why did you marry him?"

"Foolish reasons," she said. Then she went silent.

"Sorry," Sam said. He understood this, for he'd married for foolish reasons, too. Twice.

Lady Dunthorpe's gaze slid toward him and then back

to the ceiling. "I should be trying to kill you," she said bluntly.

Oddly, her words warmed him. He fought a strange twitching of his lips that might have led to a smile. "Should you?" he asked in a bemused tone.

"You are a killer."

He couldn't argue with that.

"You murdered my husband."

"No." Murder was not what he did. What he did was eliminate threats to the monarchy.

Casting a skeptical look in his direction, she continued. "I shouldn't be speaking with you. I should despise you with everything I am. If I were a good wife, I would hate you. I'd be fighting, screaming. I would not be holding what some might call a pleasant conversation with you. Not be speaking familiarly to you when you are the first thing I lay my eyes upon in the morning. Not—" She stopped abruptly, her voice catching on the word.

"Not what?"

"Not feeling...thankful."

He raised his brows at that.

"Dunthorpe is—was—not a kind man. And you, Monsieur Hawk...you are the very first person I have ever told that to." She paused until the silence stretched long. "What is wrong with me?" She directed the question to the ceiling. "You killed my husband, and now you hold me imprisoned. And I do not hate you. I *must* hate you."

He swallowed hard. He wanted to touch her, to let her know he understood exactly how she was feeling. That guilt of not caring enough—he'd been there before, with both his wives. It wasn't a place anyone should ever be forced to go. And he wouldn't wish it on her, even if she was a traitor.

"Yet I do not hate you," she continued, and he could hear the self-condemnation in her voice. "I *respect* you. How did you find me when I escaped? I tried to confuse you. I made many turns—"

"I knew where you were headed," he told her. "To Marie Rameau's house."

She released a whistling breath through her teeth. "You know much about me, monsieur."

"Yes." But not enough. Not nearly enough.

Gazing at her as she gazed up at the ceiling, he turned over the new information in his head. She hadn't loved her husband. Dunthorpe—*the bastard*—had been cruel to her.

Perhaps she wasn't working for France. But she was *French*, and through her own connections along with Dunthorpe's, she'd had access to the highest echelons of both the British and French governments.

Yet...the idea niggled at him. She could be innocent. Completely uninvolved with what Dunthorpe had done.

The intensity of his desire for her innocence hit him with such force it almost sent him reeling.

He rose abruptly. "Do you want breakfast? Smells like Carter is cooking ham and eggs. And I'd wager he's made some coffee, too." The kitchen was just a few steps down the corridor from here. The appetizing scents had wafted into the room, and Sam's stomach clenched with hunger.

She met his gaze. "I am seldom hungry," she said solemnly, "but today I feel as if I could eat a horse."

"We'll bring you a basin, to wash if you feel like it." He forced himself to turn away. He needed some distance from this woman. Some perspective. She was, without any seeming effort, causing him to risk toppling from his pedestal of emotionless calm. He felt disjointed, confused. Like she was slowly snipping away all the tightly wound threads that held him steady. "I'll join you in the kitchen when you're ready."

"Wait."

With his hand on the door handle, he looked back over his shoulder, seeing her lips had parted in surprise. "You do not believe I will attempt to fly away from you again?"

His lips curved into a rare grin. "If you do," he said softly, "I'll catch you."

Shaken yet again by his own surprising, unwelcome reaction to her, he escaped into the corridor and closed the door behind him.

* * *

Élise felt odd. Like she was walking through the thick fog of a dream. How often had she dreamed she was free of Dunthorpe? Too many times to count, surely.

Laurent brought in a steaming basin as well as a comb and a towel, and she washed her face and combed her hair. It had been many years since she'd done her hair herself, but without the help of a mirror, she managed a braid, which she wrapped into a low chignon.

She glanced at the dress she'd worn last night—the dress she'd torn to remove the ribbon. It wasn't wearable anymore, though she wouldn't want to wear it anyhow.

It was Lady Dunthorpe's dress. She would still be known by that title, but inside, she was no longer Lady Dunthorpe. No, she was Élise again. Trapped and imprisoned by one of Dunthorpe's enemies, but no longer carrying all the weight upon her shoulders as she had when she'd belonged to the viscount. And that was exactly what she'd been: a possession. A possession he'd resented and despised.

She shouldn't feel so much lighter, because the future could hold anything: long-term imprisonment, torture, even death. But she couldn't help it. Dunthorpe was dead, and she *did* feel lighter.

She rifled through the closet until she found the smallest dress. It was large, but not as ridiculous as the nightgown and the breeches had been. It was a simple white muslin with lace trimmings, and when she finished donning it, she felt...clean.

She went to the small, frost-limned window and looked outside at the sidewalk of the London street. Every so often, wheels rolled by, horses' legs pranced past, skirts swished by, and legs clad in dark wool clipped along. Her existence had been irrevocably altered last night, but the rest of the world moved on. London wouldn't stop for anyone. Not even Lord Dunthorpe.

She should mourn him. Even if she didn't love him, even if she'd spent half her marriage believing him the devil incarnate...shouldn't she mourn him?

He'd always said she was a terrible wife. A part of her had known he was right.

She pressed her cheek against the pane, the coldness of the glass biting into her flesh. Guilt was a useless, meaningless emotion. She knew this well. And yet she could not help it. It swamped her, seeped into her very skin.

She closed her eyes and stood still, just breathing for long minutes. Finally, she'd gathered enough strength to move forward. She straightened her spine and went to the door. She'd been surprised Hawk hadn't locked it when he'd left, but she knew why as soon as she emerged into the corridor.

Laurent was standing guard at her door. When he saw her, he pushed off from the wall, grinning. "I hope you're hungry. Carter has whipped up quite the feast."

"I *am* hungry," she told him. And, like she'd told Hawk, she was. She was famished. She felt like she hadn't eaten in a month.

He led her not into the dining room but just down the corridor to the kitchen, a bright and warm space with a cheerful fire roaring in the stone hearth.

A square table with four chairs was set in the center of the room, and Hawk and Carter were already seated at it and eating. There were several plates in the center, piled high with slices of ham, fried eggs, toast, butter, jam, flaky buns...

Her stomach growled as she took in all that delicious-smelling fresh food. Loudly enough to draw the attention of all three men.

Laurent chuckled and patted her arm. Hawk glanced at her over his newspaper, employing that blank expression he seemed to have perfected.

Carter was probably Hawk and Laurent's age combined, but though deep wrinkles grooved his forehead and mouth, he looked powerfully built. His hair was brown peppered with gray, his face round, and his eyes, a friendly light blue. He gave her a welcoming smile and gestured to one of the empty chairs. "Come, Lady Dunthorpe. Sit. I'm Carter, by the way. I don't think we've been properly introduced."

She inclined her head as she lowered herself into the chair. "Monsieur Carter."

"Some eggs? Ham?"

"Yes and yes," she told him gratefully, sliding into the seat. Laurent took the last empty chair, and using a large spoon, piled food onto her plate and then his.

Hawk had laid his newspaper on the table. "Would you like a bun? With butter? Jam?"

"Thank you," she murmured. "Both, please." *Dieu*, these men certainly were intent on feeding her. It was charming, in a very bizarre kind of way.

She took some egg up on her fork. It was still hot, and the pleasant, hearty taste burst over her tongue.

She closed her eyes in pleasure. She couldn't remember ever feeling so hungry. So enamored of food.

They all ate in silence for a moment. Well, she and Laurent ate. Carter busied himself with buttering one of the buns that steamed when he cut it open—goodness, had he baked bread this morning?—and Hawk had folded the newspaper and set it aside. Now he held a coffee cup cradled in his hands as he gazed at her.

His dark eyes seemed to drink her in as she ate. It was unnerving.

He lowered his coffee cup to the table, still staring at her. He was beautiful, in a most rough, masculine way. His expression was dark and inscrutable. He had a rather square-shaped face, with a strong nose and jaw. A broad forehead with thick black slashes as brows. Lovely, lovely lips. Pink and plump, they softened the harshness of his face.

His eyes were beautiful, too—darkly exotic, with thick black eyelashes.

"Coffee?" Carter asked, jolting her attention from Hawk.

"Yes, please."

Carter placed the buttered bun on her plate, then went to the stove to fetch the coffee.

Hawk sighed. "It's in the papers already."

He slid the newspaper across the table. It was the *Times*, Élise saw. And there it was: VISCOUNT DUN-THORPE MURDERED.

She lowered her fork and took the newspaper to skim the column. It told of how Lord Dunthorpe had been brutally executed by a Frenchman last night in his home in Kensington. The villain had escaped with Lady Dunthorpe, and at this point speculation abounded that Lady Dunthorpe—who'd been born on French soil and still held on to her affinity for that country—was part of the scheme to murder her husband. Perhaps she was even the architect of the plot.

The citizens of London were advised to be on the lookout for the lady as well as for a large, burly, dark-haired Frenchman.

The rest of the article was dedicated to the implications of the viscount's death on England and on the conflict with France.

Élise closed her eyes for a long moment. She shouldn't be surprised by this. She'd never been well loved—not like her husband. And she was French. Of course they would suspect her.

When she opened her eyes, all three men were watching her. Hawk's gaze was wary, Carter's concerned, and Laurent's curious.

"What if I never returned?" she said softly. "No one would miss me."

Laurent shook his head. "We're not going to hurt you. Hawk made that clear, didn't he?"

"That's not precisely what I mean," she said.

"Do you mean you *wish* to disappear?" Carter asked.

"I...don't know."

Hawk narrowed those dark, all-knowing eyes. "Why?"

She retrieved her fork and speared a piece of egg, then looked up at him. "I have finished with this game of being Lady Dunthorpe."

Hawk seemed to ponder her for a moment; then he said, "Perhaps you wish to return to France?"

She gave a low, dark burst of laughter. "Is that what you think? Do you attempt to trap me into admitting I am a French spy? I am not so foolish, Monsieur Hawk."

He shrugged. "The truth will come out eventually, *Lady Dunthorpe*." He placed special emphasis on the hated name, presumably to ruffle her feathers. But she wouldn't allow him to anger her. She let the sarcastic title scatter off her feathers like beads of water she shook free. "You'd save us a great deal of time and energy if you simply gave us what we wanted now."

She merely shook her head. She knew what they wanted. Names, dates, what information was conveyed, how, and to whom. She couldn't give them any of that.

And even if she could, she wouldn't.

She let her gaze move between the three men. "You are unfair to me, gentlemen. You kidnap me, refuse to tell me who you are, who you work for...Then you provide me with a most comfortable bed and a most excellent breakfast. But those are not enough. How can you expect me to vomit information as if to purge it from my very body?" She shook her head. "*Non.* There must be fairness in this."

Laurent gazed at Hawk. Hawk gazed at her. Carter just chuckled.

"She has a point, Hawk," Laurent said.

He was rewarded with a dark glare.

"In the event that you have indeed learned nothing," Hawk snapped, "we do not sell information. We do not negotiate with traitors."

"Well, my lady," Carter said. His voice was relaxed. Cheerful, even. "The man raises a decent question, doesn't he? Are you a traitor?"

"Hawk and I have had this discussion," she told him. "It grows tedious." She took a big bite of her bun to illustrate that point, then made a blissful noise. It was pure flaky, buttery deliciousness.

"She claims she is not a traitor," Hawk told Carter.

Had she claimed that? She didn't think so, not directly.

Hawk's probing focus remained steady on her. "So you are saying you wish to make a trade? What will you trade for information? Your safety?"

She met his gaze evenly. "Haven't you already promised me that?"

He stared at her—*Dieu*, how she wished she could read him better! Then he shook his head slowly. "No, my lady. I have told you I won't hurt you. And I can say without hesitation that Carter and Laurent won't, either. None of us is in the business of hurting women. However..." His voice faded.

She arched an expectant brow at him.

"It's possible we won't be able to protect you forever," he finished flatly.

She glanced at Carter, then Laurent. Both their expressions were grim. Hawk was telling the truth.

She focused on her food. This was something that would require some thought. What would it take for her to give her meager secrets away? Would those secrets be enough to placate them?

She didn't know. Right now, she couldn't think of what they could possibly give her...

Well, that wasn't completely true. A new identity. A new life. Freedom...

But who would she be relaying her secrets to? Would they be used for good or evil? She needed to know before she agreed to tell them. She wasn't so selfish. She'd seen war and death and mourning, and she wouldn't be responsible for any more.

"All this talk of traitors, it gives me many hints," she said casually, changing the subject, buying time. "I believe you are English spies."

Hawk arched a brow. "Do you?"

"I do." She took a bite of ham, chewed and swallowed. "You are British spies who discovered that Dunthorpe was doing something very bad indeed. So, you"—she nodded at Hawk—"disguised your voice so the French would take the blame for murdering him. I suppose you didn't want the English people to know what a very bad man he is—*was*. You wish to protect the people from that knowledge, while increasing their hatred for the French."

They stared at her. Smiling to herself but refusing to let it crack onto her lips, she looked down and tucked in to her food.

She felt the heat of Hawk's eyes on her, but she ignored how his gaze sensitized her skin, made it warm and achy, prickling with some sensation she couldn't quite name. It wasn't an unpleasant sensation, and it made her crave something she shouldn't crave at all but should fear and despise: Hawk's touch. His strength resonating around her. His powerful arms clasping her, the erotic press of his large, hard body against her smaller one...

Dieu. What was *wrong* with her?

She forced her attention off these absurd notions and focused determinedly on her plate. She ate until her belly was pleasantly full; then she finished her coffee. It was made almost as well as the French made it—it was nothing like the typical awful sludge brewed by the English.

Their silence was telling, and so was the coffee. Her theory must be correct. These were English spies who'd spent much time in France... spying and learning how to make proper coffee.

What use would English spies have for the bits of information that resided in her head?

Finally, she looked up from her plate, avoiding looking at Hawk but turning to Carter instead. The older man had taken up a sheet of newsprint and had begun to read. "Thank you for breakfast. I feel... better."

He glanced at her over the paper. "You're welcome, my lady."

"You cook like a Frenchman."

He grinned. "I take that as a compliment."

"You should," she told him.

Again she felt Hawk's eyes upon her, drawing her gaze. His presence—his gaze—was magnetic to her.

As they stared at each other, a slow, delicious heat unfurled inside her, spreading outward and through her until it washed over her cheeks.

His darkly handsome yet expressionless features made

him even more compelling. She wanted to force that impassive mask aside and discover who he really was behind it.

She stared steadily at him, the heat in her cheeks flaring as she realized he hadn't stopped looking at her. Not once during the entire meal.

Why?

* * *

Four days, and he'd heard nothing from Adams.

Sam had been sleeping in the same room as Lady Dunthorpe for four days. He'd eaten every meal with her, spent leisure time in the salon with her. Each day, each hour—hell, each minute—was an eternity.

Because . . . he'd ultimately come to accept the truth of it: He wanted her.

He'd gone mad. There was no doubt about it.

But it was there, it was a fact, and he didn't know how to stop it. She had an allure he couldn't ignore.

He, Laurent, and Carter had practically drowned her in hospitality. On that first morning, before she'd come in to breakfast, Carter had reminded him that it was easier—and far more humane—to break people through kindness. Earn a person's trust, and he or she will share everything with you.

Sam had immediately agreed, seeing the wisdom in this. Despite a rocky beginning with her witnessing Sam killing her husband, they had endeavored to become Lady Dunthorpe's friends, the people who ensured her comfort, who shared novels with her and played long games of charades with her in the evenings.

She and Laurent had formed an immediate bond. Both were French by blood—Laurent was the son of an émigré father and an English mother, and she was an *émigrée* herself. Both had lived near Hampstead and they'd known some of the same people. They conversed easily, often long into the night as they sipped at glasses of red wine.

And Sam watched them, jealous.

Jealous of what, he wasn't sure. Their easy camaraderie, he supposed. It wasn't so easy for him. He wasn't particularly friendly to anyone, but how could he be friendly to a woman he felt such conflicting emotions for?

His attraction to her was an annoyance, a nuisance. He'd tried to brush it off, ignore it. But it was persistent, and it grew more demanding with every hour he spent in her presence, until it simmered in his veins and pushed under his skin, and he thought he might explode if he didn't touch her.

Today he was leaving the house. Finally taking a much-needed afternoon leave to see his family. He hadn't met his new nephew yet, and he hadn't seen Luke and his wife for a few months.

Sam stood with Carter in the mews outside the back door of the town house, holding the reins of his saddled horse. He was ready to go, yet he hesitated.

He gave Carter a hard look. "Watch her."

Carter quirked a gray-dusted brow. "Meaning?"

"She hasn't tried to escape since that first night, but that's because she knows I will catch her. I watch her every move, and she knows it."

"As do Laurent and I."

"But you are less overt about it. She might believe you two have become lax."

Carter snorted. "She'd be wrong."

"Would she?"

The other man frowned. "What are you saying, Hawk? That you don't trust us to manage our charge?"

Sam looked at the horse—a dappled gray. He was behaving like an ass, and Carter was right to frown at him. He'd worked with the man for years—and if they didn't have complete trust in each other, one or both of them would have been dead by now.

What was wrong with him? He was nervous about leaving Lady Dunthorpe with them…not because he didn't trust them. Then why? He didn't know.

"No," he told Carter softly. "I trust you. I just…" He shook his head, not completely understanding his own uneasiness.

Carter clapped him on the shoulder. "We'll keep her safe for you."

He blinked. And there it was…complete understanding in the other man's eyes. Carter knew how attracted he was to her.

Sam froze, unsure how he felt about that. Stupid and weak, for certain. Embarrassed, perhaps. Disappointed that he'd behaved in such an unprofessional manner that his colleague had seen his emotions written on his face.

Relieved that there was no censure in Carter's gaze.

And because he needed to convince himself even more than he needed to convince Carter, he said, "She's a witness who shouldn't have been there. And probably a traitor. That's all."

"Oh, that's not all," the other man said softly.

Sam closed his eyes. "That's all it can be."

Carter was silent for a moment, and then he squeezed Sam's shoulder sympathetically. "She feels it for you, too, you know."

"Feels what?"

"Oh, you know what. She fights it. She feels it's wrong. She struggles with her attraction to the man who killed her husband because she feels she should struggle. But if it had been me or Laurent who'd killed the man ... Hell, Hawk. She would already be in your bed."

Sam's mouth went instantly dry as images of a naked Lady Dunthorpe in his bed assailed him. His body went tight all over.

He clawed his way through the haze of lust, trying to locate Carter's point.

Sam had been so overly conscious of his own conflicting emotions, he hadn't even begun to contemplate whether she reciprocated those feelings. But ... God. Was she feeling this crazy attraction, too?

"Are you sure?" he pushed out.

Carter chuckled. "Aye. There's no doubt about it. Laurent has seen it, too. In both of you."

Sam squeezed the bridge of his nose between two fingers. "I killed her husband. Nothing can come of it."

"And we'll probably be ordered to kill her," Carter said quietly.

Sam dropped his hand. "What?"

"Think about it." Carter ticked off the points on his fingers as he spoke. "She saw too much. She heard the entirety of your conversation with Dunthorpe. She knows our names—our most common aliases, at least. She knows it was the British and not the French who killed Dunthorpe. She's most likely a traitor herself. I think Adams delays in giving the order only because she's a woman. He wishes to keep the peace among us because he knows how we feel about having the blood of innocents on our hands. So he's digging for proof, for justification..."

Sam cursed, low and harsh. "I made her a promise. I intend to keep it."

"It was a promise you never should have made, and you know it. First rule, Hawk: Maintain distance from your enemies. Becoming close with them should only ever be an illusion maintained to make them feel safe and at ease enough to share their secrets."

"You do believe she is our enemy, then?"

Carter's lips pressed into a flat line. Then he shook his head. "No. I don't think so. Though I don't think she's completely loyal to the British..."

"Not that we've ever done a thing to earn her loyalty."

"Not many would agree with that, you know. We made her a viscountess. That's more than most Englishwomen have ever achieved."

Sam heaved a breath. His brother was the Duke of Trent, so he was inured to the nonsense of titles and what it all meant. Still, he knew that most of the world did not share his opinion that titles were more trouble than they were worth. And Carter's point was valid.

"In any case," Carter added, "it doesn't matter what you or I believe about her guilt or innocence. What matters is Adams's take on it. And I have a feeling he's going to pronounce her guilty."

Damn it.

Neither Sam nor Carter had ever disobeyed a direct order from Adams. Loyalty to the Agency was integral to Sam's life. The Agency was his sustenance. Without it, he'd be nothing.

If that order came... what would he do?

Chapter Five

$\mathcal{S}$am had spent most of his childhood at Ironwood Park, the Duke of Trent's seat in the Cotswolds, but his mother had brought him to London often, preferring the social landscape of Town to that of the country. When they were in residence in London, they'd lived in Trent House, a stately town house that abutted St. James's Park.

As a youth, Sam had never particularly liked Trent House; nor had he enjoyed going there. It was where the old duke spent most of his time, holed up in his study, a place the younger Sam had avoided like the plague. Sam had learned in infancy that as the illegitimate son of the duchess, his best approach to dealing with the Duke of Trent was to avoid him at all costs.

He'd managed it very well, in fact. He'd hardly ever seen the man, and when he had, the duke had mostly ignored him.

His younger brother, Luke, hadn't been so lucky. Luke had been raised thinking he was the duke's son, but had discovered last summer that he was illegitimate, too. The duke had known the truth all along, and while Sam had succeeded in avoiding the old man, Luke hadn't, and he'd paid for it dearly. Time and again, the duke had beaten him to a pulp, and Luke had somehow managed not to reveal his suffering to anyone.

Now the old Duke of Trent was dead, and the new duke was their brother—the one *legitimate* brother—who was between Sam and Luke in age. Trent was above reproach in all ways and had done his best to do right by all his siblings. Sam had always admired and respected the man for that.

Still, there was a distance between him and his siblings. Part of it was due to the secrecy involved in his work for the Agency, but most of it had to do with his upbringing. He had been raised as the illegitimate one, and that separated him by necessity from his five siblings, who had always been accepted into society with open arms.

The butler welcomed him politely when he knocked, and he entered a house that had completely changed since those days of his childhood, when he'd kept to dark corners and his attic bedchamber for fear of getting in the duke's way. Now it was noisy and boisterous, full of laughter and happiness. Just stepping into the bright, airy entry hall infused Sam with a sense of well-being—one he sorely needed after the past few days.

He might feel separated from his family, but he loved them all. They were *his*. And he missed them when he was apart from them for long stretches at a time.

As he entered the corridor leading to the drawing room, Esme, whose rapt attention was on the sheet of paper she was reading and not on where she was going, descended the last stair and nearly ran him down. He grabbed her shoulders to steady her. "Whoa there, sister."

She glanced up at him and blushed furiously. "Oh! Sam! Oh! It's so good to see you."

She rapidly folded the paper into a tiny square and tucked it into a pocket of her skirt. He wondered what that was. Correspondence from a gentleman?

He narrowed his eyes as that thought roused all sorts of protective instincts within him. Esme was his only sister. She was twelve years younger than him, and he had a difficult time thinking of her as a woman. However, he knew she had recently turned twenty, so she was not too young to be engaging in romance.

Still, due to the disaster of Esme's first and only Season, her reputation was delicate, at best. The vultures of the *ton* circled her at all times, waiting for an opening so they could sink their sharp beaks into her. She was beautiful and innocent, with a large dowry, and her brother was a duke. Probably half of the male population of London had set its sights on her.

Sam knew Trent took good care of her, but if anyone hurt her, they'd have to answer to Sam.

He kissed her cheek and then, still holding her shoulders, he held her at arm's length and looked her up and down. She was dark-haired, dark-eyed, and olive skinned. Sam had always thought that out of all his siblings, she looked most like him, although he was a great beast of a man, and she had always been quite feminine, in both body and spirit.

"Was that a letter you were reading?"

"Mm. Yes." But she didn't meet his eyes, and her flush deepened.

"Was it from a gentleman, Esme?" he asked softly.

Her eyes widened, and then she did look at him, aghast. "Sam! No! Of course it was not." She shook free of him. "I promise you, it was not."

She seemed appropriately horrified, and that placated him. He turned his lips up into a smile. "Good. Now...where's Trent?"

But he already knew—the sounds of laughter and conversation coming from the drawing room traveled all the way down the corridor. Both he and Esme glanced in that direction, then at each other. She grinned at him. "They cannot wait to see you. And you need to meet little Lukas."

"Lukas *Samson*," he corrected. Trent had named his son after both Sam and Luke.

"Right," she agreed. "Lukas Samson."

The butler had approached before they did and held the door to the drawing room open for them.

Sam's family crowded around him when he entered. His brothers shook his hand—first Trent, then Luke, Mark, and Theo. Trent's wife, Sarah, hugged him, as did Luke's wife, Emma. And then the adults all parted like the Red Sea so he could see little Lukas Samson.

The child was bundled up in a basket on the floor. Sam crouched down and gazed into the serious blue eyes of his nephew.

They stared at each other until Sarah laughed. "Oh dear. See? It's just as I told you."

At Sam's raised eyebrows, Trent explained, "He seems to possess a temperament much like yours."

"Having a child with Sam's temperament isn't a bad thing at all," Luke said. "Daresay it's far preferable to having another Luke."

"Definitely true," Mark agreed, but there was laughter in his voice. "If he took after you," he told Luke, "he'd be howling twenty-four hours a day. Though Sam *is* somewhat overserious." He batted his eyelashes at Sarah. "Don't you wish the lad had taken on my cheerful outlook upon life?"

Sam looked down at the infant, and his siblings' banter faded into the background. He gazed at the child's wrinkled features, and Lukas Samson gazed back at him like a sober old man.

An image barreled through him without warning. A vision of himself, much younger, cradling his own son in his arms right after the boy had been born. Sam had been hunched over in agony, his shoulders slumped in despair. His wife had died just minutes before. And his tiny son—who'd been born too early, was laboring to breathe, his little chest working so hard...struggling...and there was nothing Sam could do for him. For either of them.

The pain, deep in his chest, was so sharp he couldn't breathe. He stared down at the baby, his vision blurring, feeling as broken as he had on the day his son and Charlotte had died.

He'd always wanted children of his own. Even when he was a boy, he'd craved those moments when he was surrounded by his mother and his brothers and sister— his family—and he'd known he'd someday want a family of his own. He'd been thrilled when Charlotte had announced she was expecting, and watching her belly grow

with his child had made him swell with pride and anticipation.

But it wasn't meant to be. Charlotte was taken from
him. His son had lived for mere minutes after his birth before he'd been taken away, too.

Sam could never risk that happening again. He
couldn't open his heart to a family like he had to Charlotte and to his unborn child. Because he couldn't survive
that kind of pain a second time.

He heard the sounds of people around him. His siblings.
Their wives. God. He had never lost his composure in front
of them, and he sure as hell wasn't going to start now.

Still gazing down at his nephew, he patched the cracks
in his heart and found his breath. He drew himself together, blinking away the sting in his eyes, forcing his
focus to return to the here and now. He couldn't dwell on
the past. Doing so would get him nowhere—he'd learned
that lesson long ago.

Sam rose to his feet, turning to Trent and Sarah, who
had slipped their arms around each other and were grinning at him. "He is..." *So much like my own son, it hurts
to look upon him...* "Perfect," he finished softly.

Their smiles grew.

"We think so," Trent said loftily. He was a proud papa.
Sam couldn't blame him.

Trent had once been nearly as somber and serious as
Sam was. For very different reasons, of course. Trent
had not gone to war, he had not lost two wives, and he
had not seen what Sam had seen nor done what Sam
had done—thank God. But from a young age, Trent had
carried the burdens of the dukedom like heavy weights
upon his shoulders. Now it was odd for Sam to see his

solemn brother so...free. So open with his affection and his smiles. Sarah was responsible for that, and Sam was grateful.

He was happy for both his brothers who'd found contentment and peace in their marriages. He didn't hope for the same, knew that for him, some things were simply not in the cards. He'd tried twice and failed twice, and he couldn't—wouldn't—risk doing it all over again. He couldn't jeopardize another woman's safety, another woman's *life*.

For some reason, his thoughts turned to Lady Dunthorpe.

And for some reason, despite all the painful contemplations he'd just been having, his body grew hard at the thought of her.

For God's sake! This was *not* the time or place to be thinking about the woman. He'd come here to get away, and he intended to do just that.

"Let's all sit down," Sarah said to the room at large. Everyone sat save Sam, who took his regular place standing near the window. Sarah smiled at him indulgently. "Have you eaten?"

He shook his head.

"Good. I have a luncheon all planned for us."

Trent frowned. "Do you think it is wise to begin planning luncheons so soon after giving birth?"

She arched her brows. "I feel wonderful. In any case, I have never heard of a woman keeling over three weeks after the birth of her baby because she planned—not even *cooked*, mind you—a meal for her family! For goodness' sake, Simon, I do believe having children and feeding their families was what women were created to do."

"Still…"

Luke clapped him on the back. "You can stop fretting now, old man. The babe's been born, and he and his mother are fat and strong and healthy as a pair of oxen."

Sarah blushed, and Trent scowled at Luke. "Are you insulting my wife?"

"On the contrary," Luke said smoothly. "I am complimenting her health. And the lad's, too—what was he, Trent, three-quarters of a stone?"

"He was."

Sarah grimaced, clearly remembering the pain of the birth. Sam glanced again at the child, who was now being held by Esme. She cooed softly at him, and he gazed with fascination into her face. Sam hadn't thought the child was that large—he seemed miniature, even for an infant—but of course, he was no expert on babies.

Luke shrugged. "There it is, then. Proof. He's a little ox."

A maid brought in refreshments, and they all settled in for several hours of pleasant conversation. Just after noon, they shared a delicious but simple luncheon consisting of bread, sliced meats and cheeses, with sweet oranges for dessert.

After they finished eating, Mark and Theo had an engagement to attend with a friend from Cambridge. After they left, the ladies retired upstairs. They didn't say so, but Sam assumed Sarah needed to feed her infant—he didn't think she'd hired a nurse to perform that task—and of course she would not do so in the presence of the gentlemen.

As soon as the women departed, Trent asked if Sam and Luke wanted to share a bottle of brandy—one of the few remaining bottles the old duke had imported from France before the war.

Sam said he'd have some, but Luke declined.

When Sam and Trent turned to him with raised brows, he shrugged. "I am considering total abstinence from all unnatural forms of intoxication."

Both Sam's and Trent's jaws dropped.

"What? It's not so surprising, is it? You know I am no longer the pleasure seeker I once was." Luke grinned. "Or, at least, I don't leave my house to seek pleasure, I can find all the pleasure I require right at home."

Trent steered the conversation away from Luke's apparent interest in seeking pleasure from his wife. "Abandoning drink altogether, Luke? That's rather puritanical of you."

Luke's lips twisted. "Ah, brother mine. I am not and never will be puritanical. You may trust me on that." He shrugged. "I just find... well, that I sleep more peacefully when my blood has been cleansed of intoxicating substances."

"Well, then." Trent sounded amused. "What can I get you instead? More tea? Coffee? Chocolate? Water?"

"Tea, if you don't mind."

"Not at all. I'll ring for some right away."

A few minutes later, Sam stood back at the window, rotating a glass of brandy in his hands. He rarely sat in the company of others because he was generally more comfortable standing, preferably near a means of escape, even when logically he knew escape wouldn't be necessary. He supposed this was due to long-ingrained habit that had begun in his military days. His family was used to it and no longer commented on this oddity of his.

"So what do you make of this business with the Viscount Dunthorpe?" Trent asked, sitting on the sofa and nursing his own glass of brandy.

Every muscle in Sam's body went tight.

"What of it?" Luke asked disinterestedly.

"He was murdered. Hadn't you heard?"

"No, I hadn't. You know me. I'm not much of one for keeping up with everyone's comings and goings."

"Well, this 'going' was somewhat final," Trent said dryly.

"What happened?" Luke asked.

Trent glanced at Sam. "You heard about it, I suppose."

"I did," Sam said mildly.

Trent turned back to Luke. "He was murdered—shot in the heart in his own drawing room. His butler was a witness—says that it was a tall, dark-haired Frenchman that did him in." He gave a low laugh. "Actually, the description and the sketches I've seen make out the man to be rather similar in appearance to you, Sam."

Sam forced his brows upward and kept his voice mild. "Do they?"

Damn. Richards really had got a good look at him. Well, there was nothing to be done about it now. Except, as soon as this business with Lady Dunthorpe was finished, he really, *really* needed to leave Town.

"They do." Trent took a long swallow of brandy. "And they say his wife—who happens to be French—was part of the scheme. What do you make of it?"

"I'm not sure," Sam said carefully. "But I can't imagine Lady Dunthorpe could have been involved."

"She was seen with the Frenchman as they left the premises."

"My guess?" Sam said. "She was kidnapped."

"You're probably right. I've met her several times, and she never struck me as capable of such an act." Trent frowned until creases lined his forehead. "I do feel like there's something not quite right about it all. Why would a Frenchman murder Dunthorpe? It's true he's an English hero, but as a lawmaker, he's generous toward the French. Sometimes I think his proposed legislations will be of more benefit to Napoleon's country than ours. There are far more insidious targets for the French."

"But the common people haven't read that deeply into his proposals or his politics, have they?"

"No. Sometimes I think I am the only one who has."

Sam gave his brother a considering look. Trent had never been a fool. Sam turned to Luke. "What do you make of it?"

"Never liked the man. He's—he *was*—a bastard. Good riddance."

Sam nodded. Just like Luke to get right to the crux of the matter. "So perhaps we should not question who did away with him."

"Perhaps not," Trent said. "Still...something about it..."

"There are some things in life best left unknown," Sam said in a low voice.

"Very true. *Very* true." Luke raised his teacup in salute, and Sam had the distinct feeling he was talking more about his own secrets than the assassination of Dunthorpe.

"Well, I suppose the biggest concern is that this large Frenchman will go on a murdering rampage of all the aristocrats in London," Trent said. "But that seems far-fetched."

"No," Sam said flatly. "That won't happen."

"You seem very sure about that," Luke said.

"I am." With those two words, he closed the subject. Trent and Luke knew him well enough to understand that it was over, but Trent gave him a long, speculative look before he rose to pour himself another glass of brandy.

His family knew little about what he did. They all knew the basic fact—that he was employed in various missions for the Crown, but they had given up asking him for details beyond that long ago. Still, Sam always had believed that Trent knew a lot more than he claimed to know.

It was good Sam trusted his brother with his life, and he knew the feeling was mutual. Whatever Trent knew, he'd keep to himself.

"How long will you be in Town?" Luke asked him after a few moments of contemplative silence had passed.

He gave his brother a bemused look before answering. It wasn't like Luke to make small talk or to care about such things as Sam's schedule.

He supposed he'd need to eventually become accustomed to both his newly married brothers' changes in demeanor.

"I'm not sure..." He spoke slowly, thinking yet again of Lady Dunthorpe. He hoped to God she was playing an innocent game of whist with Carter and not causing trouble.

Once he'd passed Lady Dunthorpe along to whoever would deal with her next, he'd leave Town. That was the pattern. The Dunthorpe mission had been long and involved—in the interests of protecting Sam's identity in

Town, Adams would send him out of London for the next assignment.

"But I'll probably need to leave Town by the end of the month," he finished.

"Eh," Luke said dismissively. "I think you should retire."

Sam just raised a brow. There was no point in answering. There was no answer. He couldn't explain to Luke that the position he was in didn't allow for "retirement." It wasn't like a military commission he could sell and be done with.

Trent chuckled. "I can't imagine you ever leaving your occupation. What would you do with yourself if you did?"

"Good point," Sam said. It was true. He didn't have friends. He didn't enjoy the usual pursuits of London gentlemen. And what would he do in the country? Beyond his brothers and sister, who were creating their own families now, he knew no one. He would rot away in the country, alone and without purpose. He knew exactly what that would be like—after Charlotte had died, he'd been shot and had returned to England to recover. Stuck at Trent's seat, Ironwood Park, without purpose or meaning. He'd felt like he'd been withering away. It had been the worst year of his life. And then Adams had come to him, given him a reason to live again.

Now he had a purpose.

He needed to change the subject. He turned to Trent. "When do Mark and Theo intend to head north to look for our mother?"

"In a few days," Trent said with a frown. "Esme has asked to accompany them."

"Why?" Sam asked.

"She's been in London for months and is pleading exhaustion with Town."

"I can't blame her for that," Luke said. "London is damnably exhausting."

"She also wants a hand in finding our mother, I think."

Sam folded his arms across his chest and mulled the idea over. "Well, she'll bring her maid, of course, and she'll be with her brothers, who will watch over her."

"I know," Trent said, but there was still doubt in his voice. "I suppose she's just been with me so long, I consider her my responsibility. And she and Sarah are very close. Sarah looks out for her."

"Esme tends to cling to people sometimes," Sam said. "Maybe it'd be best for her to get away for a while."

"Right," Trent said. Still, he didn't sound convinced.

"I don't believe they'll encounter any threats, Trent. We've established that our mother was not kidnapped. She went willingly with this gypsy, Steven Lowell. I don't believe he's dangerous."

Trent sighed. "You're right. He's not. By all accounts, he's a quiet sort. Leaves all the ostentation to the players he hires for his troupe. He's said to be soft-spoken and personable but also a shrewd negotiator."

They were all silent for a minute. Thoughts of Lady Dunthorpe, which had been nudging at Sam's mind all afternoon, broke free. He pushed off from the wall. "I should go."

"Already?" Trent asked.

"Yes. I have ... duties to attend to."

Both his brothers gave him odd looks. But of course they knew better than to question him.

Trent rose from his seat on the sofa, setting his brandy tumbler aside as he did so. "You'll let us know when and if you leave Town?"

"If I can."

"Good enough. Try to visit again before you go."

Sam looked at Luke. "Will you be remaining in London this spring?"

Luke slanted a glance at Trent. "If Trent and the duchess are. Emma wants to stay close to help with her new nephew."

Sam raised a brow. Luke had openly avoided Trent in the past, though he'd also shown up in drunken stupors at Trent's doorstep more than once. Sam had always felt that Luke and Trent had secretly desired to have a closer relationship but hadn't known how. Maybe their wives were helping them to pave the way.

In any case, it would be good to know where Luke was this spring. Luke had spent the past several years moving about aimlessly, but Emma was definitely a grounding influence. They were happy together, and that gave Sam a feeling of deep satisfaction. Luke had been through too much pain and deserved the happiness he'd finally found.

He said his farewells and left his brothers. When the door of Trent House closed behind him, a gaping emptiness seemed to yawn in his soul.

His siblings had always done their best to bring him in to the Hawkins family circle, but the knowledge that he was truly the outsider was deeply ingrained within him. In their presence, he felt like he was an integral part of the House of Trent. But when he left them, the realization always struck him that he was truly alone. That he always would be.

He squelched the empty feeling, as he always did, and thoughts of Lady Dunthorpe came rushing in to fill the void.

Lady Dunthorpe. She made him feel...different. Like no one ever had. She'd made him smile more in the past few days than he had in the past several years combined.

He wanted—needed—to see her. He told himself it was to ensure she was all right and hadn't caused any problems with Carter and Laurent.

But he knew it was more than that.

He found himself pushing his horse, frustrated by the usual London traffic. By the time he dismounted in the mews behind the safe house, his heart was pounding in anticipation. He took the horse into the stable and brushed it down quickly.

A few minutes later, he hurried in through the back door. The house was quiet in the waning afternoon light. He paused a few steps inside, then called out sharply, "Carter?"

Silence and then, "We're here!" from down the corridor. The drawing room.

Sam released a long breath and with it a great deal of the tension that had been building within him all day.

He shut the back door and locked it securely, then strode to the drawing room.

Laurent and Lady Dunthorpe were bent over a half-played game of chess when he entered. Judging by the positions of the remaining pieces on the board, the two of them were evenly matched.

Carter looked up over his newspaper. "Welcome home."

Laurent looked over his shoulder. "Gad, Hawk. You look like you've just run all the way from Calais."

Sam gave him a wry look. "Unfortunately, I cannot walk on water."

Laurent's eyes went wide. "No! I always thought you could!"

Carter chuckled, and Sam rolled his eyes heavenward. Laurent was mature for a lad of fifteen—or almost sixteen, as he always reminded Sam—but sometimes he did act his age.

He lowered his gaze to Lady Dunthorpe. "How was your afternoon?"

"Most satisfactory." Her lips were flat but something—humor, perhaps—sparkled in her eyes. "Laurent and Carter are excellent jailors."

Laurent clutched his chest. "A compliment? Did I just receive a compliment from our esteemed guest?"

"If being called a jailor is a compliment," Sam told him.

Laurent dropped his hand and slanted him a glance over his shoulder. "You are adept at ruining a mood, aren't you?"

"Always," Sam told him. But he couldn't take his eyes off Lady Dunthorpe. And as he gazed at her, something warm and sweet flushed through him.

The sensation startled him, threw him off kilter. And he knew, without a doubt, that this woman had insinuated herself into a place inside him where he'd never allowed anyone. Not even Marianne. Not even Charlotte.

He didn't want this, but he had no idea how to stop it. How to control it. How to reconstruct those shields to keep her out.

He had to try.

* * *

Hawk was home. She'd waited for him all day, growing more worried as the hours had ticked by. Where had he gone? What was he doing? Would he be back? Each time she'd asked Laurent and Carter, they'd given her a nonanswer or changed the subject or tried in some other way to distract her. It was highly frustrating.

But then he walked into the room, and she'd been glad to see him. So glad, her heart had soared.

It had *soared*.

She must be mad. Or an idiot. Perhaps both.

There was comfort now in listening to these three men speak to one another. There was an easiness about them, a camaraderie that she'd never really witnessed among men before. These three trusted one another. The two older men protected and mentored Laurent, and he clearly worshipped them both.

She moved her bishop. "Check," she told Laurent.

"Ah, I see how it is," he said. "Sidetrack the lad, then take advantage."

"Oh, so now you're a lad?" Carter asked.

"When it suits me," he said sternly. "But only then." He moved deftly out of check.

She beat Laurent in chess, though it took another quarter of an hour. Then she played Hawk, who, after some browbeating, grudgingly took the seat across from her. It hadn't taken her long to realize the man rarely sat, and when he did, he fidgeted nonstop. This time, however, his restlessness seemed somewhat contained, and within a matter of minutes, he beat her handily.

She couldn't help her poor performance. She found his proximity overwhelming, diverting, utterly distracting.

Laurent stood over the chessboard, arms crossed, his lips pressed into a scowl. "I told you he was good. Ruthless, too." He turned to the older man. "Give a lady a chance, Hawk."

Hawk quirked a brow. "And ruin my reputation?"

Her breathing quickened. Oh, how she liked this playful side of this powerful man. There was something inordinately appealing about it.

Carter rose to make dinner—and ordered Laurent to join him because he needed to chop vegetables for the stew.

They wandered off, bickering companionably.

"Another game?" Hawk asked when the door had snapped shut behind them.

"You wish to see me desiccated in moments yet again? What a scoundrel you are," she said.

He raised his brows. "Scoundrel?"

"Yes. Scoundrel."

The edges of his lips tilted upward. "No one has ever called me a scoundrel before. Perhaps you mistake the meaning of the word."

She gave him an imperious look. "Not at all."

He looked puzzled, but he didn't comment further. "A different game, then?"

She just looked at him. They fell into silence, staring at each other over the chessboard. Her heart pounded so hard.

How could this man make her feel safe? How could she believe him when he said he wouldn't hurt her?

He killed your husband. Your husband!

She drew in a shaky breath, and he reached across the table and tucked a wayward strand of hair behind her ear, his fingers skimming the top of her earlobe and sending a deep shudder through her body.

Her husband's body was not yet cold in its grave. *Dieu*, it probably wasn't even *in* its grave.

"No," she breathed.

He lowered his hand and tilted his head. "No, what, my lady?"

"You...cannot..." She shook her head. Her voice shook. "You said...you said you wouldn't hurt me."

"Is that what you think I would do? Hurt you?" His voice was low, silky smooth, and the timbre of it sent a warm, skittering sensation tumbling through her.

He wouldn't hurt her physically. He was big and domineering, but she hadn't forgotten the way he'd held her when he'd taken her from her husband's home. He'd been strong as a rock but also as gentle with her as if she were something precious and breakable. Even though he'd thought her a traitor and probably deserving of death like her husband.

And now...did he still think that of her? She thought he probably did. Yet the way he touched her was like he was touching a fragile rose whose petals were on the verge of falling.

"Yes," she whispered. Because he would hurt her if she allowed him into her heart. She had always dreamed of love and never attained it. She was older now and wise enough to know that she could never expect to get it— *especially* not from a man who'd killed her husband.

She was insane to be as intrigued by him as she was. And yet...the way he looked at her, the way he was looking at her now, made her want to touch him. To crawl into the strong hold of his embrace.

He glanced away, a frown drawing his brows together. Her fingers itched to smooth that deep furrow above his nose with the pads of her thumbs. Touching him...it would feel so good. She felt so safe in his presence; she couldn't imagine how safe she'd feel in his arms.

Still, a part of her was appalled by the thought of touching him.

She'd known men who'd killed before. Men who were in armies, French and British alike, who'd taken lives because they had to. Because that was war.

It struck her like a blow to the chest as she gazed at him and he stared down at the chessboard. This was why Hawk killed, too. Not because he was a murderer by nature, or because he derived joy from the act. But because this was war. Somehow, the British must have caught on to the fact that Dunthorpe had been betraying them. They'd done the only thing that could be done to traitors of his ilk. They'd had him killed.

And it was true—Dunthorpe was a traitor. He was a horrible, evil man. How could she blame the English— Hawk, specifically—for ending his life? Dunthorpe had needed to be stopped. He'd been the direct cause of hundreds, if not thousands, of his countrymen's deaths. He'd done far more to deserve a death sentence than her parents and brother had—as far as she knew, they'd only been selfish and stupid in the flaunting of their wealth. They hadn't been true enemies of France. But Dunthorpe was a true enemy of England. She *knew* this with as much certainty as she knew the sky was blue.

She had forgiven Hawk, she realized. On the fourth evening after her husband's death, she forgave his killer.

It was freeing, that realization. So very freeing. An enormous weight lifted from her chest, and she felt light for the first time in days. Years, perhaps.

Still, she shouldn't allow this odd, simmering attraction she felt for Hawk to continue. He was still a spy, she was still French, and he still believed she was a traitor.

The only sane course of action would be to leave this place. Leave Hawk and this confounding attraction, leave London, leave England. Start again somewhere else, where she had no reputation, where she could be free...

"Hawk," she whispered.

The air between them seemed to crackle. He looked up, meeting her eyes, his expression dark, hard, inscrutable. He searched her face as if he could read all her secrets from her expression.

"Please..." she begged, "*please* let me leave this place." It was her only hope. Her only way to stop this...whatever was happening between them.

He gave a slight shake of his head. "You know I cannot."

"Why?" And out of sheer desperation, she blurted the truth. Most of it. "I was not involved in Dunthorpe's activities. I only suspected. That was why I returned early from Brighton. I knew he was planning something terrible—something big and something that would be devastating to this country. I came to London secretly, and I hid under the drawing room table because I'd seen a note with the meeting time and location written upon it. I thought if I hid there and listened to what transpired, I'd learn what he was planning."

Hawk's brows rose, and something like respect shimmered in his dark gaze. "That's a dangerous game."

She swallowed hard, pushing down all the desperation and pain and fear she'd felt. How could she explain her recklessness to Hawk? "I had nothing to lose. Nothing."

"Not your life?"

"I didn't care. Not just then. My life...it seemed insignificant compared to what he might have done."

He stared at her, then slowly shook his head. "And you think this is enough for me to simply set you free?"

She clasped her hands tightly in her lap. "Yes." She wished it were, though she knew it wouldn't be.

"No. I need more." He leaned forward. "Look at me, my lady."

She dragged her eyes up to his, knowing fear—and probably something even worse—shone in them. He didn't react to the look on her face; in fact, his expression held no emotion whatsoever.

"If what you say is true, then I am sorry." His voice was gentle but firm. "You were in the wrong place at the wrong time. Because of that, you may never again be free."

Just as his words sank in, the world around them exploded.

Chapter Six

───※───

$\mathcal{T}$he loud *crack* of gunfire shattered the peace of the drawing room. The walls shook. Glass splintered all around her.

Someone rammed into her. The chair toppled, and she landed hard on her side on the floor, the carpeting doing little to break the fall, with a heavy weight atop her.

"Stay down."

Through her closing throat, she vaguely registered that the growling voice was Hawk's, that he was on top of her, that he'd pushed her down behind the table.

The shot had come through the drawing room window. That by tackling her to the floor, he'd taken her out of the line of fire.

"Who?" she cried out, her voice hoarse as she gulped in air. "What—"

"Hush," he bit out.

Another shot was fired, its retort jolting through her body as it echoed in the small space. "Damn it," Hawk said tensely. His lips brushed her ear. "They're close." He moved off her, and she saw the glint of metal in his hand as he inched around the base of the table and aimed a pistol toward the window. He fired the weapon with another resounding *boom*. The sound of the gunshot ripped through her, and just like that, she started to shake.

He glanced at her, and his eyes softened as he noticed her trembling. She couldn't contain it. He wrapped his arm around her waist. They half sat, half reclined in an awkward position on the carpet.

"Shh," he murmured, gentle now. His fingers rubbed soothing circles on her back. "Can you crawl to the door? We need to get out of this room."

"*Oui*...y-y-yes."

Busy reloading his weapon, he continued to speak to her in a low voice. "Good. Stay here for now. Keep the table between you and the window. I don't want them to see you."

Another gunshot. She yelped, and he moved his hand from his gun to slip it around her waist again. He leaned close, his lips nuzzling her hair as she burrowed into him. He felt so solid against her. So big. So safe.

"Shh."

She took a deep breath, trying to calm her wild trembling. "Hush," he soothed. "You'll be all right. Just do as I say and try to keep calm."

She attempted a nod, but it came out as a random, jerky movement instead.

"All right." He continued to use that quiet, soothing voice. "Stay here. I need to go to the desk. There's another gun in the drawer."

Another gunshot cracked through the air. Glass shattered somewhere inside the room. He paused but then spoke calmly, as if the world wasn't going mad. Yet his entire body, everywhere she touched him, was as tense as stone. "When I return, you're going to crawl to the door while I cover you."

"They're going to come in," she said in a rush, her voice reed thin. "And when they do, they're going to...."

Another gunshot, and she flinched against him.

"Don't worry. Some of those shots are from Carter and Laurent. They'll be out there holding them for us."

Trying to swallow down the enormous lump in her throat, she nodded.

And then he was gone, his presence deserting her as he crawled in the direction of the desk.

More gunshots—three of them in quick succession. One of the bullets whizzed very close to the table, straight through the tablecloth, making it flutter. Thank God it was on the opposite side of the table from where Hawk was.

So many shots. It was a true battle. *Fought over what?* she wondered. Surely it had something to do with Dunthorpe's death. Were those his men out there? Was Francis attempting to kill Hawk in retaliation?

She wrapped her arms around her knees and curled herself into a small ball. It seemed an eternity before Hawk returned to her. During that time, two more shots were fired.

And when he returned, she saw his coat was torn at the shoulder, and the remains of the tattered shirt were covered with blood.

He saw where her eyes had gone and gave a low grunt. "It's nothing. A scratch. The man has no aim to speak of. I was in his direct line of fire. You ready?"

Another gunshot. She heard scrambling noises outside, grunts, then shouts.

"We're running out of time," Hawk said. "We need to go. Now. Stay low."

He took her by the arm and pulled her toward the door in a low crawl, keeping his body between hers and the gaping skeleton of the bow window that opened out onto the street, its curtains fluttering in the breeze. Cool spring air washed over her body.

Shouts sounded from the street outside the window and then a *boom* and a bullet zipped in front of Élise, inches from her nose. The shouting grew in volume— cries of pain and English words and curses her panicked mind couldn't decipher.

A little stuttering moan flew from her mouth before she could stop it, but Hawk ignored it. He yanked her forward. Reaching up, he grabbed the handle and threw the door open, thrusting her behind it just as another gunshot sent chess pieces scattering to the floor behind them.

He jumped up, pulling her to her feet at his side as he closed the door.

"Hurry," he snapped in a harsh command. He pulled her down the corridor toward the back door at a dead run. She nearly tripped over her skirts attempting to keep his pace, but as she reeled forward, he gripped her waist and hauled her back so she didn't fall.

Seconds later, they burst into the mews behind the town house. He took less than a second to scan the street up and down.

"This way." He led her behind two stables with a narrow dirt path between them. They emerged onto a small street, running full out, nearly knocking down a couple who gasped and stared at them wide-eyed. Élise could feel their gazes burning into their backs the rest of the way down the street.

They crossed the street at the corner; then Hawk opened a wrought-iron gate and led her between two houses with more mews in the back. There, he threw open a door to reveal a pair of horses already hitched to a small, black-lacquered and unmarked carriage. The driver—a man she'd never seen before, tipped his hat to them but didn't descend to let them in. Hawk opened the carriage door and ushered her inside. In the blink of an eye, he had settled next to her, closed the door, and rapped on the ceiling.

The carriage lurched into motion. She looked at Hawk. "Who is that man? The driver?"

"One of us," he said tightly. He snapped the curtains shut on both sides of them.

"Where are we going?"

"Somewhere safe."

"That is not an answer!" She was still trembling, and her breaths were coming out in sharp bursts. She knew panic was written all over her face.

He took her shoulders, one in each of his large hands, and turned her to face him. "Trust me, Lady Dunthorpe."

"Please...*Please* do not call me that."

He seemed shaken by that request. "Then what should I call you?"

"My name is Élisabeth, but call me Élise. Everyone"— everyone who mattered—"calls me Élise."

His lips pressed tightly together, but not removing that implacable gaze from her face, he nodded.

"Is Hawk your real name? I do not think it is. No parent names his child 'Hawk.' At least not proper English parents, which is certainly what you have. Your accent gives you away."

He snorted, then shook his head. "A proper English education, perhaps, but not proper English parents."

"So is it or is it not your real name? Hawk, I mean?"

He gazed at her in silence for a moment; then his decision clicked into place. She could see it on his face. His thumb brushed over her jawbone; then he said softly, "My real name is Samson Hawkins. So, yes, Hawk is part of my real name. It is what my colleagues have always called me."

"Samson Hawkins," she repeated. Then, "Monsieur Hawkins."

"Everyone calls me Sam. Everyone who doesn't call me Hawk, that is."

She nodded and tried it: "Sam."

His eyes darkened. That rough finger stroked over her jawbone again. "The way you say it... with your accent. It's..." He looked away with a little shake of his head. "Never mind."

Something caught in her throat. He'd saved her life tonight. He was so handsome. His touch was so gentle, and when he turned away with that brief flash of emotion in his expression, she melted inside.

"Where are we going?" she asked again, but this time her voice was gruff. She was still scared, but the fear had lost its sharp edge and was now a muzzy feeling that had spread into her limbs. She felt alone, bereft, frightened, and shaken. She wanted him to touch her, hold her, and continue to keep her safe.

His hands dropped from her shoulders.

"Somewhere safe," he repeated.

She gazed up at him; then she gave a resolute sigh. "I suppose I'll find out where once we arrive."

He nodded. When he began to turn away from her, she said, "But I fear you will bring me to your superiors. Where there are more of you...spy men. Who won't be as kind to me as you and Carter and Laurent have been."

"No," he said flatly. "I'm not taking you to them."

Where then? But she knew he wouldn't answer.

"What did those men want?" she whispered.

"You don't know?"

"Well...I..." She shook her head and then tried to think through the muddle in her head. "Dunthorpe's men? But were they trying to kill me or you?"

He slanted a wry glance in her direction. "Both of us, I think."

She sat back, stunned. Then she said dully, "Even Dunthorpe's men believe I am in league with you."

The thought of that—of all the powerful enemies she'd earned—caused panic to boil up within her all over again. Not only those who'd been in league with Dunthorpe would hate her, but the population in general, whose admiration for him was legendary...and she'd had nothing to do with any of it. As Hawk—*Sam*—had said, she'd been in the wrong place at the wrong time. Now his words about her never being free began to make more sense.

She drew in a long, shaky breath. "They'll kill me," she said hoarsely. "They will not stop until I am dead."

"Who won't stop?"

His face was impassive again. There he was again, that cold, calculating Hawk. The Hawk who wanted nothing from her but information.

"The English," she said.

"Which English?"

"All of them." Her breaths came in short bursts as panic threatened to overwhelm her once more. "They've never loved me, but now they must hate me. *Hate* me."

She blinked hard to try to focus her blurring vision.

All of a sudden, Sam hauled her into his lap and wrapped his arms around her. "Shh, Élise. It's going to be all right. I'm not going to allow anything to happen to you."

"How…how can…you promise that?" she gasped out. She couldn't get enough air. Her chest was constricting, closing in on itself. She couldn't take a deep breath, couldn't breathe at all…

"I promise it," he murmured. "I promise."

His big, blunt fingers pressed through the fabric of her dress and into the tight muscles of her back. He gathered her closer to him, and she curled up against the hardness of his chest. Safety. His touch brought her such comfort. Such…peace. Slowly, her breaths began to calm, and warmth traveled through her, bringing with it a deep longing, a craving she'd never experienced in her life.

A craving for more. For more *Sam*.

He gazed at her, his expression tender even as his eyes glittered. And she saw it there in his eyes. Desire climbing until it equaled her own. Ever so slowly, his fingers dragged up her back. Then his hand moved around until he cupped her cheek and tilted her face toward his. He moved closer, inexorably closer, until she could feel his strength and his heat, palpable forces in the tiny space between their lips.

Then he closed the distance. His lips touched hers, the tiniest, most erotic brush.

Her own reaction shocked her. She should have gone stiff, pulled away, slapped him. But she did none of that.

Instead she melted against him. His lips firmed, moving gently, transferring calmness and strength into her. They glided over her mouth in a gentle caress, exploring, tasting, soothing. He tasted smooth and warm and sweet.

How could such a man, such a large masculine man, taste sweet? But he did. He was *delicious*. She gripped his coat in her hands and pulled herself even closer to him. She wanted to sink into him.

He'd kidnapped her and held her against her will, yes. But despite the violence in him, there was something about this man that was pure goodness. There was something about him that she trusted completely. She had never trusted a man in her life. It seemed insane that she should trust this one.

But she did.

She kissed him harder, pushing her body to him, opening to him, allowing the heat of his breath to wash over her and through her, allowing his tongue to touch the inside of her lip. He nibbled at her mouth, from the edge to the center. Their noses brushed as they adjusted the angles of their heads so they could kiss more, taste more, closer and deeper.

The simmer in her core rose to an inferno that spread through her limbs. She was on fire, her body aching, burning...for what exactly, she didn't know. But she did know one thing...Her body wanted Samson Hawkins. *She* wanted him.

She wanted to touch him. Feel his skin under her

hands. Her fingers moved to the cloth-covered buttons of his coat. She felt for the top one and slid it open.

Abruptly, he pulled back. It took a second or two for her hazy gaze to focus upon his face.

"Élise ... we cannot ..."

She knew that. Did he think she didn't know that? But need—desire—had stolen all her logic. "One minute you are a scoundrel, but then your honorable side comes out to wage battle with that scoundrel."

"I don't know if it's honorable, but that side of me always wins."

"But I want to be the scoundrel, too, you see. It doesn't matter, does it, what we do in the confines of this little space? No one but us will ever know ..."

He released a low groan. "But it does." He shifted in the seat, and she felt the hard ridge of him under her thigh. The press of his erection against her flesh made her breath stutter and her body give a dark, delicious pang of anticipation.

This scoundrel had seduced her thoroughly, and without even trying. But her body was anticipating what her heart knew would not be happening. Not now. Not tonight, and most likely not ever.

Ever so gently, he lifted her and settled her onto the seat beside him. She clasped her hands in her lap as he pushed the curtain open a sliver to look through the window.

"We're almost at the meeting point," he said softly.

"The meeting point?"

He nodded.

"We are meeting someone?"

"Yes. Laurent."

"And Carter?"

"No. He has different duties in the event of an attack on the house."

"What are those?"

He shrugged. "Reporting the incident. Cleaning up any possible difficulties if I am not present to do so. We plan for every contingency."

"I see."

Her face heated as she imagined what it would have been like if Sam had allowed her to continue...if she'd stripped off his coat and shirt and felt his body—his skin—beneath her palms.

Laurent would have opened the door and seen her wantonly pressing herself against his mentor.

As the carriage drew to a halt, she knew she should be glad that at least Sam hadn't lost his senses. Because she certainly had.

She still ached with unfulfilled passion, but another part of her burned from his rejection. She'd been too carried away to stop, but he clearly hadn't...And that hurt a part of her she'd never known was capable of hurting.

"Stay here," Sam ordered. He opened the door and stepped outside. Élise gazed at the door closest to her, her eyes dropping to the handle, her chest a confused tangle of emotions—embarrassment, shame, hurt, desire, and more she couldn't unravel.

Maybe she could do it—escape from these beguiling, confusing men. Run. Find a safe place where she could be free of all this.

She thought about the implications of tonight's attack. If it was Francis who'd been trying to kill them—and who else could it be?—there was nowhere she'd be safe.

But Sam had promised he wouldn't let harm come to her.

It would be no use running, anyhow. She hadn't forgotten how easily Sam had caught her when she'd run before.

No. This was not the time. She knew these men now—what they were capable of. They would catch her in the blink of an eye.

She couldn't—wouldn't—succumb to being a prisoner forever. Eventually, she'd be given the right opportunity to escape. When it came, she'd take it. And the odd feelings she was beginning to have for her captor did not make a bit of difference to her plan. Not one bit.

They didn't dally long. Within a few minutes, Sam slid in beside her once more. Seconds later, the carriage lurched into motion again.

"Laurent's driving now," he explained. "We're leaving Smithy—he was the first driver—here in London."

"So . . . we are leaving London?"

"Yes."

"But you will not tell me where we are going?"

He sighed. "We're going north. To a safe house in a remote location where hopefully no one will be able to locate us."

"Were Laurent or Carter hurt?"

"No. Laurent is here and in one piece. Carter will remain in London, and he is also unhurt."

But Sam had been hurt. He'd gotten shot—she remembered the ragged tear at his shoulder. *Bon Dieu.* She'd been so muddled, she'd forgotten, and she hadn't been able to see it clearly in the dimness of the carriage. She closed her eyes. "What about you?"

"What about me?" Surprise was evident in his voice.

"You are not in one piece."

"Of course I am."

"Your arm..."

"I told you," he said, "it is nothing."

"I must look at it. Show me, please."

With a sigh, he turned, exposing his left shoulder to her sight for the first time since they'd entered the carriage.

She swallowed hard. It was a ragged, bloody wound. She was shocked he hadn't flinched, hadn't favored it when he'd held her.

He was a strong man. Now it was her turn to be strong.

"Is there any cheap gin to be found in this carriage?" she asked.

He gave her a bemused look. "Gin? What do you intend to do with gin?"

"I shall give you a great deal of it to drink; then I shall splash it profusely over your injured flesh."

He raised a brow, but he bent over and pulled a woven sack from beneath the seat and proceeded to rummage through it. Finally he was favoring his arm, she noted. Perhaps his reaction of pain had been delayed by all they'd gone through tonight.

He pulled out a corked bottle of red liquid. She frowned. "That is wine, I believe."

"Will it do?"

"No. Not well. But begin to drink it, if you please."

"Gladly," he said. "I was beginning to get thirsty anyhow." His lips quirked in a rare smile. "There's a bit of dried salted herring in there. Not quite the dinner I'd hoped for, but it's all we have."

"No, thank you," she clipped out. Food had never

sounded more unappealing than it did at this moment. And salted herring? Just...no.

He uncorked the bottle and drank a hearty swallow straight from it before handing it to her. "Thirsty?"

Actually, she was. She took the bottle and took her own healthy swallow, feeling rather pleasantly barbaric. She hadn't drunk wine from anything but crystal in many years.

She wiped her mouth with the back of her hand, realizing for the first time that the only items she had in her possession were her undergarments, her shoes, and the too-large simple cotton dress she wore. No pelisse or coat, no gloves or hat. The moment she stepped out of this carriage, she would be completely conspicuous to any passerby.

She gazed down ruefully at the simple dress that hung on her like a sack. At least no one would accuse her of being the elegant, untouchable Lady Dunthorpe. She'd hated the role for so, *so* many reasons.

"Thank you," she said politely, handing the bottle back to him. "Now...Is there anything else in that satchel? A jug of water, perhaps?"

"There is."

She pondered for a moment, debating the wisdom of using water or wine. "Pass me the water, then."

"Of course."

He handed her a jug, this one corked as well. She set it aside and put her hand to the waistcoat she'd almost ripped off him in the throes of lust just minutes ago. Their eyes met.

"I'll need to remove your waistcoat and shirt."

"Are you serious about this?"

"There is no doctor in this carriage, is there? And I do not think I am a fool for assuming that you have no intention to stop for one."

"You're right," he admitted, "on both counts."

"Then I propose I do my best. I am, in fact, not a doctor, but I do possess some limited medical knowledge."

Marie was the one who'd helped the injured and ill *aristos* who came to her in Paris during the Terror, usually wearing dark cloaks and skulking to their door at night, afraid of going to a "proper" doctor. She and Marie had lived in hiding, pretending to be commoners, for two years after Élise's parents and brother were killed and before she and Marie were able to escape, with Élise's uncle's help, to England.

Élise had been quiet in those days, watching Marie, helping whenever she could. Terrified to open her mouth for fear that her aristocratic accent would expose her. The patients had thought of her as Marie's mute little sister. She'd absorbed as much knowledge as she could, and Marie had fostered her curiosity. Together in England, they'd continued to share an interest in healing, but on a more academic level, since they'd seldom had the opportunity to practice it.

Her gaze locked on to Sam's wound. Here was an opportunity, oozing with blood, right in front of her. She slid off the seat and crouched in front of him in the small enclosed space of the carriage.

Sam reached up to help her with his waistcoat buttons, but she shooed his hands away. She slipped the black buttons through their holes and slid the wool over his broad shoulders, careful not to touch the wound on the left side. But her hands did skim over the front of his upper chest, and her body leapt back to life at the feel of the powerful muscles beneath her fingertips.

She folded the waistcoat and set it aside. She didn't meet his eyes, just gazed at where his shirt was tucked into the waistband of his trousers.

"Now the shirt," she murmured as she grasped the linen and began to pull it out. He held himself rigid, perfectly still, but she felt his eyes on her.

The carriage dipped through a rut in the road and she began to tumble to the side, but his arm whipped out to steady her. She gripped the edge of the seat beside his thigh—his solid, rock-hard, thick thigh—and glanced up at him.

"Do not use your arm again until I have assessed the wound," she scolded him. "I forbid it."

"Do you, now?" Humor edged his voice. He let her go and took another deep draft of wine.

"Hold still," she snapped.

He laughed. He actually laughed! It was the first time she'd ever heard him laugh, and her gaze snapped to his face in astonishment.

"How you may laugh at a time like this is beyond my comprehension."

"A time like this? What do you mean?"

"A time of danger."

"We are out of danger, my lady," he reminded her.

"Élise."

"We are out of danger, Élise." The way he said her name, with that perfect French accent, made a shudder of desire run down her spine.

"But we are not out of danger," she insisted. "I am well hated. Obviously, someone has decided that I am the enemy and he has determined that you must die, too."

"He won't find us," he said in a tone of supreme confidence.

"Ever?"

He blew out a breath, and his dark eyes studied her, all seriousness now. "I prefer to focus on the present. It's safer that way. For me, the most direct road to madness is sitting still and attempting to conjure possible futures. And for the present, we are perfectly safe."

"Why would you do that? It is unreasonable not to consider the future." She'd finished untucking his shirt and began to pull it upward, revealing miles of muscled, olive-toned, deliciously hard male flesh.

He was so beautiful. Her thoughts trailed off for a protracted moment as she focused on her task. A few scars marred his perfect flesh—there was a jagged one in the rough shape of a circle just below his right shoulder. And a trio of long, slashing ones over his right hip.

"Because most of the futures I conjure up are not pleasant ones," he said quietly.

She paused to gaze up at him. "Why?"

He shrugged. "Think of what I do."

She swallowed hard and returned her gaze to her task. "Ah. That. Raise your good arm, please." He did, and she maneuvered the shirt over his head and off his arm. As she began the process of drawing it over his wound, she said, "I believe, monsieur, that I prefer your laughter over your melancholy."

"Sorry to disappoint you."

"No, you do not disappoint me. I do not think you are a man who laughs frequently. It makes me happy that I can cause you to do so, even if it is not very often."

She finished pulling the shirt off, leaving his heavily

muscled torso completely bare. She forced herself not to stare, however; instead she focused on the wound. The bullet had torn across his outer arm, taking bits of cloth and flesh with it. Clearly, it hadn't lodged inside his body, which was a good thing.

"It would be better if I could stitch it, but I will assume you do not have the proper implements for such a task."

"You are experienced in stitching wounds?" he asked in surprise.

"Somewhat."

"Well." He paused to take that in, then said, "No. I don't believe there is medical equipment like that in this carriage."

"That is very stupid," she told him.

"Oh?" There it was again, that tiny edge of humor in his voice. "Why?"

"Because this is your vehicle of escape. Did you believe you were all untouchable? That even fleeing a group of men intent upon murdering you, you would not be injured?"

"We certainly never intended to become injured," he said. "In any case, none of us have surgical experience. Nor did we anticipate fleeing with a noblewoman who did."

She blew out a frustrated breath. "Stupid, as I said. What if the shot had gone through your shoulder, lodged in a bone, nicked an artery? You would be very dead by now."

"But I am not."

She made a small growling noise.

"Does it make you happy, Élise?"

"Does *what* make me happy?"

"That I am not dead?"

"Infinitely happy," she grumbled. "Now. I will be picking the fabric from your wound thread by thread. It will be very unpleasant."

And he laughed again, that deep, low, throaty laugh that *did* make her happy. Her lips twitched, fighting to smile, but she tamed them into flatness.

"Be still," she ordered, tearing at the tattered remains of his shirtsleeve. "It is time to make this clean."

Chapter Seven

Given her lack of proper implements, Sam couldn't fault Élise's work on his arm.

The wound definitely wasn't a serious one. He'd experienced more severe injuries in his lifetime. Compared to some of those wounds, this was a scratch. But he couldn't deny it—he gobbled up her careful attentions like a starving man. He watched her as she worked, focus deep in those blue eyes, her lips pressed into a straight line.

She picked all the debris from the wound, cleaned it with plentiful amounts of water, then dried it and wrapped it with strips taken from his ruined shirtsleeve and pieces of cotton she tore from her petticoat.

She was efficient, competent. She was serious. She was the most beautiful thing he'd ever laid eyes on.

After she finished, they sat for a long while in companionable silence. It had long since grown dark, and erotic thoughts crowded in Sam's mind. The way she'd responded when he kissed her. Impassioned, fiery. She was a little ball of heat. What would it be like when she exploded under his hands? Under his mouth? With his cock buried deep inside her?

He tilted his head back on the cushion, swallowing a groan.

He was so damn debauched. He tried to thrust the images back, but her warm body was so close. Her sweet smell, like violets, permeated the small space. Her upper arm brushed over his. Her thigh pressed against his. He knew, from when she'd worn the breeches, how feminine that thigh was. What would it look like when she was naked? Pale and shapely...

The coach came to a sudden halt, jolting Sam from his thoughts. They had left London behind and were now on the London Road heading north. Toward Lancashire and Lake Windermere, where the safe house was located.

"Stay here," he told Élise. They needed to change out the horses, and he needed to give Laurent a rest.

She glared at him. "You cannot expect me to remain inside this very small space until time comes to an end."

"I can expect you to remain here until we arrive at our destination. You cannot leave the carriage. You're not dressed appropriately, and you'll arouse suspicion."

"And if I require...a private moment?"

He sighed. "I don't intend to torture you. Of course we will stop if you require it."

She made a disgruntled noise.

"Do you need one now?"

"Well. Yes. I do. However, it is not urgent. Not yet."

"Good. We'll stop on the road as soon as we leave this town."

To his surprise, she let out a low laugh.

"What's so funny?"

"I am becoming a true barbarian," she said. "Drinking straight from a jug. Tearing up my petticoats for bandages. Pissing, so to speak, upon the side of the road."

He raised a brow.

"I believe I will enjoy this barbaric life," she said primly.

He shook his head at her even as a smile played at the edges of his lips, then took his leave of her and went outside to the innyard. He and Laurent made quick, efficient work of exchanging the horses for fresh ones. As they led the new horses back to the carriage, Laurent covered his mouth against a huge yawn, and Sam clapped him on the shoulder.

"Long day, eh?"

"Long evening," Laurent admitted. "The day wasn't so bad. Spent most of it playing chess with Lady Dunthorpe, after all. Not an unpleasant way to pass the time."

Sam didn't find spending time with her unpleasant, either, but he still scowled.

What was this feeling? Possessiveness, he realized. He felt like he didn't want anyone to speak with her or to enjoy her company, except himself. And he damn well didn't want her enjoying anyone else's company.

That was ridiculous. He'd never felt that way about any woman before. It would be idiotic to start with this one.

He took a deep breath through gritted teeth. "Right."

"But..." Laurent turned troubled eyes on Sam. "Hawk..." He swallowed hard, his throat making a jerking movement with the action. "I think...I think I might've killed one of them."

Something inside Sam went cold. Laurent's first kill.

He'd known it would come someday, but...Hell. It wasn't something to celebrate. "How are you?" he asked in a low voice.

"I...don't know."

Damn. The boy was so young, and he sounded shaken to his core. Sam squeezed his shoulder. "You did well. You kept Lady Dunthorpe safe. Without you out there, I'm not sure we could have escaped from that room."

Laurent nodded, then blinked hard. "Right."

"You did what you needed to protect your own, lad," Sam said in a low voice. "I'd have expected nothing less."

Laurent gave him a somber smile; then he seemed to shake it off. Or perhaps he just wished to change the subject. He gestured to Sam's arm, obviously seeing the bandage through the hole in the sleeve. "Lady Dunthorpe's handiwork?"

Sam nodded.

"She did a fine job. I was a bit worried."

"It's nothing," Sam muttered. He took a breath. "Get some sleep. I'll wake you a few hours before dawn."

"Right."

Laurent opened the door and disappeared into the carriage compartment, and Sam climbed up to the driver's perch.

He didn't push the horses but allowed them to walk at a slow pace. The lanterns at the front posts of the carriage helped, but it was a dark night with heavy cloud cover and no moon to speak of.

It was quiet out here, the clomping of the horses' hooves over the packed dirt of the road making the only sound. The cold night air felt heavy and thick around him, as if it were going to snow.

He thought about Laurent, about how he'd often wondered if the boy was cut from the cloth that would make him successful in this line of work. He'd handled himself well this afternoon, performing his duty without hesitation. He hadn't even told Sam about the possible fatality until now, when they were out of London and safe.

The fact was, though, Laurent was softhearted in a way, given to powerful ideals about the distinction between right and wrong. He was a believer in the work they did, in the rightness of it.

But sometimes, Sam knew well, the lines between "right" and "wrong" grew hazy. What would happen the first time Laurent was ordered to do something he didn't believe was entirely right?

No telling what would happen. And that was Sam's worry.

He focused on the dimly lit road, brooding, hoping the boy had fallen into a peaceful sleep in the carriage.

Eventually, his thoughts drifted back to Lady Dunthorpe. *Élise.* How he'd been inexorably drawn to her sweet, trembling lips. His desire to taste her had reached a peak, and he hadn't been able to deny the impulse to bring his mouth to hers. He'd wanted to be close to her. He'd wanted to drive away her fear, make her forget. He'd wanted to taste her.

In retrospect, his thoughts at that moment had not been at all rational. He supposed he was still worked up from the events of the mad dash from the town house.

Her thoughts hadn't been rational, either.

Or...had they?

Carter had said she'd be in Sam's bed already if not for that fact that he'd killed her husband. In truth, she should never want to go near his bed. That one act he'd committed—that she'd *seen* him commit—should have put her off him forever.

Had she hated Dunthorpe to such an extent that she could forgive his killer so easily? That she could kiss her husband's murderer?

Something about her weakened him, made him want to open up to her, to trust that she'd never been involved in Dunthorpe's treachery and had been only a victim of his villainy. He had no proof of her guilt.

No proof of her innocence, either.

Sam had dropped his guard. He'd told her too much. For God's sake, he'd even told her his name.

A part of him had decided she was innocent, but that didn't mean she was. It could be his heart doing the thinking—his *cock* doing the thinking. A very real possibility remained that she'd been working with Dunthorpe and was still in league with Dunthorpe's men.

If that was the case, what would her plan be? Certainly to discover as much about Dunthorpe's killers as possible—including who had employed them to do the job. She'd come uncomfortably close in her guess, too, when she'd told them she'd thought they were British spies.

How would she insinuate herself into their good graces? By playing the innocent, the woman who was terrified of gunfire and who thought her husband a traitorous beast.

She'd rouse their protective instincts. Next, she'd seduce them, starting with Sam. He was the leader; he'd killed Dunthorpe; he knew the most. If she got to him, she'd get to Carter and Laurent by extension.

God. He closed his eyes. He didn't want her to be that

woman—that cold, calculating creature. He wanted her to be the intelligent, feisty, deeply vulnerable woman who so intrigued him. But how could it be real? How could she kiss him—*kiss him*!—four days after witnessing him shoot her husband in the heart? Whether or not she'd loved that husband...

He pressed his fingers to his temple, trying to hold back the headache forming there.

He remembered his promise to allow her some privacy to relieve herself. With a sigh, he drew the horses to a halt.

He needed to proceed with the utmost caution.

* * *

They drove for three days and three nights, not rushing per se but not stopping for anything except to change horses and buy food, which they ate in the carriage. The weather was dreary and overcast, promising but delivering neither snow nor rain.

Sam and Laurent wouldn't allow her to join them on the perch—they said it was too cold, that she didn't have the proper clothing, that passersby would make note of her appearance.

So, except for those brief times when she took care of the necessities of her toilette, she was trapped in a tiny space. She tried not to resent this, but if Laurent or Sam had been imprisoned in here for as long as she had, they'd certainly feel resentful, not to mention angry.

When Laurent shared the carriage with her, he was as charming as ever but less talkative than usual. Most of the time, he simply sprawled on the cushion and slept while Élise jammed her body into a corner and tried not to disturb him. The boy could sleep in any uncomfortable position, it seemed, and he always fell asleep in a matter of seconds.

She often watched his innocent-looking face as he slept, reflecting that for such a young boy, he was involved in quite a dangerous profession. And he was French, too. How had he started in this? In more ways than one, this occupation seemed contrary to Laurent's sweet nature.

That innocent look his face took on in repose was an illusion, though, she knew. Laurent was old beyond his years. As cheerful and harmless as he appeared, he was a competent young man, and Sam trusted him implicitly.

Sam.

In contrast to the boy, the man never seemed to sleep. She'd woken this morning with her head on his lap as he stroked her hair. More than once, she'd opened her eyes to see his dark gaze on her face, tenderness in his expression that melted away as he realized she'd awakened, turning into his usual emotionless flatness.

It was early afternoon, and Sam had promised they'd arrive at their secret destination by dusk.

Laurent was driving, so Sam sat beside her in the carriage now. His wound had healed rapidly. It had scabbed over, and Sam said it itched like the devil, but she was happy with her handiwork. It would leave a small scar, but otherwise, he would soon be good as new.

"You are silly to keep our destination from me," she announced, breaking an extended silence.

"I am, am I?" She heard a smile in his voice.

"You are," she confirmed. "For I will know it once we arrive, will I not?"

He sighed. "Knowing you, yes, you probably will."

"And I know quite a lot already."

"Do you?"

"Of course. I know we have gone very far north, but not so far as Scotland. We passed through Birmingham day before yesterday and Preston this morning."

"You are correct."

"Well, then. You might as well tell me what our final destination will be."

"How extensive have your travels been in England?" he asked her.

"I have been here many years, monsieur," she said dryly. "This is my home."

"That doesn't answer my question."

"I have traveled extensively, of course. To my husband's country estate and house parties all across the country."

"Tell me some of the places you've been," he said. "I know you spend most of your time in London. But you have also spent time in Brighton."

"Yes," she said. "My uncle, the Compte D'Ambert, owned a house in Brighton. He had no children of his own, so he left it to me, you know, and it is my house now. It is a large house—very large for one small woman—but it is mine, and I like it there."

Another benefit, of course, had been that Dunthorpe *didn't* like it there.

"Mmm," Sam said.

"And Dunthorpe's country house is in Yorkshire. I have spent much time there over the years, though it is not my house of preference."

"Why not?"

"Because," she said simply, "it is Dunthorpe's."

"So you don't like it just to be disagreeable?"

Dropping her elbow from the window ledge, she turned to him. "It is not that simple, as I believe you are aware."

He shook his head, and there was an odd, determined gleam in his eyes. "I know very little about you and Dunthorpe, my lady."

She gave him a tight smile. "That is for the best. There is not much worth knowing, especially..." She hesitated.

He bent close, which in this small space, was very close indeed. She could feel the warm wash of his breath over her cheek. "Especially?"

She clenched her hands into fists in her skirt and straightened her spine. "Especially for you, Monsieur Spy. Not because you are a spy, or because he was your enemy. But because there are private things between a husband and a wife that no one outside of a marriage has a right to know."

He raised his hand and brushed a finger down her cheek. His finger was rough. Callused. It left a tingling trail in its wake. Her heartbeat surged, heat flushed through her, and she looked down at her lap.

She'd avoided touching him as much as possible the last few days. She wanted to touch him, but the wrongness of it kept replaying in her mind. He'd avoided her, too, and that gave her the strength to keep her distance. Perhaps he'd never wanted her.

But those insecurities faded when she woke to him cradling her head in his lap and stroking her hair...

"What sorts of private things?" he asked.

She blew out a frustrated breath, thrusting away that

annoying, persistent excitement she felt whenever he came near. "You have never been married, monsieur. If you did, you would know."

"I *have* been married," he said.

She drew back, eyes wide with shock. "You have?"

"I have."

"Where is your wife?" she asked suspiciously. Coldness washed over her, dousing that warm flush of arousal. Images of a woman waiting for him somewhere assailed her. *Dieu.* He hadn't behaved like a married man, but—

"Dead," he said. "They both are."

"Both?"

"Yes. I was married twice."

"And they both died?" She couldn't quite comprehend that. Certainly he was too young to be a widower twice over.

"Yes."

She stared at him in stunned silence for a moment. Then, "Did you love them?"

He seemed taken aback by her bluntness. He blinked at her; then his lips tightened. "I cared for both of them. They were *mine*."

The way he said *mine*. Such a possessive tone. And despite the topic of their conversation, heat flushed through her yet again. *Dieu*, but a part of her so wanted him to say "mine" just like that . . . in reference to her.

She pushed her focus back to the conversation at hand. "What were their names?"

"Marianne. And Charlotte."

"How did they die?"

"Marianne died at war." He closed his eyes in a too-long blink. "She inadvertently walked into an army training area. She was killed. It happened in Malta, where I was stationed at the time."

"And the other?" she asked quietly. "Charlotte?"

"Charlotte...she died in childbirth in Portugal, both she and our son. It happened a few days before the Battle of Vimeiro...which marked the end of my military career."

"*Bon Dieu*," she murmured, reeling with all this. She gazed at him, thinking about the flat expression on his face, about the monotone of his voice.

Two wives, both dead. A dead infant son. He had been at war. She swallowed hard. "Why was it the end of your military career?"

"I was shot and stabbed by a bayonet. I returned to England to recover."

The mangled scar on his chest. The slashes...they had been from a bayonet. In battle. Her breaths grew short as her mind circled from his scars back to his losses, how they must have affected him. It explained so much about him, about his seriousness, his lack of emotion. Even now, his face was schooled to blankness...and suddenly that blankness held so much more poignancy. Suddenly, those moments in which she'd seen him smiling or laughing seemed much more special.

"That—all of it—must have been very terrible," she murmured. Her heart ached for him. "I am sorry."

He acknowledged her condolences with a tilt of his head, but his expression remained stoic.

She reached up to cup his cheek, wanting to provide comfort by touch. "You were a good husband."

He gave a snort. "What makes you say that?"

"I just know it. But me..." She drew in a deep breath. "I was not a good wife."

"Why not?"

"I did not love my husband, and I did not like him, either. I married him when I was seventeen years old, which is young—too young. At seventeen, I did not understand that some level of mutual respect is required in a successful marriage."

He leaned in to the hand cupping his cheek and closed his eyes. "I always wonder if you're lying to me when you talk like that about Dunthorpe."

She dropped her hand. "*Non.* I do not lie." Not about that.

His eyes opened, and they gleamed at her, dark as obsidian in the dim carriage. "Did you manipulate Dunthorpe, too, then? As you manipulate me?"

"How do you mean?"

"You tell me," he murmured. There was a silkiness in his voice that rubbed at her nerves and sent her senses into high alert. "In every way, perhaps?"

"I do not know what you are talking about."

"Don't you?" He leaned closer, so close his lips brushed her cheekbone when he next spoke. "You beguile, Élise. You seduce. Is that how you manipulate men? Is that how you manipulated Dunthorpe?" She stiffened, but he didn't seem to notice. "You seduced him with your wiles, turned him traitor? People will do that for the love of a beautiful woman, you know. Ever so easily, they will turn on everything they once held dear. Recall Helen of Troy?"

"Move away from me, monsieur," she said tightly, even though her heart pounded and the heat from his proximity grew almost unbearable as her body cried out for her to touch him. But she didn't like what he was saying. It was offensive. Cruel.

"Why? Don't you want this?" One finger trailed along the edge of her dress's neckline, and damn her body, but his touch lit it afire.

She swatted at his hand. Ineffectually. His large palm curved around her shoulder, clamping like a shackle, leaving her virtually incapable of movement.

She glared up at him, angrier than she'd ever been in his presence. Could he really think she was some wanton who seduced men to manipulate them? "What are you doing?" she grated out.

"Giving you what you want." He stroked her jawbone with his thumb.

Her anger grew. So did her arousal.

"And what is that?" she snapped. His touches did mad things to her body, but his words...they infuriated her.

"Me." He bent his head and brushed his lips over the shell of her ear. A deep tremble resonated through her body. "I'm burning for you, Élise. You're driving me mad. I can hardly restrain myself from laying you flat on this bench and taking you right now. I want to rip this ill-fitting dress from your skin. I want to roam over your body with my hands and my mouth. I want to—"

"*Non!* None of that is true. You avoid me." Ever since she'd gone mad and kissed him like a starving woman with a feast laid out before her, he'd sat beside her, spoke to her, played his role as her gentleman jailor to perfection. But there was no doubt he'd been avoiding her ever since that moment he'd pulled away from her kiss.

He gave a short bark of a laugh that held no humor. He lifted his head, and his dark gaze bored into hers. "And why do you think that is? If I touch you, I want to touch you more. If I look at you, I want to see more. When I'm away from you, I want you near. You're driving me mad, Élise."

She was silent. Speechless. Her lips parted in shock as she stared back at him.

"Isn't that your intention? To become my obsession? If it is, you've achieved your goal, love." His hand roamed over the top of her bodice, cupping her breast through the layers of material.

Bon Dieu.

She was on fire. Want, need, desire, lust—they all raged through her, a drowning swirl that threatened reason. She couldn't help it—she pressed against his hand. It felt so good—so *right*—cupped around her like that.

"What is your price?" he murmured.

"My...price...?" she repeated through a thick haze of arousal.

"Would you turn me traitor, too?" he rasped. "Would you have me reveal all the secrets I know? Would you have me kill the men I work for, those I work with? Would you have me slit Laurent's and Carter's throats in payment for one night of pleasure?" His hand slid around to the back of her dress. He began to flick open her buttons with expert skill.

"You are a fool if you think that is what I am," she managed.

"Isn't that what you're doing? Kissing me four days after I killed your husband? What other motivation could you have? You want vengeance, I think. You've made me pay dearly; you know you have. You have cracked my control. My sanity. But it's not enough for a life. You need more—everything I have."

"*Non*," she whispered. Angry tears pricked at the backs

of her eyes. "You think I offer myself in payment for...something."

"For everything. What is it you want besides vengeance? Your freedom? Our deaths? Information? There is so much for you to gain from your seduction, Élise."

She closed her eyes as he flicked the last button open and drew her sleeve down over her arm. His mouth went to her bare shoulder, his lips nuzzling. So soft, so warm, just like when he'd kissed her before.

She loved the feel of his lips.

But she did not like his words. His words were...terrible. They were wrong. The implications of them sent shards of ice slicing through all the heat his touch elicited. "You believe that is what I did? Forced Dunthorpe to become a traitor?"

"Mmm..." His tongue touched the ridge of her collarbone. "Is it?"

"Sam..." She groaned as his lips moved up the side of her throat. Her body moved without her approval, and she tilted her head to give him better access.

She had been too flippant with him. Making light of her relationship with Dunthorpe, as she had with everyone since the beginning of her marriage. But Samson Hawkins wasn't a man to be trifled with.

"I did not turn him into a traitor," she pushed out. She felt like sobbing...She wanted to shut out his words and focus on what he was doing to her, how he was touching her, how it made her body ache and scream for his touch...but she wouldn't. She *couldn't*. She needed to explain. He had brought the ugliness that was Dunthorpe into this moment, and she couldn't ignore it.

THE SCOUNDREL'S SEDUCTION 125

She didn't want to speak of Dunthorpe to anyone. Not even to herself. If she could, she'd lock away the last eleven years into a place even she couldn't reach.

She drew back from his lips and scooted away from him as far as she could. But it was a small carriage and she couldn't put nearly as much distance between them as she would have liked. "He was a traitor long before I married him. He thought...he thought marrying me would gain him influence with certain men of power in France."

He'd been wrong about that. She carried the blood of French royalty and was related to many key political figures in post-Revolution France. But she was an *émigrée* who had spent the better part of her life in England, and those ties that had once been so important in France held less weight these days. The English were slow to understand this basic shift in the culture of her country.

The French had used Dunthorpe. They had seduced him with promises of power and money, but they knew him for what he was—a traitor. They paid him his money, they kept promising power, but in the end, they held no respect for him.

Dunthorpe had always pretended this hadn't bothered him, but it had made him furious. And of course, she often bore the brunt of his verbal whips, because she was French and she made a convenient object for his anger.

"Was he right? Did you help him gain influence in France?" Sam's strong arm slid behind her back, drawing her closer to him. He kissed along her jaw, then, ever so gently, his teeth grazed her earlobe. Something clenched inside her, warm and needy and wanting.

"Do...do not do this to me, Sam," she pleaded.

"Do what?"

"Make me into something I am not."

"What are you then, little minx?"

"Not a minx..."

"But you are."

"Non."

"Why, then, Élise?" His fingers moved over the skin of her shoulder, his rough touch so erotic she nearly moaned. "Why did you kiss your husband's murderer four days after the deed was done?" His tongue traced the shell of her ear.

A tear squeezed out of her eye and trailed down her cheek. She swiped it away before he could see.

"I...I do not know," she pushed out. And that was the truth. She didn't know. She'd been drawn to Sam, compelled by the strength and safety he offered.

"Shall I tell you why?"

She didn't answer.

"Because you are a siren. You intend to lure me to certain death."

She shook her head. "That is not it." She sucked in a breath. "It is true that I want my freedom. I do not enjoy being a prisoner. Does anyone?"

"We haven't kept you in shackles in a dungeon. We haven't starved you or tortured you."

"But you have kept me prisoner."

"Yes," he agreed. "A pampered prisoner; that's what you are." His lips moved to her hairline, nuzzling along its edge. Her body was on fire, demanding to move closer, to push herself against him, to use her own lips and hands on him. Instead she contained herself, holding herself rigid, clenching her hands into tight fists at her sides.

"But a prisoner nonetheless," she said. "All I desire is freedom. All I want is to be away from all of this."

"All of what?"

"Spies. Traitors. France and England. I never wished to be involved."

"Yet you were."

He was right. She'd been involved since before her parents' and brother's heads had rolled at the guillotine.

"Not consciously," she whispered. "Dunthorpe used me. Now you use me, too."

He pulled back, his eyes narrow, angry slits. "Don't ever categorize me with him. I am nothing like him."

"Yet you want the same thing from me."

"No." His voice was flat and cold, his expression harder than she'd ever seen it.

"Even if I tell you everything I know— which is not very much—you won't let me go. What motivation does that give me to tell you? You hold me prisoner, perhaps forever, perhaps until you receive orders to kill me, so why should I reveal any of my secrets to you?"

He took her shoulders in his hands, his fingers pressing hard into her skin. "Tell me. Did you know what Dunthorpe was planning? Were you in on it?"

"Which plan?" she asked dully.

"The plan to assassinate the Prince Regent."

Shock slammed into her so hard, it took her breath.

Sam shook her slightly, clearing the red haze from her eyes. "Did you know about it?"

"No," she croaked out. "I told you—I knew he'd planned something...something very big. I was married to that man for eleven years, and I knew he was evil. His hubris truly knew no bounds. I knew this scheme was one to surpass all his previous ones. His behavior had been so odd. There was an excited gleam in his eyes I did not like at all.

"I thought if I hid there, his meeting with the Frenchman—you—would tell me what I needed to know. Then I could take that information to someone, perhaps...perhaps the Duke of Trent."

She wrapped her arms around herself, closing herself to Sam—to the world.

Silence.

Then he said quietly, "The Duke of Trent?"

"Yes. I have met him more than once, and I have spoken to him at length. I know he is a kind man and very loyal. He would have done the correct thing with the information I would have given him. He would have stopped Dunthorpe."

"Do you know what would have happened had the duke been given proof of Dunthorpe's dealings? Your husband would have hung."

She drew in a stuttering breath, then whispered, "I know."

Sam groaned. "God, Élise. You don't know how badly I want to believe you."

She gazed directly at him. "Believe me. Because it is the truth."

He stared at her, his face twisted with some emotion she could not define.

Then he cursed, low and harsh. And he pulled her into his arms and kissed her.

Chapter Eight

She tasted sweet. Ripe. Like the grapes that grew so readily in the country of her birth.

Like she had last time, she wrapped her arms around him. She emitted a little gasp and opened to him.

The wrongness nudged at his mind—Why would she let him kiss her? Even now?—but he shoved it aside.

He wanted this woman. He wanted to kiss her. To hold her, to touch her, to bring her pleasure, then to possess her.

She was his weakness, probably his downfall. But at this moment, he didn't care. He needed, on a primal, instinctual level, to make her his.

He took her mouth first, exploring with lips and tongue, closing his eyes as the pleasure of her touch permeated his whole being. He'd hauled her petite body onto his lap, and she pressed against him now in all the right places. His cock hardened against her bottom. Her breasts pressed against his chest.

So sweet. So damn beautiful. He couldn't get enough. He wanted more.

He dragged the sleeve of her dress farther down her arm, exposing the top mound of her breast, her stays just barely covering the top edge of her nipple. He brought his lips to that soft top curve and kissed her. She was so perfectly pale there, and God—so sweet. He could lose himself in her softness.

She arched into him, her fists tightening in his coat, her body molding to his.

He slid his fingers beneath the edge of her stays and yanked down. The stiff boning sewn into the material resisted the movement but gave a few inches to the strength of his tug, exposing her nipple.

He drew back to look at it. A perfect circle of pink, with the taut bud in the center, already rigid from his attentions. He brought his mouth back to her breast, rubbing his lips over her flesh. She pressed into him, panting now, so receptive, so hot for him...He circled his lips over her and suckled.

God, how he needed this. He didn't think he could stop it. As he kissed her breast, he tugged her sleeve all the way off. He drew his fingers up and down her arm, unable to get enough of her silky skin. He could touch her all day and want to touch her more.

Her nipple puckered, grew tighter beneath his ministrations. She released one hand from his coat and thrust her fingers through his hair, cupping the back of his head and pushing him tighter against her.

While he stroked her soft, smooth skin with one hand, he palmed the curve of her bottom with the other, drawing her ever closer, shifting beneath her in a vain attempt to relieve the pressure in his cock. There was no relief to be had...The only place to find it, he knew, was inside her.

He groaned against the plump flesh of her breast, imagining plunging inside her, how it would feel to have her hot, wet, velvet flesh close around him.

"Ahem."

The sound of a throat clearing jerked Sam's head up. He whipped around to see Laurent had opened the door and was staring at them with wide eyes. Élise scrambled to get her clothing in order, yanking the cotton back up over the nipple that glistened from his attentions.

Sam just wanted Laurent's gaze off her. "Give us a moment," he snapped out.

"Er. Yes. Of course." Pink-cheeked, Laurent slammed the door, and Sam turned back to Élise. In silence, he helped her draw her sleeve up over her arm. Then he murmured, "Turn round so I can do your buttons."

She did so mutely. He quickly buttoned her up, then took her by the shoulders and turned her to face him. He looked into her smoky blue eyes for a long moment. Then he tucked a few stray blond hairs behind her ears.

"We're here," he told her. He hadn't been aware of turning down the drive, of the carriage stopping. His entire focus had been upon her.

He couldn't lose himself like that again. Damn it—he was smarter than this.

She slipped her hands behind his neck and pulled him forward until his forehead touched hers. "Do you believe me, Sam?" she whispered. "Tell me that you believe me."

"I...want to." God, how he wanted to.

She held still for a moment, then pulled back and gave

a little nod as if to say his desire to believe her was
enough . . . for now.

She tidied her skirt, which had bunched up over her
legs. "I thought I'd be so happy to finally arrive, to finally have my freedom from this little prison. But I find
I am not as happy as I imagined. I wish . . ." She hesitated, then met his gaze and murmured, "I wish we had
more time."

Time for what? he wondered. Time for pursuing their
desire or time for pursuing the truth?

Either way, they'd have time. They were in a remote
location, and they'd be here for several days, at least until
Adams sent further instructions.

"Come." He slipped his hand over her sleeve until he
closed his fingers over hers. "I'll show you the house."

He helped her down from the carriage. As soon as her
feet hit the ground and she saw the cottage, she gave a little gasp.

"It is lovely!"

He agreed. His mother had owned a house on Lake
Windermere, and some of his happiest childhood memories had been on this lake. It was probably because of
his familiarity and pleasant feelings about the place that
he had chosen this particular cottage as his northernmost
safe house in England.

From where the carriage was parked beneath a leafy
tree, they faced the small, square stone structure beyond
the clearing. The clouds had cleared while he'd been
overcome by Élise inside the carriage. Beyond the cottage, the lake glimmered deep blue under a bright spring
sky.

Daffodils and other bulb flowers bloomed in a border

around the house, lending bright splashes of yellow, red, orange, and purple. Far in the distance, green hills rolled along the horizon—the other side of the lake a mile away, clearly visible on such a brilliant day.

A breeze rustled the leaves in the forest of trees behind them, but otherwise, there was a calm about the place. A sense of peacefulness Sam tried to soak in whenever he was here.

"This is Hawk's favorite place," Laurent told Élise.

She did not seem embarrassed about the scene Laurent had discovered in the carriage. She flashed him a smile. "I see why that is. It is a most beautiful setting."

Sam squeezed her hand. "Come inside. I'll show you the rest."

"I'll take care of the horses," Laurent said. "You go ahead."

Sam turned his gaze to the lad. He seemed somber but accepting. In the close space they'd shared over the past few days, the tension between Sam and Élise had grown stronger. Surely Laurent had sensed it, but he had never mentioned it.

Sam was grateful the topic hadn't been raised, because he knew what he'd say to Laurent if the situation were reversed—if Laurent were the one being beguiled by their prisoner.

"Don't be a bloody fool. Keep your distance."

God knew, Sam had tried. But she was forbidden fruit, sweet and ripe and utterly tempting. His attraction to her was dangerous for both of them, and it needed to be squashed. But he wasn't sure if he could squash it. There was no denying the essential nature of his growing need for her.

He turned away from Laurent and led Élise into the house. The place smelled unused, somewhat stale, but he remedied that by opening some windows.

They entered into a tiny parlor, which opened into the salon. A window overlooked the lake to their right, and straight ahead was a stone fireplace. The space was carpeted and furnished comfortably with small tables and chairs and a chaise longue. At the far end of the room a staircase led up to the second level and a doorway led to the kitchen and dining room.

Élise turned to the window. She drew the gauze curtain aside and gazed out. Sam moved to her side. For a long minute, they both looked out over the water. The sun had begun to set over the hills on the opposite bank, and it cast a golden stream of light over the lake, its beam ending at the cottage.

With a heartfelt sigh, she turned to him. "I might almost feel free here."

Good, he thought.

"But I will never forget that I am not."

What could he say? He couldn't tell her this would be temporary, that she would be back to her home and to her friends soon. How could that work? She was a risk— not only from the British perspective, but also from their enemies'. He couldn't throw her back to the wolves in London to fend for herself. Someone, on one side or the other, would make sure she was silenced.

Would she ever be safe anywhere?

Resolve hardened within him. He'd get to the bottom of this. Learn those secrets she didn't trust him enough to share. After their encounter in the carriage this afternoon, he believed deep in his soul that whatever those secrets were, they wouldn't expose her as Dunthorpe's accomplice.

Then he'd find a way to keep her safe. He slipped his arm around her and tugged her close to him. She fit against his body as if they were perfectly matched puzzle pieces. He angled his head and pressed his lips into her hair, breathing her in. She had a scent that seeped right into his blood and heated it—utterly feminine with hints of violets and erotic sweetness.

He heard the door latch and straightened, stepping away as he dropped his arm from where it held her tucked against him. There was no point in hiding, but he had no desire to make either Élise or Laurent uncomfortable.

Laurent strode into the salon carrying two bags—one he'd had when he'd met them in London and the other the bag containing a few basic items they'd kept stored in the boot of the carriage.

He grinned at Sam. "Good to be home, isn't it?"

Sam glanced at Élise, whose gaze searched the room.

"This is your home?" she asked.

"Close as I'll ever get to having one, I suppose."

"It's a lovely choice."

Laurent winked at her and walked to the stairs with the bags. Sam and Élise followed him up.

Sam showed her the three bedrooms, all of which had windows that looked out over the lake.

She glanced at him from under her lashes when he took her into the largest room and told her this was where she'd be sleeping. "And you will be my guard?"

"Of course."

"There is a room just next door," she pointed out.

"Yes." There was. But that didn't make any difference.

The fact that they felt such a mad attraction for each other had not diminished her desire for freedom. She still might try to run.

He didn't blame her for wanting her freedom; he respected her for it. It didn't mean he was going to let her escape.

"I'll go start dinner," Laurent said. "It'll be good to have something warm tonight."

Their meals had consisted mostly of cold meats, cheeses, and breads since they'd left London. But when they'd passed through Kendal just over an hour ago, it had been market day. Laurent had purchased enough provisions to last a week, and he had also bought a gallon of hearty stew for dinner. Sam's stomach grumbled at the thought of it.

Élise insisted on helping Laurent, so they all returned to the kitchen, where Sam built a fire in the stove and Laurent tended to the pot of stew. Sam went with Élise to fetch water from the well. Élise rinsed dusty dishes and silver while Sam roamed around the pantry, finding a bottle of wine and a jug of ale.

They worked in an easy silence, murmuring occasional questions and suggestions to one another. Soon the kitchen was filled with the savory scent of the stew. Élise put the bread Laurent had bought into the oven to warm, and then she went into the dining room, her arms laden with clean napkins and silverware, to set the table.

As a daughter and a niece of *comptes* and the wife of a viscount, she was accustomed to being waited upon hand and foot, but she was surprisingly self-reliant and adaptable. And despite the fact that her entire life had been turned upside down a week ago, she still faced the world with a cheerful outlook that Sam found refreshing. He'd forgotten long ago, even before his marriage to Marianne, how to be positive.

Laurent chuckled, and Sam realized he'd been standing stock-still, gazing at the empty doorway Élise had just disappeared through.

"Never thought I'd see you like this, Hawk," Laurent said in a low voice.

Sam had never thought he'd see himself like this, either. Being smitten like an untried greenling...and without having complete knowledge of the woman or her motivations. Hell, it was unlike him, and it was also rather pathetic. He gave a heavy sigh. "Leave it alone, Laurent," he grumbled.

"'Course," the lad said lightly. "Won't mention it again."

"Good."

"But..." Laurent said, and there was a hint of boyish mischief in his voice. "It makes me happy."

"What do you mean?"

"I like her," he said bluntly. "I don't believe she is to blame for any of what has happened to her."

"Don't you?"

Laurent shook his head as he swirled the long wooden spoon in the pot. "Nah. She's innocent as a child. But now..." He whistled through his teeth. "Dunthorpe's friends are her enemies."

"You believe that's who attacked us in London?"

"Sure, I do." Laurent slanted a glance in Sam's direction. "Don't you?"

"Probably. But we can't be completely certain."

Laurent snorted. "Who else could it be? The poor lady

has earned powerful enemies in this world through her association with Dunthorpe and through no fault of her own." Laurent blew on a spoonful of stew and took a testing sip. With a nod, he took a pair of thick cloths and pulled the pot from the flame. "I'm glad with so many powerful enemies, she's gained a powerful friend in you."

"And you?" Sam asked quietly.

"Aye, of course she has a friend in me, but powerful?" Laurent shook his head.

"Give yourself more credit, lad. You are more than capable of protecting a defenseless woman."

At the doorway, Laurent looked over his shoulder back at Sam. His brown eyes were sad when he said, "I know."

They sat around the square table. Laurent ladled soup into their bowls while Élise sliced the warm bread she'd fetched from the oven. Sam buttered his bread generously, and they ate in relative quiet for several minutes, savoring the flavors of the meat, barley, and vegetable concoction.

Eventually, Élise sighed. "It is so delicious. It was very wise of you to choose this tonight, Laurent. There couldn't be a more perfect dinner."

He flashed her a grin. "Did you hear that, Hawk? The lady believes I am wise."

"I'd have to agree with her in this case," Sam said mildly.

"I hope you will remember me as the wise one," Laurent told Élise.

"Remember you? Why do you say this, as if I will never lay my eyes upon you again?"

"You may not," Laurent said gravely. "I must leave tomorrow, to return to London."

"What?" Élise's eyes were as big and blue as a wind-tossed sea.

"I must submit our report to our superiors and receive orders about how to proceed."

"Ah. I understand. But you will be back, yes?"

Laurent's uneasy gaze met Sam's.

"Possibly," Sam said. "Or they might send someone else."

"Carter?"

"Possibly," Sam said noncommittally.

Élise frowned. Then she looked down into her half-empty bowl. "I will miss you, Laurent. You are the friendliest of my gentlemen jailors."

Laurent cocked a brow in Sam's direction. "You see? Friendly *and* wise."

Sam gave a low snort.

"Don't worry, my lady," Laurent said. "Before I depart in the morning, I will prevail upon Hawk to be on his best behavior."

She gave a ladylike huff, as if to expect Sam to be on any sort of good behavior was preposterous.

She was right about that. Good behavior wasn't something that would come easily to him—not when he was alone with this woman in this place.

But while he was a bastard by blood, he was a gentleman by nature. He wouldn't harm her. He would protect her with every bit of himself.

Élise knew that, too, but still, there was a spark of concern in those blue eyes when she glanced at him.

Several minutes later, he rose, his chair scraping over the hardwood as it moved back. He gathered the plates and bowls, raising a brow at Élise before taking hers. "Finished?"

"Yes."

"I'll wash these, then."

He escaped into the kitchen, where he washed the dishes in the water they'd hauled in from the well.

Having a few feet of distance between him and Élise helped bring his boiling attraction to a low simmer, though he knew it wouldn't be so easy once Laurent was gone.

His longing for her was a deep ache under his skin, a never-ending pulse of need. He didn't think he could ignore it for long.

* * *

Sam woke at dawn to see Laurent off. He'd pulled the mattress from the bed in the adjacent bedroom to the floor of Élise's bedroom the night before, and at the first sign of a lightening sky, he slid out from under the covers. He pulled on his trousers and slipped out into the corridor, closing the door behind him. Unlike the London house, this one did not have locks on its bedroom doors. Fortunately, though, the front door did have a lock, and with the lake bordering the house on two sides, there were few routes of escape.

Still, Sam didn't like leaving her alone. He intended to keep his eyes and ears open...just in case.

He hurried downstairs, slipping on his shirt and tucking it in as he descended. He found Laurent in the kitchen, grabbing a water skin and a few slices of dried beef for his saddlebags.

"About ready?" he asked the boy.

"Yes. Horse is all saddled and ready to go."

They'd agreed that Laurent would take one of the horses, leaving the second horse and the carriage. Sam felt more comfortable having the animal here, because even though the chances were slim of anyone finding them, the horse would provide a faster means of flight, if necessary.

"Good," he said. "Laurent...I need you to do me a favor."

"Anything," the lad said.

"I need you to deliver a message to my brother."

Laurent raised a brow. "The duke?"

"Yes. I need you to tell him he can send correspondence to the King's Arms in Kendal."

Laurent frowned. "Correspondence regarding the search for the dowager duchess?"

"Yes, and anything else he might need to tell me. I don't know how long I'll be gone, and I think they're close to finding some real information about my mother's whereabouts."

Sam hadn't mentioned to Laurent that his mother's last-known whereabouts were relatively close by, in Preston, which they'd driven through early yesterday morning.

His brothers and Esme were on their way to Preston, too, though they were probably traveling in a much more leisurely fashion than he, Laurent, and Élise had. They would likely arrive a few days from now. He would consider sending them a message, too, depending on how things went here and how long he would need to stay, but for now, informing Trent was the best he could do.

As isolated as this house was, he felt close to something here. Closer, at least, to finding his mother.

Not for the first time, he wondered what she was doing

right now. Where she was...If she was happy...For so long he'd truly believed she was dead, but since the Hawkinses had learned about Steven Lowell, everyone's hope had shifted.

If they found her, Sam wanted to know. He wanted to see her in the flesh. Make sure she was well and then discover why she'd left them in the way she had.

Laurent frowned. "You've never let your brother know your whereabouts before. I mean, I know you're not telling him the location of the cottage, but Kendal is very close—"

"True, but I think it's the right thing to do this time. Definitely don't tell him anything about Lady Dunthorpe or the situation that led us here."

Laurent looked affronted. "I wouldn't do that."

"I know." Sam gave the lad a crooked smile—the closest thing to a genuine smile he could conjure on the best of days. Unless Élise was nearby. Smiles seemed to come more naturally to him in her presence. "Go on, then," he said gruffly.

He walked Laurent to the front door. Laurent unwound the reins from the hitching post and stood beside the horse. "Take care of her," he told Sam in a low voice.

Sam gazed at the young man. He'd known Laurent since he was eleven years old, when he was brought to Adams's house, the illegitimate son of a lady and a French émigré. His mother had wanted him to be fostered by gentlemen. Her ambition had been for him to become something, someone who made a difference in the world. She'd wanted nothing more than for Laurent to be a hero. Illegitimate though he was, his mother had adored him. Just like Sam's mother had adored him.

Perhaps it was the similarity in their upbringing that had forged the bond between Sam and Laurent. From the beginning, he'd looked after the boy. When Laurent was thirteen, Sam had begun to take an active role in training him.

He'd been innocent and eager then. And now he was almost a man.

"I will, lad," he said softly.

"I'll try to return as quickly as possible." Laurent's lips twisted. "If Adams allows it."

Sam nodded. He hoped Laurent would return, and he hoped Carter would be with him. The three of them were of a mind about the moral basis of their position. Together, he knew, they'd make the best decision about how to handle Adams's orders—no matter what they might contain.

"Do you have your pistols?"

"Of course," Laurent said smoothly. He patted his right pocket, presumably where he was keeping one of them.

"Good. Be on the lookout for Dunthorpe's men." As far as they knew, none of the enemy had seen either Laurent or Carter, but one could never be too careful. Sam was quite sure they'd seen him—and clearly—which put him at a great disadvantage the moment he entered their sphere again. Especially considering that Dunthorpe had been very good at hiding the identities of those who'd been in league with him. Sam might not know he was facing an enemy until it was too late.

"I will," Laurent said.

"You'll be spending the night at Masterson's?"

Masterson was one of them, but he kept a stable façade as a tollgate-keeper on the turnpike north of Preston.

They had several such men scattered throughout the country. This particular posting kept Masterson in a position to keep an eye on travelers heading north.

Sam and Laurent had briefed the man on the circumstances as they'd passed through the tollgate on the way here, though they hadn't dallied long, not wanting to reveal Masterson's true identity to Élise.

"I don't know." Laurent's fingers restlessly stroked the edge of the saddle. "I could probably make it a good twenty miles farther—"

"No," Sam interrupted. "Stay there tonight. We're safe here, so you needn't push yourself. From here to Preston is a good day's ride, and you'll need to give Masterson the full details, as well as question him to ascertain if anyone suspicious has passed through."

A slight frown pulled at Laurent's brows at that thought. "All right. I'm to Masterson, then."

Sam nodded and squeezed the boy's shoulder. "Good. Be careful. I'll await your word."

Laurent nodded in return and mounted the horse. In moments, he had disappeared into the wood and the *clomp* of hoofbeats faded into the encroaching dawn.

When he could no longer hear the retreating horse, Sam returned to the house and closed the door behind him before locking it securely.

Alone, at last, with Élise.

Chapter Nine

❧

Six days had passed, and the ridiculous man hadn't so much as looked at her. He had thrust the scoundrel part of himself aside until it didn't exist, until all that remained was the stoic gentleman.

Élise sat on the shoreline now, hugging her knees against her chest, breathing in the crisp, clean afternoon breeze. Sam was on the bank behind her a few yards back, watching her every move, no doubt, but she'd grown accustomed to his presence there and was no longer self-conscious under his constant scrutiny.

Élise pressed her lips together in frustration. It was not like she had expected Sam to throw himself at her the second Laurent left them. But this—this was absurd. He went through the motions as a proper gentleman jailor should do, but he spoke of nothing more significant than the weather, and when he looked at her, he seemed to look through her. His expression never wavered from that irritating emotionless look he was so skilled at presenting to the world. It was as if his body was present, but his mind, his soul, was somewhere else.

That frustrated her to no end. It was insufferable that she was being kept prisoner, but this ignored-while-being-watched state was beyond endurance.

She'd kept her annoyance—or perhaps if she were being honest with herself, her hurt—to herself in order to pretend to be the docile prisoner these last few days. Sam's lack of "presence" was only solidifying her desire to escape, and she'd spent many of her lonely hours occupying herself with scheming thoughts.

As a result of her outward passivity, Sam had grown more lax in the way he watched over her. He still slept on the mattress he'd kept in her bedchamber, and he still hovered over her for the majority of the day. But there were times he left her alone for short periods, which seemed to be growing longer every day.

Despite her confused frustration about Sam's withdrawal, she found it easy to play the part of a contented soul. This isolated spot soothed her, the lake a balm to her agitated thoughts. She'd spent long hours here at the shore watching the tiny waves lap over the pebbles and making her peace with Dunthorpe.

She was free from Dunthorpe forever, but the question was, what did she intend to do with her freedom? Dunthorpe had left her nothing. All she had was the house in Brighton, which would need to be sold. She could live off the proceeds for a good long while.

But where would she live? Not London, not Brighton. Too many enemies would know where to find her in those places.

Maybe here, she thought wistfully. If she'd come here

by choice, if it weren't a prison to her, she'd feel quite at home.

But maybe she could find a place like this, a place far from a large town, a little cottage—

First she needed to escape.

Her fingers, which had been sifting through the pile of pebbles beside her, found a flat one, and she tossed it with a flick of her wrist, sending it skipping over the water.

She chewed on her lip.

She would escape from this place, but she refused to do so stupidly, as tempting as it might be to simply take flight with no direction in mind. She needed a plan—a solid one.

She could not go to Marie. Her friend was certainly being watched, so any contact with her might prove dangerous to both of them. The last thing Élise wanted was for the most treasured person in her world to get hurt.

Her thoughts kept circling back to the Duke of Trent. She wished she hadn't brought up his name to Sam. He was one of the few people she'd mentioned since knowing him, and Sam remembered everything. If she disappeared, Sam would know to check with the duke. But maybe she could plead her case to the duke, and he would help her to disappear before Sam or his fellow spies could find her—

"What are you thinking about?"

Élise let out a startled yelp, then glanced up and behind her at Sam's wide, large body hovering over her. "*Dieu!* You frightened me."

"You knew I was here. Or were you so deep into your thoughts that you forgot?"

"Yes," she mumbled. "That was it."

"Penny for them?" He lowered himself onto his haunches beside her.

She'd heard that expression somewhere... What did it...? Oh, yes. "My thoughts?"

"That's right."

She cocked a brow at him. "I demand an actual penny, in truth. Not one that is imaginary."

The corner of his lip twitched, which she considered a great success. It was the closest he'd come to a smile in many days.

"Now, what would you do with a penny out here?"

"I can always find a use for money. We will go to market tomorrow, yes? I shall find something exquisite to purchase with my penny."

He released a low puff of laughter, and Élise wanted to pump her fist in victory. "I believe I have one in the cottage. If you share your thoughts with me, it will be yours."

"Excellent." He sat close to her, not touching her but mere inches away. So close, his warmth washed over her skin. She liked him being beside her like this. After so many years of keeping her distance from all men, her husband included, it was a foreign sensation to crave this kind of closeness.

Sam cocked a brow. "So...?"

She forced her mind to scroll through all the topics that she'd considered in the last several minutes while sitting here.

None of those thoughts was entirely safe, that was for certain. And perhaps a devilish part of her wished to get a rise out of him, because she sighed. "Well... I was thinking about you."

He cocked one dark brow and looked at her in amusement. "Me?"

"That is correct."

"What about me?"

"How you have been ignoring me," she said simply. She dug her hands into the pile of pebbles again, found a flat one and flicked it out over the water. She didn't watch it skip; instead she watched Sam's face, his reaction to her words.

All traces of amusement vanished, and he turned his head away to gaze at the spot in the lake where she'd flicked the stone. "I haven't been ignoring you."

She tried to lighten her voice. "Ah, but you have."

He turned back to her, his eyes so deep and dark, a tremor flicked up her spine. He was so beautifully fascinating. She could gaze at him forever.

"You know why, Élise." The tenor of his voice was low, and there was an edge of intensity to it that made the tiny hairs on her arms rise.

"Do I?"

"Don't toy with me."

She pursed her lips and blew out a puff of breath. "Is that what I am doing? Toying with you?"

"I think so."

Tilting her head, she seriously considered this. The truth was, she thought she did know why he was ignoring her. It didn't make it any less vexing.

"I have a notion as to why you are behaving in this fashion," she conceded. "However, I don't know for certain. I could be wrong."

"Tell me what you think, and I'll let you know one way or the other."

"I think," she said carefully, "that the part of you that is a scoundrel..." She swallowed, suddenly having to force the words out through a closing throat. "That part of you wants me. And you are ignoring me because you believe if you ignore me, the want will go away."

Silence. Her face burned, but she raised her chin at him, gazing at him directly. She'd never been accused of cowardice, and she wouldn't start now.

Still, she felt like she'd torn a part of herself open. She'd given him the power to either mend that gash or stick a knife in it and twist. When had she become so connected to this man—this *jailor*—that he had gained the ability to hurt her?

Fear bubbled in her chest as he stared at her, his expression completely stoic, revealing nothing. She regretted her words, but she couldn't—wouldn't—show him that.

"Am I correct?" she whispered after a long minute.

"Yes." His voice shook slightly and his lips twisted, and the flat expression he'd had moments ago transformed into something that brimmed with emotion. There was anguish and confusion and something else she couldn't quite define.

Seeing emotions on Sam's face, though...Her heart melted.

"Have you succeeded, then? Has the want gone away?" Her own tone was even, but inside she was in turmoil. *Please...please tell me it hasn't gone away...that you still want me, because heaven help me, I want you, too. Desperately.*

"No," he said softly, his answer coming quickly this time. "It hasn't gone away."

Relief flooded her.

Dieu, the man had seduced her without even trying.

"So then you may stop this foolish nonsense."

His brows rose in question.

"Since it is not working," she clarified, "you may stop speaking to me as if I am the strangest person in the world to you."

His lips twitched again. "It's that easy, eh?"

"Of course."

He wrapped his arm around her and drew her close. It was the first time in days he'd touched her, and she sank against him, into the comfort offered in the circle of that powerful arm.

"Why do we fight it?" she asked him softly after a long moment of silence. Because she'd been fighting it, too, this intense attraction, this desire to be as close to him as a woman could be to a man. She'd been waging this battle since they'd been in London.

And she was tired of fighting.

His arm tightened around her. "Do you fight it, too?"

Gazing up at him, she nodded. She spoke in a quiet voice. "I have finished making my peace with Dunthorpe. I am ready to move past that dark time with him. It is time for me to move forward instead."

"The world wouldn't agree with that."

"Perhaps it would not. But I have never been much for caring what the world believes about me. If I had, I would have crawled into a deep hole, locked the door, and thrown away the key long ago."

"You were married to him for eleven years, Élise. He died less than a month ago."

"It is eleven years I am very glad to have behind me."

He released a long, slow breath. "Tell me why."

A deep shudder ran through her. Would Dunthorpe always be this ugly presence between them? There was no simple answer to his question, and she couldn't even fathom where she might begin. "Why must I tell you? Why do you not simply believe me when I say that it is so?"

"I want to understand you better." He was silent for a moment, then said, "He was not a good man, Élise. I can't imagine you...and him..." He shook his head.

"It is not something that is pleasant to imagine. For me also."

"Tell me how you met."

"At a ball. When I had just turned seventeen, my uncle gave me a London Season. Did you know that? As if I were an English debutante."

"Dunthorpe danced with you at this ball?"

"He did. Twice. He was very charming. And my uncle the *compte*—who was still alive back then—knew he was looking for a wife and believed he would be a good match for me. My uncle was of an old-fashioned mind and very impressionable when it came to bloodlines and money, and Dunthorpe was in possession of both."

"So Dunthorpe began to court you."

She began to relax against Sam, taking comfort from his solid presence. "He did. There were obstacles on all sides. I found him rather old—he was sixteen years older than me, and I told my uncle it should be forbidden for a man to marry a woman when he is almost twice her age! My uncle liked everything about him when they were apart. When they met face-to-face, my uncle did not particularly approve of his demeanor. He found Dunthorpe to be a pompous, arrogant man—which he was. And Dunthorpe himself, well, there was the matter of my Frenchness, you see. He always imagined he'd marry an English rose."

"But the obstacles were overcome, clearly," Sam said.

"Yes. I decided his title and his money made up for his ancient age. I was much influenced by my uncle back then, you see. My uncle was of the mind that a man's disposition did not matter when he possessed as much blue blood and as much money as Dunthorpe. And Dunthorpe..." She rolled her eyes. "He told me himself when he proposed marriage to me that he had come to the conclusion that my beauty surmounted my Frenchness, and because of that, he deemed me worthy."

"So you married him."

"I married him, little fool that I was." She turned to him, her lips pressed together. "Children of that age should not be allowed to make such decisions."

"They're not," he said dryly. "According to the law, both the bride and groom must be twenty-one years of age. If one of them is younger, the marriage requires consent of the party's parent in order to be a legal one."

"Or the party's guardian. My uncle gave his consent, of course. Which proves he was just as foolish as I was."

"So you married Dunthorpe that autumn?" His voice was a low rumble in her ear. His fingers played with the edging of lace on the short sleeve of her dress. There had been a crate filled with women's clothing up in the attic, and Élise was pleased to learn that once upon a time, a woman of a similar stature had resided in this cottage.

"Tell me about the beginning of your marriage," he murmured.

"It was not so bad, for the first year. He handled me rather like a prize, a trophy he might display upon his mantel. But I did not begrudge him that. I did my best to be a good wife to him. My uncle and Marie had trained me in the ways of this, but... well, my uncle was a man, you see, and had been a widower for a long time. And Marie... her marriage was very different. Very passionate and full of love."

Sam frowned. "What happened to her husband?"

"He died. In the early days of the Terror, he was killed attempting to protect my family."

Her words brought memories of the Terror to the forefront, and she drew in a shaky breath. She and Marie had lost everything. She'd clung to Marie, who was ten years older than her—a mother and sister both during those years and the ensuing years in England.

She continued, her voice lowering as she struggled to keep it steady. "He and Marie had been our trusted servants for many years. They met in the service of our family as children, and they'd married just a year before the Terror. They were madly in love, and young, too, so I suppose it is possible all young marriages aren't stupid ones."

She looked down at the small space between her and Sam's thighs, where her fingers sifted among the pebbles. She drew her fingertips over the smooth stones and blinked the sting from her eyes as sadness claimed her, like it always did when she thought of those times.

Sam's lips pressed against the top of her head. "It hurts you to remember."

"Ah, yes. It makes me melancholy. My life...It was long ago, but it was different before the Revolution. When I was a small child, there was always much joy and laughter in our house."

"And after you married Dunthorpe, you weren't able to gain it back?"

"No. After the first year, he began to resent me. Because..." She stared down at the stones, wondering why, even now, after so many years, this was so painful for her to discuss. It was common knowledge, after all. "Because I am barren." She swallowed hard. "Of course, I wanted a child...very badly. I went to many doctors and took many foul-tasting potions to remedy this affliction. But"—she gave a definitive shake of her head—"there is naught to be done about it. My body refuses to allow a child to grow within it. And Dunthorpe, he hated me for this."

"Did he hurt you?" Sam's voice was low and steady, but a sudden tension surged around them, and she hesitated before answering.

"No. Not...physically."

"But in other ways?"

"He was very cruel." She squeezed her eyes shut and laid her cheek against the front of Sam's shoulder. She felt wrung out, twisted dry like a stocking coming out of the laundry. "I don't wish to speak any more of it."

His fingers stroked the outside of her arm, up and down, up and down. Such a soothing motion.

"I have often wondered if I was being punished by God," she whispered, "though I was never sure if I was being punished for failing to bear him a son or for marrying him to begin with."

"I've felt the same way," he said. "Wondering if I've been punished."

"Punished for what?"

He shrugged. "For being who I am."

"Because you have killed men?"

He shook his head. "It was that I was—*am*—illegitimate. I am a result of an affair my mother had before she was married, and I never knew the identity of my father. My mother's husband used to say that bastard children were devil's spawn. That they were inherently wicked because they'd inherited the wickedness of their parents."

She cocked a skeptical brow. "And you believed this?"

"Not really, no. But when Marianne was killed, I—" He stopped, then took a deep breath and finished. "I began to wonder if it was because of me, because I deserved to suffer. And then when Charlotte and...and our son..." He pressed his lips together and shook his head, clearly unable to continue.

She didn't push him. How could a man bear the deaths of two wives and an infant son upon his soul? It would be a crushing weight to anyone. It would make anyone think desperate, painful thoughts.

"So happiness and joy, they have been elusive to you, too," she said somberly.

"They have," he agreed, staring out over the water. "But...I do have a family. I have four brothers and a sister—none of whom are fully of my blood, yet they have never treated me as anything less than a brother to them."

"Will you tell me about them?"

He slid her a glance. "Maybe another time."

"Now you do not play fair, monsieur! But..." She pulled back slightly and smiled up at him. "I believe I now understand why."

"Do you?"

"Yes, I do. It all becomes clear to me with this revelation of your illegitimacy."

"Oh?" he asked, and there was an edge of amusement in his voice. "Tell me what you have puzzled out."

"Well, it is in your accent, you see. I know you have a powerful ear for accents—I have heard you play the Frenchman and the coachman, for example. But your natural accent is very, very aristocratic. You, my jailor, are an English *aristo* by blood."

"Am I?"

"Oh yes, you are. Your mother was the aristocrat, yes? She took a lover, as many of her generation were wont to do, and"—Élise made an elaborate gesture toward him— "*voilà*! Here you are. Yet you were raised as an aristocrat's son, were you not?"

He shook his head in wonderment. "You never fail to impress me, Élise."

She gazed hard at him. "Who was she?"

"Hm?"

"Do you forget? I am of the English aristocracy, too. I have met a great number of the other women of the *ton* over the past eleven years. I am certain I must know your mother. Who is she?"

He gave a low grunt. "You know I cannot tell you."

"Why not?"

He simply sighed. His arm slipped from her shoulder, and she felt his withdrawal once again.

She gave his thigh a little pat. Touching that rock-hard

slab of muscle gave her heartbeat a jolt. "Never mind it. You will tell me in due time."

"I hope so," he said quietly, and she felt the truth of it resonate in his voice. "I hope I can."

She slipped her arms around him and tugged him down to her, pressing a kiss to his jaw when she could reach it. "I hope you can, too."

When he turned his head, their noses bumped. And then his lips were on hers, warm and hungry and impassioned. He brought his big hands up to her face, cupping her cheeks in his palms to angle her head just so. Just so he could kiss her to utter perfection.

She floated away on the tide of desire his lips wrought upon her. He was so hard, so firm. So very real. He made all those years of her miserable marriage float away until they were a distant memory.

All there was now was Sam. Holding her, protecting her, kissing her as if she were the only thing in the world that had ever mattered to him.

But then, slowly, he drew away, and she watched the impassivity wash over his features as he removed his body, his heart and soul, from all contact with hers.

Within seconds, his withdrawal was complete.

She wanted this safety, this desire, this deep, intense feeling she felt growing between them to be real...She wanted it with a ferocity that was staggering.

But it *wasn't* real. The struggle against their desire for each other—*that* was real. And the conflict wasn't over; it wasn't close to being over. For a moment, desire had been victorious, but it was a fleeting victory, a tiny battle in an enormous war.

He was broken, and so was she. By their terrible

pasts, their bleak futures. By their first meeting, which had cemented the hopelessness of anything real between them.

Happiness and joy, as always, slipped away before she could grasp them.

"It's growing cold," he said flatly, looking away from her stricken face. "We should return to the house."

Chapter Ten

❦

The following morning, they dressed in modest clothing—Sam wearing none of the rich fabrics he'd donned in London and Élise dressed in a dark cloak over a simple white sprig muslin—and hitched the horse to a cart. They sat side by side on the perch—looking like any country gentleman and his wife to passersby.

Sam enjoyed the sheer simplicity of it. It was a glorious day, clear and crisp, with puffy white clouds offsetting the brilliant blue of the morning sky.

They rode in comfortable silence, though perhaps it was more an illusion than reality. For Sam's part, he was torn with the same torment that had beset him for the previous seven days. Yesterday, she'd pulled the reasons for his behavior toward her out into the open. She'd given him a good argument to cease his cool indifference.

Yet it felt like his last line of defense. When he let that stiff veneer that covered him melt away, he would do something stupid. He knew he would.

Maintain a professional distance. He was trying. He had thrown every bit of energy he had into that task.

He knew it made him seem like an ass to her. Hot and out of control, then cooling quickly as he was able to rein himself in.

Better an ass than...

Than a what?

Than a stupid fool who allowed himself to get carried away by blind lust.

Than a man who allowed himself to care and then inevitably had everything torn away from him.

He needed to close himself off. But he was doing a poor job of it with his hot-and-cold behavior, letting himself get so deeply drawn in by her allure before he was able to regain control.

As for Élise, she appeared perfectly composed, perfectly relaxed as they drove into Kendal.

But he'd known the woman for almost a fortnight now, and he recognized the sharpness in her gaze, the tightness at the corners of her lips. She was on edge. Perhaps it was simply because they would be together in a public place for the first time. Perhaps it was because his behavior was confusing her. Hurting her.

Hell. He didn't want to hurt her.

It was probably already too late for that. He really was a bastard.

"Stay close to me in the market," he told her softly. "I will hold your elbow like a solicitous husband, for the most part. But there might be times when I am forced to let you go."

She didn't say anything, but her chest rose and fell as she drew in a deep breath.

"Don't try to run," he told her, using that same low, flat voice. And hating himself for it. "I *will* catch you."

She shuddered visibly.

Did it mean she wished to be caught? Caught and then...

No. He shook off those thoughts, knowing full well the direction in which they'd take him.

They drove for a moment in silence. Then, he said, "Élise? Do you understand me?"

"Yes." She turned to face him. "Do not worry, Monsieur Jailor. I am not foolish enough to try to run. Not today. Not here."

"Good."

He stopped among the many other horse-drawn conveyances at the edge of the market. He dismounted, secured the horses, then helped Élise down. When she was steady, he took her arm and steered her toward the stalls.

The Kendal market was crowded and noisy—and as they passed down each aisle, weaving through the crowd, the scents of raw and cooking meats, spices, and herbs assailed them. Sam stopped at a stall selling an assortment of fresh foul and bought a large turkey.

Élise approved of his choice. Grinning, she said, "That will be delicious for our supper tonight."

"And tomorrow, and the next, likely."

"I shall buy some herbs to season this bird. The cottage is stocked for those who wish their food to taste like paper."

He nodded, rather bemused, then stood to the side as she haggled over herbs and spices, many of which he'd never heard of prior to today. She was a tough negotiator, and finally the herb seller threw up his hands in disgust.

"Very well, then! One shilling, sixpence, and no' a penny less!"

"Very good," Élise said. She turned to Sam, arching an expectant brow. "I require a shilling and five pence, I believe, monsieur."

He fought a smile, remembering the penny he'd given her last night over their sparse dinner of dried beef, crusty bread, and cheese. He fished in his purse and handed her two full shillings—in case she wanted to spend the extra sixpence on something else.

She flashed him a brilliant smile that went straight to his gut and then turned back to the hawker. They exchanged money for a—rather enormous—bag of fresh and dried herbs and spices.

As they walked from the table, he said, "I had no idea you were such a connoisseur of food."

She gave him an arch look. "I am French, my Sam. Need I say more?"

He did smile then—compelled by the "my Sam" along with her directness. "No," he said. "There is no need to say more."

They wandered around the market for a while longer, Sam purchasing everything they might require for the next week. With Élise's help, he chose a variety of vegetables they could cook that would go well with the turkey—celery and onions and turnips, not to mention two heads of cabbage, some carrots, a half pound of walnuts, extra porridge, a loaf of bread, coffee, tea, and sugar.

With his arms loaded with parcels, he couldn't keep his hand on Élise, but her arms were also full, and she remained close to him of her own volition, for which he was grateful.

He wouldn't hesitate to drop everything and run after her, if necessary. No doubt she knew this, for she gave no hint of even considering attempting to run.

Laurent should be back before market day next week. In truth, Sam expected him any day. Perhaps tomorrow.

"Sam? Is that you?"

Sam froze, his body going stiff at the sound of his sister's voice. His *sister*. Good God.

His gaze slid toward Élise. She looked up at him with wide eyes and raised brows. But she didn't make a peep as he turned slowly in the direction of Esme's voice.

She stood there, all young freshness and pink cheeks, strands of shining, dark hair curling out from beneath her bonnet brim. Her eyes were alight with pleasure at seeing him. A quick glance beyond her verified that she was with her maid, who stood just behind and to the side of her.

He wondered if Esme and Élise knew each other. She'd mentioned being acquainted with Trent—but everyone knew the Duke of Trent. On the other hand, Esme was uncomfortable in social situations, and because of that, the Hawkins family had taken great pains to keep her sheltered. She'd had a London Season two summers ago, but it had been cut short, and she hadn't been out in society much since then.

He hoped they hadn't met. And if they had, well, Élise looked far different from that night Sam had first seen her at the opera. Then she'd been a glimmering vision of rich, titled perfection, dressed in shimmering satin and wearing sparkling diamonds. Now she wore no jewels, and her dress was simple and outmoded.

She was still perfect, though. Perhaps even more so, he thought, because like this, Élise was not only beautiful; she was human. She had an approachability that the icy vision of flawlessness at the opera could never hope to have.

He shifted his parcels into the crook of one arm and held out his hand to his sister. "Esme," he said, letting pleasure he didn't feel infuse his voice. Not that he wasn't happy to see his sister—he always enjoyed seeing her. But not like this. There was too much danger associated with this. For all three of them. "I didn't expect to see you here."

"I didn't expect to see you, either." Her gaze flicked from him to Élise.

"Esme, this is a friend of mine, Madame Élisabeth de Longmont." He used her maiden name, and Élise didn't so much as flinch.

Esme's lips curved in a shy smile.

"Madame, this is my sister." He paused, then said simply, "Esme."

He avoided her title and her last name, because while it wasn't surprising that Élise hadn't connected "Samson Hawkins" to the House of Trent, Esme's identity was known in *ton* circles. Élise's clever mind would certainly connect "Lady Esme Hawkins" and Sam himself to the Duke of Trent.

To her credit, Esme didn't flinch, either, though her lashes did flicker in surprise. Sam was sure she'd never in her life been introduced in such a fashion.

It didn't seem as important as it once had to keep his family's identity from Élise. He was beginning to believe that his secrets would be safe with her. But his cautious nature was too ingrained. He never allowed his occupation to cross over into his personal life. There were many reasons why, not the least of which was that he refused to put any member of his family in danger.

Élise smiled at the younger woman. "Oh, Mademoiselle Esme. I would embrace you were I not carrying all these annoying parcels! It is so wonderful to meet the sister of my good friend. And you are so beautiful, too!" She gave Sam a chastising look. "You did not tell me, monsieur, that your sister was such a lovely creature."

Sam tilted his head in acknowledgment of this fact. "You are right, madame. I have been remiss."

Inside, a warmth grew within him. Élise was not going to disappoint him.

Esme's pink flush deepened. She gazed down at the muddy, trampled ground. "Well...er...thank you," she murmured.

"But what brings you here?" he asked her. "You're supposed to be in Preston with our brothers." Again, he did not name names deliberately.

"Well, yes, we did go to Preston for a few days. But..." Esme looked up, and he saw the flash of uncertainty in her eyes as they flicked to Élise and then back to him. "Well, we found something there that led us here," she said cryptically.

"I see," he said. And he did see. Mark and Theo must have discovered a clue in Preston that had brought them to Kendal.

Excitement welled within him, like it did every time someone in his family found evidence regarding the whereabouts of their mother. But he tamped his excitement down and maintained his outward façade of calm.

"Where are you staying?" he asked his sister.

"At the Crown Inn."

"Good."

"You must join us for dinner," Esme said. Then she seemed to realize she hadn't included Élise in the invitation. "Oh! Both of you, of course."

"Thank you," Élise said graciously. "You are so very kind."

"It is kind, but we cannot." He leaned forward and murmured, "I am not at liberty to go. I'm sorry." He was tempted anyhow, because not only would he have liked to see his younger brothers, but he was damned curious what they had found to bring them here.

But it would be beyond foolish to be seen with the Hawkins siblings in public—and with the missing Lady Dunthorpe, no less.

Speaking of—they'd been out in this public setting for too long already.

"We need to go, Esme, but I'm glad you found us here."

Surprisingly, he *was* glad. He was only disappointed that he couldn't spend more time with her and see his brothers.

Trent would eventually let him know why they'd come to Kendal. But God knew how long he'd have to wait for his brother's letter.

Sam bent forward—awkwardly, thanks to all the packages he still carried—and kissed his sister's cheek. "I'll try to find you at the inn before you leave."

"It was a pleasure to meet you, my lady," Élise said.

Sam nearly choked. Of course the blasted woman had somehow discerned that Esme held a title. The blasted, *clever* woman. He slid his gaze in her direction to see a smile playing about her lips.

He shook his head and flicked his fingers, gesturing in the vague direction of the cart and horse. "After you, madame."

* * *

Élise insisted upon preparing the turkey herself. Since Sam had taken her from her home, she had passively allowed the men to cook for her, first Carter and then Sam himself. This passivity was due to habit more than the fact that the men had simply taken those tasks upon themselves without comment.

The truth was, Élise hadn't touched an unprepared morsel of food for many years, and entering a kitchen with the goal of creating a meal felt odd. Like she was stepping back in time, into those uncertain days between her parents' and her brother's deaths and the day, two years later, that her uncle had met her in Dover and had taken her under his wing.

Even after she'd begun to live with her uncle, she'd remained close to Marie, often going to her house and helping her cook meals and run errands and whatever else needed to be done. But when she'd become the Viscountess Dunthorpe, Marie once again had become conscious of the separation between their classes and had insisted she put an end to doing even that much.

She had returned to the kitchen tonight not to reunite herself with the joys of cooking, nor to create a delightful feast for the man she was growing to... *admire* far more than she should.

She gazed at the herbs lined up before her, studying each of them, remembering.

Many people, old and young, rich and poor, had suffered from nightmares and the inability to sleep during the Reign of Terror. Marie, using herbal knowledge passed down from generations of women in her family, had created a sleeping tonic that had given her a reputation that extended far beyond Paris.

That had been inadvertent. Marie had never wanted to draw attention to herself and Élise. Nevertheless, they had survived for months by selling tiny bottles of Marie's tonic to hundreds of their countrymen whose eyes glowed with fear and sadness and were weighted down by heavy bags.

Élise had collected the ingredients from the herb seller at the market while Sam looked on with a patient expression on his face. He'd thought he'd been indulging her by buying her all these herbs. Surely he'd known that not all of them were intended for the turkey.

It was the turkey itself that had given her the idea, though. She remembered how her mother would always smile and tell Élise that nothing gave her father a sound sleep like a meal of turkey. Élise had paid attention when she'd eaten turkey in later years and found that it did indeed seem to give her a sedated, sleepy feeling.

So when Sam had purchased the turkey, an idea had taken root. And it had grown when she saw the variety of herbs on the seller's table.

She knew, at that moment, how she would escape. And she had the key ingredient tucked into the pocket of the apron she'd worn to the market. She pushed her hand into it and felt the small vial she'd swiped from the chemist's table.

Laudanum.

They'd been leaving the market when they'd passed by the chemist. She'd pushed the worry of the sleeping draft from her mind, knowing that she had many of the ingredients promoting somnolence, if not the most powerful one. She'd been thinking about Sam's lovely young sister, Lady Esme, and how she'd looked at Sam with such adoration.

And then she'd seen it. The chemist's table, piled high with medicines and remedies. And on the edge, with large, neat black lettering, a sign that read LAUDANUM.

She didn't have time to think, to worry, to second-guess herself. She had made a very large scene by pretending to slip and scattering her parcels everywhere. On the way down, she'd grabbed Sam's arm, and his parcels had gone flying, too.

The vial had stood on the edge of the man's table, along with a dozen others. Everyone had been bending over collecting her packages for her when she'd slipped this little vial into her pocket. This, along with the turkey and the herbs she would prepare it in, would put Sam in a deep slumber for a good long while.

She pulled her hand out of her pocket and turned to the turkey to remove it from the brine.

She'd prepare Samson Hawkins a fine turkey tonight. The best meal he'd had in weeks.

She'd make him happy tonight, because tomorrow he was going to hate her.

Chapter Eleven

$\mathcal{S}$am took the last swallow from his glass of wine and leaned back in his seat. He felt uncommonly peaceful tonight. Good food, good wine, good company.

Through half-lidded eyes, he glanced over at that company. As always, she sat erect in her seat, a lovely little creature but larger than life, full of boundless energy, full of light.

No one had ever made him feel so alive.

"Did you like it?" she asked softly. God, he adored her voice. With that melodic lilt, that soft rhythm of her French accent. It was a gliding caress over his skin.

"I loved it," he said, hearing the simple satisfied pleasure in his own voice.

She smiled. "Excellent. I myself am so full I am likely to burst at any moment."

With effort, he rose, knowing that while he'd much rather relax with her in the salon, he needed to take care of the cleaning up. Since she'd spent all afternoon cooking, it was the least he could do. He went to her side and bent down to kiss her cheek as he took her plate and silverware. "Thank you for dinner."

"You're welcome." She started to rise, but he stayed her with a hand on her arm. "No. I will take care of it. You rest."

She smiled up at him. "If you feel I am exhausted from my extreme exertions in the kitchen this afternoon, my Sam, then you are mistaken indeed."

He squeezed her arm. "I can't imagine I'll ever see you exhausted, Élise."

"I am touched by your confidence. Now, allow me to help you."

He sighed. "If you wish it."

"I do." She put her hand on her wineglass, then removed it. "But I will leave the wine out, yes? We will have another glass when we are finished."

"Yes," he agreed.

They worked in companionable silence, Sam washing and rinsing the dishes and Élise drying them and putting them away. As always, they made short work of the mess, and once again—as he had been every other night—he was impressed by this woman's lack of spoiled affectations. Sinking wrist-deep into grease and turkey bones didn't bother her in the least.

Her true personality was a surprise to him. From that first long-distance glimpse he'd had of her that night of the opera, all sorts of assumptions had clicked into place. Very few of them had proven true.

He went outside to dump the dishwater, and when he returned into the warmth of the cottage, he found her in the dining room, pouring them two glasses of wine. She handed him his. "Salon?"

"Yes," he said on a half sigh, half groan. His limbs felt heavy. He hadn't had that active a day...Perhaps the events of the past weeks had begun to catch up with him.

They retired to the salon, where Sam built up the fire, then joined Élise on the sofa.

He took his wineglass from the side table and took a deep swallow. The wine, which he'd retrieved from the small cellar here at the cottage, had a rather odd bitter aftertaste, but otherwise it was very good.

He set the glass on the table and in a moment of true weakness, slung his arm around Élise. She cuddled against him. The rounded flesh of her breast pressed against his side. His cock, the damned thing, grew hard and tight and hot.

He wondered if she knew exactly what kind of an effect she had on his body.

He took a long, slow breath. He wouldn't lose control. He wouldn't. Each day had been a greater challenge to him, because she grew more appealing to him with every hour. More lovely, more attractive. And as his interest in her grew, so did his hunger for her.

He slid his fingers up and down her arm. He liked the feel of her slender arm beneath his fingertips. She was so feminine...

He reached for his wineglass and took another sip of wine. His cock was still rock hard. So hard it was beginning to hurt.

"When do you think Laurent will be back?"

"Any day," he told her. "Tomorrow, perhaps. Or the next day. Probably not longer than a week. Remember, though, it might not be Laurent who comes to us. It might be Carter, or someone else."

She sighed. "I hope it is Laurent or Carter. I like them."

"You like your jailors?"

"They are not very wicked jailors. They are both gentlemen."

More so than he had been, no doubt. He sighed, and the release of air left his body feeling heavy and weak. He glanced over at the wineglass, trying to recall how much he'd had to drink. Surely not enough to feel as sotted as he did. He could hardly keep his eyes open.

She pulled away from him, looking at him with those lovely ocean-blue eyes.

"Are you tired?" she asked him softly.

"I am, a bit," he admitted.

She took the glass from his hand, and he realized it was empty. Odd, that. He couldn't remember drinking the rest.

She leaned forward, her lithe body moving over him, to set the wineglass on the table.

Her little hand stroked down his sleeve; then her elegant fingers curled around his hand. "Perhaps we should go to bed."

He knew what she meant. He did. But hell if those words didn't release all kinds of carnal images to flood his mind. He squeezed his eyes shut.

After a moment, she said, her voice flooded with uncertainty, "Sam?"

He opened his eyes. He'd managed to stanch the flood of erotic pictures. Almost.

"Yes?"

"Shall we go upstairs?"

He had to think a moment, translating her words through the muddle in his brain. Then he nodded. That was probably best. He was damned tired.

"Élise?" he murmured, stopping her by tightening his grip on her hand as she began to rise.

She sank back down onto the sofa. "Yes?"

He gazed at her, all seriousness now. "I want to kiss you," he said gruffly.

He just wanted a kiss. Just one little kiss to take the edge off this biting hunger for her.

She stared at him. And then she swiped the tip of her tongue over her bottom lip. He groaned softly and dragged her to him.

He tried not to be a boor. A part of him wanted to eat her up, to be greedy and take, take, take. But another part wanted to cherish her, wanted to show her all the protective instincts she brought out in him.

He wanted her to be his. God, how badly he craved that. Knowing she was his, all his, would be the sweetest feeling...

Her lips were soft and warm under his, tasting of wine and the herbs from their dinner but still ripe with her innate sweetness. Her body fit so deliciously, perfectly against his, like she was made for him.

He drew back a scant inch, whispering against her mouth, "You're so lovely. So perfect."

Hell, he wasn't one to spout pretty words to a woman, but she needed to know—he needed to tell her—

"So are you, my Sam."

"No," he groaned. "I am a killer. I killed your husband."

And there it was, in black and white. He drew back

farther, his arms slipping from where they'd been holding her tight against him.

She cupped his cheek and pushed at it, forcing him to look from his lap up into her face.

"You are a defender of your king and of your prince," she said softly, "and I do not hold that against you."

Something melted inside him, making him feel languid and oh so tired. She brought her lips to his again and kissed him softly. "Come," she murmured. "I will take you upstairs."

She took his hand again and tugged him up from the sofa. It felt like his body weighed a ton.

He just wanted to go to sleep. He'd feel better—refreshed and awake—in the morning. It had been a long day. A long month. A long *life*.

She doused the lantern but left the fire going. He gave a heavy sigh as they started walking up the stairs. It seemed to take forever to get up to the short corridor at the top. She pulled him to her bedchamber, and they went inside. He pushed his makeshift bed against the door, then sank down onto it.

Something nudged at his brain, told him this wasn't right, to beware. But, God, he was so...damn...tired. He rubbed harshly at his eyes, but it made no difference. He needed to close his eyes. Just for a few minutes, even, and all would be better.

Élise knelt before him and was removing his boots.

That was kind of her, he thought.

And he didn't remember anything more.

* * *

When Sam lost consciousness, Élise found herself unable to leave right away. She finished tucking him in bed, ensuring he would be comfortable. She straightened his limbs—no easy feat given the difference in their sizes—slipped a pillow under his head, and pulled the covers up around him. Then she simply looked at him.

He looked peaceful in sleep with the harsh, serious lines of his face relaxed. But he didn't look young. He looked like a mature man who'd been through hell and who'd come out of it burned and scarred but still in one piece.

He was a survivor. Like she was.

She stroked her fingers down the side of his face. He didn't budge, and she might have been worried if not for the steady rise and fall of his chest and the puffs of air she felt against her fingers when she moved them over his lips. Just to be sure, she checked his pulse and was further pacified by the slow, strong, and steady beat of his heart.

To her, he was beautiful. Strength, determination, intelligence, and loyalty. She'd never before met a man with that particular combination of qualities. To her, they were most compelling. They proved to her that he was special.

And now she had betrayed him.

No, not really, because she'd never made him any promises. She'd made it quite clear to him that she still wanted—and intended—to escape. Still, she couldn't completely thrust away that tinge of guilt.

She tugged, pulled, and yanked at the mattress, finally creating a space just barely wide enough for her to squeeze though. Through it all, Sam didn't move.

She rose, opened the door as quietly as possible, and slipped out of the room through the narrow gap. She went straight to the attic, where she'd covertly laid aside a boy's costume not dissimilar to the one she'd worn when she'd tried to escape back in London.

She wasn't a fool. A lone woman would draw far too much attention. She needed to dress like a boy—again. She'd probably still draw attention, but it was the best she could do.

Hurriedly, she discarded her dress and petticoat and replaced them with the gray woolen trousers, shirt, and coat. She tucked her hair under the matching gray cap and slung the old-fashioned, layered cape over her shoulders. The benefit of this costume was that she'd also found a pair of boots that had probably once belonged to a youth of thirteen or fourteen. Still too big for her, but certainly better than going barefoot. After she'd pulled on the boots, she gathered her clothes and then climbed down the narrow steps from the attic as quietly as she could.

And then she went to check on Sam one more time. Just to be sure he was all right.

He hadn't moved from where she'd left him, but his chest still rose and fell with steady regularity. Resisting the urge to crouch down and touch him, she turned away and left the bedchamber, closing the door softly behind her.

Using hot coals from the hearth, she lit a lantern. She fetched some food and wine from the pantry.

Then she stole two crowns and a shilling from Sam's purse, which he kept in the desk drawer in the salon.

She had become a thief, she thought, with a choking surge of guilt. He could have her prosecuted and hanged for this, if he caught her.

He might be angry enough at her escape to do it, too.

With her heart pounding and her arms full, she hurried to the stable. In the gelding's stall, she set to saddling it. She was by no means an expert at saddling horses, but she rode them often when she was in Brighton, and she'd watched her groom saddling her mare any number of times.

Of course, that had been a sidesaddle. Chewing on her lower lip, she lowered the lantern on a shelf and the other items she'd brought on a bale of hay, then focused on her task, first cinching the saddle on, then attempting to bridle the animal. Encouraging the gentle bay to take the bit took six tries, but finally, she managed it. It had taken too long for her to do that, she knew. A half hour, at least. Sam might right now be stirring, realizing she was missing...

She found the saddlebag she'd seen on one of the shelves and stuffed it with the food and money as well as her feminine change of clothes. She opened the door to the stall and to the stable, propping them open as best she could, using large rocks to hold the doors in place, then she stood on the bale of hay and mounted.

Once she was up, she held still a moment, adjusting herself to the awkward position of riding astride with her legs splayed awkwardly on either side of the horse.

She had ridden astride as a child with her brother. Her mother would have been horrified if she'd found out, so it had been a secret between her and Anton.

Thinking of him, she found the stirrups and tucked her booted feet into them. Anton had been the kindest of big brothers. Though he'd been five years older than her and off at school throughout most of her childhood, he always had a hug and a kind word for her when they were together. And he'd always taken time to be with her, to play with her, to teach her things no one else would, like how to ride a horse astride.

He should have grown into a kind and generous man. But no. The guillotine had taken his life at the age of fourteen.

"All right, *mon bon ami*," she murmured to the animal, reaching down to pat its withers. "Are you ready to escape from this place?"

The horse shifted on its feet, which was more of a response than she'd expected, and she took it as a definite "yes."

"Very good, then," she whispered, taking up the reins. "Let us spread our wings and fly."

She walked the horse out of the stables and down the long, lonely drive that led from the main road to the cottage.

The night was deathly quiet, but the half-moon peeked through a shifting layer of clouds, giving the road a faint, silver-limned glow to help light her way.

The ride to London was a long one, and it would probably take her a week, at least. London wasn't the ideal place for her to go—knowing she had so many enemies there did not make it an appealing objective in the least. But the Duke of Trent lived in London, and her mind had kept returning to the man for a reason. He was the one she must go to for help.

She faced a week or longer of hard riding, concealing her identity, and sleeping in forests and fields at night, but she had done all that before, long ago, in France. She could do it again. And in a week or so, she'd be in London, and the Duke of Trent would help her.

If Sam didn't catch her first.

Chapter Twelve

Sam clawed his way through the thick veil of sleep, slicing long, jagged lines and pushing his way through to the lucidity promised on the other side. He pried his eyes open, but they slammed shut again as acute dizziness washed through him.

Good God.

He caught his breath, forcibly settled his stomach, and cracked his eyes open once more. The dim morning light cut into his head like daggers, and he gave a low groan.

He struggled up onto his elbows, trying to remember how he'd ended up in bed. He remembered dinner, sitting in the salon with Élise, coming upstairs, her taking off his boots...

His boots were sitting side by side next to the mattress. Élise...

He pushed the blankets aside and staggered to his feet so he could see the bed.

Empty.

The shock to his system was as jolting as if someone had poured a bucket of ice water over his head. It also made the situation clear—so damn crystal clear that the revelation stabbed into him.

She'd drugged him. And then she'd left.

His lips went tight as the coldness washed over him. He wouldn't shout, scream, indulge in fury or panic. He would face this with frigid, icy precision, as he had with so many other problems over the years.

It was why he did what he did. It was why he was one of the best.

He searched the house methodically for clues. She'd taken the boy's clothing and boots from the attic. She'd taken enough food to last her a day on the road. She'd stolen two crowns and a shilling—an odd amount. If he were her, he would have taken the entire purse.

He didn't need to check the stable, but in the interest of being thorough, he did.

She'd taken the horse. Of course she had.

So, as dawn turned the cloudy eastern sky a dull gray, Sam set off on foot.

He went south, because that was the only direction she could have gone. There was nothing for her in the north. The south would be more dangerous, but Élise wasn't a coward, and everything she knew was in the south. He walked in that direction with confidence.

Within an hour, he was mounted on a horse he'd purchased from a yard in the village of Windermere.

Within two hours, it had begun to rain, and he rode through Kendal in a torrential downpour.

He stopped at the King's Arms Inn, which had not yet received any correspondence from Trent. After a brief debate with himself, he went across the town to the Crown Inn, where his sister and brothers were staying.

His brothers were still abed when he arrived, but Esme was up and breakfasting in the common room. He strode into the room, which was populated with several tables, most of which were taken by other guests enjoying their breakfasts. She was seated at a small table, scribbling away in her notebook, while her maid sat in a shadow in the corner, waiting patiently.

He was at his sister's side when she finally looked up and saw him. "Sam! Um…" She hurriedly clapped the notebook shut and placed it atop a similarly sized package beside her plate.

"Good morning, Esme."

"I didn't expect to see you here! Where is Madame de Longmont?"

It said a lot about the assumptions Esme had made about his relationship with Élise when she expected her to be at his side this early in the morning.

"She is not with me." He wasn't going to volunteer any more information than that.

"Oh…uh…" Esme glanced down at her half-empty plate. "Oh, please do sit with me."

"All right. I will for a moment," he told her. As soon as he was settled in the chair across from her, he removed his hat and placed it on the table. Then he leaned forward and murmured, "I don't have much time, but I wanted to be sure all was well with you and Mark and Theo as I rode through town today."

A line appeared between Esme's brows. "Oh? Are you leaving the area?"

"I'm not sure. I might return; I might not."

She gazed at him, her look turning speculative as she studied him. Then she simply said, "I see."

"Tell me why you're here. What have you discovered about our mother's whereabouts?"

"First we should see to getting you some food—"

He reached forward, closing his hand around her wrist. "I don't have time to eat."

The line between her brows deepened. "Some coffee, then?"

"Yes, coffee." He looked up, and as chance would have it, a woman was passing by hefting a coffeepot. He hailed her, and a moment later, she placed a steaming cup before him.

Esme pushed over her plate of toast. "Here, eat this, at least."

He took it gratefully. His stomach was still twisted up from whatever the hell Élise had given him last night, and maybe the toast would help. He glanced up at his sister. "Now tell me about our mother."

She sighed. "We came here to Kendal because Mark found a witness who'd helped disband Steven Lowell's camp in Preston. The man told Mark that the players had traveled in a southeasterly direction. Except for two of them: Steven Lowell and a woman. Those two had headed north."

"But why Kendal?"

Esme gazed down at her food but didn't take a bite. "We didn't know at first, but then we found a man in Lancaster who'd encountered a gypsy named Steven Lowell, and the woman, whom I'm sure is our mother. He'd heard them speaking of visiting the Lake District. They said they wanted to go there because..."

She hesitated, and he tried to wait patiently, though he knew that every second he dallied, Élise was drawing farther away from him.

Nevertheless, he knew he had something that Élise didn't. She wasn't experienced in flight. He was, however, quite experienced in the pursuit of his prey.

He took a deep breath. "Because our mother's old house is at Lake Windermere?"

She shook her head. "No. I don't think they intend to visit her house. It would be too obvious, you know." She clasped her arms over her chest and blushed deeply. "Well...evidently, the lakes are the most sublimely romantic place in all of England."

He blinked at her. Swallowed his mouthful of toast and washed it down with hot, bitter coffee. Then he said slowly, "Our mother and Steven Lowell...have gone to the lakes...for a romantic interlude?"

Looking appalled to be discussing this with him, Esme nodded.

Sam rubbed the bridge of his nose. "Good God."

"And Kendal is the gateway to the lakes if one is arriving from the south, so they must have journeyed through here. Mark and Theo are questioning everyone to see if they can discover exactly where they went."

"And you, Esme?" He glanced at the pen and ink bottle and the notebook lying on the parcel beside her plate.

She followed his gaze and sucked in her breath. "I...er...Well, I am questioning people, too. I questioned several at yesterday's market."

"What's that package?" He was only mildly curious, assuming it was something she was sending home to Sarah or the baby.

"Um..." Panic flared in her eyes, and everything within Sam went on high alert.

"What is it?" he asked, more sharply.

"I..." She swallowed hard and whispered, "I can't tell you."

He raised his brows. "I'm your brother. Of course you can tell me."

Curving her arm protectively around the package and notebook, she pressed her lips together and shook her head, dark resolve settling in her gaze. "I cannot."

He studied her for a long, drawn-out moment. This was beyond odd. Esme had never been rebellious before—

It hit him over the head like a hammer, and he bit out, "It's for a man, isn't it?"

Her eyelashes fluttered as she blinked at him several times. "No!"

"Esme..." He infused a heavy dose of fatherly warning into his voice. God, what kinds of examples of proper behavior had the poor girl been given? He and Trent were much older and had been gone throughout her forming years, living their own lives. Their mother had had dozens of lovers, and she'd practically flaunted them under her daughter's nose for most of her life. Esme had never known her father, the old Duke of Trent; he'd died before she was born.

"It's not... It's not a man. I promise you. It's not!"

"What, then?"

"I can't tell you!" Her voice was a low wail.

"Then I'll just have to see for myself." Lightning fast, he reached for her with both hands. With his right, he lifted her arm, and with his left, he snatched both the parcel and the notebook from the table.

She jumped to her feet, her chair scraping over the wood floor, and rushed to his side. "Please, Sam, no!"

He held both items firmly, and though she attempted to grab at them, her efforts were futile. Tears welled in her eyes.

God. He'd never made his baby sister cry before. But then, he'd never been given reason to believe she was anything other than completely angelic prior to this moment.

"You're drawing attention to us, Esme," he growled in a low voice. "Sit down."

His tone brooked no argument, and she did as she was told, plunking her body heavily in the opposite chair. Her hand shook as she rubbed at her eyes. "Please…"

"Calm down." He tried to infuse gentleness into his voice. "Just tell me what this is about."

She took several deep breaths, as if trying to compose herself; then she said, in a mournful whisper, "You will not approve."

"I am already aware of that. Otherwise you wouldn't have tried to hide it from me."

"But…" She rubbed her eyes again. "You'll make me stop…and…and I don't want to stop, Sam. I *can't*."

"Stop what?"

She hesitated; then she murmured, "Writing."

He looked down at the package and notebook he clasped in his hands, then back to his sister. "Writing? This is your writing?"

"Y-yes."

He looked at the package. The address in London was not one he recognized. "Where are you sending it?"

"To…my publisher."

It took a moment for this to sink in as he gaped at her. "Your *publisher*?"

She nodded.

"You have published your writing?"

She nodded.

He still couldn't wrap his head around this news. "So...you have written something that a publisher has accepted and made into an actual book?"

She nodded yet again.

"And...this book is available for sale? And people have read it?"

"Them," she whispered. "People have read them. There are three of them now. This is the fourth." She gestured to the package.

He stared at her. His sister had just turned twenty, and she was a secretly published author. Of *three* books.

"Have you told Trent about this?"

She shook her head. "No. No one outside of those directly involved in the publishing of the books knows my identity."

"Esme...what kinds of books are these?"

Her flush deepened to a dark rose color. "They are...well...I'm afraid they are torrid romances, Sam. Please...do not read them."

He blinked at her. His sweet, innocent, unmarried sister, his sister who'd never even had a suitor, had written torrid romances under a *nom de plume*. Bloody hell.

He didn't know what to say. Words completely eluded him.

"Please don't tell Trent," she whispered.

And then, surprisingly, a tiny, grudging respect for his sister bloomed. Young as she was, she'd written stories that a publisher had deemed publishable. "Well," he said shakily, "I must congratulate you, then."

Her eyes widened.

"I will obey your request and not read them. I believe it shows a great deal of bravery to do what you have done. How long have you kept this a secret?"

"More than a year, now." Pride crept in to cover the fear on her face. "The first one was published just after Mother went missing."

"And you plan to continue to publish these . . . stories?"

"Oh, yes. For as long as I possibly can."

He slid the package, along with the notebook, across the table to her. He felt almost dizzy. His world had been knocked out of kilter this morning when he'd discovered what Élise had done, but now there was an even greater sense of unreality.

His sister was no longer a child. She was a published authoress who had successfully kept her identity hidden from the world—and from her overprotective family—for more than a year.

He needed to spend more time with Esme. To learn more about his baby sister, who had, somewhere along the way, become a woman.

Unfortunately, though, it couldn't be now.

She gazed down at the package. "I was planning to get this into the post before Mark and Theo woke."

"Don't let me keep you from that task." He sighed. "I really do need to go." Again, the image of Élise riding farther and farther away from him pushed through his mind.

He clapped his hat upon his head and rose. Then he bent down to kiss his sister's cheek. "We'll talk again. Soon."

She nodded. Then whispered, "You're not telling Trent?"

"It is not my secret to tell, is it?"

She smiled. "Thank you."

He returned her smile. "Good luck with the search for Mother. I hope to join you in the search very soon."

"I hope you will," she told him.

He walked out of the common room feeling bemused and unbalanced. But as soon as he stepped back into the rain, determination twisted into a hard knot in his stomach.

It was time to find Élise.

* * *

Élise wrapped her arms around her body and stumbled down the road.

Everything that could have possibly gone wrong had gone terribly wrong.

Before she'd reached Kendal, the horse had gone lame. She'd had to walk the beast the remaining way into the town.

She'd waited until the mail coach arrived at seven o'clock in the morning, her panic mounting that Sam could be on his way at that very moment.

But she'd managed to board the mail coach, and they left Kendal on time. Still dressed in her boy's clothing, she'd avoided the askance looks from the other passengers. She was certain they'd all suspected she wasn't really a boy.

And then it had begun to rain in buckets, and around noon, when they were just to the north of Preston, the mail coach sank into the mud, and in the continuing downpour, more mud flowed over the road with every minute that passed. Though the drivers and passengers had all banded together in an effort to disengage the coach from the knee-deep bank of mud, it was an entirely fruitless endeavor. The coach was hopelessly and irrevocably stuck.

As a group, the passengers chose to walk back to the village they'd just passed through to wait for the coach to be dislodged and the rain to abate, but Élise had no desire to go backward. Instead she had decided to continue south. She could manage the rain a bit longer. Preston was a large town, and she'd find a warm, dry place there to rest before heading on to London.

But as she walked, the rain fell harder. It was a deluge. It seemed everyone else in the world had been wise enough to stay off of the road today—the cold and wet permeated her clothing, her skin, and then her very bones until she couldn't control the chattering of her teeth.

All she wanted was to find a warm, dry place, curl up into a ball, and sleep. She hadn't slept at all last night. She hadn't realized that one night of missed sleep could make a person feel so wretched.

Her muscles ached—every one of them, from the tips of her toes through to her neck. Her head throbbed. Her throat felt hot and parched, and when she swallowed, it felt as if she were swallowing pieces of glass.

She stopped in her tracks, gazing into the sheeting rain at the ribbon of gray road that seemed to go on and on before her.

Lovely, she thought sarcastically. This was not just lack of sleep. She was getting sick. A cold, perhaps, although if it was a cold, it was the worst cold she'd ever had. Perhaps it was made worse by the chill and the rain. Usually, people weren't foolish enough to brave the elements like this when they were afflicted with a cold.

She trudged forward, her steps heavy, slow, and very deliberate. Preston couldn't be too far. The driver had said it was only three and a half miles. She could walk three and a half miles any day.

Except, perhaps, today.

She stumbled over a fallen branch in the road and fell to her knees. Her right knee smarted as she returned to her feet, and she looked down at it to see blood seeping through a tear in her trousers.

Just a skinned knee, she told herself. *Just a small cut, like the ones you had countless times as a child.*

Unaccountably, tears blurred her vision. The world around her went out of focus. The rain stung her cheeks like little pinpricks of ice.

She tripped again. This time she stayed down longer, breathing through the sharp burst of agony of the knee she'd cut the last time.

After several moments, she rose again. She looked around her hopelessly. On both sides of the road, there was nothing but endless fields. No shelter to be seen.

But on the right, a stone slab lay on the side of the road. A perfect bench. She could rest there for a little while, gather her wits and her energy, and then forge onward.

She limped over to the slab and sat upon it. Letting the saddlebag that had been slung across her back fall to the ground, she hugged her arms around herself, shaking too hard and feeling too exhausted to examine the damage to her knee. All she knew was that it hurt like a hound of hell had sunk its teeth into it.

Shelter. She needed shelter. She was sick, and she was cold, and she was tired. She wouldn't be able to walk much farther.

The driver had said Preston was three and a half miles away. She'd walked at least two already—maybe even two and a half. One more mile, and she'd be in Preston, safe and dry.

The thought was enough to bring her to her feet, resolutely strapping the bag over her shoulders once more. One more mile. She could do that.

One more mile was nothing at all.

Chapter Thirteen

$\mathcal{L}$ate that afternoon, Sam plodded onward. He couldn't push the horse too hard in this driving rain, but damned if he didn't want to.

She was out here somewhere. He hoped to hell he caught up to her before she reached Preston. Preston was a larger town, and it'd be more difficult for him to find her there.

Foolish, stubborn woman. When he'd encountered the mail coach, a sinking feeling had contracted his gut. The drivers, unable to leave their cargo, had been huddled inside, waiting for the rain to let up and for assistance to arrive.

Sure enough, a "slender, effeminate" young man had come aboard the coach in Kendal. And that young man, when the coach had become stuck, had mumbled—in a rather feminine voice—that he intended to continue on to Preston instead of returning to the hamlet a quarter of a mile back, as the rest of the passengers had done.

As alert as if he'd not been drugged near to death just the night before, Sam's senses were sharply attuned to his surroundings. There was little movement besides the pounding rain, the gathering puddles of water and mud in the road, the flutter of tree leaves as the rain lashed at them. There was no sign of life—no birds, no forest animals ducking into the bushes as he passed. Every living thing with any sense had found shelter and had tucked itself away to wait out the storm.

Clearly, Élise had no sense whatsoever.

He turned the horse down a tight bend, and on his next visual sweep of the road, he stopped dead at the sight of a huddled form off to the side. He pulled the horse to such a sharp halt, the animal reared. By the time it regained all four of its legs, Sam had already dismounted and was running toward the dark figure.

"Élise!" he shouted with a cracking voice. The figure was a dark blob of wet wool and virtually unidentifiable. But he knew it was her. He skidded to his knees beside her and rolled her over.

She was unconscious and deathly pale. He cupped her cheeks in his hands, all the anger and frustration that had accumulated within him over the past twelve hours draining from his body in a furious rush.

Her skin felt clammy under his palms, and her lips were a disturbing shade of blue. "Élise, can you hear me?"

She gave a low moan, and he released a harsh breath at the sound.

She was alive. That was something.

He gathered her into his arms and walked her to the horse. He knew exactly where he was—where the closest shelter was.

Masterson.

Fifteen minutes later, Sam stopped the horse in front of the gatekeeper's tollgate.

Élise had woken for a moment on the short journey. Gazing at him through shining eyes, she'd given him a faint smile, whispered, "My Sam," in a croaking voice, and then had snuggled more tightly against him before drifting off once again.

"Masterson!" he barked out.

The man stuck his balding pate out the door of the little shack he kept beside the gate. His eyes widened when he saw Sam, and he rushed out into the rain, pulling an oilskin coat over his shoulders.

"Hawk, what the hell're you doing out here?"

Sam glanced down at the unconscious woman in his arms. "She tried to escape."

Masterson gave a disapproving grunt. "Couldn't have chosen a better day, could she?"

"Evidently not," Sam said dryly.

"What's wrong with her? Did you shoot her?"

"No, I did not shoot her. She's ... I don't know, exactly. I think chilled to the bone, possibly ill. And she's bleeding—I think she cut her leg. I need to get her warmed up."

"Of course." Masterson held out his arms. "Hand her over, then."

Sam's arms reflexively tightened around Élise. But he took a deep breath and handed her down, an awkward proposition given the depth of her unconsciousness. The thought crossed his mind that she might have taken some of whatever she'd given him last night.

He dismounted and exchanged the horse's reins for

Élise. Masterson secured the horse and then led Sam down a muddy path to his cottage, which was hidden behind a thick row of pines.

Masterson led them inside to a small bedroom. "Lay her down here. I'll fetch some towels for you, but I've got to return to the booth. You've anything you wish here at your disposal."

"Thanks."

Masterson nodded and left the room. Moments later, he returned with the towels and then disappeared, telling Sam that he'd be back at six and they could talk more over dinner.

When Masterson had finally closed the door behind him, Sam turned to the drenched, unconscious woman he'd laid atop the bedcovers.

He'd already removed her cloak, so he started on her feet, peeling off the leather boots that had molded to her skin. She didn't budge as he removed the trousers, the coat, and the shirt. All were completely soaked through. He left them in a sodden heap on the floor.

He'd have to strip her completely bare in order to warm her up.

She was a practical woman. When she returned to consciousness, she'd understand why he'd done this.

He went to work on her stays, then her chemise.

And then she was naked. He tried not to look, to keep a businesslike calm about him, but she was perfect. Beautiful. Absolutely exquisite. As he'd known she would be.

Quickly and efficiently, he toweled her dry, then covered her with blankets. A few moments later, she began to shake. These weren't feminine little shivers, but full-blown spasms of her body that looked so painful they made his heart contract.

He took a few moments to prowl around the cottage, searching for something that might heat her, might warm her, but the fire was cold—and too far from the bed-chamber to make any difference anyhow—and he couldn't find so much as another blanket, unless he meant to steal the one off Masterson's bed. He snatched it off. He'd deal with Masterson later.

He returned to her. He laid Masterson's blanket over her and stood watching her for a moment, cringing at those awful spasms. Helplessness clawed at him.

And then it came to him. He knew what he must do. He threw off his own clothes—even his smallclothes, because the rain had somehow found its way beneath everything and made them damp, too.

Fully naked, he climbed into bed beside her and covered them both with the blankets. He drew her clammy, shivering body against him. God, but she was a shock of cold against his skin.

He closed his eyes and bent his head against her wet hair, holding her firmly against him, touching her with as much of his own skin as he could manage. His cock hardened almost instantly, but he gritted his teeth and ignored it, throwing all his focus instead onto Élise, on bringing warmth and color back into her lovely fair skin.

* * *

Élise was hot. She was burning. It felt like someone had thrown her into a giant oven and shut the door. Her skin was on fire.

She couldn't stand it anymore. With a huge force of will, she kicked, trying to relieve the oppressive weight that rested over her body. A dull pain throbbed in her knee, but it was nothing compared to the pain in her head.

She heard a low grunt of disapproval; then she felt arms wrap around her.

Someone's skin pressed against her own. It was an odd feeling. She had been touched, skin to skin like this, infrequently in her life.

Her eyes flew open as she heard the words, "Here now. You don't want to be cold again."

Who was that? Sam? But she had escaped from him! She had gone to Preston...

Her thoughts fizzled away as she struggled to rise, blinking in the darkness to try to gain her bearings. How was it that she was on a bed? She remembered the mail coach becoming stuck in the mudbank, and she remembered walking... and feeling terrible...

Oh... her head ached. Her body ached. She still felt terrible. And terribly hot.

"Hot..." she pushed out through her dry, cracking throat.

Strong arms helped her to sit. A light flickered—a candle, and she saw Sam's shadowy profile. He'd been lying beside her.

"*Comment*... How... did you?" *Dieu*, it felt like she needed to learn how to speak again. And every word she uttered hurt.

"Shh." He twisted away to reach for something from the small table beside the bed. "You've been ill. Here, have some water."

He pressed a cup to her lips. She took a sip of the cool liquid, and it felt good against her lips and tongue, but swallowing it was torture.

She'd been ill? She was so confused. She rubbed her temple. "What...happened?"

"I found you in a heap on the side of the road about half a mile north of Preston."

"Ugh," she groaned. Had she fainted? She must have. She had never arrived at Preston, because she had *fainted*, and Sam had found her first.

What would have happened if he hadn't found her?

She couldn't think too hard about that. It made her already aching head pound.

She leaned back weakly against the headboard. "What time is it?"

"Almost dawn. Here," Sam ordered. "More water."

Again, the cup pressed against her lips. Again, she sipped at it, and again it scraped over her throat. She winced.

"Hurts, huh?"

"*Oui.*" She didn't have the energy to say the English word.

"You were chilled to the bone when I brought you here," he told her. "Once I got you warmed up, you developed a fever. Masterson will summon a doctor in the morning."

She didn't know who Masterson was, but she couldn't bring herself to care.

She closed her eyes and nearly nodded off, but...

He was being awfully kind. Wasn't he supposed to be angry with her?

All of a sudden, urgency pulsed through her. She

didn't know why exactly, and she didn't have the mental capacity to consider the logic of it—but she didn't think she was ever going to reach London and the Duke of Trent. And someone needed to be told. Francis would need to be stopped.

She needed to tell Sam. *Now.*

"Je dois te dire…" She shook her head. *English.* Though she knew he spoke French, they always spoke English together. "I must tell you something," she murmured.

"Later."

"Non…maintenant. Now."

Lines of disapproval were carved around his eyes, and brackets of annoyance deepened around his mouth. Her gaze flickered over the bulging muscles that etched his bare shoulders. But the fact that he wasn't wearing a shirt seemed utterly insignificant compared to what she needed to tell him.

"It's his brother," she whispered.

Sam shook his head, uncomprehending.

"His younger brother, Francis. He will inherit now that Dunthorpe is dead."

"Yes," Sam said, still not understanding. "He was Dunthorpe's heir, so he's the new viscount. By all accounts, Dunthorpe intended to will everything to him."

"Yes, that is all true, but there is more." She gripped his arm, desperate to tell him everything. "Dunthorpe did not care about the monarchy. He did not care about England. All he cared about was his own financial gain, and he used whatever means he deemed appropriate to obtain his goal."

"Right. I know all this, Élise." Though Sam's voice

held strained patience, he shifted on the bed, and his brows knitted, hinting that patience was about to come to an end.

She tried to glare at him, though it took almost more energy than she possessed. "I am attempting to tell you my most valuable secret, my Sam, so growing impatient with me is not at all brilliant."

He blew out a breath. "Tell me, then. What does Dunthorpe's brother have to do with this?"

"He is—*was*—Dunthorpe's chief lieutenant. He has been for the past six years. Once Dunthorpe informed him that I would never bear children and that he would be the recipient of everything upon his death, Francis grew obsessed. Just as obsessed as Dunthorpe himself was."

Finally, understanding dawned. "He knew about the plot to assassinate the Regent?"

"He must have. He knew everything. They were very close and very secretive. They planned everything together. He was Dunthorpe's protégé."

"I see."

"There was another man, too. Someone you must be wary of. His name is Edmund Gherkin. He is the opposite of Francis, who is emotional and inconsistent. Gherkin is intelligent. He is cold and calculating, and I do not believe I have ever seen a hint of emotion from him."

"I know who he is," Sam said. "Dunthorpe's solicitor."

"Yes."

Exhaustion had been creeping through her body throughout the conversation, and now it weighted her down. She felt her shoulders slump as she leaned more heavily against the headboard. Sam's lips tightened. "This isn't a good time for you. You need to rest. We'll talk more later."

"But Dunthorpe—"

"I understand, Élise, and I am glad you told me this. We'll take the appropriate action."

"Good," she murmured. "Just...don't let him find you again...They will try to kill you. I don't want them to..."

"Here now." His arms, gentle but firm and so very strong, went around her. "Let me lay you back down."

He helped her onto her back and settled in beside her. Then he pulled her into his arms. He was...she was...*naked*. An electric jolt shot through her, her body going stiff.

"Your...my...our clothes!"

"Shh. It's all right," he murmured.

And, forgetting why being naked with Sam might be of any concern, she melted into the comfort of his arms and drifted off to sleep again.

*   *   *

"It's the influenza," the doctor told Sam in a low, serious voice.

Sam glanced over at the small form on the bed. She remained motionless, for though she was awake and lucid, she was almost too weak to move.

He grasped the doctor by the elbow and led him out. When they were in the passageway, he closed the door behind them, then turned to face the man fully.

"What are her chances?"

The doctor blinked at him owlishly through his spectacles.

Sam leaned forward, grinding his teeth before repeating, "What...are her chances?"

The doctor puffed out his cheeks, then released a breath. "The next day will tell. The wound on her knee isn't significant thus far, but it will become so if it festers. I have wrapped it tightly, so you needn't bother with it any further. You need to reduce her fever as much as possible. Keep her cool."

"Being cold was what did this to her," Sam said.

"That may be, but if you encourage warmth now, it will raise her fever ever higher."

"Fine. How do I reduce her fever?"

"Cool water on her fevered skin. Sponge baths are best, repeated as necessary whenever the skin is hot and dry to the touch."

Sam nodded. "What else?"

"Cool drinks. Barley water is preferred."

"And?"

"I would highly recommend bleeding her."

"No." Sam had been bled when his gunshot wound had festered. Not only had it been the worst experience of his life, it had made him so weak he'd fallen into a coma for a day.

"Blistering is a possibility—"

"No." He remembered soldiers being blistered—that looked just a touch less horrid than being bled.

"A dose of prussic acid might alleviate—"

"Absolutely not." He'd seen a man killed by prussic acid once. The stuff was poison.

The doctor sighed.

"What else?"

"Just keep her cool, Mr. Hawkins. Lukewarm broth might help, but no heavy foods."

Sam's lips twisted. He could hardly get her to take tiny sips of water. Heavy foods were not going to be a problem.

"That's all?"

"And simply wait it out. As I said, the next twenty-four hours will be telling."

Sam gritted his teeth. "How will I know if she is getting worse?"

"Her temperature will rise. She is clearly exhausted, but she has her wits about her now. If she grows worse, she will become delirious. You will know things have become dire if she is seized by convulsions. If that happens, then death invariably will follow."

Sam froze. Red anger crept into the edges of his vision. Hearing death discussed so flippantly referring to Élise…No, he wouldn't tolerate it.

He gave the man a brusque, dismissive nod, then turned away and slipped back into the bedchamber. The doctor could find his own way out.

He closed the door on the doctor and sat on the edge of the bed. Élise looked so small, so frail and harmless lying there. But she was a woman who brimmed with life, who virtually vibrated with it. He wasn't going to allow that life to be snuffed out.

She gazed up at him, her eyes preternaturally bright. "What did he say?" she rasped out.

He didn't want to scare her, but he wouldn't lie to her, either. Their days of lying to each other were over.

"Influenza," he said softly.

"Ah." She didn't seem overly perturbed by this news.

"The good news is that the doctor said the fever should be gone in a day or two."

"Good," she said, a note of wistfulness in her voice. "But he is a fool. He wrapped my knee too tightly. You must remove the bandages."

He frowned at her, and she looked at him, exhausted but lucid. "Remember the wound I dressed for you in the carriage, my Sam?" she asked softly.

"Yes." He'd almost forgotten about it, it had healed so well.

"I know how to dress a wound. That man was a fool. If you keep this dressing on me, it will fester."

His lips pressed tightly together, he removed the damned bandage; then, as she gave him careful instructions that seemed to take every last drop of energy she possessed, he redressed it.

Finally, he tucked a stray strand of hair behind her ear and rose. "Rest. I need to go fetch some things for you and talk to Masterson. I'll be back in a few minutes."

She turned her lips to his palm and pressed a kiss there. Her eyelids flickered shut, and he removed his hand, though as he did so, he allowed his fingertips to slide over the softness of her cheek. Soft but so hot his fingertips felt scalded.

He went into the kitchen, where Masterson was clearing the breakfast dishes. He glanced over his shoulder when Sam walked in and reached up to put a clean plate into his dish cabinet. "What'd he say?"

Sam put the kettle on the stove. "She has the influenza. He said the fever should go down soon. If it doesn't..."

He shook his head, his throat closing at the thought of the worst happening to Élise. Damned doctor had given him these dire thoughts. He could wring the bloody man's neck.

Because, the truth was...he cared for Élise. To see her looking so defeated and weakened by this illness made him want to punch the wall. To have it kill her...

He squared his shoulders. "Have you got a sponge?"

"I do." Masterson disappeared into his pantry, returning a moment later to hand Sam a large sponge. "What for?"

"Doctor said she's to be given sponge baths."

"Ah." Masterson turned away, but not before Sam saw a smile playing around the man's lips.

"Don't even think it," Sam growled.

Masterson raised his hands in a gesture of surrender. "I'm not thinking anything."

"Oh yes, you are."

Masterson chuckled. "Ah, Hawk, you've got it bad for this one."

Sam didn't respond to that. What could he say?

Sobering, Masterson took his coffee in hand and sat at the small table. "I've a minute before Tom leaves the gate. I need to talk to you about something."

With a weary sigh, Sam sat across from the man. He had a few minutes while the water heated. Still..."Make it quick."

"You were rather preoccupied last night—"

"Just say it. I need to get back to her."

Masterson seemed to wage a valiant battle against his twitching lips. Sam glared at the man, who was evidently wise enough to manage to keep a smirk from forming on his face.

"I know it's a change of topic, but I've been thinking about the dowager duchess."

"What about her?"

"Well, I told you how I remembered your brothers questioning me as they came through the tollgate. At the time, I'd no recollection of seeing the Dowager Duchess of Trent or the man who was with her."

"Steven Lowell. Yes?"

"But something you said last night sparked a memory. You mentioned they were heading to the lakes for a romantic interlude. I do recall an older couple passing through—about a month ago. They seemed"—he coughed and gazed into his cup—"to have a powerful infatuation with each other."

Sam raised a brow.

Masterson lifted his gaze and observed Sam with steady brown eyes. "If that woman was indeed the Dowager Duchess of Trent, she is a master of disguise."

"How's that?"

"No one would mistake her for a duchess, Hawk. Her hair flowed down to her waist, her feet were bare, and her dress was homespun, made of the brightest colors. She and her man were riding on a cart drawn by nags, and they were all wrapped up in each other—"

Sam held out his hand. "All right. That's enough."

Masterson shook his head. "Anyhow, the more I think about it, the more I think that woman was her. And the man must be this Steven Lowell chap."

Sam nodded. His mother and the gypsy must have passed through Masterson's tollgate if they'd indeed gone north. "Did they say anything about where they might have gone?"

"They were talking about waterfalls."

"Waterfalls?"

Masterson nodded. "Aye. As I stepped up to take their toll, he was murmuring about showing her all the falls in England."

"Starting with those in the Lake District?" Sam asked.

"It seems the natural starting point. My guess is if you want to find the Dowager Duchess of Trent, try the falls."

Sam nodded. "Might be a little far-fetched, but it narrows the area down somewhat. I will send my brothers to perform a thorough search."

Masterson raised his ashy brows. "Or send yourself, perhaps."

Sam glanced toward the bedchamber where Élise was. He really needed to get back to her.

"Take her with you," Masterson said, and he finally let the smirk show fully on his face. "Falls are very romantic, you know."

As Sam turned a scowl on the older man, Masterson took his leave, chuckling.

Sam took the water from the stove and made Élise some tea. He poured cold water into a basin, which he took into the bedchamber along with the sponge and the tea. Élise had evidently been dozing, but she stirred when he stepped beside her.

"You're back," she murmured, her blue eyes shining with a silvery sheen as she gazed at him.

"I am." He lowered himself to the edge of the bed and studied her. Her chemise had dried, and he'd helped her into it before she'd seen the doctor. She lay under the sheet but refused to have more on top of her. "I'm going to give you a cool bath."

She raised a brow, managing to look cynical despite her obvious pain and exhaustion. "Oh? Is that so?"

Her voice was lower than usual, with a harsh rasp to it, and he knew that every word she spoke was painful to her.

"It is," he said mildly. "Doctor's orders. But first I want you to drink this tea."

She eyed it unenthusiastically. He helped her sit up, and then he patiently forced her to drink the entire cupful, despite numerous pauses and several complaints. When the cup was finally empty, he set it beside the basin. Then he reached for the sponge, which he dipped in the water before squeezing out the excess.

She made a scoffing noise as she eyed the sponge. "You are going to bathe me," she said. "With that."

"Yes. We'll start here." Speaking mildly, he moved the sheet aside and untied the neckline of her chemise before tugging it open, keeping her breast covered but exposing an expanse of creamy skin. Ever so gently, he swiped the sponge over the hot, pale skin of her shoulder, then down her arm.

She shivered.

"Too cold?"

"Ah...no. It feels...very nice."

He glanced at her to see her bright eyes steady on his face. His heart kicked against his ribs, and he looked away again to focus on his task.

He worked in silence for long moments, gliding the sponge over her heated body, feeling her gaze on him.

The sponge quickly grew warm, and he dipped it in the cool water once again. As he squeezed the water out of it, she blinked at him, her lush eyelashes fluttering as if she was attempting to focus.

"How do you feel?" he murmured.

"Very terrible, mostly," she said. "But...better. It is very soothing, your touch."

He wanted to take her focus off how terrible she felt. Off her fever and her pain. He could soothe her body with the cool water and the sponge...and perhaps he could soothe her mind, too.

With the truth.

Chapter Fourteen

Elise's head had never throbbed so violently in her life. Every part of her skin burned with heat, and a deep ache resided in every one of her muscles.

But when Sam swiped the cool sponge over her, it was sweet relief. She felt like arching in to his touch and purring like a kitten. She probably would have, if she'd had the energy. As it was, she allowed her lids to sink and simply appreciated his soothing touch.

He moved away to rinse the sponge again. "I'm going to pull your chemise down so I can bathe your chest."

She didn't say a word, focusing on ignoring the bright flash of self-consciousness. She knew the man had taken off her clothes while she was unconscious—he'd had to, of course, if he didn't intend for her to freeze to death. He'd slept beside her last night in the nude, presumably to warm her.

It wasn't that she was ashamed of her body. It was just that she wasn't accustomed to others looking at it or touching it. Especially men. The only man who'd ever seen her naked was her husband, and he hadn't looked at her or touched her in a very long time.

It was strange and odd, but so comforting and so pleasant. In any case, she was too ill to argue.

She managed a brooding sigh, and against her will, she stiffened as he tugged the chemise down to her hips.

He gave a soft laugh. "You've never struck me as shy."

"I am not," she huffed.

"No." His voice was husky, and his gaze locked on her torso. "You're the most beautiful thing I've ever seen."

"I fear I would make a poor bed partner right now, my Sam."

"Never."

She pulled in a deep breath and winced. Even breathing hurt.

He saw it, because his eyes darkened and his lips pinched together. "Don't worry. You're too beautiful for me not to notice, but I will push those thoughts away. The important thing is to heal you. We can..." His gaze met hers. "Discuss those matters later."

Deep longing resonated in him—in his voice and beyond his darkened eyes. Her heartbeat seemed to stutter. "Yes," she murmured, "later."

When she was better... when she was herself again... she would want him. She would want him so much she'd never want to let him go.

"For now..." His gentle, cool stroke passed between her breasts. "There are some things I want you to know."

"What things are those?" She gave in to the heaviness of her lids and closed her eyes. His touch was soothing, but his voice made her feel safe. After a life that had never offered much in the way of safety, she craved the safety he offered.

"I don't want there to be secrets between us anymore."

She tried to remain perfectly still, but she knew he sensed her stiffening again.

"I know you weren't in league with Dunthorpe. I believe you."

She sighed, a part of her relaxing in relief. Another part of her remained tense and on edge, anticipating what he might say next.

"This morning," he said quietly, "before the doctor came, you told me you'd been planning to go to the Duke of Trent in London to ask him for help."

"Yes," she whispered.

"The Duke of Trent is my brother."

Her eyes flew open, and a hoarse sound of surprise flew from her mouth before she could stop it. "What?"

He was looking down at her, his face serious, the sponge gripped in his fist, for the moment not in use.

"Yes. I am the duke's illegitimate half brother."

She remembered all he'd told her about his family, about how close he was to his siblings, about how they treated him as if he were a full brother to them.

The Duke of Trent's brother.

She blinked up at him in astonishment.

"I am eighteen months older than him, and we were raised together. When we were grown, he bought me my commission, and I went into the army. I married Marianne and brought her to Malta; then I married Charlotte in Portugal. After she and our son died . . ." He stopped and turned away. She watched him as he soaked the sponge and then squeezed it out, her heart twisting. She couldn't see his face, but she did see the defeat in his posture.

He turned back around, wet sponge in hand, and spoke in a low voice. "After she died, I was wounded in battle. The wound didn't heal properly, and I was sent home to England to recover. When that ordeal was over, I sold my commission. I was recruited to join a secret agency by a colonel I'd served under."

"Your spy agency?" she whispered.

"We aren't spies, in that we do not attempt to learn enemy secrets. We work to protect the interests of the king and the monarchy. Shortly after the Revolution in France, certain key political figures secretly created the Agency. Very few people know of its existence."

The odd fact that she was one of them now did not escape her. Why was he telling her all this? She'd attempted to escape from him! Her actions were certainly not the usual way to earn someone's trust...

"There is a network of agents that extends to everywhere in the world where Britain wields influence. Our sole purpose is to preserve the integrity of the monarchy and to quell any attempts at treason."

"Such as Dunthorpe's," she murmured.

"Such as Dunthorpe's." He stroked the cool sponge down her side.

"You were ordered to kill him because he was a threat to the monarchy."

"Yes."

"And now you await your orders regarding me."

He studied her for a long moment, then, gazing at her evenly, he said, "Yes."

What if his superiors decided she should suffer the same fate as Dunthorpe?

Their gazes held for a long moment. Then he looked away. Her thoughts must have been written all over her face.

Would he do it? Would he take out a gun and shoot her as he had her husband? She couldn't bring herself to believe that he would. And yet...He was a soldier. A warrior and an agent of the British government. He followed orders; he did not disobey them.

This was the man who made her feel safe. What an illusion. He'd kidnapped her, pursued her, and he could be ordered at any moment to kill her.

She'd always fought to survive, to endure, through her parents' execution, the Terror, poverty, and ultimately Dunthorpe. But if Sam could do this...if he could murder her in the name of his country...

She wasn't angry. She wasn't even afraid. She felt defeated. She felt...so very tired.

But she wanted to know more. She wanted to know everything about him, to understand him. He was in a mood to share the truth with her. When she woke up, when her fever went away, would he feel the same? Would he feel the same when he was ordered to eliminate her?

"Your mother...she is the Dowager Duchess of Trent, then?" she murmured, her eyes closed. She shuddered as he nudged the sheet over her thigh and the sponge stroked down the length of her leg, avoiding the bandage wrapped around her knee.

"Yes."

"She is the one who disappeared last year, isn't she?"

Sam released a long sigh. "Yes."

"Then...she...you were born before she married the Duke of Trent?"

He nodded. "The duke tolerated me in his house. It was a condition he agreed to in order for her to marry him."

"She wouldn't have married him unless he accepted you into his home? She must have loved you very much."

"Yes," Sam said simply.

"And then the new duke was born..."

"Trent was born, and Luke followed two years later. Then Mark and Theo, and finally Esme, whom you've met. I was twelve years old when Esme was born."

"Lady Esme," she murmured, teetering on the edge of unconsciousness. "I knew she was a lady. I know these things, you see. I am ever so clever."

"You are, Élise," she heard him say as if from miles away. "The cleverest and most beautiful woman I have ever..."

* * *

From the subtle relaxation of her shoulders and the slight change in the tempo of her labored breaths, Sam could tell the moment she slipped into slumber. He continued his ministrations, turning his focus to her lovely body.

He was an ass for lusting after her when she was so ill. But he was a red-blooded male. And she was...she was *perfection*.

Perfection that was still burning hot. As soon as he swiped the sponge over her skin, the water seemed to evaporate away. He was shocked steam didn't billow in the sponge's path.

Two bright spots of color flared on her cheeks, but otherwise, she was too pale.

He took an unsteady breath. Worry wound like a rampant, uncontrollable weed through him.

He checked her skinned knee, then covered her leg and breasts with her chemise and the sheet. He continued bathing her body, just trying to infuse her skin with the coolness the sponge attempted to deliver.

It didn't work. Nor did she wake. By the time Masterson returned to the house, Sam was pacing the room, feeling like pulling his hair out with helpless frustration.

She wasn't getting better. She was growing worse. Her skin was hotter and drier than ever. Her breaths grew more and more uneven. She whimpered occasionally in her sleep, but she didn't wake.

He despised this intense feeling of helplessness. He'd experienced it once before, when Charlotte was in childbed—and that hadn't turned out the way anyone had hoped.

Sometimes happiness appeared to hover within reach, as it had in the cottage at Lake Windermere with Élise, but it always, always slipped away when he grasped for it.

He had learned to stop trying. It was easier that way. But with Élise, happiness seemed to have reached for him, and he hadn't had the strength to shut it away.

And now he was on the verge of losing it yet again.

The door cracked open, and Masterson's face appeared in the narrow space. His brown eyes took in the situation in the bedchamber. "She sleeping?" he asked in a low voice.

Sam, who'd drawn to an abrupt halt in the center of the room, nodded.

Masterson cocked his head. "Come outside," he said. "I need to speak with you."

Sam glanced at Élise to find she hadn't moved. He followed Masterson into the corridor.

The older man turned to him, concern etched in his brow. "Just had a very interesting carriage pass through my gate."

Every sense in Sam's body flared into alertness. "Did you?"

"Aye. It was Dunthorpe's carriage."

Sam narrowed his eyes. "Carrying the new viscount?"

"Aye."

Sam frowned. "What business does he claim to have in the north?"

"That's just the thing, right? Dunthorpe had few ties to the north and seldom traveled in this direction. I did ask, but the coachman was tight-lipped and said it was a matter of private business."

Sam's frown deepened until he could feel the pull between his brows. It was as Élise had told him. Dunthorpe's brother was his associate—most likely his second in command and now in charge.

"Dunthorpe's after us."

"Looks that way." Masterson gave him a crooked grin. "Little does he know he was within a hundred yards of you and now headed, no doubt, toward an empty cottage."

"And still no word from the Agency?"

"None."

The Agency was usually decisive on such matters. The fact that it was taking so long with this one gave Sam a twisting feeling in his stomach.

"So what are you going to do?" Masterson asked him.

"I need to send Adams a message. Can you ensure it's delivered?"

"Of course." Masterson led Sam into his tiny parlor, where he gave Sam a sheet of paper, ink, and a pen.

Sam wrote a long letter to Adams, telling of all he'd learned since he'd come north, including the information he'd received from Élise regarding the new Viscount Dunthorpe and Edmund Gherkin.

He rushed through the end, informing Adams frankly of his belief in Lady Dunthorpe's innocence, then asking for his orders to be sent directly to Masterson, since he and Lady Dunthorpe were going to be at undisclosed locations for an indeterminate amount of time.

It was the first time in his association with the Agency that his superiors wouldn't know his exact location. Given what they were considering ordering him to do, however, it was for the best.

He finally sealed the letter and gave it to Masterson, who left right away to have one of his people in Preston take the message to headquarters in London.

Sam stopped by the kitchen to fetch a bowl of broth for Élise, and when he walked into the bedchamber, he knew right away that something had changed.

Élise sounded terrible. Her breaths emerged in pained pants. The temperature of her body had heated the air throughout the entire room.

Sam threw open the window and breathed in the blast of cool air, then turned to look at her.

She was so pale. The earlier spots of color on her cheeks had drained away completely. Her eyes were closed, but her thin arms were above the sheet, and her hands gripped fistfuls of the sheet on either side of her body.

He lowered himself on the edge of the bed. "Élise, love, are you awake?"

"Sam?" Her voice emerged weak and thready, but her eyes didn't open.

"I'm here." He smoothed his hand over her brow, brushing away the strands of hair stuck to her skin, and almost drew away at the temperature. His heart kicked in his chest. She was so damn hot.

"Thyme…"

"It's just after eight…"

"*Non*…no! Thyme…the herb. Tea. Good for fevers. And licorice root. Tea."

Her mumbles became incoherent, and panic rose within him.

She was too hot. She was delirious, and she still hadn't opened her eyes.

He sat rigid for a moment, attempting to get his pounding heartbeat under control. Then he stood and dipped a towel in a new basin of clean water. He wiped her brow in a useless attempt to cool it, then folded it and placed it across her chest.

She's going to die. She's going to die, and there's nothing you can do.

He took a steadying breath. He wasn't going to give up. Not yet. She was still here, still beautiful, her chest rising and falling as she fought for every breath.

She was a fighter, and he would help her fight.

"Élise," he said gently, "what do you need?"

"I'm…cold," she rasped out. "So…cold."

He blinked at her. What did she mean, she was cold? Her skin scorched his hands wherever he touched her.

Her body lied to her. Yet as she lay there, she began to shiver and shudder beneath the sheet.

He strode out of the room and found that Masterson did have a bit of thyme, though he couldn't find any licorice root. He made a strong tea of it and hurried back to Élise. She hadn't moved a muscle since he'd left her. It would probably be hopeless trying to get the liquid into her.

And yet...

"Élise, I made you some thyme tea. I need you to drink."

She made a small noise, and he almost smiled, realizing that was a scoff of disbelief. He could hear her regular, non-sick voice saying, "Oh, my Sam, how ridiculous you are!"

Tenderly, he propped her up with the pillows. He took a spoonful of tea and held it to her lips. Her eyes flickered, opened, and then, as if she found it too difficult to keep them open, they slid shut again. But her lips parted and she took the spoonful of tea. It seemed like forever before he saw her slender throat move as she swallowed.

It took her the better part of an hour before she'd had half a cup, and she turned her head, pressing her lips together and refusing any more.

He stroked the sponge over her temple. "Do you need the privy?"

"No," she croaked out. He tried to remember the last time she'd used it. More than twelve hours ago, at least.

"You're not drinking enough."

She made a low, grating, sobbing noise. He wouldn't

push it. Not now, when she'd just had tea. In a little while, he'd try to get her to take some more.

But for now, she was shivering even harder, and she needed to rest. He took away some of the pillows that had been propping her up and started sponge bathing her again. But the cool water only seemed to make her shudder harder.

"Stop," she moaned. "Please."

He squeezed his eyes shut; then he dropped the sponge into the basin before turning back to her. "What do you want, Élise? What can I do?"

"Hold me, my Sam," she murmured.

He stripped down to his shirt and smallclothes and slid beneath the sheet beside her. Pressed up against her like this, he could feel the depth of her body spasms. She whimpered with every few breaths. He tugged her against him, murmuring, "Shh. It's going to be all right."

"I am dying," she whispered a few minutes later.

He stiffened. "No."

"Please. Tell Marie...tell Marie that I love her. Tell Sam that I love him."

Something surged in his gut, poignant and all consuming. But he held very still as she shuddered against him. Because if he moved, he'd break.

"Please," she said on a weak sob. "Please tell them. Please."

"I will," he said roughly, his arm tightening around her.

An hour later, she began to convulse, and Sam could do nothing to help her, except hold her. And pray to a God who had never listened to him before.

Chapter Fifteen

※

Élise's mind was so groggy, she had to pick her way through the fog, grasping on to bits of memory.

She was ill. Very ill.

Sam had been there. Sam had taken care of her.

She'd been sick before. Once, during her marriage. Maids had taken care of her then. Dunthorpe hadn't paid any attention whatsoever. But this time, Sam had been at her bedside constantly.

At her bedside and in her bed.

There was a heaviness slung across her hip. A pleasant, warm heaviness. But she was wet. Soaked through.

She'd been in the rain. Was she still wet from the rain?

She was so confused. She made a little noise in her throat as she tried to understand.

"Élise?"

Sam's voice. Low and gruff with sleep. It was his arm that lay over her waist. She wiggled restlessly. It would feel nice... if she wasn't so very *wet*.

The arm moved up her body until a hand smoothed over her forehead. He released a sharp breath, and she cracked open her lids. He was gazing at her in the dim light. It was nighttime, but a single lamp was burning on the bedside table on his side, haloing his head with golden light.

"Sam," she murmured.

"Your fever is gone," he said, his voice full of wonder.

She frowned. "How long have we been here?"

"Three days."

She took a moment to absorb this. Three days. She'd been sick for a very long time. "Where are we?"

"At my colleague Masterson's house. Just outside of Preston."

"Oh yes. I remember." *Vaguely.*

"How do you feel?" he murmured.

She thought about this. It felt like moving a muscle would require every ounce of energy she possessed. "Very tired," she said.

"But better?" he asked, and her lips twitched when she heard the note of hope in his voice.

He wants you to be well. And his arm was stroking up and down her side in a soothing motion. She gave a contented sigh. Or, it would have been contented had she not been so very, very wet.

"Why am I wet?"

"You're sweating."

"It's...uncomfortable."

"Here." He shifted, then peeled the sheet and blanket from her body. Cool air whispered over her body, but her chemise was so damp, the wetness made her cold. He placed a hand on her hip. "Ah. You're going to have to take this off, love. Let me help you."

"You have stripped me many times by now, yes?"

"Yes," he confirmed.

With a wistful sigh, she raised her arms as he tugged the chemise up and over her body. "This is highly scandalous."

"I know. But nobody knows about it but us."

"Your Masterson does," she grumbled.

He gave a soft laugh. "Masterson keeps secrets for a living. He won't be exposing ours to the scandal sheets, trust me."

Now she was cold. It was a cool evening, and her body was not only damp, but also naked. She wrapped her arms around her torso and shivered.

Sam just grinned. He...grinned! She grinned back at him, because when Sam smiled, a responding joy shot through her.

"You're better," he whispered gruffly.

She nodded. "I think so. I am tired. But I feel very much better."

"And you're cold again."

She nodded, and he tucked her naked body against his clothed one. Her body was much smaller than his, but when she pressed against him, she simply fit. It was comfortable, and it was warm. And she didn't care that she was naked.

Except, a few minutes later, she snuggled deeper into his arms. And his hardening cock pressed against her belly.

She sucked in a breath and began to pull back, but the arms wrapped around her were like iron. She didn't try to move away again. She didn't want to.

* * *

Fighting the sickness had sapped all of Élise's strength, and it took a week after the fever broke for her to regain enough strength for Sam to pronounce she would be well enough to travel in another few days.

As she recovered, he told her about how his missing mother, the Dowager Duchess of Trent, might be close—in the Lake District—and how he was considering returning to the lakes to search for her. And Élise told him about her years with Dunthorpe, about her vague knowledge of the past schemes and secrets he'd sold to the French, and about the friends and family members she thought might be in league with him.

Sam knew all her secrets now, but she was content with that. There was no denying he'd saved her life, and her meager secrets felt silly and insufficient in comparison.

Now Sam wanted to turn his focus to finding his mother, and she couldn't blame him for that. There would be time for collecting evidence and capturing the men who were in league with Dunthorpe. Plenty of time, since they wouldn't try to do anything treasonous anytime soon, now that their master was dead. They would require at least a few months to reorganize their plans and their hierarchy.

Sam had told Élise that the new Viscount Dunthorpe had passed through Masterson's tollgate, evidently searching for them. Somehow, Francis had learned she and Sam had gone north. Fortunately, he hadn't had the faintest idea that Sam and Élise were here with Masterson, so whatever information he had been given was incomplete.

"Dunthorpe was evil," she murmured. They were outside, strolling on a path adjacent to the road that led away from Preston. Bluebells bloomed along the edges of the path, and the air was sweet smelling and redolent of spring. "But Francis..." She hesitated.

"What is he like?"

"He is different, but no better, I think. He was always jealous of Dunthorpe, but he also loved Dunthorpe, and he looked up to him. There were very vast swings from love to hate." She sucked in a breath. "I don't believe he is quite sane. But ultimately, he worshipped Dunthorpe. Which is why Dunthorpe trusted him with his secrets. Francis never would betray his brother, and my husband knew this."

Sam pressed his lips together, and she could see his mind churning.

"You did not have any evidence against him?" she asked.

"No. Dunthorpe was very careful."

She nodded. "I wish I could tell you who was a part of the scheme against the Regent. I could not even confirm that Dunthorpe himself was part of that."

"He was the ringleader," Sam said. "But he couldn't have planned it alone."

"He planned it with the French, no doubt."

Sam nodded, but then he frowned at her. "Why do you speak of the French with such distaste?"

She made a snorting noise. "I am disgusted by it all. By their meddling. By them attempting to infiltrate our country and kill our Regent."

Sam slipped his arm through hers and led her around a boulder that nearly blocked the path. "*Our* country?"

She slanted him a glance. "I have lived here most of my life. I have been an English viscountess for much of that time. Why can I not be English?"

"I think you can be whatever you consider yourself to be," he told her. "But people will always see you as French."

She sighed. "I know. But I am not. England kept me safe when I was a child. Now England is mine. A part of me will always love France and will always be French. But I will never love Napoleon nor the madness of my countrymen during the Revolution."

"I understand," he said. And she knew he did.

* * *

That night, she took a bath for the first time in days. It wasn't an actual bath, since Masterson wasn't in possession of a proper bathtub. But Sam gave her some privacy for a while, and she washed herself using the sponge he'd used on her when her skin had burned with the fever.

She even managed to wash her hair using soap and pans full of warmed water. Then she dried herself, donned her chemise, and tucked herself into bed.

She was pleasantly drowsy, and she'd just about nodded off when Sam entered. He came straight to the bed and sat on the edge, looking down at her with a soft smile on his face. He tucked a stray strand of damp hair behind her ear.

"Are you tired?" he asked.

"No." She yawned. "Which was why I was nearly asleep when you just came in."

"Ah. Should I go?"

She looked straight into his twinkling dark eyes, and something pulled inside her, straight to her womb. Heat crept under her skin, and she knew exactly what she wanted.

"No," she whispered. "You should stay."

* * *

Sam knew he shouldn't. She was still recovering, and he had been beating down his desire for her for so long, he wasn't sure if he could do it again tonight, especially when she was looking at him like that, with those blue eyes that made promises she shouldn't be making.

If he gave his desire free rein...Hell. He didn't want to hurt her.

He should probably sleep on the sofa in Masterson's parlor.

But he couldn't move. He was trapped. Spellbound under that smoky blue gaze.

Her beauty clenched his gut. Her color had returned and her cheeks had rounded once again. She'd regained her strength quickly. He should have expected that, because she was young and strong, and a fighter.

She reached out a hand to him, and he took it, squeezing lightly. He'd wanted her so much and for so long, a deep, yawning, aching hunger had begun to reside inside him.

"Come to bed, my Sam," she murmured in a husky voice that seemed to go straight to his cock. He was hard in an instant.

He pulled in a breath, hesitating. "You need rest."

"Yes, I do," she agreed. Then she flashed him a smile. "After."

He stared at her for a moment longer, his gut churning; then he gave a brisk nod. He turned away to remove his coat, shoes, and trousers before slipping in beside her.

She wrapped her arms around him until her body, clothed only in her thin chemise, pressed against him. She'd lost weight during the illness, and her hipbone pushed against his stomach. She'd been thin before, but now he wanted to feed her, to serve her breakfasts in bed...

He looked down at her, once again brushing away a heavy curl that had fallen over her face. She smiled at him. "I miss your kisses."

"Do you?"

"I do indeed. Your kisses are..." She gave a wistful sigh. "They are very good. They make me happy. They make me want more." She gazed straight into his eyes. "I've wanted more ever since the first one."

How could he deny this woman? He bent down and kissed her.

His body flared to life. Though he couldn't forget that he needed to be gentle with her, that she was recovering from an illness that could have been fatal, he kissed her like a bumbling youth. Like a boy who was discovering the pleasure of a woman's body for the first time.

Truth was, he couldn't get enough of her. Of her violet scent. Of her sweet, ripe taste, which reminded him of grapes. Of her body. Of her sharp intelligence, her snapping eyes, her wit, her feisty personality, her...

God. He'd never wanted anything like he wanted her. Never. He could hardly breathe for wanting her.

He pulled back, his breaths coming in unsteady puffs. Somehow, during the kiss, he'd ended up on top of her, pinning her body down with his bulk.

He searched her face, looking for any sign that she wanted him to stop, that this was too much, that she was in pain...

"Tell me to stop," he whispered.

Her eyes widened.

"This isn't right," he said. "Tell me. Tell me I need to stop."

"Sam..."

He gritted his teeth, bracing himself for it. He'd lost his mind for her, but he hoped she'd held on to some bit of sanity.

She pulled in a shaky breath. "Sam. I...I don't think I can live another day without feeling you inside me."

Her arms had remained firmly around him and now they tugged his body closer. Her gaze smoldered, and her eyes grew hooded with desire.

He shuddered. His cock pressed against her thigh, so heavy and hard and hot, it hurt. He knew she felt it, because she shifted restlessly against him.

"Inside me," she whispered again. "I need you."

He shook his head, but he moved against her leg, unable to stop himself. "I don't want to hurt you."

"I am a very strong woman, my Sam," she said in that carnal, husky whisper. The edge of her lips turned upward. "Do your worst. You cannot hurt me."

He shook his head, the edges of his lips fighting to smile, too. He kissed her, still moving erotically over her. "Not my worst," he said against her lips. "I can't...Not tonight."

She sighed. "I know this. Your sense of honor is too strong, *n'est ce pas*?" And then he felt her chest move subtly as she laughed.

He stroked his hand down her side, feeling her body, the curve of her waist, the flare of her hip. He curled his fingers in the material of her shift and pulled upward, slowly dragging the skirt up her leg as he continued to sample her mouth, drugged by her potent taste.

He moved his lips over her cheek and then down under her jaw to the column of her neck, nibbling and sucking as she arched her neck, exposing it to his lips.

He moved farther downward, licking along her collarbone and the tops of her breasts at the neckline of the chemise. Then he gripped that seam between his teeth and tugged in impatience.

"You want this off, do you?" she asked, humor in her voice. "Then it will be my pleasure. But you must take off that ridiculously enormous shirt. And your drawers as well."

He released the neckline of her shift and rose up over her, balancing himself on his hands. "Is that an order, *madame*?"

"*Mais oui.*"

After he helped her out of the chemise, he slipped out of the bed to take off his drawers and shirt. She watched his every move, and he slanted her a glance, his lips twisting into a wry smile.

"Do you like what you see?"

"Every inch of it. You are very tall, and you have very big muscles, and a very, *very* big—" She broke off abruptly, and he laughed as he crawled into the bed beside her, once again pulling her flush to his body. They both went still at the collision of their bare skin. She was smooth and soft and warm against him, and she fit so perfectly. He felt like he could hold her here forever.

"My size doesn't worry you?" he murmured, burying his face in her hair and breathing her in.

"Not at all, my Sam," she purred. "It excites me. Very much."

He nearly groaned aloud. God, this woman was going to kill him.

He slid his hand down her back and cupped the warm, round curve of her buttocks, drawing her closer to him.

She rubbed wantonly against him. Slipping her hand around the back of his neck, she pulled him to her lips, kissing him deeply. So damn seductively.

He moved his hand around her thigh, then cupped her sex in his palm. She released a puff of breath as she pushed into his hand.

"Such a vixen," he teased.

"No, never. Except when I am with you. Except when you are Sam the Scoundrel, and I want you with such intensity it hurts."

That response sent a deep satisfaction through him, and he crushed his lips to hers.

As she wiggled against him, he slid his fingers between her legs. Her arousal instantly coated his fingers, lubricating his path. He stroked her, reading her responses from the twitches and trembles her body made and from the whimpers that emerged from her throat.

She liked it... right *there*. He stroked above her opening, testing. Yes. She preferred the soft glide over a hard press of his fingers. So he did it again and again until she vibrated against him, and he took her harsh releases of breath into himself as he continued to kiss her.

Her movements grew ever more restless. "Sam..." she breathed out.

"Come for me, love."

She gripped his arm tightly, as if she needed to hold something solid. And then she slowed, went stiff against him and gave a low, keening cry, and her body began to undulate.

He slid his fingers over the spot, drawing the spasms out for as long as he could until she went limp, burying her face in his chest. He kissed the top of her head, unable to stop the masculine pride that swept through him. He'd made her come. He'd given his woman pleasure.

He slid his hand around to her buttocks again, squeezing her against him, and she looked up at him, a saucy expression in her eyes.

"Inside me," she told him, an edge of hoarseness in her voice. "You think you made me come to make my body ready for you, but you are wrong, my Sam. I have been ready for you for many days."

With a low growl, he flipped her onto her back. "Impatient vixen."

"Seductive scoundrel," she shot back.

He couldn't wait. Not a second longer. He needed to be inside her. *Now.*

He found her entrance. There was no fumbling, no need to direct himself to the proper location. Like everything else, despite the differences in their sizes, they simply matched. They fit. They *belonged* together.

He stared into her eyes, his cock hovering at her opening. She gazed back up at him with those lovely blue eyes, and then she gave him a small smile. She gripped his shoulders, but otherwise she held her body still, waiting.

"Élise," he said gruffly. And then he pushed home.

She arched up into him and cried out, and he froze. Her heat wrapped him in a viselike grip, and the pleasure was so overwhelming that a tremor gripped the base of his spine.

But fear also consumed him. He'd gone too fast. Too hard. Forced her little body to accommodate him too quickly.

"God, are you hurt?" he rasped out, shaking from pleasure, his arms trembling with restraint. "Did I hurt you? Do you want me to—"

"No," she groaned. "No, no, no...do not stop, you foolish man. *Dieu*, you make me feel so full, so *complete*. It is so good, my Sam. Do not stop. *Move*."

And he did. He slid out slowly, then in again. He held on to his control now, knowing that if it snapped, his body would demand that he rut with her like some wild animal.

So he moved slowly, sinking into the hot clasp of her, then drawing out again, her body bringing him such pleasure that stars blinked at the edges of his vision.

Beautiful Élise. She held on to him, meeting him thrust for thrust, exhaling harsh breaths whenever he locked deep inside her. He kept his eyes on her, watching her lips part, her eyes glaze over, the expressions of rapture move over her face.

He wasn't bringing her pain; he was bringing her pleasure.

Knowing that, he moved faster. The sweet edges of completion furled at the base of his spine, hardening his cock, making his muscles tense all throughout his body.

"Yes," she said, her arms tightening around him, her

sex tightening around him, her muscles tightening beneath him. "*Yes*. Give me more of you, Sam."

"I need to..." He ground out the words, his voice almost refusing to cooperate with his effort to create words. His entire world had narrowed down to the pleasure Élise's body was bringing him. "I need to pull out."

Her arms tightened even more, and her legs wrapped around his thighs. "Oh no."

He pushed in and held still. Damn, his entire body was trembling with restraint. He was close. Too close. "I don't want to—"

"You cannot. I am barren, remember?" Her voice was soft but sure.

He closed his eyes against the edge of pain in her voice. "Élise," he groaned.

"Come inside me, my Sam," she said. "That is what I want."

Just like that, his control snapped. He surrounded her, a heavy fortress, his muscles tight, his thrusts deep and hard. He lost himself to the pleasure.

God, it felt so good. So right. She was his heaven.

She came again, crying out as her body squeezed tight, then arching and pulsing. He faltered for the briefest of moments, but she clasped his cock so tightly, he lost himself to the pleasure once again. He thrust once, twice, three times. She grew hotter, silkier around him.

He pushed in one more time and came hard, pleasure ripping through him.

The sensation ebbed slowly, and it seemed hours before he came back to himself, though he knew it was only moments. Realizing he was probably crushing her, he gathered his energy and rolled to his side, keeping her with him, his body still locked inside hers.

She gazed at him, flushed and deliciously rumpled. "God, you're beautiful," he said to her.

"So are you, my Sam," she murmured with a serene smile. "So are you."

Chapter Sixteen

*S*am received his instructions from his superior at dawn three mornings later. He and Élise had just made love and were lying on the bed wrapped in each other's arms when there was a knock on the door, and a tentative, gruff voice called, "Hawk?"

Élise recognized the voice. *Carter.*

Sam had turned to look at her, his dark eyes fathomless in the early-morning light.

"He comes with orders for you," she breathed.

"Yes. But rest easy. It doesn't matter what message he bears." He spoke in a voice too quiet for Carter to hear. "I won't let anything happen to you."

She nodded and watched as he slipped out of bed and quickly donned his clothes.

Whatever might happen, she would remember this moment—Sam dressing in the increasing light of dawn, the golden glow coming through leaves of the trees outside dappling his strong body with golden color and enhancing the ripples of muscles across his torso. He was so beautiful. Not thin and soft like Dunthorpe, but virile and strong.

He bent down and kissed her cheek. "Stay here."

"Tyrant," she murmured playfully.

He drew back, gave her a hard warning look, then turned and left the room.

She got out of bed and washed, dressed herself in the simple walking dress Sam had somehow procured for her while she'd been sick, then twisted her hair into a chignon at the base of her neck using the comb Masterson had given her.

She had decided that she liked Masterson, even though he had mostly avoided her and had never become as friendly with her as Laurent and Carter had. Of course, she had been ill most of the time she had been here. But she could tell that Masterson held a deep and abiding respect for Sam, and that was enough for her.

She wondered if Laurent had come with Carter. She hoped so. She rose from the chair, intending to go out to the parlor and greet the newcomers, but as soon as she took a step toward the door, Sam threw it open.

She stopped short at the thunderous look on his face. His gaze snagged hers and held, his eyes dark and dangerous. "We're leaving," he bit out. "Now."

Too startled to do anything else, she nodded her agreement. But a sour feeling curdled deep in her belly.

Adams had sent the order to kill her.

Blindly, pressing her hand to her stomach to stanch that awful sensation, she went through the motions of preparing to go. The clothes she'd arrived in had been thrown away, and Sam hadn't brought her saddlebag, so she didn't have much. Just the second dress and the underclothes Sam had bought for her.

When there was nothing more to do, Sam grasped her hand and led her out of the bedchamber. She stumbled after him, giving a brief glance behind at the mussed bed where he'd loved her for the first time.

Moments later, they hurried down the drive in front of Masterson's house, headed for the carriage waiting at its end. Small, dark, and inconspicuous, it was much like the carriage they'd ridden north in—but that carriage was still in the stables at the cottage by Lake Windermere.

Laurent was already seated on the driver's perch beside Carter. Both men tipped their hats and nodded at her as she approached, but even Laurent's usual lighthearted demeanor had darkened.

She had time only to give them a little wave before Sam hustled her into the carriage, and the vehicle lurched into motion.

Sam was stiff and still, looking straight ahead. She laid her hand on his thigh to find it tense and unyielding— solid as a rock. "That was . . . abrupt."

He turned to her slowly. His eyes were dark in the gloomy interior of the carriage. His body resonated with an energy she couldn't define.

The Agency wanted her dead.

She should be terrified. Horrified.

But she was with Sam. And she was safe, as she'd never been safe before. He'd allow no harm to come to her. She knew this as intrinsically as she knew she'd take her next breath.

Suddenly, Sam grabbed her waist and hauled her into his lap. And then his mouth was on hers, kissing her as though he were a man dying of hunger and she was his ambrosia.

She loved him so much. It seemed impossible that she could say this about a man who'd killed her husband, kidnapped, pursued, and recaptured her, but in spite of all that, he was so utterly *good*.

Arousal flooded through her, heat pulsing between her legs. She wrapped her arms around him and kissed him fiercely.

"It's all right," she said against his lips. "It will be all right, my Sam."

Because it would be. She *knew* this.

He fumbled with his trousers, then with her skirt, yanking it up, kissing her all the while. Then his fingers pressed between her legs, and she moved against him, dry at first, but the wetness came quickly in response to his insistent touch.

She shuddered in his arms. He had learned her body so quickly. He already knew how to touch her, what made her mad for wanting. Her husband had never known these subtle details about her.

He pushed his free hand into her chignon and pulled the pins free, scattering them on the carriage floor. "I love your hair," he said hoarsely. "I love it down and free, like your spirit."

He combed his fingers through the curls that now tumbled over her shoulders as he stroked her sex.

When his fingers slid over the slickness of her growing arousal, he shifted her so she straddled him. Then he positioned her above his cock, and she groaned as he lowered her body over the length of his erection.

Her eyes nearly rolled back into her head, so powerful

were the sensations his penetration wrought upon her body. It wasn't only her sex, which squeezed over him, but the glowing strands of pleasure that seemed to undulate throughout her body. She'd never known that carnal congress could be this pleasurable for a woman, but Sam—he made it so... *exquisite*.

He pushed into her hard, his face against her shoulder, his hands clasped around her buttocks, regulating her movements, lifting her and then pressing her down over him. So hard and deep were his thrusts from this angle that she emitted a small whimper each time he fully lodged himself deep inside her. She held him, too, clutching his wide shoulders and murmuring, "Sam, Sam," over and over again.

He was so big. So large that she'd hidden her feelings of trepidation when she'd first seen him in all his naked glory. She wasn't sure he'd fit. But he did—oh so tightly. Like he was made for her, like a key fitting into a lock. And when he moved inside her, the stroke against her inner walls was so powerful it wrought all kinds of wicked sensations on her body. On her mind. On her *heart*.

The orgasm struck without warning, and as her body clenched, she threw her head back, forgetting to breathe. White-hot pleasure burst through her. She lost control, but that was all right. Sam would keep her safe.

She rode the pleasure as if it were a shooting star, hot and powerful and all consuming. There was nothing but the wicked, exquisite sensations shooting through her and Sam, keeping her whole, preventing her from exploding into a million pieces.

Slowly, she came down, sucking in breaths as she realized she'd starved her lungs for air.

Sam was relentless, though, positioning her so his cock moved deep and deliciously hard inside her. *Bon Dieu.* It was overwhelming. And before she completely came down from the previous orgasm, another one began to well.

His cock seemed to grow, touching her everywhere. Within a few moments, she felt his body tense, and then he pressed her hard against him, burying his face in her neck as he came. His cock pulsed deep, bathing her inner walls with his seed.

That knowledge was enough to take her over the edge again, too. Her whole body tightened in a sweet climax that rushed through her body like a powerful flood.

And they held each other through it, basking in mutual release, mutual pleasure.

When it was over, he crushed her to him, his lips caressing her ear. "You're mine. Mine."

She closed her eyes, sinking deeper against him. He spoke the truth. "Yes," she murmured. "I've never wanted to be anything else."

She knew that now. The knowledge of it was a balm to her soul. All that she had been through: the loss, suffering, war, death, abusive marriage. It all narrowed to this point. When she was with the man she was meant to be with. When they'd both just reached the pinnacle of pleasure, and he was still inside her.

She was meant to be his. She was born to be his. There was no greater truth—not for her.

How silly that she had tried to run from him. Twice!

She held him close, breathing him in. He smelled faintly of salt and sweat. He smelled of masculine, virile man, and his scent made her sex twitch with pleasure.

He smoothed her hair back from her face. "Look at me, Élise."

She pulled her face back so she could gaze into his eyes.

"I won't let anything happen to you."

She stared at him. "It came, then. The order to...kill me."

He was silent for a moment, and then he said the one word that turned her heart into stone. "Yes."

She closed her eyes, still clutching his shoulders. "What shall I do?"

"We'll figure something out."

"Everyone wants me dead. Dunthorpe. England. If Dunthorpe has sent word to them, then France, too."

"I will protect you with everything I have. My weapons, my strength. My family ties. My heart, my soul. My life is yours, if that's what it takes."

She swallowed hard, and tears sprang to her eyes. "That is very much to give, my Sam," she said in a rasping voice. "Too much."

His fingers tightened, digging into the flesh of her buttocks. "Not too much."

"Why would you do this for me?"

"Because, love," he murmured in a low voice, "you have brought me back to life."

Her head fell onto his shoulder as she released a low moan. "I will fail you."

"No."

"I have failed you twice already. By running away from you."

"You were held prisoner against your will, and you wanted your freedom. I would have done the same if I were you."

"What if I were to run again?"

"Is that what you want?"

She sighed. "I don't know. Am I your prisoner again? Your orders are to assassinate me. Perhaps it would be best if we parted ways. You could inform them I escaped—"

His arms went tight around her. "No. Don't run from me, Élise."

"It seems the rational solution," she argued.

"How I feel about you—it's not rational." His voice was strained. "I need you with me. I need you near me. There will be no more running."

"What if I do not wish to be your prisoner?"

"Is that what you think you are?"

Anger tinged his voice, and she pressed her forehead against the hard flesh at the front of his shoulder. "No."

This was no time for games, she reminded herself. She needed to be honest with herself, and with him. England wanted her dead. Dunthorpe wanted her dead. Sam would help her. He was a master spy of sorts, so he had some reasonable expertise on these matters of killing and murder.

"No, I am not your prisoner," she said again. She raised her head to search his face with her eyes. "I am your lover."

She gazed at him with uncertainty, terrified he might laugh at her. But he didn't laugh. He caught her chin in his fingers and tilted her head up until she faced him.

"You're more than my lover."

She gazed at him for a long moment, then whispered, "Yes."

Her face burned. He *was* more than a lover she'd use

for physical pleasure and then discard. Not that she'd ever done that, of course, given that she'd never had a lover. He meant so much more to her...too much, perhaps. So much it was...*terrifying*.

Clearing her throat, she moved off him. She didn't look at him as he fixed his trousers while she arranged her skirts. Her hands went up to her hair, and she sighed. As she slipped off the seat with the intention to rummage around for the pins he'd dropped, he caught her forearm.

"Leave it down," he said gruffly. The look he gave her made her belly clench. Trying to appear casual, she slid back onto the cushion.

"All right, then."

They sat in silence for a few minutes, but Sam didn't release her arm.

"Where are we going?" she finally asked him.

"To the Lake District. As planned."

She lifted her brows. "Not to sound self-important, my Sam. And I know how critical it is for you to find the duchess your mother. But there are a great number of people hunting for me. I do not mean to be ungrateful, but perhaps I should go somewhere else whilst you perform your search. We could meet up again, perhaps..." She considered, then continued. "In Ireland?"

"We've been over this," he said with an edge of a growl in his voice. "You'll stay with me."

She sighed.

"There's nowhere safer than with me."

"You are very stubborn, Sam Hawkins."

He nodded, seeming unperturbed by this.

"Dunthorpe is in that area searching for us. And who knows how long it will take before your superiors determine that you don't intend to kill me and they send someone else?"

"Dunthorpe is looking in the wrong place. There's no way he can know where we'll be. Even *I* don't know where we'll be, exactly. And as for Adams...he will have his hands tied for a while, considering Masterson knows nothing of the order or of my intentions, and Carter and Laurent are with me."

She swallowed hard. "Do Carter and Laurent know?"

"Yes."

"And," she said in a small voice, "they do not wish to kill me, either?"

Sam's lips twisted. "They believe in your innocence, as I do. Carter...he has been in this game longer than I have, but he is a good man with a strong sense of honor. Laurent..."

"Is a baby," she murmured.

He looked surprised. "Right. That's exactly it. He's an innocent in many ways, and he came to us with many preconceived ideas about right and wrong. And eliminating any woman at all is unconscionable to him. But an innocent woman? Never."

"And Masterson?"

He paused, then looked directly at her. "Masterson is his own beast. He has always worked in seclusion, never forming lasting bonds with any of us."

"But Masterson respects you."

"The respect is mutual," Sam said.

"But do you believe his conscience would allow him to kill an innocent?"

"If those were his orders, yes."

She pondered this in silence. Eventually, Sam sighed.

"You must understand. We all—well, most of us— consider the acts we perform abominable. But we do what we do for our country. The ends justify the means."

"Like any soldier," she said, stroking his arm. "I understand."

She liked to touch him. He was so very *solid*. An indomitable force.

"So you have recruited Carter and Laurent to help us?"

"Hardly. They insisted upon joining us, and I agreed, though I will send them away tomorrow. After we travel through Kendal and pass the northern part of Lake Windermere, we should be out of danger."

"Do you believe we might encounter Dunthorpe?"

"Not likely, but it is a possibility. And if we do, Laurent and Carter will be invaluable."

She shuddered as images of a shootout between these men and Dunthorpe's invaded her mind.

Sam wrapped his arm around her and drew her to him so she fit tightly against his body.

"We'll take care of you, Élise," he promised.

Chapter Seventeen

They did not encounter any sign of Dunthorpe that day, and when night fell, they made camp in a crag that hid them from the road leading to Ambleside, a town at the north end of Lake Windermere.

If the greater majority of England wasn't trying to kill her, Élise would have thought it was wonderful.

"I have never slept outside before," she told the men as they huddled together on a blanket and ate dried beef, bread, and cheese and shared a bottle of wine. Sam had told her he would have caught her a trout or two from the River Kent, but by the time they'd stopped, it was twilight, and they'd hardly had time to start a fire before the world had lost its light completely.

Someday, she hoped she could fish with Sam, and they'd cook a trout over an open fire and lie under the stars. She couldn't imagine anything more idyllic. But the future was as nebulous as the stars themselves. And she knew better than to discuss it with Sam. He'd warned her that he didn't like thinking of the future, because the only futures he could imagine were deadly ones.

Even she didn't want to think of a future that might be deadly. She didn't want to think of the men lurking out in the darkness hunting for her. Wanting her dead.

For now, what they had was enough.

"Well, I *have* slept outside before, my lady," Carter told her, pulling her from her dark thoughts. "Far too much. Nowadays, all I need to do is send a glance toward the ground, and my back shouts an immediate protest."

Laurent snickered. "Poor old man."

Carter gave Laurent an affable shove. "Watch your mouth, greenling. I might be an old man, but I can still squash you."

Sam was silent beside her. Earlier, they'd gone down Kendal's high street in such a state of quiet that the rattle of the carriage's wheels over the cobbles had been almost unbearably loud.

Nothing had happened in Kendal, though. They had driven through without incident. She knew Sam had been looking not only for Dunthorpe and his men, but for his brothers and sister, who had been lodging at the inn there, but there had been no sign of them, either.

But the new Lord Dunthorpe was somewhere out on one of the lakes. Élise could *feel* him nearby. Looking for them.

She shuddered and pressed herself closer to Sam.

"I want the two of you to return to London tomorrow," Sam told Carter, slipping his arm over her shoulders.

Carter released a weary sigh. Laurent, who had been cutting off a hunk of cheese for his bread, whipped his head up, his eyes wide. "What?"

"I need you to return to London. It's too dangerous for you to be with us."

Carter remained impassive, but Laurent scowled. "We are your partners, Hawk. We cannot leave you."

"You can," Sam said mildly. "And you will. Tomorrow." He took a decisive bite of dried beef.

Carter looked at Sam, his gaze even and calm. "We want to help you. Both of you."

"Listen, this is the choice I have made. Once Adams discovers what I have done, I will be blacklisted. *Hunted.*" Sam turned to Laurent. "You've just begun your work for the Agency. I don't want you dead before you've even begun."

Laurent frowned. He looked away from Sam and poked a stick into the fire, brooding. "I don't want to be part of the Agency. Not anymore. Not after this."

"You have no choice," Sam said quietly.

Carter clapped the boy on the back. "You already made your choice, son. You are one of us. You knew that changes of heart wouldn't be accommodated."

Élise's own heart constricted for Laurent. He'd most likely joined the Agency when he was eleven or twelve... He'd been just a boy, and to make a permanent decision like that at such a young age...

"I don't want any of you hunted because of me." Élise pushed the words out through her scratchy throat. "There must be something I could do to..."

"No," Sam said bluntly.

"I could tell your Mr. Adams everything I know—"

"You've already told me everything, love. It's not enough," he said gently.

It was the first time he'd called her "love" in the presence of others. Her cheeks heated, and she looked down at her knees clasped to her chest. But a part of her grew warm and soft, filling with affection—no, something stronger than that—for the man who seemed to have no fear of sharing how he felt about her with his friends.

"So your agency will not listen to you?" she asked quietly. "Surely you are one of its most loyal and trusted agents."

"Several days ago Hawk wrote Adams a letter proclaiming your innocence, my lady," Carter said. "But in London, a very strong case has been building against you."

Just as quickly as the blood had rushed into her cheeks, she felt it draining.

Carter continued. "The new viscount has been feeding the rumors about how you conspired with the French to kill your husband. He's been giving 'evidence' from your unhappy marriage to Dunthorpe to strengthen his position that Hawk was the mercenary you hired to do the deed and that the two of you escaped together."

Élise bent forward, pressing her kneecaps into her eyes. "And I suppose your Adams believes this nonsense?"

"Not the part about you being in league with Hawk, of course. But Adams believes you must have been in league with Dunthorpe, which was why you were present at the meeting that night."

"So your Adams believes Francis is nothing more than the rakish dolt he portrays so expertly? No one who behaves in such a foppishly *British* manner could possibly be a traitor." Élise's voice was bitter.

Carter nodded. "The only evidence we have against him is what you've told Hawk."

Laurent made a scoffing noise. "I met him once, in passing. Not only is he a dolt and a fop, but he's a snobbish one. The very worst kind."

"But if we prove him to be the villain? If we prove that he has been in league with Dunthorpe since the beginning?"

The three men exchanged glances. Laurent heaved a sigh and went back to poking his stick in the fire.

Finally, Sam spoke in a quiet voice. "Adams has never revoked an elimination order, Élise. Never."

* * *

Later that night, Élise lay awake on the blanket. Sam was beside her, probably awake as well, since she couldn't hear the deep breaths of his sleep. Laurent and Carter slept on the other side of the fire, half hidden behind a hawthorn bush. Though, even from here, she could hear the drone of Carter's snore.

Sam didn't snore at all. She was glad for that.

Behind her, he turned over and slung his arm around her, tugging her close so that her body fit into the curve of his.

She sighed with pleasure. He felt so good, so warm and hard, against her.

His hand stroked down her side, then brushed over her stomach. Then it moved upward until he cupped her breast in his palm.

Élise's eyes sank shut, and when his thumb passed over her nipple, she wiggled her behind against him. His growing arousal pressed against her buttock cheek, and she released a shaky sigh.

"Shh," he whispered in her ear. He pinched her nipple

gently, until it pebbled, becoming warm and sensitive under her clothes. Then he moved to the other, giving it the same teasing attention.

Élise bit her lip to keep from moaning as his hand shifted, moving downward to pull her skirt up in handfuls. Finally, his fingers moved between her legs and found the opening in her drawers.

He stroked her gently, exactly the way he knew would have her panting and moaning within seconds. Then he slipped a finger inside her, pumping into her as he had with his cock last night and this morning. She reached back, grasping the hard muscle of his buttock and pressing it against her, rubbing wantonly against his erection, which was now rock hard.

"Mmm," he said quietly. He pressed another finger into her, and her breath caught as she clenched her teeth to stop herself from crying out.

He pumped those fingers into her, the delicious friction driving her to near madness. And then they left her, and he was clasping her leg, moving it upward. His cock, hot and heavy, nudged at her entrance.

With one solid thrust, he was buried inside her. She held back another cry, but she couldn't contain it completely. A whimper escaped from her throat. Sam breathed harshly, nuzzling her neck from behind her as he moved his hand back to her breast.

He took her on a slow, deliberate journey to her peak, wiping her mind of everything—all the fear and worry—until once again, there was only Sam. He caressed and squeezed her breast, pinched and stroked her nipple, kissed and sucked her neck, all the while sinking his cock into her with deliberate, powerful thrusts.

From this angle, he stroked a part of her that made delicious sensation resonate through her. It took all her willpower not to squirm and cry out with each and every caress he made inside her body.

The pleasure built and built, and then she was there, on the cusp. Her fingers dug into the hard flesh of his arse, and he buried himself inside her again, stroking her so deep and so hard, it pushed her over. She flew, her body soaring.

It went on and on. He kept moving, rubbing against that spot inside her, keeping her aloft on a long, drugging, delicious orgasm.

It wasn't so much that it ended, but she came down in fits and starts, drifting on the pleasure as a feather dropped from a tall tower drifts on gusts of wind.

It was beautiful, what her Sam could do for her.

Her channel heated for him now. It had grown slick for him, welcoming him into its depths. And within a few minutes, Sam found his release, too. Unable to stay completely quiet, he, too, released a low, wrenching groan. His body went taut behind her, then he came in a pulsing flush of fluid and spasms.

They lay there for some time, Sam lodged within her, both of them trying to quietly catch their breaths. Then he slowly pulled free, but he slipped his arm around her, and as he turned to his back, he pulled her with him until she was tucked against him.

She snuggled into his shoulder and wrapped her arm around him. Drowsiness overcame her instantly. Before she drifted into oblivion, she murmured, "Good night, my Sam."

His response sent sweet tingles resonating through her heart.

"Good night, my love."

* * *

The following morning, they went into Ambleside, where they parted ways with Carter and Laurent, not without some additional grumbling on Laurent's part. It was decided that Laurent—who assured Élise he was an excellent liar—would return to London with a story of how Sam and Élise had disappeared in the night. Carter would head north to Penrith and then to Carlisle, supposedly "searching" for them.

Sam watched as Élise kissed them, first Laurent, who blushed furiously when her lips pressed against his cheek, then Carter.

"I hope I will see you both again soon," she said with feeling, "and in better circumstances."

"I do as well, my lady." Carter came up to shake hands with Sam. "Good luck, Hawk. I'll do what I can."

Carter knew just as well as Sam did that he was doomed. Still, it was kind of him to say it, and Sam clapped his friend on the back. "I know you will. Thank you. For everything." He might never see Carter again. God, that was a dismal thought. The man had been a significant part of his life for a long time.

He watched him climb onto the perch as Laurent approached with a scowl on his face.

Sam reached up to shake the boy's hand, but Laurent kept moving forward until he held Sam in an embrace. "Don't let her get hurt, Hawk. I don't want to have to kill you."

Sam reached up to return the embrace awkwardly. "I'll do my best."

"And don't you get hurt, either..." Laurent pulled

away, and a sheen of tears glossed his eyes. He shook his head as if to fling the emotion away. "I wouldn't be happy if you did."

"Good to know," Sam said, mildly bemused, even as affection for the boy pummeled through him.

Laurent straightened. "All right, then."

They nodded at each other, then Laurent joined Carter on the perch. Carter clucked to the horses, and a few moments later, they disappeared behind a limestone and blue-slate-covered building as they turned a bend in the road.

* * *

Élise watched Carter and Laurent go with a heavy heart. She'd miss them. She hoped she'd see them again.

When they disappeared around a bend in the road, she turned to Sam. "What now?"

"We need to leave town."

He was right. They needed to stay ahead of Dunthorpe and of Adams.

She looked down the street. Ambleside was an agreeable village set on a sloping hill, its buildings tall and narrow in the Tudor style, pleasant and welcoming, with geraniums blooming in bright red clumps in windows up and down the street.

Buildings and trees down the street obscured the view of the lake. Up the street, hilltops peeked up from behind the houses, their spring growth spanning every shade of green of the spectrum.

Sam clasped her shoulder. "There's a waterfall not far from here. Let's go see it and ask the residents if they've seen my mother and Steven Lowell."

She smiled at him. "That sounds excellent."

As they walked toward the cascade, which Sam told her was called Stock-Gill Force, they discussed their strategy for the next few days. They would present themselves as a newly married couple come to the Lake District for their honeymoon. They were particularly interested in the falls, forces, and cascades.

The sky was blue today, with white, wispy clouds, and the air was cool, but it had a pleasant, soft quality to it.

"I will enjoy pretending to be your wife," she announced to Sam as they progressed uphill.

He raised a brow at her. "Will you?"

She squeezed his arm closer to her. "Yes. It is better than being your prisoner, I should think."

She'd said the wrong thing. His face lost all trace of humor. It turned hard and cold. "No," he said tightly, "it is worse. Much worse."

Her throat closed. It had been a stupid thing to say. Of course he remembered his wives.

It squeezed her chest tight to think that something she'd said had hurt him. Maybe talking about them would help.

"Tell me about them," she murmured.

"No."

The word jolted through her, leaving her cold inside. Unaccountably, tears rose to her eyes, and she took a staggered, unsteady breath.

"I am sorry, Sam."

"What for?"

"You know."

"You did nothing."

"I made you think of them…of what happened to them."

He stopped short. They'd turned up a less populated road, clumps of grasses blooming on either side. "I don't want to talk about it," he ground out.

She pressed her lips together to hold back anything else that might be trying to emerge, nodding.

It was none of her business, his life with his wives. None at all. She was madly curious, though. And oddly...*jealous*. Jealous that they'd known Sam when he was younger and less jaded, when he'd looked toward the future with hope.

She was also sad for another reason. Because he did not wish to share more details of his past with her. It was no business of hers...but still. They'd shared much over the last few weeks. She'd shared so much...perhaps too much?

He began to walk again, but he didn't link his arm with hers this time, and the lack of contact left her feeling strangely bereft. They passed a building with a sign on the front painted in bold black lettering: THE SALUTATION INN.

Sam hesitated, frowning. "It's near here, I think."

"Let's ask the innkeeper."

They went inside and introduced themselves under their new aliases. Sam asked about the falls, and the jolly and rotund master of the place directed them to go "just out the back and through Mrs. Braithwaite's garden."

"Thank you, sir," Élise said. "We are hoping to see as many of the cascades as we can."

"Of course you are. Many people go through here with the same intention."

"Is that right? Has anyone come through lately?"

"Indeed they have. Several, in fact."

"Oh? Has anyone come by in the last few days?" Élise sidled up against Sam and smiled lovingly into his face. Neither action was difficult to enact. "Were there any newlywed couples like me and my Mr. Samson?"

The innkeeper scratched the white tuft of hair at his chin. "Can't say as I've seen any newlyweds like you two. But you should ask Mrs. Braithwaite." He chuckled and tapped his temple. "She keeps good records of all who pass through her property to see the falls. She's considering charging a tariff, I daresay."

They thanked him again and headed out the back door of the inn. Past the stables, a cottage appeared through the dense wood, and as they approached, a lawn and flower garden bracketed by trees appeared beyond the cottage. The sound of rushing water was a touch louder out here.

"We're very close to the waterfall now," she said.

Sam shrugged. "We don't need to see it at all, really. All we need to do is find out if this Mrs. Braithwaite has any information—"

"Oh, you are very wrong! We must go to the falls. Not only to keep up appearances, but because I have never seen a waterfall."

He raised a brow at that. "Never?"

"Not once in my life."

He took her hand and pressed it onto his arm, and the comforting pleasure of his touch washed over her once again. "Then you shall see this one."

Sam knocked on the door to Mrs. Braithwaite's cottage, and when the old woman answered, he introduced them and said they had traveled from Birmingham for their honeymoon and that his wife had never seen a waterfall.

The woman had a kind face and clear blue eyes that

seemed to take everything in. When she smiled, her face collapsed in a sea of wrinkles. "Oh, my dear. How lovely. Your first waterfall? We must make it special for you. Come in. Come in..."

It was as if Mrs. Braithwaite had prepared for their arrival. She packed them a picnic of a pigeon pie, berries, and wine, gave them a blanket, and told them exact directions to a place where they could lay down the blanket and have a beautiful and romantic prospect of the falls as they ate their luncheon.

The woman was such a chatterbox that Sam and Élise could hardly get a word in edgewise. But when she paused for a brief moment to draw in a breath, Élise jumped in. "Are there many couples that come to see your falls, Mrs. Braithwaite?"

Mrs. Braithwaite's forehead dissolved into deep wrinkles as she attempted to recall. She was very lovely, Élise decided. She wished she could live in Ambleside and be this woman's friend. The innkeeper's comment about her planning to charge a tariff for crossing her property was completely ridiculous, because Sam had already offered her money, and she'd declined.

"Well, there was a couple of a more advanced age about a week past. A *gypsy* couple."

Élise felt Sam go stiff beside her.

"A gypsy couple?" Élise infused just the right amount of mild curiosity into her voice.

Mrs. Braithwaite beamed, and her blue eyes glimmered. "They were on their honeymoon, too. Or at least, that is what the wife told me. I don't rightly know if the gypsies have the same traditions we do when they marry, but"—she waved her hand airily—"that's not of import.

They seemed like rather *English* gypsies, if you catch my meaning. Maybe they were part English, but then again, I am not an expert of the race.

"Anyhow, they came here, and they were sweet as peaches. They said they, too, wished to explore the waterfall to begin their tour of the cascades all over the district. I could tell right away that they were very much in love. So I made them a picnic luncheon, too!"

"Did they stay in town?" Sam asked.

"Oh, no, they made off straightaway after returning from the waterfall. In their gypsy way." Mrs. Braithwaite laughed.

"Did they say where they were going next?" Élise's heart thrummed with excitement.

"Well, yes, they did. They had quite the itinerary, and I helped them with it, of course. I told them about Skelwith Force, which is quite a lovely cascade, and not far from here. Then I said they needed to walk up Tom Gill—oh, and you two mustn't miss that one, either! After that, I think they planned to ride up to Lake Ullswater and see a few falls there."

"And then?" Sam pressed.

Mrs. Braithwaite gave him a playful frown. "You are rather serious about your waterfall explorations, son. I think they mentioned Derwent Water, but I cannot be sure." She threw up her hands. "By then my poor old mind was near drowning in lakes and falls. So many locations had been tossed about that I couldn't keep up."

She handed Sam the picnic basket and patted him on the arm. "Now, go. Your wife looks hungry, so feed her well."

"I intend to." Sam thanked her for the basket, and they left the cottage.

It took only a few minutes. They followed the sound of water and Mrs. Braithwaite's directions, and it was easy to find the flat, grassy plateau where she'd said to spread the blanket.

Élise stood on the edge of the plateau and gazed at the cascade as Sam laid out the picnic. It was so lovely. And it wasn't one waterfall, but two. Two lines of frothing, pouring water, separated by a moss-covered, rocky island in the center and tapering into one large fall below, where the water crashed into a placid pool at the bottom. Trees and ivy and ferns grew densely around the cascade, feeding off its nutritional waters, no doubt.

Sam came to stand beside her. "What do you think?"

She sighed. "It is so beautiful."

"It is."

They watched in silence for a long moment. The water never stopped—an endless flow. And while she knew that water constantly trickled down from the earth into the streams that fed the falls, something about it felt magical. That if it were of this world, it should slow, then eventually stop. But no. The water kept coming, endlessly falling with foamy power into that pool.

"Come," Sam said softly. "You need to eat."

She sighed. That had been the most difficult part of her recovery. She hadn't really regained her appetite. But when she sat and smelled the savory pigeon pie, she managed to eat half a piece.

Sam scowled down at her plate. "That's all?"

"I am very full."

He sighed. Then he popped a blueberry into her mouth.

It was a burst of sweet flavor on her tongue, and she

gasped with pleasure. "*Bon Dieu*, I could eat every single one of those!"

"Then you shall."

And she did, one by one, as Sam fed them to her with implacable patience. At one point, she tried to push his hand away, saying she could feed herself, but he scowled at her and wouldn't hand her the bowl of berries when she demanded it. So she relented. She snuggled up against the hard body of her more-than-lover and watched the waterfall as he fed her blueberries.

And even though all kinds of terrible things might happen to her tomorrow, in this small, beautiful slice of the world, she was with Sam, and she was safe and content.

Chapter Eighteen

❧

Sam and Élise forewent Mrs. Braithwaite's recommendations of Skelwith Force and Tom Gill because Sam assumed his mother and Steven Lowell would have gone to see those cascades days ago.

Instead, that very afternoon, after Sam had procured two horses and a cart, they headed north. Soon they entered the village of Rydal, and while there'd been no sign of Dunthorpe, Sam learned that his mother and Lowell had been seen here as well—they had visited the two waterfalls to the northeast of the village the day before yesterday.

People tended to notice gypsies, and after having left their band of traveling players, the dowager duchess and Steven Lowell seemed to have abandoned caution. Once again, Sam and Élise were told of how "English" the two of them seemed, though they were clearly not, given their colorful gypsy dress and flamboyant ways, and how very much in love they were.

Sam knew his mother well. She'd had many lovers, and when she loved, she loved fiercely and openly. But this situation—it was beyond odd.

When the dowager duchess had vanished from Iron-wood Park a year ago, she'd left no trace of where she'd gone. Sam and his siblings had thought the worst—that she'd been kidnapped and held for ransom, or that she had been murdered in a robbery.

She'd vanished with two of her servants, and Trent and Sarah had made the first significant strides in finding her when they'd managed to locate one of them. The man had informed the family that the duchess and her servants had been taken to Wales by a man driving a cart drawn by asses. Further investigation on Luke's part had revealed that that man, Roger Morton, had been employed to deliver her to Steven Lowell.

The dowager duchess hadn't been taken from her house by force. But the questions still swarmed in Sam's head. What had prompted her to disappear like that? To leave her life and her family in such panic and upheaval? Could it be just another affair? This was not how their mother had handled her affairs in the past. But perhaps since this one was a gypsy...

A duchess engaging in a romance with a gypsy from a troupe of traveling players—hell, it was almost unthinkable.

Sam wanted—*needed*—to find his mother and this man. He needed to close the book on this past year of grief and fear. He and his siblings deserved answers.

He and Élise found the low falls near Rydal Hall, where they ate a warm dinner he'd had wrapped at the inn in the village. Then they walked uphill for a few hundred yards and stopped at the high falls. The place was deserted, and dusk was rolling in slowly. The days were growing longer, the nights warmer as they inched toward summer.

If Sam were alone, he'd press on, but Élise was still recovering from a serious illness. Procuring a room at the inn would be too conspicuous with Dunthorpe hunting for them. Instead he found a flat, dry area with a good view at the base of the falls and told her they were stopping for the night. She looked at him, brows raised.

"No! We cannot! Your mother and her...gypsy man are *very* close. We must keep going."

In response, he merely unrolled the bedroll and went to gather wood for a fire. As he turned away, he heard her make a frustrated growling noise, and he smiled.

Élise tried to help him set up camp, but he waved off her assistance. When he finally got the fire going, he looked up to find her seated on the grass a few paces away, hugging her knees against her chest as she gazed at the waterfall.

He watched her for a long moment, and something in his chest constricted.

His feelings for her cut straight to his core. They were so intense he knew they could destroy him.

But how could he tell her that? How could he wish for her to feel the same way when he'd promised himself never to encourage any woman's affections?

He'd chosen a life that wasn't at all conducive to loving or being loved. He'd made that choice for a reason.

If something happened to her...

By choosing to protect her, he'd made another choice. He'd avoided thinking about the repercussions of that choice on purpose. Because it was impossible to ignore the fact that the only escape from the Agency was death. And it was also impossible to ignore that until Élise had come into his life, the Agency had been everything to him.

Pushing those thoughts aside, he went over to Élise, and bending down, he touched her shoulder. She looked up at him, a faint smile playing about her lips. But her eyes were shining.

"What are you thinking about?" he asked.

She shrugged and gave him a soft smile. "Some things."

He cocked a brow. "What things?"

She reached a hand up. "Sit with me."

"Come closer to the fire. It's getting cooler."

She glanced wistfully back at the waterfall. "Soon I will not be able to see it."

"But you will hear it all night long."

That made her smile. "Yes. That will be good."

She took his proffered hand, and he pulled her up and led her to the blanket he'd laid beside the fire.

She sat and removed her leather gloves to warm her hands.

Her hands. They were pale and long-fingered. Delicate. Unscarred and uncallused. They were the hands of an aristocratic lady. Lately, he often forgot about her aristocratic connections. Her past associations and history had fallen away to reveal Élise as she really was—a complex, fascinating, beautiful woman.

She gave him a wry look. "And now *you* are thinking. About what?"

"About you," he said softly.

"Good things, I hope."

"Very good."

She smiled and laid her head on his shoulder.

"Now you tell me what you were thinking," he said.

She sighed. "Just that today has been a dream. Everything is so lovely and wonderful. I wish I could forget that the world outside all this wishes for me to be dead."

"Not the whole world," he corrected.

She made a scoffing noise. "Besides Marie, nobody cares." His heart squeezed, but she continued. "I realized long ago that I am not the sort of woman who is welcomed into English society with open arms. I have accepted that truth."

And now she believed that if Dunthorpe or Adams killed her, no one would mourn her.

"I care," he said softly.

She looked up at him through her long lashes. "That is very odd, don't you think?"

"Why?" he asked in surprise.

"No one has cared for many, many years. Then you came to kidnap me and hold me against my will. I have deliberately frustrated you at every turn. And yet you insist that you care."

"You don't believe me?"

"I do," she murmured. "And that is the oddest part of all."

He watched the fire and the fading waterfall beyond, wondering how it had come to this. He was in love with this woman.

He couldn't love her. He couldn't love anyone.

Too late.

"Sam?"

"Yes?"

"Make love to me. Here, in front of the waterfall. Before it is too dark and we cannot see it anymore."

His breath caught as he stared at her. He'd never known a woman as forward as this one. She was a woman who was clear about what she wanted. He loved her for that, and for so many other reasons.

He turned to her slowly, raising his hand and pressing a finger under her chin to tilt her face up to his. He kissed her long and languidly as the water crashed just a few yards away.

He pressed her down until she lay on the blanket in front of the fire. He pulled back and commanded, "Look at it."

She turned her head to gaze at the cascading water, then looked back up at him. "I cannot decide which is more beautiful. You or the waterfall."

He laughed. The way her mind worked never ceased to charm him. "The waterfall, Élise. Keep watching it until you can't anymore. You've only a few minutes of daylight left."

She wrapped her hands around his neck and dragged him down for a quick kiss, then capitulated with a sigh, turning her head so she could watch the falls.

"Good girl," he murmured. "Watch. And feel."

He moved down her body, pressing kisses over her clothes. When he reached her feet, he took off her shoes. Then he untied her garter and removed her stocking, rolling it down her calf, kissing her skin as it was exposed, gentling over the new scar on her knee. He rolled the stocking off her heel, the arch of her foot, then her toes, pressing firmly with his fingers as he did so.

She moaned with pleasure. "I will be your captive forever, my scoundrel, if you continue to seduce me like this."

He smiled, kissing the top of her foot, then her toes, trailing down from the biggest to the smallest.

He repeated the treatment on the other side, pressing her flesh until she was as moldable as putty in his hands. Then he moved back up her leg, stroking her inner thigh beneath her skirts until he found the drawstring of her drawers. He untied it and pulled the waistband. She lifted her bottom so he could pull the garment all the way down her legs and off, leaving her completely bare beneath her skirts.

He glanced at her as he laid her drawers aside to see that she was gazing at him again.

"The waterfall," he reminded her.

"I know," she said, "but I cannot help but imagine what you have planned next for me."

Pleasure, he thought. He wanted to bring her unimaginable pleasure. He wanted to brand himself in every part of her.

"The falls, Élise," he said sternly.

With a smile playing about her lips, she turned to look at the cascading water once more. He turned her to her side so he could unbutton her dress and petticoats. Then he went to work on her stays, touching her whenever he could as he loosened the laces. Finally, she was dressed only in her chemise, and he went behind her, pulling her back until her body molded against his front.

"Are you cold?"

"*Non.* It is a warm night."

Good. But he still worried about her growing too cool, so he covered them with one of the woolen blankets he'd brought for them to sleep under. When they were both situated beneath it, he ran his hand up the curve of her waist, then across her front and higher until he cupped her breast over her chemise.

God, he loved how her breast fit in his hand. Not too big, not too small. Utterly feminine.

He took his time, exploring her breasts one at a time, teasing her nipples into taut peaks as she gasped and wiggled against him. She followed his order, though, never taking her eyes from the falls.

He bent down to kiss the shell of her ear, nuzzling and licking as he removed his own coat, then his trousers and drawers, keeping his shirt on. He withdrew the pins from her hair, setting them in a neat pile beside the blanket this time. He unwound her hair and fanned it out in golden glory over the blanket.

Then he moved her hair off her neck and kissed the slim column, traveling down, kissing the backs of her shoulders and trailing his lips down her spine over the fabric of her chemise.

"You are a tease." Her voice had grown husky with desire.

When he reached the top curve of her buttocks, he nudged her onto her back and pulled the skirt of her chemise up, situating his body between her legs.

He dragged his tongue against her inner thigh. She went stiff—the higher he licked her thigh, the more ticklish she was, and he tortured her, kissing and nipping the insides of her legs until she shook and made gasping, complaining noises above him.

He laughed against her skin but wrapped his hands around her thighs to hold her still.

And then, finally, he went to her sex. She moaned at the first touch of his tongue. He licked her thoroughly, then added his fingers, sliding them into her as he moved his lips over the slick area above, first slowly and languidly. As her movements became more frantic, he moved quicker, pressed his fingers deeper as he tasted her.

He didn't need to hold her thighs anymore. They were locked tight around him.

She grew wetter, hotter, stiffer. He pushed his fingers deep, and she cried out. "Yes. There. Please. There."

He did it again and again. Her sex clenched around him, viselike. Then she came, her body squeezing and releasing, pulsing around his fingers and beneath his tongue. He continued his thrusts and his licks until she relaxed around him, her thighs falling away.

He kissed her sex one last time, gently, and then kissed his way down one of her legs until he arrived at her foot, which he pressed and rubbed for several minutes, ignoring the demanding pulse of his cock.

He gave the same attention to her other foot, then moved up her body, finding her watching him.

"It is too dark to see the waterfall," she murmured. "It disappeared when... when..."

"When you came?"

"Yes." A wide smile spread over her face. "Exactly then."

He grinned.

"Oh, my Sam," she chastised. "You look far too satisfied. Like the cat who ate the canary."

Raising his brows at her, he licked his lips. "Mmm."

She grabbed his shoulders and flipped them over before Sam knew what she was doing.

"Now it is my turn." Her eyes, flecked golden from the firelight, gleamed wickedly.

She crawled down his body, giving it the same attention he'd given hers earlier. She tugged up his shirt, her hands playing over his torso, teasing his nipples, gently pressing her lips around his scars. She followed her touches with teasing, playful kisses.

His cock was so hard it felt like it might burst. As she kissed his chest, she rubbed wantonly against it.

The vixen knew exactly what she was doing.

She trailed downward until her lips feathered against the head of his cock. He groaned aloud. He'd never had a woman's lips there before. Not for lack of fantasizing about it. And holy hell, it felt good.

She took his cock in both her hands and began a sweet torture that he was fairly certain might just kill him.

She kissed, licked, sucked. She fisted him in her hands and worked her palms up and down. She took his cock deep into her mouth and stroked him with her lips and tongue, mimicking the motions of carnal intercourse.

The pleasure...it was too much. Too strong. He was...

He groaned loudly. His hips moved now, out of his control, thrusting in her hands and her mouth as she hummed against him, the vibrations traveling all the way to the tips of his ears.

"Élise," he moaned. "Stop. Stop."

He should pull away. But she gripped him harder, took him deep into her mouth. So deep. His cock tightened, heated. And then the orgasm crashed through him, rushing like the waters of the nearby falls, filling his every pore with pleasure.

She didn't move away. She kept sucking him, milking every drop from him. It seemed to last forever. Her throat worked as she swallowed, pressing more seed out of him each time.

Until, finally, her movements gentled and her lips slipped off him. He lay spent, half dead, the crashing pleasure still ringing in his ears, though a tiny voice of reason told him it was probably just the waterfall.

She kissed her way back up his body as he had done with her earlier. Then she settled against him, pulling the blanket up over them.

Cradling her in his arms, he squeezed his eyes shut.

He loved her. He *needed* her.

He hadn't wanted either. He would never wish his love or need on anyone.

"Sam?" she asked in a low voice.

"Hm?"

"Are...you all right? Did you...not like it?"

He pulled her tighter against him. "No. I loved it. It was..." He shook his head. There really were no words to explain what it was.

She sighed. "What's wrong, then?"

"Nothing."

She was quiet for a moment. Then, softly, "You lie to me."

Yes, he did. She was too clever.

She stroked his chest, moving her fingers up and down. He couldn't help but find her touch soothing.

He squeezed his eyes tighter. Then he said in a grating whisper, "I didn't love them."

Her hand stopped, held still for a moment, then started again. "Whom?"

"Charlotte. And Marianne."

He felt her body move as she released a long breath. "I'm sorry."

"Marianne and I were children. Only seventeen when we married, the same age as you when you married Dunthorpe. She was eighteen when she died."

"Oh, Sam," she whispered.

"I married her because my mother and Marianne's father thought it would be a good idea, and I wanted to appease them."

"As I married Dunthorpe partly to appease my uncle. It is a valid reason for many to marry. Those kinds of matches are certainly more common than love matches."

"Nevertheless, she died, Élise. I didn't love her. I hardly knew her. And she died because she married me."

"It wasn't your fault."

He was silent for a minute. "And then . . . Charlotte. I married her to appease the colonel. For advancement in my military career." He gave a scoffing laugh. "I was a damn fool. It didn't take long for me to realize the mistake I made. Charlotte was sheltered—an innocent in all things. But she always resented me." Élise stiffened against him, but he continued. "She despised the fact that I was a bastard, and I think that tarnish on me, and by extension on her, ate at her until she began to loathe me."

"I hate her," Élise said stiffly. He could literally feel her bristling against him. His protective little fireball.

"She was also very young," he said softly. "She never had the chance to become wise."

Élise blew out a breath through her clenched teeth. "I shall not speak ill of the dead. Even though I am tempted. Very tempted."

"But I...I didn't love her. And she died because of the child she carried. Because of me..."

She squeezed him tight. "That isn't your fault, either. How could you have known?"

"I always th-ought..." His voice broke, but he pushed through, needing to tell her this, to confess to her what he'd told no one in his life. "I thought she and our son were taken from me as a punishment because I didn't love her enough. If I had, if I'd paid more attention to her instead of working all the time, if I'd encouraged her to leave her bed more instead of languishing in it all day..."

"Sam. How could you have known? Even if you'd loved her more than life itself, she would have died."

He was silent. That logic had crossed his mind in the past, only to be pushed away by his guilt.

"I cared about them both."

"Of course you did. Because you are you. You are caring by nature."

"But I never loved them," he said quietly. "And they both suffered and then died. Because of me."

"No." She seemed very confident in that rejection of his guilt. But she hadn't been there to see the plethora of mistakes he'd made with both his wives.

He loved Élise. He *needed* her.

But to have her would be selfish, as he'd been with Marianne and Charlotte.

"I can never form a connection with another woman. I...I am no good for women. I am...*lethal.*"

"That is utter nonsense," she said.

"Is it?" He sighed. "You have several people who want you dead, thanks to me."

"My Sam, you have saved me from those people, and

more than once. It is because of Dunthorpe they want me dead, not because of you."

"This is why I joined the Agency. It doesn't lend itself to family life. As I am sure has been made obvious to you."

"Yes, that seems very clear."

"Then you can see... You can see why this can only be temporary between us." He tried not to flinch. Hell, but it cost him to say those words.

"No."

He blinked down at her. "No?"

"No, I cannot see why it can only be temporary."

He sighed, surprised he'd need to spell it out for her. "My line of work is too dangerous. Even more so now than when I was in the army."

"Well then." He could hear the smile in her voice as she snuggled closer to him. "It is very good that you are no longer in this line of work."

"What do you mean?"

"You have left it, no? To become my knight in shining armor. You have made that your new line of work. For which I am grateful," she added.

It felt like something yanked his heart in two different directions, pulling him apart from the inside out. He wanted Élise like nothing he'd ever wanted in his life. But forging a deep connection with a woman would lead only to suffering in the end.

Élise had suffered enough. He couldn't bear to see her suffer anymore.

"You don't understand," he told her gruffly. "It'll be even worse—"

She pressed a kiss onto his pectoral muscle. "You are forgetting something, my Sam."

"What's that?"

"We're together now. That makes us twice as strong. I'm afraid. Of course I am." Her lips brushed over the front of his chest as she continued. "But I trust you, and you must trust me. If there is any possibility for us to escape this dire situation we have found ourselves in, we will find it. Together."

Chapter Nineteen

Sam and Élise didn't find the dowager duchess the next day. Nor did they find her the day after that. While Sam had kept an unhurried pace, Élise would have preferred to gallop across the countryside in pursuit of his mother and running from the men she knew were after them. She wouldn't have stopped until the duchess was found once and for all, and then she and Sam would have escaped somewhere to hide where Dunthorpe or Adams would never find them.

Sam, however, insisted on being slow and steady. She knew why—he was concerned for her health. He touched her often, and Élise knew it was not just for the pleasure of it. He was checking for fever.

He was very careful, too, asking subtle questions about the visitors to any given place, not only to find out whether the gypsy and his mother had been there, but if Dunthorpe or anyone from the Agency had been looking for them.

While they found hints of the dowager and Steven Lowell, all was quiet when it came to Dunthorpe and the Agency. If Élise didn't know better, she would have guessed they'd given up on the search. But she did know better. They were out there. Somewhere.

Late on the fourth day of their waterfall explorations, they approached Ullswater, where Airey Force was located. Airey Force was a celebratcd waterfall, arguably the most famous of the cascades they'd visited. They left the horses and cart at the edge of the road and walked to the falls on a well-trodden, rocky path, the greenery overhead like a ceiling blocking the sunlight.

"Ooh," Élise murmured when it came into view. They stepped onto the wooden footbridge spanning the stream and stared. It was majestic—taller and heavier than any of the others they'd seen. It carved a chasm into the wall of rocks it cascaded over and crashed into the large pool below with such force, the water seemed to vaporize. Far above them, another footbridge connected the two ledges of the steep chasm at the top of the falls.

There was no sign of Sam's mother, or anyone else, for that matter.

Frustrated, Sam thrust a rough hand through his hair.

Élise slipped her hand into his and squeezed. "We will find them," she said loudly so as to be heard over the roar of water. "We are very close."

He sighed and squeezed her hand back.

Hand in hand, they gazed at the falls for a long while. "I wish I could paint, or at least draw," she said. "Then I could capture this moment. But as it is, I must engrave this picture into my memory and only hope that time doesn't wear it away."

"You don't draw?" Sam asked.

"No. I am very bad at all those feminine pastimes. I cannot draw or sing or play an instrument. I am dismal at sewing and embroidery, and I've never in my life touched a knitting needle."

He chuckled. "What interests you, then?"

"Oh, many things!" she exclaimed. "But I am sorry to say that not very many of them are acceptable in society."

That brought a wicked gleam into his eyes, and his gaze dropped down her body.

She swatted him good-naturedly. "I meant things like reading books in Latin and grouse hunting. I did not mean *those* things! You are a scoundrel, after all."

"With you I am."

"Well, he finally admits it. Perhaps you will also admit that I knew it properly from the beginning."

"Perhaps." He slanted her a glance, a grin playing on the edges of his lips. "Perhaps not."

She made an unladylike, disgruntled noise. "Difficult man."

He bent down and kissed her temple. "We should move on. There's another cascade about half a mile from here, and then we need to find a safe place to make camp for the night."

She nodded, and they turned away from Airey Force. The path to the second falls was slightly more treacherous, the rocks on the ground slippery with moss and the angle of the slope increasing. Sam kept a firm grip on Élise's elbow, ensuring she didn't fall. But it wasn't long before they came to the second cascade.

This was a pretty waterfall with a lovely prospect but far less significant than Airey Force. It wasn't nearly as tall, but it was slightly wider. The pool at the bottom was small, with large moss-covered boulders erupting from its surface.

A couple sat on one of those boulders. They reminded Élise of her and Sam, the way their arms were wrapped around each other and the way they gazed at the falls. Élise turned to Sam to tell him they should leave and give them some privacy, but just then, he lurched to a halt.

He stared at them, his lips parted. Élise's heart began to thud against her ribs, and she turned slowly back to the pair.

They were about a hundred feet away and had their backs to Sam and Élise.

His mother. Could it be?

As if she'd felt the weight of Sam's stare, the woman turned her head to glance behind her. She, too, froze. Then she jumped up, half stumbling on the moss-covered surface of the flat rock. Élise couldn't hear her over the sound of rushing water, but she saw the word form on the woman's lips: "Sam."

She lunged for them, slipping on the wet rocks, splashing in shin-deep water but not seeming to care. She wore a heavy indigo blue woolen skirt that went to just above her ankles, and no shoes. A colorfully striped shawl was tied about her waist, and another shawl, this one of pale yellow, covered her dark, gray-streaked hair, which was loose and tumbled to the middle of her back.

Sam dropped Élise's arm and strode toward the woman with strong, determined steps.

Élise picked up her skirts and hurried after him. Seconds later, the woman—well, Élise supposed she should admit to herself that this unassuming, handsome woman was indeed the Dowager Duchess of Trent—hurled herself into Sam's arms at the edge of the stream bank.

Élise watched, fascinated, as the duchess burst into tears.

"Oh, Sam. Sam, my darling. I thought I'd never see you again!"

Ever the strong one, Sam stood tall, holding his mother in his arms as she dissolved against him.

Élise glanced beyond them to see the man picking his way over the rocks, making his way toward them at a much slower pace than the woman had.

The man was tall and large-boned, more conservatively dressed than the woman, in dark trousers, white shirt, and a simple dark coat. Though he didn't wear shoes, either, he would have been more likely to pass for an Englishman than the duchess in her exotic garb. He had a thick head of shock-white hair, dark only around the temples. His face was round, though he was by no means fat, and good-humored, and his dark brown eyes were vibrant and brimming with curiosity.

Sam patted his mother's back. "Shh, Mama. Shh."

The man came to stand beside her. She pulled back from Sam slightly, glanced at the man, glanced back to Sam, and then burst into fresh tears.

The man took a deep, fortifying breath and spoke loudly to be heard over the combined noises of the falls and the duchess's weeping. "Good afternoon." His English was perfect, with only the slightest inflection of a Roma accent. "I am Steven Lowell."

Sam hardly spared him a glance. "I know." He hesitated, stroking his mother's hair, then added, "I am Samson Hawkins."

The man gazed evenly at him. Then said simply, "I know."

* * *

It took some time, but Sam managed to calm his mother down. He wanted to shake her, to demand answers immediately, but he knew there would bc no point to it. His mother wouldn't be able to communicate with him until her emotions had run their course. The sound of crashing water was too loud to be conducive to conversation anyhow, and not only was his mother emotional, but the bottom of her skirts was soaked, and if she stayed out here she'd catch her death.

"Let's go dry off and find a place to talk," he said into her ear.

Snuffling, her eyes bleary from all her tears, she nodded. She stepped away from him, still gripping his arms tightly, and as she gathered her composure, she caught sight of Élise and asked in a clear voice loud enough for Élise to hear, "Who is that, darling? She is familiar to me."

So, she hadn't lost her directness. "Mama, this is Lady Dunthorpe. Lady Dunthorpe, my mother, the Duchess of Trent."

How odd to make these introductions in these circumstances. There was a false ring to the words as he said each woman's name. For his mother certainly had sloughed off all the skin of the Duchess of Trent. And Élise...hell, it almost hurt to call her by her legal name, but he was beyond calling her Madame de Longmont. She was important enough to him now that he couldn't imagine deceiving any member of his family about her true identity.

"Ah," his mother said crisply. "I remember now. Lord Dunthorpe's French wife." She wiped away another tear with the back of her hand and turned back to Sam.

"There's a grassy area around the bend in the path," he said gently. "Let's go sit there...I think we all have some explaining to do."

"May I suggest we return to our camp and have some dinner," Lowell interjected. "I caught a few fine trout this afternoon, and we would be happy to share a meal with you."

When his mother vigorously agreed to this plan, Sam nodded, though he could hardly look at the older man without his hands curling into fists. But he refused to lose his temper. Once he heard the explanation of his mother's disappearance, he'd decide whether the kidnapping bastard required a pummeling.

The four of them tramped back down the hill in relative silence. He let the older couple lead, and he followed, grasping Élise's arm firmly. Not that she came even close to stumbling. She was the nimblest woman he'd ever known. Still, he intended to keep her safe, even if his efforts proved excessive.

Near the road, they fetched the cart and horses, and Lowell led them another half mile to the location of his camp at the edge of Lake Ullswater. It appeared as though people had made camp there before—a large sunken fire pit dominated the clearing. Lowell had erected a simple tent under the shelter of an ancient oak.

As Sam secured the horses, the older man got the fire going quickly as the duchess expertly fileted the trout.

He could do nothing but gape at his mother—a woman who'd been waited upon hand and foot her entire life—covered in fish guts. He couldn't quite wrap his head around the change in her. Still, she was undoubtedly his mother—emotional and direct and larger than life.

She and Lowell were like a long-married couple welcoming friends into their beloved home. "Sit, sit," Lowell told them, gesturing flamboyantly to a pair of flat rocks adjacent to the fire as if they were fashionable, silk-upholstered armchairs. Uncharacteristically quiet, Élise obeyed, and Sam followed suit.

Lowell withdrew several small new potatoes from a burlap sack and began to juggle, first with three, then adding more until he juggled seven at once while Sam and Élise watched, speechless. Then, as he continued juggling, he tossed them one at a time into the fire until his hands were empty.

Meanwhile, clearly immune to Lowell's juggling expertise, Sam's mother set a long pan filled with globs of fat on the flames. When the fat began to sizzle, she added the trout and then hurried to the lake to wash her hands. She returned a minute later to lower herself beside Sam on his rock, arranging her brightly colored skirt around her.

He hesitated, uncertain how to begin this monumental conversation.

The truth was, he needed answers. He needed them now.

"Why did you leave?" He glanced at Lowell, who was placidly watching them from the other side of the fire. "Did he take you against your will?"

She laughed, a pleasant tinkling sound. He'd always loved the sound of his mother's laughter. He'd missed it.

"Well, Steven did not have the best timing. I'll grant you that. I was angry when his man came to take me away. I was given no warning and had left so much undone. But"—she cast a fond glance at Lowell, and they shared a secret, intimate smile—"that is all settled now. No, darling. He did not take me against my will."

"But why?" Sam asked. "Why did you leave Ironwood Park? Do you understand how your disappearance affected us? You cannot know what it did to my brothers and Esme." *And me, Mama? Do you know how it affected me?*

She blinked, her eyes filling again. "How is my dear little Esme?"

"She is well." She was also writing torrid romances for a publisher in London under an assumed name, but that was Esme's secret, not his.

"And the boys?"

He hesitated. So much had been revealed, and there was so much to tell, not the least of which was that in the past year, both Trent and Luke had found love and had married.

He leveled his gaze on her. "Mama. You must tell me why you left."

Lowell cleared his throat, and Sam glanced at him to see the older man had narrowed his eyes slightly at him in a clear warning not to upset his mother. Respect bubbled up from the well of deep suspicion Sam felt for him. Very deliberately, Lowell turned from Sam to Sam's mother. "Why don't you serve up the trout, Maddie."

Maddie. It took a moment for Sam to translate the

name. It was a nickname for his mother's given name, Madeline. But Sam had never in his life heard anyone call his mother "Madeline," not to mention "Maddie."

His mother used a spatula to scoop the fried fish from the pan into bowls, which she handed first to Élise, then Sam, then Lowell, and finally herself. Lowell deftly dropped a few small, hot potatoes into each of their bowls.

Élise looked around for utensils with which to eat, and Sam's mother laughed again. "Oh, no, my lady. We've no forks. You are to eat it in the Roma way—with your fingers." She wiggled her bare, callused fingers at Élise.

Now it was Sam's turn to narrow his eyes. Was his mother testing Élise? Expecting her to throw a tantrum as most ladies of the *ton* would?

She passed the test, because she grinned at Sam's mother. "That is a most excellent way to eat, I am sure." And she blew on the hot food for a moment before taking up a whole potato between her fingers and taking a bite.

His mother had been attempting to scandalize Élise, but he'd learned she was very difficult to scandalize. He'd succeeded in scandalizing her to her bones when he'd shot Dunthorpe, but since then, she'd managed just about everything he'd tossed her way with good humor.

His mother eyed Élise, an expression of surprise flickering over her face before she quickly masked it.

They all ate in silence for a moment. The food was excellent—far better than the dried meat, bread, and cheese that had become Élise and Sam's standard fare over the last few days.

Finally, his mother sighed. "I never thought I would need to explain."

He could only snort in response to that.

"I thought you would note my absence eventually, then perhaps wonder at it for a short while, and finally you would go on with your lives."

He stared at her for a moment, flabbergasted. Then he shook his head, tamping down the anger bubbling within him. "That's so foolish."

She closed her eyes. "Perhaps it was only wishful thinking. I thought you'd continue with your lives and I'd begin my own. But it has been difficult for me, darling. I have missed all of you more than words can express. The distance between us has created a deep, aching void in my very soul."

"Then why didn't you come home?"

"I . . . cannot. Don't you see?" She gestured at herself, then at Lowell. "This is who I am now. I am no longer the Duchess of Trent. How could I possibly explain this to anyone? I left the way I did because I knew that making a public spectacle of it would ruin my family, ruin my beloved children. A duchess running off with a gypsy isn't the sort of thing a family is able to recover from, Sam. You know this.

"The way I did it . . ." Her face crumpled a bit, and tears pooled in her eyes. She sniffed and blinked them back. "I know . . . I *do* know it was a cruelty to all of you, but the other way would have been even more cruel. I chose the lesser of two evils. I knew you'd be sad for a while, but in our world you can recover from the loss of a mother. You cannot recover from the loss of your position in society."

Sam stared at her, unable to hide the shock that must be written all over his face. "You're saying that you disappeared without a trace because you didn't want to bring scandal down upon the House of Trent? Because you might *embarrass* us?"

"Embarrass you...perhaps. But more than that, it would scandalize you, *ruin* you..." After a long silence, she added, "You know how vehemently Trent despises scandal. And having his own mother choose the life of a gypsy traveling player over the life of a duchess...I am not sure his pride could endure the blow. Luke was on the brink of utter failure already. I knew the news of Lowell just might push him over the edge. Mark and Theo, with their shining futures lying ahead of them like bright stars—I did not want my actions to snatch it away from them. And Esme..." She shook her head. "I had done all I could for the poor dear. She needed the apron strings cut, once and for all."

Sam was speechless. He shook his head. The woman simply did not fathom the upheaval she'd caused over the last year as they'd all desperately tried to make sense of what had happened.

Élise placed her hand on his forearm and squeezed gently, a gesture that did not escape his mother's keen notice. But she—wisely—kept her mouth shut on the subject of him and Élise. For now. Though he had no doubt that the questions would be flowing later.

Sam still couldn't find any words, so Élise rescued him. Over the last few days, he'd told her in great detail of what he and his siblings had gone through in the quest for answers regarding their mother.

She spoke in a quiet voice. "Sam and his brothers and sister have been searching desperately for you for the past year. They thought you'd been murdered. They've been overturning every stone in England to find answers."

His mother frowned. "For the past year? For an entire *year*?"

"Yes," Sam said. "We didn't intend to give up until we found you, no matter how long it took."

"But..." She shook her head, her brows drawn together in an expression of befuddlement. "You have your own lives."

"That doesn't mean we forgot we had a mother." The words came out harsher than Sam had intended, and his mother flinched as if he'd struck her.

Twin tears crested over her lower lids, then trailed down her cheeks. Across the fire, Lowell was watching them, his lips pressed together. Sam glared at him. He was finished trying to contain his anger. "And what have you to say about turning an entire family upside down for more than a year? Or do you not care since you know nothing of us?"

Lowell took a deep breath. "I know much about you. More than you think, boy." His expression was mild, but the warning in his voice was unmistakable.

Sam turned back to his mother. "It was Esme who discovered you were gone. She and Sarah called the family immediately to Ironwood Park. Luke didn't receive the message, but the rest of us rode straight there.

"We searched everywhere. The grounds. The village. We dragged the lake. Mark came up to Lake Windermere, thinking you might have gone to your lake house. Trent and I pursued clues in London, and when Luke was finally informed that you were missing, he threw himself into the search as well."

"Oh, Luke," his mother murmured. "My poor Luke. How desperately I miss him."

Sam continued. "We wrote to all of your relatives, all of your friends. Word eventually spread, and soon all of London was talking about your disappearance. And then…" He hesitated, but he assumed his mother was just as ignorant of this as she was ignorant of the lengths they'd been going to in the search for her. In any case, the truth needed to be known. "And then Trent found your maid's body."

His mother's eyes went wide and she clapped a hand to her mouth. "Binnie?"

He nodded. "She had half your jewels in her possession. I see now why you gave them to her—you had no need of them any longer, correct?"

"Yes, but…"

"She flaunted them, and she was robbed and murdered."

"Oh no," his mother whispered, her eyes filling with tears yet again. "My sweet, loyal Binnie."

"We thought your manservant had suffered the same fate, but Sarah eventually found him. He told us about how Roger Morton had taken you from the dower house."

"Roger Morton." His mother pressed her lips together in distaste, making it clear she'd disliked the man.

"Luke went after Morton," Sam continued, "chasing him from Wales to Bristol to Scotland and back to London, where he finally caught him. Morton was guilty of several crimes unrelated to your disappearance, including having Luke falsely arrested for theft. He ended up dying in prison of the wounds Luke inflicted upon him. But before his death, he revealed the name of Steven Lowell."

His mother glanced at Lowell. "I told you that blackguard couldn't be trusted," she murmured.

"You were right about that," Lowell agreed placidly.

"Trent was the one who learned where we might be able to find Lowell. He discovered that your last-known location was in Preston, so Mark and Theo traveled up here to continue the search. I happened to be here for different reasons." He gestured to Élise. "We've been following your trail from waterfall to waterfall for the last few days."

His mother drew in a deep breath. "Good God. Sam, I had no idea. Truly I didn't. I thought—"

He cut her off. "I know. You thought we'd mourn your loss for a few days and then go on with our lives. You have a very low opinion of your children."

His mother looked from him to Lowell and back again. "Eat," she said huskily. "You've hardly touched your food."

It was a command from his childhood, and before he knew it, he was obediently taking a bite of the roasted potato.

After he'd swallowed, he cocked his chin toward Lowell, but he didn't look at the man again. "Who is he, Mama? What possessed you to leave us behind for him?" He tried to keep his voice even, but he failed. It cracked and wavered with emotion. "For this? Did you have an association with him before last year? An assignation of some kind?"

Sam had no recollection of meeting this man at Ironwood Park, though he had met some of his mother's lovers, both there and in London—which had always been a more-than-awkward experience. But he'd never seen Lowell before.

His mother hesitated. Again, she looked at Lowell,

who gave her a succinct nod, then back to Sam. "You were never meant to know this," she murmured.

"Know what?"

She gazed at him with shining golden brown eyes. "My darling Sam." She held her hands out toward Lowell, blinked hard, and then whispered, "I'd like you to meet your father."

Chapter Twenty

Sam froze. Beside him, Élise tensed, and he felt her hand come to his forearm again in a comforting gesture.

He wrenched his gaze to the older man.

My father.

No.

He'd never thought of himself as having a father. And now this man sat before him, in the flesh.

My father.

He stared at Lowell, who gazed back at him, an implacable expression on his face. Judging by that expression, it seemed the man had known about him all along.

His father had been aware he had a son for the past thirty-two years. And he had never tried to know him.

Sam blinked. The words pounded against his skull—*meet your father*—but his skull was thick, and the words couldn't penetrate. Not completely.

He didn't have a father. He was the bastard son of the

Dowager Duchess of Trent. He was simply a product of one of her many affairs.

"No," he croaked out.

"Yes," his mother said firmly.

"I...don't understand." His voice had gone low and hoarse, sounding foreign to his ears. Élise squeezed his arm. He turned to her, saw the expression of sympathy on her beautiful face. "I don't understand," he repeated to her.

"I know," she said.

He turned helplessly back to his mother. "Explain," he croaked out.

"Oh, my darling"—there was sympathy in her voice, too—"it is a very long story."

He shook his head. "I...I need to know."

She ducked her head to take a bite of her food, her gaze meeting Lowell's again. The silent communications between them were driving Sam mad.

"It is your story to tell, Maddie," the older man said quietly. "We have discussed this. You know what you must do."

She sighed dramatically, then turned back to Sam. "It was better you didn't know. So much better. Despite your illegitimacy, you have gone far in your life. You were an officer in the army, and now... Well, I don't know *exactly* what it is you do now, but I know you hold a position of great importance."

She placed both her hands over the fist he'd clenched in his lap. "I know you, my darling. If you'd known your father was who he was, you wouldn't have kept it to yourself. You'd allow the world to know, to beat you down with its prejudices. As it stood, you rose quickly through the ranks of the army. Would any of that have happened if the world knew you were not only illegitimate, but the son of a half-breed gypsy?"

Sam glanced at Lowell again, who gazed back at him with those fathomless dark eyes. So the man was a half-breed. It explained quite a bit, not the least of which was why he didn't seem to be connected to a tribe. They'd probably rejected him for being half *gadjó*. As the English had undoubtedly rejected him for being half gypsy. Being a half-breed meant you were accepted by no one.

Sam closed his eyes. His mother was right. Without Cambridge, without the army, knowing he was a quarter gypsy, what would he have become? He had no idea.

"It was a secret that needed to be kept," she said.

And yet she told him now. She'd chosen this moment to destroy him.

Élise must have seen something in his expression, because her fingers tightened over his arm. "You're still who you are, Sam," she said. "Nothing you learn today or any other time can change that."

Sam took a long moment to absorb her words.

She was right. Bolstered by this, he opened his eyes.

"I kept it from you," his mother continued, "not because I felt you would hate me for the truth, but because I knew the world would heap abuse upon you for it. I did it to protect you from that."

It made sense. He had been known as a fatherless bastard, which was bad enough, but being known as the bastard of a half-breed gypsy would have been worse.

Still, a headache pounded between his brows. He raised his eyes to meet Lowell's yet again. His *father's* eyes. The man was so quiet, allowing Sam's mother to run the conversation. But what did he think about all this?

It seemed clear that he didn't care. If he had, he would have done something to reveal his identity to Sam long ago.

Sam looked away. He knew nothing of Lowell, had no connection to him beyond the basic bond of blood. A blood bond meant nothing when there was no substance to fortify it.

He turned back to his mother. "Tell me...how this came about."

She nodded. "Very well. As you know, before I married the Duke of Trent, I lived in Northampton at Tarn Hall, your grandparents' estate."

Sam nodded. He knew about Tarn Hall but had never gone there. His mother had never told him why she didn't take him there, but he knew anyhow: His grandfather had forbidden his bastard grandson to set foot on the property.

His mother continued. "Steven and his players came to Northampton one summer. I had just turned eighteen. I went to watch them, and when I saw him, laughing and juggling..." A flush rose on her cheeks, and she glanced at Lowell. Sam refused to look in that direction again, just stared stoically at his mother. "Oh, darling, it was love at first sight. I knew my father the earl was angling for me to marry the Duke of Trent, whom I disliked immensely. Steven—and all the players—they were so free, such lighthearted and happy people. I wanted nothing more than to join them."

She sighed, then continued. "I was a young lady of noble birth, constrained by society's expectations. My life...Oh, Sam, I was a very unhappy girl. I felt stifled.

Imprisoned. Steven was wild. He was happy, and he was free. I wanted that so badly for myself. I *craved* it. I intended to run away with him that very night. He came out to Tarn Hall, and I sneaked out of my bedchamber window. We ran and ran across the fields.

"We spent two days running. They were the two best days of my life. I learned so much—about living, about congress of the sexes, about the world." Her hands, which were still over his fist, squeezed tight. "But then my father found me. He literally tore me from Steven's arms. He returned me to the house, where he beat me, then locked me up in my bedchamber with a boarded window for the next several months. My metaphorical prison had become a prison in truth. And the only way out was to agree to marry the duke."

Sam realized he was clenching his teeth so hard, his jaw was beginning to ache. Forcibly, he released the pressure, making himself relax. His fist opened under his mother's hands, and she threaded her fingers in his.

"The duke wanted me, Sam. He wanted my dowry, which was enormous—the largest the country had seen in years. By the time I agreed to marry him, I knew I was with child. I told him that I would not marry him unless he accepted my baby into his house. I told him he didn't have to be a father to the child, but he needed to accept his existence and give him his name. I was firm on this one point, darling. I would not be that mother who gave her child away to be raised by some farmer or crofter. I wanted you." Intense certainty resonated in her voice.

"Where was he all this time?" Sam gestured roughly to Lowell.

"Steven tried to come back to me, but he was turned

away by my father, who threatened to shoot him if he ever appeared at Tarn Hall again."

Sam took an unsteady breath. Élise, who had kept quiet this whole time, stroked her fingers across his arm in a soothing motion.

"I gave birth to you," his mother said. "My beautiful, dark boy, who reminded me so much of his father, whom I continued to love with all my heart. And two months later, I married the Duke of Trent."

Sam knew the rest. He blew out a slow breath, as if he'd been holding it in throughout the entire story.

There were still so many questions. "What I don't understand is how you knew he was coming back. After more than thirty years... how did you wait so long? How did you communicate during all that time? What made you agree to go to him?"

"There's more to the story, my darling," his mother said. "Steven and I saw each other twice in the first several years of your life. Both times were..." She hesitated, then looked down. "Difficult. I was married to someone else. I was a duchess. He was a traveling player. I was raising his son, and I didn't wish said son to know the truth of his paternity. I needed to keep up appearances as the duchess. I needed to perform my duties, not for my own gain but for that of my children."

Her voice lowered. "You remember those years, Sam. They were full of turmoil. I wanted to hold you children together... to give you the best lives I possibly could—"

"By lying to all of us?" Sam cut in incredulously.

That stopped his mother cold. She studied his face, panic flaring in her dark eyes.

He stared back at her.

"What do you know?" she whispered.

He gave a humorless laugh. "More than you'd like, I'm sure."

"Tell me." Her voice sounded raw. "Tell me what you know."

He disengaged his hand from hers and rubbed his temple. "What do I know?" He shook his head. "Let me tell you what happened soon after you disappeared, Mama. Our old neighbor, Baron Stanley, approached Trent and attempted to blackmail him into marrying his daughter. Do you know what information he held over Trent's head? That all my siblings, besides Trent himself, are illegitimate. Lord Stanley himself is Luke's father, and Mark and Theo aren't even yours but the issue of the old duke and his mistress. He even conjectured that Esme was illegitimate, but he had no proof of that."

Everyone was completely still around him. Even Élise. He'd shared much with her, but not the secrets of his siblings' illegitimacy.

"Trent was prepared to marry Stanley's daughter to shut him up. Because we all know what would happen to Luke, Mark, Theo, and Esme if the truth were revealed."

"Oh God." The duchess seemed to curl into herself, bending over and holding her face in her hands. "Oh God. I didn't intend for this to happen, Sam. You must know this."

"We sought out his proof, and we know that his accusations are true. Luke is the result of your affair with Baron Stanley. Theo and Mark are the result of the old Duke of Trent's affair with his mistress. Esme? Well, her parentage remains a mystery."

"Esme is your sister," she sobbed.

"I hope so," he said coldly.

She looked up at him, tears flowing freely from her eyes once again. "No, Sam, you don't understand. Esme is your full sister. Steven is her father, too."

Sam held himself rigid. How many blows could a man take in one night? If he let himself go—if he let one muscle relax—he just might shatter into a million pieces.

He took several gulping breaths, trying to keep himself together. "How?" he pushed out.

His mother sniffed, rubbed her nose. Lowell rose and fetched her a handkerchief, which she took from him gratefully. He then knelt beside her and held her in his arms, murmuring soothing words Sam couldn't decipher into her hair.

Sam watched it all with a sort of horrified fascination. His mother. And his father. Embracing in front of him.

The truth still hadn't quite penetrated.

"I have made a mistake, Steven. Another one. Oh, I've made so many mistakes."

"You did what you thought best, Maddie. For your children. For all of them."

"But it wasn't the best. They know. They all *know*."

"Shh," Lowell murmured, rubbing circles into her back. He glanced at Sam, then looked quickly away, refusing to meet his eyes.

His father.

God, would his mind ever accept this? Could *he* ever accept it? He wasn't sure. He'd lived his whole life without a father, and he'd come to a certain peace with that. Now...his existence had been altered. The way he looked at the world needed to be altered.

Lowell pulled Sam's mother into his lap. He held her

and rocked her, and his mother suddenly looked older. Older, more fragile, and more vulnerable than he'd ever seen her.

She'd always been the strong one. The one they'd all turned to when they had a skinned knee or lost a toy or were pushed by one of their siblings. She was brash, she was eccentric, and she was the most *real* person any of them had ever known. And she'd loved all her children—even Mark and Theo, who weren't technically hers—with a passion and vehemence rarely seen in aristocratic circles.

They'd leaned on her, he realized, but when had she ever had someone to lean on like this? When had she ever had the opportunity to cry? To be vulnerable? Who had held her when she'd cried?

Sam thought of the string of lovers that had gone through their house. Had she been searching for this? For something she knew Lowell could give her but was never able to find in anyone else?

Maybe.

"Tell him," Lowell was urging her. "You need to tell him the rest."

Well. At least Lowell wasn't encouraging her to continue to lie.

Sniffing, she looked back at Sam. But she kept her arms firmly around the older man, clinging to him as if to a lifeline.

"When you were eleven years old, he came to me." She laid her head against Lowell's shoulder. "Trent was ill, and everyone knew he was dying. Steven...he wanted me to leave, to run away with him, but again I told him I could not." She was quiet for a long moment; then she closed her eyes. "Esme was the result of that meeting.

"We saw each other infrequently over the next years. But each time he came to me, Sam, it was like I was reuniting with a piece of my soul I had been missing. I knew, as I'd known from the beginning, that Steven was who I wanted. Who I'd always wanted. But I couldn't leave my life as the Duchess of Trent. Not until my children were grown and settled.

"I waited as long as I could. And then, one day, I received a message from Steven. He asked me to be with him finally. Once and for all. I had borne my life without him for so long, and I didn't think I could bear it much longer. Esme was grown—she was nineteen years old—and the rest of you were older. Theo was at university. Mark had just had his commencement from Trinity College and was beginning his life. Luke was struggling to find his way, but I no longer had the power to set him upon the correct course. Trent had settled in as the duke years earlier. And you, Sam darling—I had seen you go through so much, but you were thirty-one years old, and I knew that your path was your own, that nothing I could do as your mother could change it.

"So there it was. My children were grown and had ventured out into the world. It was time for me to leave. To be who I always wanted to be, with the man I'd always wanted to be with."

Sam shook his head. Then he said quietly, "They might have been grown, Mama, but Esme had not ventured out into the world."

"But she had, Sam. She'd had her Season the previous year."

"Her failure of a Season," Sam corrected.

"Yes. That was my fault. I pushed her too hard. If

she'd needed another Season, if she'd needed more guidance from me, I would have stayed at Ironwood Park. But Esme…" She shook her head. "She has always been a mystery to me. I did my best with her, but I'd reached the limit of what I could do. I always felt that Sarah was better for her than I ever could be. I knew I was leaving her in Sarah's capable hands."

Well, she was right about that. Sarah had proved herself as Esme's companion and true friend.

"How is Sarah?" his mother asked, her eyes misty.

Sam hesitated; then a smile quirked his lips. "You really don't know, do you?"

"Know what?"

"Trent married her. They have a son."

Her hand slapped to her heart. "No!"

"Yes."

"No. You cannot be serious. You must be lying. I know the girl worshipped the ground Trent walked on, but…are you saying…are you telling me he deigned to marry his head housemaid?"

Sam shook his head. "There was no deigning about it, Mother. Trent married her as his equal. They are very much in love."

"Heavens." She gazed up at Lowell. "I don't believe I have ever been on such a stormy sea of emotion…but this…this makes me so happy. Sarah Osborne—the housemaid of Ironwood Park—is the new Duchess of Trent. I couldn't imagine anyone better suited for the role." Her lips twisted. "Though I am sure society does not agree."

"It doesn't matter what society thinks. Trent would agree with you, and that's *all* that matters," Sam said.

She gave a heartfelt sigh. "I believed Trent was on the verge of marrying one of those *ton* debutantes—someone like the Stanley chit. That was one spectacle I was glad to leave behind. But I cannot tell you how happy I am that he came to his senses."

"Luke is married, too, Mama," Sam said softly.

She sat up straight, looking at him hard. "Now I know you are joking."

Sam shook his head. "I'm not."

She pressed her lips together. "Allow me to guess—he was caught tupping some innocent country milkmaid and was dragged to the altar, gun pointed at his head, by the poor girl's enraged father."

Sam chuckled. "That's how I would have guessed it, too. But no. How it actually happened was quite different from that."

She leaned forward. "Tell me."

"In his search for Roger Morton, he met Emma Anderson, a woman who was also hunting for Morton. The man ruined her family."

The story was a complex one, and this was not the time to go into detail about it, so he cut to the chase. "The two of them traveled up and down the country together in their search for Morton. She seemed to dig through that dissolute shell that had always covered Luke, to the core of him. He thought her too good for him for the longest time, but she helped him see the error of that thinking."

The duchess sighed. "Are they happy together?"

"Very."

"So my leaving Ironwood Park led to something good, after all."

Sam shook his head, bemused. "If you'd like to think of it that way, then for Luke, yes it did. He's a changed man. You'd hardly recognize him."

Sam glanced upward, realizing that somewhere in the midst of this conversation, the sky had grown dark and the temperature was dropping rapidly. Stars were popping out in the clear indigo darkness, and the full moon hung low over the lake.

He slipped his arm around Élise and drew her close. She locked into place against him, making that perfect fit, like she always did; then she snuggled even closer.

His mother's dark eyes took this in, but again she didn't comment. "Are you finished with your dinner?"

He nodded, then checked Élise's bowl. She'd eaten about half the meal, and the temptation to order her to eat more was strong. But half the bowl was about twice as much as he'd eaten, so he could hardly complain.

His mother collected the bowls and, without another comment, bundled the dirty dishes in a large pan, then carried them to the lake to wash them.

The three of them watched her for a moment; then Élise rose. "I will go to assist her."

Before Sam could protest, she'd lifted her skirts and hurried after his mother.

Leaving him alone, for the first time in thirty-two years, with his father.

They sat in awkward silence for a moment. Then Lowell asked, "Did you procure a room at the inn?"

"No." Sam knew his answer sounded abrupt—even clipped—but he wasn't about to explain how Dunthorpe and the Agency were after Élise and him.

Lowell didn't seem affected by his terseness. "Then

you must stay here tonight. If it will not offend your lady, of course."

Sam nodded. "We will stay." He didn't comment on Élise. His mother and Lowell would soon learn that, though she was an aristocrat both by marriage and by blood, she wasn't easily offended, especially not by lack of servants and a soft bed.

Truth was, it was already dark, and it would be difficult finding a new camp tonight. Plus, Élise must be tired.

He and Lowell sat for a few more minutes in silence, Sam staring broodily into the fire. He didn't know how to go about this business of having a father. What could he possibly say to the man?

"She told me all about you," Lowell said.

Sam slid him a glance. How was he supposed to respond to that?

"She is very proud of you." Lowell hesitated, then added quietly, "And so am I."

Something clenched inside Sam, and anger welled up in him. This man didn't know him. He didn't have the right to have feelings of pride for a son he'd never bothered to know. But he pressed his lips together and didn't say anything. He was well versed in keeping his silence, in keeping his emotions to himself. He had learned the necessity of doing so during his childhood. His *fatherless* childhood.

After a moment, Lowell added, "I wanted to marry your mother, Samson. I wanted her even more when she told me about you. I asked her to take you and run away with me, so we could be a family together. She would not do it."

Sam forced his head to move in a nod.

"She believed it would be better for you to be raised in a duke's house with all the rights and privileges that upbringing could offer you. She felt the same about your sister."

"Yet she ultimately chose this life over that one." Sam gestured around them. The fire crackled; the air was fresh; stars glittered overhead. This was a kind of peace that had never been found at Ironwood Park, especially when the old duke was alive.

"Most would not choose this life if given the option," Lowell said.

Sam couldn't argue with that.

"Sometimes it isn't such an easy life. We work hard, and the work is constant. Your mother and I are taking a honeymoon of sorts, but we will return to the endless toil soon enough."

"So, you finally married her."

"I did." Satisfaction played around the edges of Lowell's lips.

"And where is your troupe now?"

"Manchester," Lowell said. "Most of them have family there. They are taking a respite before the flurry of the summer season."

"You intend to join them there?"

"No. They have only a few more days. They will spend the next weeks performing between Manchester and Birmingham. We will join them when we are finished."

"Then you must have someone else running it?"

Lowell nodded. "My assistant of many years. He is up to the task, though it is only the second time I have left him alone. The first was last spring, when I went to Maddie in Wales."

Sam didn't respond to this, and the two men sat in silence for a while. Sam wondered why his mother and Élise were taking so long. Perhaps they were having their own awkward conversation down at the shore.

"She's right, you know."

Sam quirked an eyebrow at the older man.

"At Ironwood Park, you were given more than I could have ever offered. You and your sister both."

Sam ground his teeth to prevent himself from making a noise of disgust. The man didn't know a thing. How could he compare being raised fatherless in the cold halls of Ironwood Park to being with a whole family?

But neither this man nor his mother would ever understand how his childhood as the bastard son of the Duchess of Trent had shaped him. They might think they'd done right by him by making the choices they had. He knew differently.

But why resent them now? What was done was done. And poor Esme still didn't even know whether her father was the Duke of Trent or someone else.

"You need to tell Esme," he said.

The older man's brows crept upward.

"Tomorrow, I'm going to take you and my mother to her. And then you're going to tell her everything. Just like you told me."

Chapter Twenty-One

❦

"What is your game with my son?" the duchess asked.

The older woman had handed Élise a towel to use to dry the dishes, and she'd been working on the second bowl when the question broke through the silence.

Élise swallowed. How odd, to feel the need to defend herself from an overprotective mother. Overprotective of Sam, too, who was the most capable man Élise had ever known.

She kept her voice mild. "There is no game, Your Grace."

The dowager snorted. "Don't call me that. I'm just Maddie now. Or Madeline, if you prefer formality."

Calling a dowager duchess by her given name didn't particularly strike Élise as formal, but she held her tongue.

The duchess continued. "No game, eh? Well, you are a married woman, so—"

Élise's cheeks burned at the thought that the duchess

believed she was having an adulterous affair with her son. "I am no longer married."

The woman's brows shot up. "No?"

"No. Dunthorpe is dead." Élise hesitated, then added in a low voice, "Murdered."

The duchess's brows remained firmly arched high on her forehead. "How did you end up with Sam, then?"

"Circumstance," Élise said cryptically.

The older woman's brows lowered, and she gave Élise a hard look, as if trying to search under her very skin. Élise simply dried the bowl the duchess had handed her and pretended she didn't feel the heavy weight of the woman's gaze.

"Something to do with his secretive occupations, then?" the duchess asked.

"Perhaps," Élise said elusively. She guessed she wasn't nearly as good at evading this kind of question as Sam was.

"I see," the duchess mused. Then, "You protect him. Good."

Always. But Élise kept her mouth shut. Her need to protect Sam, even from his own mother, was so surprising to her as to be overwhelming.

Because I love him.

And that was what love meant. Part of it, anyhow. She was learning as she went.

"Don't worry about me, Your Gr— Madeline," she said, speaking the French name with its proper accent. "I want what is best for Sam. Just like you do."

"Is that so?" the duchess said slowly. "No one has ever felt that way about Sam before, though I cannot imagine why. His is a heart of honor, yet he has been hurt again and again. By society, by his country and its enemies, by his wives, and by the old Duke of Trent. He has suffered enough. I should like to see him happy."

Élise's heart twisted, thinking of all these hurts. Some of them she understood completely; others, not as much. "He told me the duke ignored him."

The duchess gave a mirthless laugh. "That's true. Perhaps you have never been ignored, Lady Dunthorpe, but sometimes it is as harsh a punishment as being beaten."

Élise considered this for a moment; then she nodded. "I understand."

"And his wives were frivolous creatures. Both of them, though in entirely different ways." She gave Élise a side-long glance. "I don't believe you are frivolous, though. You seem quite . . . *earthy* under that perfectly honed shell. Though I must say, 'earthiness' was not my first impression of you. I think we met at Lord Symonds's ball a few years ago."

"Yes, I believe you're right." Élise sighed. "I wore the mask of Lady Dunthorpe as well as I could. Though at times it was excruciating."

"Oh, I understand that, my dear," the duchess murmured, handing Élise another bowl. "More than you can possibly know."

*   *   *

Late that night, Élise lay beside Sam under the stars. Hours ago, the older couple had retired into the tent, and all was silent in that direction.

She was awake, her mind tumbling with all that had been said earlier. Most of all, she thought of Sam, who lay silent but alert beside her. Sleep was elusive to him, and she couldn't blame him for that. Tonight he'd been introduced to his father for the first time in his thirty-two years. A father who had never made an effort to know his son.

That kind of blow couldn't be easy to recover from.

She lay, as she did most nights, in the crook of his arm, and she turned to press a hard kiss against his chest.

"I am so sorry, my Sam," she whispered.

He tensed. "For what?"

"Hearing all that you heard. To deprive a boy of his father... what deeper pain can there possibly be?"

Sam released a long, stuttering sigh, and she squeezed him tighter.

"How is it that you understand but they do not?" he asked her quietly.

"I don't know."

His lips pressed into her hair. "It's been like this between us almost from the beginning. You believed you should feel a certain way since I was holding you against your will, but deep inside, there has always been an understanding between us."

"Yes," she murmured. "There always has. It is inexplicable, really. But it is true."

"I don't want to be without you, Élise."

She closed her eyes, letting the words float through her like sweet balm. "I don't want to be without you, either."

"I have never said this to a woman before... but I..." He hesitated, and she waited, as if on the edge of a cliff, wondering whether he'd pull her away from certain death or push her over.

"I love you," he finished, his voice rough with emotion.

"Oh, my Sam. I love you, too," she said, squeezing him tight.

"There is so much," he began. "Dunthorpe. Adams and the Agency. They'll do their best to kill me. If I cannot keep you safe—"

"Stop." She pressed her fingers against his lips and whispered, "Stop. We will keep each other safe."

He shook his head, and when she pulled her fingers back, he said, "We are just two people. They have money, men, resources. There is no way—"

"If I can prove I was never in league with Dunthorpe—"

"We told you. Adams never rescinds his orders."

She ignored the pang of despair that shot through her. "We could go somewhere. America, perhaps—"

Sam shook his head.

"Something. There has to be something we can do—"

"No," he said. Pain laced his voice. "There's nothing. I will fight for you until the end, but you need to promise me something."

"What's that?"

"That you will go to Trent. He will be able to protect you like no one else can."

"I want to stay with you—"

"If I'm not here, you must go to Trent. Promise."

She was silent for a long moment. Then she whispered through her dry throat, "I promise. But it won't come to that."

He began to shake his head again, but she caught his cheek in her palm and forced it in her direction so she could press a hard kiss to his lips.

And...all of a sudden, it became more. That hard kiss

turned into something needy and desperate. The desire to be with him, to be *one* with him, exploded within her.

He must have felt it, too. His arms drew her against him, over him, strong iron bands pulling her to him as if he couldn't get close enough. As if he couldn't get enough of her. "Élise," he whispered. "Élise, my love."

Her eyes sank shut as pleasure washed through her. There was no greater joy to her than being Samson Hawkins's love.

She kissed him harder, then moved her lips over his jaw, rough with the day's growth of beard, then to his ear, which she nipped.

His erection grew quickly, straining against her leg. She pressed kisses down his jaw and the side of his neck, then over his shirt, her lips gentling against the jagged scar from his battle wound, then lower, against the thick muscles at the front of his chest.

She moved down his body, soaking up his essence with her lips. He was so intrinsically strong. So masculine and muscular. Such a protector. So different from any man who'd ever been in her life.

She reached his drawers and kissed his cock over the linen as she fumbled with the string. Finally she had it undone. She pulled his drawers open, then jerked them over his sex, exposing the long, hot length of him. He was fully erect and magnificent under the light of the moon.

She kissed him, breathing him in. His masculine, musky essence was so much stronger down here. She licked him, moaning with pleasure at his taste. Not only that, his texture, his length, his hardness. The sheer magnitude of his masculinity.

She swung her leg over him, then pulled the blanket up

over her shoulders. She took his heavy length in her hand and probed between her legs until she found the slit in her drawers with the head of his cock.

She slid him over her slick flesh, up and down until she had to bite her lip to keep herself from groaning. Then she fitted him at her opening and pressed her body downward.

She took him in. All of him, until she could feel him reach the limits of her body, until she could feel him throughout every bit of her being. She stretched to accommodate him—a sweet, pleasurable pain that caused her to blow out a harsh breath.

He grasped her buttocks in both his hands, squeezing the flesh, spreading her and opening her for him.

Then she began to move, grinding over him, against him.

He filled her. She loved how he touched her. How he gripped her buttocks with one hand and moved the other to fondle her breast. Even over the fabric of her chemise, he teased her nipple until the sensation collided with the pleasure he wrought between her legs.

He was beautiful, her Sam. He made her feel whole, complete. Cherished, and . . . *loved*.

Tears stung at her eyes. Because the truth was, no one had ever made her feel those things until he'd come into her life. Sam was special. He was real, and he was inside her, and he loved her as fiercely as she loved him.

She could never give that up. No matter the cost.

She moved, sliding her body over him, feeling him glide through her body, almost all the way out before filling her completely again and again.

He felt so good inside her. So very, *very* good. Exquisite. Beautiful.

She ground against him, rubbing that sensitive nub above her entrance over him. The orgasm curled within her, tightening her muscles, condensing in a fiery ball at her core. She drew in, her muscles growing taut, her channel growing slick and hot and tight over Sam.

His fingers dug into the flesh of her bottom and her breast, and the pleasure-pain of his grip only added fuel to the fire.

And then she exploded, the ball of heat inside her fragmenting into fiery sparks that shot through her every limb. She slammed down over him, drawing him in deep. He held her tight against him as she pulsed and shuddered, gasping with the intensity of her release.

As the spasms ebbed, she sank over him. He was still wedged deep inside her, and he moved gently, causing sensation to rocket through her with every small motion of his body.

She moaned out loud before she could stop it. She was very sensitive now, so soon after such a powerful orgasm.

He gripped her tightly, both his hands sliding up her back over the fabric of her chemise and pressing her body against him. He rotated his hips, digging his cock wholly, deeply inside her, and she shuddered, burying her face against his neck, breathing him in.

He held her like that, locked against him, his movements starting slow and then increasing in intensity until he was thrusting upward, spearing into her, filling her so completely she began that rise to orgasm once more.

She began to move with him, matching his pace and his thrusts until a second orgasm washed over her, sweet and sharp, her body squeezing him, holding on to him as if she'd never let him go.

And then he came, too, with a low moan, pushing up into her, locked against her. He pulsed inside her tight heat, and they were both so slick and hot, it was like the sweetest inferno overcame them both, encapsulating them in white-hot pleasure.

She buried himself in the warmth of his neck, and as the residual spasms racked her body, she whispered, "I love you, my Sam. I love you so very much."

*   *   *

It was just past noon the next day when they rode into Kendal—Sam, Élise, and his mother riding in Sam's cart while Lowell drove the second just behind them.

Sam stopped in the yard of the Crown Inn and spent a few moments assisting the hostlers with the carts and horses. When he finally went inside and asked for Mark, Theo, and Esme, the innkeeper said they weren't in.

"Do you know where they've gone?" Sam asked.

"Not at all, sir." The man eyed his mother and Lowell up and down with a slight curve of disgust to his lip.

"Do they plan to return this evening?"

The man's gaze jerked back to Sam. "Oh yes. I assumed they'd be back by nightfall. The gentlemen are always in for dinner."

Sam nodded. "I would like to reserve two additional rooms for tonight, please."

The man's eyes flickered once again to his mother and Lowell, lingering on the duchess's feet. Sam had noticed that she hadn't worn shoes once. It was so odd—he tried to recall ever seeing her barefooted in the past, and he couldn't remember one instance.

The innkeeper leaned forward. "A room for you and the lady"—he gestured to Élise, who was standing beside Sam—"of course. But I am afraid we do not cater to their sort here."

Élise, who'd had her hand on his arm, squeezed hard, but it took a moment—a long moment—for Sam to register what the man was saying. When he finally understood, he gaped at the man in disbelief. Did he know he was talking about the Dowager Duchess of Trent?

He opened his mouth to say just that, but his mother hurried up to him. "Sam," she said warningly, placing her hand on his shoulder.

Sam blinked through the red haze tingeing his vision.

"You mustn't say a word," she said soothingly. "It is all right. Steven and I will make camp somewhere outside town. It is how we prefer it."

If not for the last few words, Sam would have said something—would have made that self-righteous innkeeper eat his words. But she was right—this was the life she had left, because evidently, she did prefer sleeping outside.

"It is how I prefer it, too," Élise murmured beside him.

He turned cold eyes on the innkeeper.

"Never mind," he said, his voice chilly. "We will obtain different lodgings." Superior ones, according to his three traveling companions. "We will wait outside until my brothers and sister arrive."

The innkeeper turned away without saying another word, and the four of them returned outside.

Lowell gazed at him, and his voice was low when he spoke. "I see the anger on your face, boy. But don't you see? This is exactly what your mother *didn't* want for you. It is what she wished to protect you from."

Sam looked away from him. He recognized the truth in what Lowell said, but still . . . it wasn't enough.

He leaned back against the brick siding of the inn and crossed his arms over his chest, prepared to wait for his siblings.

His mother gave a hearty sigh. "We will need to set up a camp outside town."

Sam nodded. "Go ahead. Élise and I will wait here."

"We will be back."

"Try to be quick about it. They could return at any time."

His mother nodded and hurried over to Lowell, who was retrieving the horses. Sam noticed the hostler hadn't even unhitched Lowell's horses.

Something clenched within him.

This wasn't new to him. He knew how society refused to accept people's differences. But this was his *mother*. And his father.

He watched them drive away, feeling his shoulders deflate a bit when they turned a corner and disappeared from sight.

Élise stood beside him in silence. And he realized she'd had to endure a bit of that, too. Not to the extent of the gypsies, but she was still different, still considered an outsider. She was French, and France was currently England's most hated enemy.

Even so, the British and French had a long-standing, complex relationship, and while she was an enemy, there was something familiar about her to any given British person. She wore the same fashions. She looked very similar to an English lady. She was an aristocrat, through and through.

Sam closed his eyes.

Beside him, Élise said in a low but vehement tone, "That man was hateful."

Sam nodded.

"But very many people will treat them that way, I am afraid."

"Yes."

"It is her choice," Élise mused. "I often hated my life as Lady Dunthorpe, and I do like sleeping under the stars when the weather is fair and the air is balmy. But abandoning the modern conveniences forever? I do not think I could do it."

"Neither could I." Sam had been absent from those conveniences enough to appreciate wholeheartedly a soft bed and a warm hearth whenever he returned to them.

"There. Then it is a fact," Élise announced. "Your mother is a singularly special person."

Sam slanted her a glance, feeling a smile curve the corner of his lips. "You know . . . you're right about that, love. She always has been different. Special."

She nodded in agreement and slipped her hand into his.

*   *   *

Élise and Sam stood outside the inn until Élise's feet started to ache and darkness began to draw its veil across the sky. Mr. Lowell and the duchess had returned at midafternoon, parking their cart in the innyard even though that hostler—who was as awful as the innkeeper—kept shooting them nasty glances.

The duchess had brought them a supper of cold potatoes, corn cakes, and dried beef, and Sam bought them
each an orange from a street hawker.

And they waited.

It was nearing eight o'clock when a man rounded the
street bend on horseback, traveling dangerously fast.

He halted the horse abruptly and the animal reared
back slightly, but the man held on. Then he slipped off
and called for the hostler without sparing a glance at the
party of four loitering in the eaves.

Sam stepped forward. "Theo?"

The man whipped around to face Sam. He was young,
tall, and handsome but with a serious face. He had dark
eyes and dark hair, but he looked nothing like Sam. His
eyes were lighter, as was his hair. His build was slighter,
his face narrower, and his complexion didn't contain any
of the olive shades of Sam's.

"Sam, is that you?" There was a desperate edge to
his voice as he strode toward Sam. "Thank God! Esme
is—" He broke off suddenly as his eyes came to rest on
his mother. "Mama?" he gasped out. He blinked several
times as if not quite believing his eyes. "Mama?" he repeated.

The duchess blinked, too, but Élise knew she was
blinking to hold back tears. "Oh, Theo. You do not hate
me?"

"Hate you?" The poor man sounded utterly confused.
He looked at the duchess with unfocused eyes. "Mama, is
that really you?"

And then, much as she had done with Sam, the older
woman threw herself at her son—it clearly was of no con-
sequence that he wasn't her son by blood—and began to

sob. Sam and Mr. Lowell gathered around her as if to protect her, and all three men soothed the older woman as Élise stood back and watched, her heart melting.

The duchess was surrounded by men who loved her. This was a family. It reminded her of her own family, so long ago, before the Revolution and before the guillotine...

They all seemed to be talking at once.

"Are you all right, Mama?"

"Where are Esme and Mark?"

"Why don't you have shoes?"

"Can you ever forgive me, darling Theo?"

"Wait." Theo pulled back from his mother but cradled her hand in his and kissed it. "I am so glad Sam found you. I want to know everything. We all do."

Both the duchess and Sam stared at him, and Élise could see Sam's spine stiffening.

Something was wrong, she realized. Sam sensed it from the way his brother was speaking.

"But it can't be now," Theo continued. "It's going to have to wait."

"Why?" Sam asked. "What has happened?"

Theo gazed at Sam, and deep grooves appeared in his brow.

"Esme is missing. She disappeared from her bed four nights ago. We believe she was kidnapped."

Chapter Twenty-Two

Élise watched how Sam changed after that. He turned into a brusque, efficient leader of men. So hard and commanding, no one dared to disobey him.

Theo described how Esme had been taken from her room early in the morning before her maid had come to wake her. To them, it was clear she'd been kidnapped because she hadn't taken her notebook with her, and according to Theo, she took her notebook *everywhere*.

Currently, Mark was out searching the countryside. Had been all day, though Theo expected him back as soon as he grew too tired to continue. They'd already sent word to the duke, who had evidently gone to Ironwood Park for a brief holiday, and they expected him to arrive late tonight or early tomorrow. As when the duchess had disappeared, they hadn't enlisted the help of the authorities, although Mark planned to go to a constable if the duke didn't arrive by tomorrow.

Sam glanced her way, and their eyes locked.

"Dunthorpe?" Élise mouthed. Certainly Adams held enough respect for Sam and for his family that he wouldn't stoop so low. Dunthorpe, on the other hand, would possess no such qualms.

Sam gave a short nod.

Their interaction caused Theo's eyes to fall on her for the first time, and hasty introductions were made, to both her and to Mr. Lowell. The suspicious look Theo gave the older man did not escape Élise's notice. Of course, he didn't know the duchess and Steven Lowell's story yet.

After the introductions, Sam turned back to his brother. "Theo, I know who took Esme—"

"Who?" at least two voices cried out.

"Here on the street is not the place to discuss it."

"We will go into the inn."

"No," Sam said. "Our mother and Lowell aren't welcome here."

Theo turned wide eyes on the older couple. "But—"

"Come to our camp," Lowell interrupted mildly. "It is close, and outside of hearing range of anyone in town."

"Thank you," Sam said, but he looked warily around them, searching, no doubt, for one of Dunthorpe's men who might be watching.

Élise's breath caught. Dunthorpe would be a fool not to post men in town. They'd probably been watched all afternoon. The thought of it sent a cold shiver up her spine.

Fifteen minutes later, they had all gathered around a fire pit in which Mr. Lowell was patiently fanning the flames. Sam had brought two boys from town, both of whom he'd hired to watch the area surrounding the clearing and notify him right away if they were pursued here.

All of them were seated except the dowager, who was pacing the clearing restlessly, and Sam, who stood in front of the fire.

Sam didn't waste any more time. He met each of their gazes, one by one. "I have a plan. As I said, I know who took Esme."

"Who?" his mother asked again, an edge of panic in her voice.

Sam sighed. "Please sit down, Mama. To make a very long story short, the new Lord Dunthorpe has kidnapped Esme to get to me. The bastard is using *my sister* to get to me." Rage bristled in his voice, so sharp that it abraded something in Élise's chest.

And it didn't escape her that he didn't make her a part of his story. But she was—she was deeply mired in it. In fact, Dunthorpe had probably used Lady Esme more to get to her than to Sam.

She wrapped her arms around her body to contain the roiling feelings of anger and fear.

Theo's lips flattened to a tight white line. "How can we find him?"

Sam glanced at Élise. "If I am correct, and he's using Esme as bait . . . I know exactly where he is."

Élise nodded. Yes. Dunthorpe would take Esme to the cottage. It was the most obvious place if he wished to draw Sam and Élise to him.

His mother held up a hand. "Wait. Would this man hurt my dear Esme?" Her voice pitched higher. "Would he hurt you? Does he . . . does he intend to kill you?"

"I can answer your last two questions," Sam said. "Yes and yes. He intends to kill me; that is for certain. But"— he gave his mother a grim look—"I won't let him."

"And...Esme?" his mother asked weakly.

Sam looked to Élise. And when he did so, everyone else turned to look at her as well. She thought hard about Francis, about how low he really would stoop in order to get to her and Sam.

"I would say no," she said finally. "I don't believe he would hurt an innocent lady. But..." She gnawed on her lip for a second, then looked up at Sam. "There is a madness in him, Sam. Similar to...to my husband's madness, but more unstable. He knows what is right and what is wrong, but at times it's as if he ceases to care."

Sam rose to his feet. "I'm going to get her back." He turned to Theo. "Did you bring your pistol?"

Theo nodded. "Mark and I both have one. We brought them"—he glanced at Mr. Lowell and his cheeks grew rosy in the firelight—"er...in the event we needed them."

"Good." Sam turned to Mr. Lowell, but before he could say anything, the older man rose, too.

"I would come with you," he said gruffly. "But someone needs to remain with the ladies, so I will stay here. I've a pistol, too, if it comes to that."

Sam stared at him for a minute, then nodded. "You will remain out here with my mother. I don't think we were followed, but you can never be too careful. Don't sleep until I return." He turned to Theo. "Return to the inn with Lady Dunthorpe to await Mark and Trent. I hope to be back by the time either of them arrive, but..."

He let that final word hang, but Theo nodded. "I understand. But you will need help—"

Sam shook his head. "I won't involve you unless there is no other option." He turned to Élise. "If I don't return, you will need to guide them to the correct place. You know where he has taken her?"

Élise nodded. She knew the cottage on the lake very well. She also knew the exact route to take from Kendal.

Sam held out his hand to Élise. "Walk with me a moment."

She took his hand, and he pulled her up.

He nodded briskly to his family. "We'll get her back," he told them solemnly.

He led Élise to the clearing where the horses were grazing. She watched in silence as he saddled one of them, her heart hammering.

How many men did Dunthorpe have? He'd have Edmund with him, surely, but how many others? Sam would be completely outnumbered. How could he possibly have a chance?

He cinched the belt beneath the horse and turned to her.

"Sam," she choked out. She went into his welcoming arms, and they folded around her, strong and large, offering some reassurance. But she didn't like the look in his eyes. He was going to rescue his sister at all costs. *All* costs.

"Take Theo with you," she begged. "I can wait for the duke and Lord Mark alone. Please."

She felt him shake his head. She squeezed her eyes shut and pressed her face into his chest.

"Listen to me, Élise. If I don't return—"

She made a choked noise, but he continued in a steady voice. "I'll take care of Dunthorpe. You won't need to worry about him. But Adams still has the order on you. Speak to Trent. My mother knows what you are to me, and she will tell him. Trent will help you. He'll find a way for you to change your identity. Or a place for you to go—"

"Nooo," she groaned. She couldn't think this way. Of hiding from this Adams while Sam no longer existed in this world. She drew back from him, wrapped her hands behind his neck, and pulled him down to her. She kissed him hard on the lips. "You will come back to me. Do you hear me, Samson Hawkins? No more of this talk. Do you understand?"

"Élise, you must—"

"*Non!*" she said firmly. "I will listen to no more of this. You will fetch your sister, and all will be well. You need to survive, because without you..." Suddenly her chest seemed to collapse in on itself, and the next words were so painful she almost couldn't push them out. "Because...without you I...I am nothing."

"Élise." He groaned softly. His lips pressed against the top of her head.

"Bring your sister home to us," she murmured. "That is your only choice, Sam. Your only choice."

* * *

Two hours later, Sam dismounted a half mile away from the cottage. He secured his mount a good distance from the road and then wound through the forest.

Finally, through the trees and brush, the cottage came into view. The moon was completely full tonight, and the sky clear, which was both a blessing and a curse. A blessing because he'd be able to see danger coming. A curse because danger would be more easily able to see *him* coming.

Sam withdrew the pistol from his coat and checked the chamber. Then he did the same with the smaller gun tucked into his boot. He'd have two shots. It was doubtful they'd give him time to reload. Two shots and then his fists against an unknown number of men.

He tucked away the smaller gun and straightened, gazing at the cottage. No lights glowed in the windows. All was quiet.

Too quiet, he thought. He crouched down in an opening between two bushes, where he could get a good view of the land surrounding the cottage.

He scanned for several minutes. Patient, as his training dictated. And then there it was...a movement in the trees on the south side of the drive. His breath released in a long, low hiss.

He'd been right. Dunthorpe was here, lying in wait for him. A man had been placed on watch—in a good location, with a view of not only the cottage and the surrounding clearing, but also of the long drive leading to it.

Sam felt the familiar calm coldness wash over him. Calmer and colder than usual, for this wasn't obeying an order. It was for his family. For himself. For Élise. And for Esme. These men were holding his sister, possibly abusing her. Hurting her.

He'd kill them all.

He fell back into the forest, retreating to the first bend in the packed-dirt drive, where he crossed in a crouch. The lookout wouldn't see him from here. He approached on silent, well-trained feet. He was a large man, but he was adept at being invisible when the occasion demanded it.

He approached the lookout from behind. The man was

a fool. He didn't look in Sam's direction; nor did he hear him coming. Sam scanned the environs, made his decision.

He came at the lookout from behind, leaping on him, covering his mouth with a solid palm. Taken completely by surprise, the man grunted as Sam twisted his body and rammed his head into the solid trunk of the oak he'd been leaning against. He immediately slumped into unconsciousness.

Sam searched him, found a gun, which he took. He'd have three shots now.

One man down. How many more? From his new perspective, Sam studied the cottage and its surroundings. No movement, but that didn't mean there wasn't anyone there.

He needed to get to the cottage, but he'd be completely visible by the light of the moon as he crossed the lawn. There was no escaping it, though. He'd chosen this cottage as a safe house because its prospect was not only private but allowed for excellent visibility for someone defending it. However, in this case, Sam wasn't there to defend his castle, but to raid it.

He couldn't remain out here forever. Certainly not until morning when everyone would be awake and more eyes would be watching and waiting for him. This needed to happen now. He checked the lookout again. He was breathing but deeply unconscious. It would be a while before he woke.

He held the man's gun at his side, ready.

Then he took a deep breath and sprinted for the cottage door.

* * *

Theo and Élise returned to the Crown Inn, where Theo asked the innkeeper to send anyone who came to see them upstairs immediately. They ignored the man's curious stare as they went upstairs to the suite of rooms the siblings had procured. There were three bedrooms and a connecting sitting room, where Theo and Élise made themselves comfortable, preparing for a long wait.

The place was lavishly decorated—it was obvious that travelers from the upper orders visited this place frequently. A marble fireplace trimmed with gilt adorned the sitting room. The sofas and chairs featured carved oak armrests and upholstery of the finest light yellow silk.

Theo was silent and broody at first, obviously shocked about finding his mother, concerned about his sister, and wary about Élise.

She was quiet, too. She was too worried about Sam to attempt small talk with his brother. But eventually Theo ordered dinner sent up, along with a bottle of wine. A full glass of the stuff seemed to lubricate Élise's voice. She gazed at the young man sitting before her. The poor boy had hardly touched his food and kept glancing at the door as if expecting one of his brothers to throw it open at any second.

"They'll be here soon," she said in a soothing voice.

"Right," Theo said. "If the waiting doesn't drive me mad first."

"You should eat, my lord. You will need your strength."

He looked down at his food, his lips twisting, then back up to her. He stared at her for a long moment, and

Élise recalled what Sam had told her about his youngest brother. He was the studious one. Academic, always with his head in books of chemistry and mathematics. He was intelligent and thoughtful, and the closest of all of them, not only in age but in spirit, to Esme.

"I cannot eat." With a sigh, he laid down his fork, giving up on the roast of beef on its bed of vegetables, which had surely grown cold and soggy by now. Élise glanced down at her own plate. She had done far better than him, for which she was proud, as she'd had to go searching for her appetite when the food had arrived.

"You're worried about your sister," she said.

"Yes. And Sam."

She closed her eyes briefly. She was desperately worried about Sam, but she said, "He knows what he is doing."

Theo leaned forward, curiosity emerging from behind his frown. "You know what Sam does, then? Exactly what he does?"

She didn't want to give away Sam's secrets, but she didn't want to lie to any of his family members, either. "Yes."

"What does he do?"

She shook her head. "I cannot say."

Theo's eyes narrowed. "How, exactly, do you know my brother, Lady Dunthorpe?"

She wondered at the possessive way he spoke of Sam. He was the son of the old Duke of Trent by his mistress, while Sam was the son of the Duchess of Trent and Steven Lowell. The two weren't related by blood.

Though there was a seven-year age difference between Sam and Theo, they had been raised together in the same house, by the dowager duchess. Having met the woman who'd raised these men, she supposed she shouldn't be surprised by the brothers' loyalty to each other.

She pondered how to answer the youngest Hawkins brother's question. "He killed my husband" would give away too much, certainly, and raise about a million additional questions.

So she kept it as close to the truth as she could without revealing too much. "He"—she hesitated; a few weeks ago, she would have said, *kidnapped me*, but now she realized he'd done something altogether different— "saved me."

Sam had told her she'd brought him back to life, but the truth was, he'd brought *her* back to life.

Tears stung her eyes. She clasped her hands in her lap, struggling to keep them at bay.

"You care about him, don't you?" Theo asked in a low voice.

She couldn't look at him. She couldn't speak, either, because if she did, she'd start to cry.

She didn't cry often…but this…this was different. She felt different. Her feelings were almost too strong to contain. She blinked hard, twisted her hands together, and stared down at them as she nodded.

"Ah, my lady." Suddenly Theo was beside her. He slipped a comforting arm around her shoulders.

How odd that he should comfort her. He had his own worries, for his sister and his brother. And yet here he was, comforting *her*. The outsider.

An errant tear slipped down her cheek, and she wiped it away, frustrated by her weakness. "I am sorry," she said. "Pay no attention to me, if you please."

He squeezed her shoulder. "It is obvious that my brother cares for you. Which means I must pay attention to you. My brother doesn't care easily."

She did cry then. She turned to Theo, and he, the young man with his own overwhelming fears, held her as she wept.

She didn't want to lose Sam.

She *couldn't* lose him.

* * *

Sam reached the stoop of the cottage and turned sharply, intending to flatten his back against the side so he could assess the activity inside. As he rounded, a dark figure flashed in his periphery.

Sam spun around, but it was too late. The man grabbed him around the waist, twisting, trying to tackle Sam to the ground.

Sam resisted, at first stumbling, then planting his feet and regaining his balance. He lifted his gun. But before he could aim, another man pummeled him from behind, slamming Sam against the side wall. His fingers opened involuntarily, and the gun landed on the dirt with a *thunk*.

Sam rounded on his first adversary, landing a hard punch to the man's jaw. The man grunted and swung at Sam, but he ducked away from the blow.

Someone—a third man, he thought—grabbed his arm from behind him, wrenching him back. A body rammed into him, and he fell back, landing so hard on the ground his breath left his body with a whoosh and his lungs seemed to constrict, leaving him gasping for air.

At least four men held him down. A gun pressed hard

against his temple. Sam looked past the black barrel and into the narrow face of Edmund Gherkin, Lord Dunthorpe's solicitor, his skin glowing a ghastly gray in the moonlight.

"Well," Gherkin said in a quiet, deadly calm voice. "Look at what we have here."

* * *

Lord Mark appeared just after midnight, exhausted and disheveled. Theo introduced him to Élise and filled him in on all that had happened.

And then they sent Élise to bed, where she tried to sleep but ended up tossing and turning the night away. Just after dawn, she heard sounds in the sitting room.

Sam!

She rushed out of the bedchamber in her chemise. But it was not Sam who was in the sitting room talking with Mark and Theo. There were two other men there. One was a blond man Élise had never seen before. The other was a handsome green-eyed, sandy-haired man who held authority about him like a cloak. A man she'd met before on two brief occasions.

The Duke of Trent.

His eyes widened when he saw her. He blinked several times, then frowned. "Lady...Lady Dunthorpe? What are you...?"

He'd recognized her.

The man behind him tilted his head in curiosity as his blue eyes scanned her up and down. He turned to Mark and Theo with raised brows.

She blinked, then flushed, remembering her unkempt,

undressed state. She managed a fumbling curtsy, realizing that the brothers had been telling the duke the story of what had happened last night, but they hadn't reached the point where Lady Dunthorpe was sleeping in one of the bedrooms.

"Your Grace. Good morning. I am...so sorry. I was expecting someone else."

"She was expecting Sam," Theo supplied.

The blond man stepped toward her, brows raised in question.

Mark coughed. "This is our brother, Lord Lukas Hawkins."

"Lord Lukas," she murmured with a bow.

"Where did Sam go?" the duke asked Mark and Theo.

"We don't know," Theo said.

"But I do," Élise said softly.

As the four brothers turned to her, she straightened her spine, determination rushing through her. Now was the time to be strong.

"I will take you to Sam and to Lady Esme."

Theo started to speak. "My lady, you should remain—"

She raised her hand to stop him midsentence. "No," she said quietly. "I will show you where he is. But I *must* go with you."

Chapter Twenty-Three

❦

Cool, moist air sent shivers of trepidation down Élise's spine. A watery morning sun dueled with a thick layer of clouds, struggling to shed its warmth and light over the landscape. It was the first overcast day since she'd been ill, Élise realized.

They rode in a carriage most of the way to the cottage, but when they reached a tree she recognized as being about a half mile away, she rapped on the ceiling of the carriage, giving Lord Lukas, who was driving, the signal to stop.

He pulled to the side of the road, and they all disembarked. No sooner had they huddled together at the side of the carriage than Luke's head shot up. His eyes narrowed toward the tree line, and his jaw tensed. "There's something out there. I'll be right back."

Before any of them could move, he'd sprinted into the trees. He emerged a few moments later leading Sam's horse. Sam had had the same idea as Élise, leaving the horse out here and walking the rest of the way to the cottage.

She looked from man to man. Their leader was clearly Trent. He was confident and sure, but he was a politician, not a warrior. Not like Sam.

A flutter of trepidation shot through her, but she thrust it away. These four men might not be warriors, but they were Esme and Sam's brothers. And she'd learned enough about them in the last eighteen hours to know, without a doubt, that they'd give anything to save their siblings. They were loyal and caring men, and she understood exactly why Sam was proud to call them his brothers.

They huddled together on the side of the quiet, abandoned road while Élise described the layout of the cottage and the surrounding lands.

When she'd finished, the duke assigned everyone their duties. Theo and Mark were to deal with any guards or men outside the cottage, covering Luke and Trent as they gained access through the front door.

The two younger brothers would remain outside while Luke and Trent located Sam and Esme inside and freed them.

"What about me?" Élise asked softly.

"You will guard the carriage." Trent's tone brooked no argument.

Élise pressed her lips together, knowing better than to naysay him. These men possessed certain masculine notions about leading a lady into danger. If she argued, they'd only tie her to the carriage.

So she forced herself to grind out, "Very well," and

she actually succeeded in making the words sound rather bland and believable.

She stood by the horses and watched the men, the four of them in a tall, strong line across the road, as they walked toward the cottage.

She'd be devastated if any of them were hurt, she realized. She cared for all of them, because Sam cared for all of them, and because they were good, loyal men.

She bent her head and said a quick prayer.

Then she hurried after them.

*   *   *

Sam attempted to stretch his aching limbs, but his range of motion didn't allow for much, since he'd been trussed to a beam in the cottage's attic.

Esme had been used as bait; now he was being used as bait. And it infuriated him to no end.

He yanked hard on the rope that tied his hands behind him, looping several times around the horizontal beam. He'd been attempting this all night. His wrists had started to ooze with blood from his efforts. It was no use. The knots were too strong.

He glanced over at Esme, who lay curled on the floor, her arms tied in front of her and then to the second beam on the other side of the room. She'd finally fallen asleep a few hours ago, after she and Sam had spent most of the night talking.

They'd kept his sister locked up here in this dismal attic, frightened nearly out of her wits, for four days. Anger surged in him again, but he bit it back.

Noises sounded outside, and Sam raised his head, listening. Men were talking, but he couldn't hear the words, and he couldn't define who was speaking.

The voices grew louder, and suddenly there was a shout.

"Drop your weapon!"

Sam straightened as much as his bonds would allow. Theo and Mark must be outside.

Esme jerked awake with a low cry. She blinked hard to clear away the sleep. Panic suffused her brown eyes as she turned to him and struggled awkwardly to her knees. "What was that?"

He spoke quietly. "Theo's out there, and so is Mark. Probably Trent, too." Maybe even Luke, though he couldn't be sure.

"They've come for us?" Esme asked. "Like you said?"

Sam nodded.

Esme shuddered. "I just want to see Mama. Then I want to go home."

He'd told her the story about their mother in its entirety last night. She'd taken it well, considering she'd believed that she was the legitimate daughter of the Duke of Trent for most of her life. Last summer, she'd been warned that that might not be the case, and Sam knew questions about who she really was had been eating at her.

When he'd told her that they were in fact full siblings, she'd gazed at him with rounded eyes, then told him in a soft voice, "I don't know what to say. To discover I am not who I thought I was..." She shook her head. "At least I am given this, Sam. I am proud to be your sister."

She'd always believed she'd had full siblings, so he knew the fact that they were full-blooded brother and sister hadn't affected her as deeply as it had affected him. He had a mother, a father, a full sister, two half brothers, and in Mark and Theo, two "adopted" brothers. It was as full of a family as he ever could have wished for.

"We'll be home soon," he told her soothingly. "But you're going to need to be strong, Esme."

"Wh-what do you mean?"

He spoke carefully. "They're going to attempt to use us to get what they want. Don't listen to them. Block whatever they might say from your mind. Listen only to me and our brothers. Do you understand?"

"Yes."

He couldn't say anything more because just then the door burst open. A very disheveled Edmund Gherkin strode into the room. The man was thin and short, with pointed features and slick black hair that stuck up at odd angles as if he'd just been yanked from his bed.

He gestured to Esme and spoke to the three men who had entered on his heels. "Untie her and bring her downstairs with us."

"Keep her out of this," Sam growled. "Bring me downstairs instead."

Gherkin gave him a sour look. "Why would I do that?"

"Because you've already used her as bait, haven't you? It's my turn now."

Gherkin's thin lips quirked upward. "You're forgetting something, Hawkins. When given a choice between pretty ladies and snarling giants, the fish is more likely to bite at the pretty lady, wouldn't you agree?"

Sam knew what Gherkin and Dunthorpe wanted. They wanted Élise.

"You're reeling in the wrong fish," he told Gherkin.

"The one you really want isn't here." Because his brothers certainly wouldn't have allowed Élise to stroll into this danger.

"Hm...perhaps you are right. Perhaps we have lured the gudgeon when what we really want is the trout."

"Exactly."

"And how will sending you downstairs instead of the lady help us in our endeavor to ensnare our juicy trout?"

Sam narrowed his eyes. "I know where she is. I can have them bring her to you."

Gherkin threw back his head and laughed. "How stupid do you think I am?"

Actually, Sam didn't think the man was stupid at all. He'd handled ambushing Sam with a finesse he hadn't expected.

"They came for Lady Esme. They came for their sister," Sam pushed out.

"And not for you?"

Sam shrugged. He glanced at Esme to make sure she was all right. Her hands were clenched in fists, and she was looking down, evading eye contact with any of the men. Good.

"They won't leave without her," Sam warned.

"Then, unless they turn over what we want, they'll find themselves sorely disappointed." Gherkin turned back to the men guarding the door. Sam recognized the man he'd knocked out last night. He glowered at Sam, his blue eyes shining with hate. This one would be dangerous.

Gherkin gestured to him. "You, Jack, take the girl. The rest of you, bring the man. Be careful," he added wryly. "He bites."

Still glaring at Sam, Jack stomped over to Esme. Sam

released a relieved breath, glad Gherkin had decided to bring him downstairs. He sure as *hell* didn't want to be trussed up here and helpless while his brothers fought for their lives with his sister possibly caught in the crossfire.

He tried not to prove Gherkin correct and moved as docilely as a trained pup as they untied him from the beam and led him and Esme downstairs.

At the bottom of the first flight of stairs, Gherkin disappeared into a room halfway down the short corridor. Dunthorpe was hiding there but too much of a coward to show his face. Sam was sure of it.

He let Gherkin's men guide him down the second flight of stairs as he considered his enemy. Gherkin and Dunthorpe, plus three additional men. Possibly others.

They pushed Sam into the salon, where another man stood with a gun trained on Trent and Luke. Neither of his brothers held a gun—they had probably been stripped of all weapons before entering the house.

Damn it. Six men—at *least* six—with weapons versus three without. Not good odds.

But Mark and Theo must still be outside, and as far as Sam knew, they were still in possession of their weapons. Five against six evened the odds a bit more.

Sam and his brothers exchanged slight nods of greeting before Trent and Luke turned to Esme. They both appeared serious and grim as they studied their sister, searching for any sign of injury. But she held her spine straight and her head high.

"Are you all right?" Trent asked her softly.

She nodded.

Several minutes passed before Gherkin joined them.

During that time, the men stood crowded in tense silence in the small room. Trent and Luke stood beside the fireplace, with the man standing in front of it pointing the gun at them. Esme was to the right of the door with Jack, and Sam and the two other men were to the left of the door, adjacent to the sofa.

Sam spent those minutes alternating between strategizing and attempting to listen to the muffled conversation upstairs.

"No!" someone cried. Dunthorpe, if the whiny voice was any indication.

"It's imperative that we…" The rest of the sentence was muddled, but another whine from Dunthorpe cut it off halfway through.

He wondered if Dunthorpe and Gherkin were aware of how obvious it was that they were quarreling. Perhaps they didn't care.

Eventually, Sam heard the stomp of boots, and then Gherkin appeared in the doorway. He reminded Sam of a rat, small but strong. And wily.

He gazed at Trent and Luke, then turned to Sam. "You know what we want."

Trent raised a brow. "I have no idea what you want, what you expect, or what game you're playing, but I know what I want. I want you to release my brother and sister. Immediately."

Gherkin sneered. He gestured to Sam but kept his slitted eyes on Trent. "What? Your bastard brother didn't fill you in on the game? It's a fishing game. I throw out the bait; then I reel in my fish."

Trent crossed his arms over his chest, looking bored. "Well, you've reeled us in. You win, sir. Now let them go."

Gherkin rolled his eyes heavenward. "Gad, you aristocrats are so dense. I don't know why I am surprised. I thought you'd be a little quicker than this, Trent."

"What the hell do you want?" Luke's hands clenched into fists at his sides, and his blue eyes were snapping sparks as he took a step toward Gherkin.

Gherkin gave Luke an assessing glance. "The infamous Lord Lukas, is it? What I want, my lord, is Lady Dunthorpe."

Luke's face went blank. He looked at Trent. "Lady…Dunthorpe? Who the hell is that?"

Trent shrugged. "Wife of Lord Dunthorpe, the viscount who was murdered last month in London. Though I can't imagine how we'd have anything to do with her whereabouts." He turned to Gherkin. "I believe she's in London. I heard she was there the night Dunthorpe was murdered."

Their act was so well performed, Sam was almost convinced they didn't know anything about Élise. But that couldn't be true. She'd been with Theo. Luke and Trent must know exactly where she was.

"You don't know her? Really?" Gherkin slid Sam a look. "Why don't you ask your brother?"

Sam kept his face completely placid as Trent and Luke gave him expectant looks. Lying about Élise wouldn't get him anywhere. Neither would revealing anything.

"Your brother and the lady were in league. They killed Viscount Dunthorpe, then ran away, to this cottage, in fact. When they learned we were after them, they swam away yet again, like frightened little gudgeons." Gherkin made a fluttering motion with his fingers. "So you see, all we seek is justice. We'll take your bastard brother and we'll take Lady Dunthorpe. We'll ensure justice is served; then the rest of you can be on your way."

Luke gave a disbelieving snort. "If you think we're going to leave Sam in your hands, you're insane."

But Trent gazed at Sam, a clear question in his eyes. Sam nodded slightly. *Yes. Do it. Play along.*

Trent laid a hand on Luke's arm. "If we give you information, will you release our sister?"

"Not just information, Your Grace. You will need to procure Lady Dunthorpe. A viperous French bitch for a lovely, sweet, young Englishwoman. I have grown to know your sister these past few days—"

Luke gave a warning growl, and Gherkin shrugged. "Anyhow, it is more than a fair trade."

A muscle in Trent's jaw moved. "Release my sister, and I'll tell you where you can locate Lady Dunthorpe."

"I have a better idea. You bring the French whore to me, we'll make the exchange, and that'll be that."

Trent's eyes flickered toward Sam, and Sam moved his head slightly in the semblance of a nod.

Trent threw back his shoulders. "Very well." Luke gaped at him, but Trent ignored him. "She's down the road a piece."

"Trent!" Luke spit out, shocked that Trent would agree to these terms and completely unaware of the byplay that had been happening between his two older brothers.

Trent ignored Luke's protest.

Gherkin nodded. "Good. Let's go." He gestured to the man holding the gun on Trent and Luke. "Shoot them if they try anything."

The man nodded grimly.

Sam was glad they'd be leaving the house. More space

out on the grounds to fight. Not to mention Theo and Mark were certainly somewhere outside with weapons, and they'd be able to help.

Gherkin turned to the men holding Sam; then he met Sam's gaze, giving that spine-chillingly bland grin. "You'll stay here. No need for you to come, after all. Is there, Hawkins?"

Sam stepped toward him, a deep scowl forming on his face. "If you hurt her—" But one of the men held the tail of the rope wrapped around his wrists, and he jerked back hard. A spasm of pain shot through Sam's shoulders. He fell backward, twisting his body as best as he could to break the fall. He leaned up on his shoulder just as the man holding the gun on Trent and Luke exited the room.

"No!" Sam shouted. But it was too late. They'd gone after Élise.

*   *   *

Élise had watched Trent and Luke "surrender" while Mark and Theo remained hidden in the shadows. After the guards had ushered the two older brothers inside, Mark and Theo had rushed across the clearing. She'd held back until they'd settled against the wall of the cottage; then she'd darted after them.

She'd turned the corner, and she must've been difficult to see with the way the dim morning light shone through the trees, haloing her body. But the gun barrel had glinted in the light of dawn as Theo had instinctively raised his arm to point it at her, and she'd heard the click as he'd cocked it. But Mark, bless him, had recognized her and nearly tackled his brother to the ground while hissing out, "It's Lady Dunthorpe, you idiot!"

Since then, Mark had kept close by her side, seeming resigned to her presence. Of course, initiating an argument in their current position wouldn't be wise.

Now she held her body flat against the outside wall of the cottage. Beside her, Mark stood stock-still. Neither of them wanted to draw the attention of the party emerging from the front door.

Throughout the entire exchange between Edmund Gherkin and the brothers, Élise had been crouching in the bushes, peeking into the salon window. From there, she could hear just about everything that was said, and she could see Edmund through the tiny crack in the curtains.

The sounds of footsteps retreated quickly as Edmund, his men, Esme, Trent, and Luke marched down the drive. Élise turned to Mark. "We need to get Sam," she whispered.

He nodded. "Back door?"

"Yes." She hoped it wasn't locked.

They inched around to the back of the house, where Theo waited. "We're going in to get Sam," Mark told him in a low voice.

Theo nodded, but his brown eyes were large in the dimness. "How many men?"

"Two men guard him." Élise was trembling all over, but a sort of peace had come over her, quelling the shaking to a manageable tremor. There was a time for fear, but now was the time for action. She could give in to the fear later.

She didn't look at the brothers; instead she gazed down

the bank and out over Lake Windermere, which sat placid and gray under the overcast sky. She let its calmness infuse her. "But there might be more men in other parts of the cottage. We will need to be very careful."

Pressing his lips together, Theo nodded. He was just as frightened as she was. Perhaps more. She had been in a few terrifying situations recently . . . but had he? Probably not.

"Stay here," Mark growled.

She blinked at him. "Really?" At this point, he had to be joking.

"Really. Sam will kill me himself if he discovers I brought you into such danger," he said.

Élise pressed her lips together. Mark was right, and she didn't want Sam to be angry with them. This was her choice, not theirs.

And maybe it was for the best if she remained right here for now. If whoever was in the cottage didn't know of her proximity, that was to everyone's benefit.

She sighed. "Very well. I will await you here; then we'll go help Esme and the others."

Mark gave a tight nod. Theo tried the handle, and the door opened easily. Dunthorpe and Gherkin had probably thought there was no need to guard the back door, since there was no real access to it unless you passed by the front of the cottage first.

As soon as Mark and Theo disappeared inside, closing the door quietly behind them, Élise tiptoed back around to the salon window. She wedged herself into the bushes, crouched down beneath it, then gripped the sill and pulled herself up just enough to see inside.

She could see a sliver of one of the guards, arms crossed over his chest and a smug look on his face.

There were several seconds of still silence; then the door banged open. The guard spun around, then lurched forward, as if someone had kicked his knees out from under him. It must have been Sam.

And then a gun fired. Élise's entire body jolted. It was so loud, it seemed to explode within her head. She jerked to her feet, uncaring if anyone saw her. "Sam!" she cried softly. Had he been shot? Had the other guard killed him?

She hesitated for scant seconds, resisting the urge to punch through the glass pane with her fist, trying to parse out all the emotions and thoughts and fears flowing through her head and sort out what she needed to do—how she could help.

Theo rushed into her line of sight. He bent down and then rose, Sam coming up along with him. He stood tall while Theo undid his bonds.

He wasn't injured. Praise God. Élise pressed her forehead against the glass pane, the relief washing over her weakening muscles.

"Hurry," Sam told Theo. He looked over his shoulder. "Is that one down?"

"Yes," Mark said. "He's unconscious, at least."

"This one's dead," Theo said, his voice strained. "I got him in the heart, didn't I, Sam?"

Untied, Sam turned and put his hands on his youngest brother's shoulders. "You did well, Theo. Do you have more ammunition?"

He crouched down, evidently searching for one of the fallen guard's weapons. But Élise spun about at the sound of rapid footsteps approaching.

It was Trent, followed closely by Edmund, who was

pressing a gun into the duke's back. They were followed by Esme, with her hands tied in front of her, and the guard who had been with her all along, and Luke and another man, who held a gun trained on him.

They were coming to investigate the gunshot.

"Kill him!" a high voice screeched from inside the house. "Trent knows too much! You must kill him!"

Élise's blood ran cold. She recognized that voice. Francis, mad with his own cowardice.

Edmund and Trent were just a few feet away from her. They hadn't seen her yet, but she saw them clear as day. Her vision homed in on the weapon pressed to Trent's back.

Edmund always followed orders. That was why her husband had trusted him. And he was going to follow orders now. Élise saw it in the thinning of his lips, the narrowing of his eyes, the slight movement of his fingers on the weapon—

"No!" she screamed. She lunged forward. Edmund turned, surprised, just as she leapt upon him. Thrown off balance, he crashed to the rocky path with Élise on top of him.

He bucked, throwing her off. She landed on the grass with such force the breath was knocked from her lungs. When she looked up, dazed, she saw that the duke had pinned Edmund to the ground. Everyone was shouting. Screaming. Grunts and the dull smack of flesh on flesh as punches were thrown. Sam, Mark, and Theo burst out of the cottage and joined the melee.

She heard Francis's reedy scream and scrambling footsteps inside the cottage. Was he trying to escape? But there was nowhere for him to go.

And then, above all the other noises, there was an ominous *click*.

Everyone paused, turning toward the sound. The man standing with Esme gripped her arm tight. He held a gun to her temple. She stood frozen, literally scared stiff, her face an unearthly white—even her lips were pale. Her eyes were huge, dark pools in her face.

"Jack!" Sam snapped. He'd run past Trent, who had subdued Edmund, and stood on the path halfway to Esme. "Let her go. She's done nothing to you."

"Aye, but ye have, guv." He rubbed at a spot above his forehead.

"I was only trying to help my sister. Do you have a sister, Jack?" Sam took a slow step toward them, his voice calm and level.

"What's it matter?" Jack bit out.

"You love your sister, don't you? Just like I love mine." Jack spat on the path.

"Kill her, and you're taking my only sister from me," Sam said quietly. "You know I will never let you survive."

Jack shifted uncomfortably.

"It won't be an easy death," Sam continued in that low, deadly voice. "I'd make you suffer. I'd extend your hell on earth for as long as possible before you die."

Jack's light blue gaze shifted between Sam and Edmund, who lay motionless on his back. Trent's knee was dug into his solar plexus and a thin line of blood streamed from his mouth.

"And if I don't kill 'er?"

"Your fate will be much more tolerable," Sam said simply.

Keeping his eyes on Sam, Jack began to lower the gun.

But Sam moved so fast, he was a blur. Esme stumbled back, and Sam and Jack slammed to the ground. It took no more than a second for Sam to wrestle the gun from the other man. And then the butt of it crashed against Jack's head, in the same location he'd rubbed seconds ago. Immediately, he went limp. Sam leapt to his feet, still holding the gun.

His gaze assessed the situation quickly. Mark had done something to the guard who'd had the gun on him—he was holding his stomach and groaning. Jack was unconscious. Edmund was alive but pinned flat on his back by Trent.

And none of the Hawkinses had been hurt. Élise nearly sobbed with relief. The *bon Dieu* had been on their side this day.

Esme stood on the grass near Élise, sobbing quietly into her bound hands. On shaky legs, Élise rose and went to her, first undoing her bonds with trembling fingers, then taking the taller woman into her arms and patting her back, murmuring, "There, there. It's over now, my lady."

But it wasn't. Francis, the new Lord Dunthorpe, was still inside.

Sam realized this at the same time she did, it seemed. His gaze arrowed in on the cottage's doorway even as he strode toward it. Without another word, he disappeared inside.

Theo looked at Trent with questioning eyes, and Trent nodded. "Go. He might need your help."

Theo disappeared next, and the rest of them waited. Élise couldn't take her eyes off the door. Her heart was starting to pound, fear overtaking the mask of calmness that had settled over it earlier. What if Francis was lying in wait for Sam? What if...?

Boom!

The shot rattled the eaves of the cottage, and nearby, a flock of sandpipers soared into the air, startled from the water's edge and screeching their displeasure.

And then all was silent once more.

*   *   *

Sam emerged from the cottage's front door, Theo at his heels. His gaze scanned the people scattered about on the lawn, searching for Élise.

She stood beside Esme. As soon as their eyes met, her legs seemed to give out from under her. She sank to her knees, her shoulders heaving.

Sam sprinted to her. Kneeling down, he gathered her in his arms and held her close. "Shh, my love. All is well. All is well... Shh."

It took some time, but finally he managed to soothe her enough that she pulled back. Her beautiful face was tear streaked. Her eyes were rimmed with red.

He'd seen what she'd done. She'd tackled Gherkin to save Trent. That took no small measure of bravery. Pride and love surged through him, and right there, in front of all his siblings, he pressed a gentle kiss to her lips.

"Wha—what happened?" she whispered. "Where is Francis?"

"He was upstairs. When he knew there would be no escape, he killed himself. Shot himself in the head."

"*Mon Dieu*," she whispered. She slumped against him, her body shuddering violently.

He held her and comforted her as his brothers moved around them, securing the four of Dunthorpe's men who still lived. Theo comforted Esme, who was crying quietly. Mark fetched the carriage and Sam's mount while Luke went to the stables, where he found another carriage and two more horses.

A few hours later, they arrived back in Kendal. Sam and Theo spent another good hour speaking with the constables while their brothers, eager to reunite with their mother, took Esme and Élise to Steven Lowell's camp. By midafternoon, Dunthorpe's men were secured in the Kendal Borough Jail.

God only knew if Dunthorpe had positioned more men around Kendal and the environs. If he had, they had scattered to the four winds by now. But Sam was satisfied. Neither Dunthorpe nor Gherkin would be a threat to Élise ever again.

After they finished their business in town, Sam and Theo walked to Lowell's camp. When they arrived, everyone turned to face them, and one by one, Sam looked into the exhausted but hopeful faces of each member of his family: Trent, Luke, Mark, Theo, Esme, his mother, his father, and Élise.

All that was missing were Trent's and Luke's wives and Trent's infant son. But they were safe at Ironwood Park, and they'd all be together soon.

He went straight to Élise and wrapped his arm around her shoulder. She snuggled against him, fitting there as perfectly as ever.

They ate a dinner of a hearty stew their mother had prepared in anticipation of their arrival, and then everyone retired for the evening. Trent, Luke, Theo, Mark, and

Esme returned to the inn, but Sam and Élise chose to remain in the camp with his parents.

Élise lay tucked up against him in the bed they had made on a soft pile of leaves surrounded by tall bushes and trees to give them privacy. The clouds had cleared, and millions of stars lit the night sky overhead, but Sam couldn't take his eyes from the woman beside him.

There was still the danger from Adams, but maybe Élise was right. Maybe if they were together, they'd find a way.

There, as the stars shined down on them, he allowed the dam to break. He stopped fighting the fear of being too close to her. The fear that there would be no future for her if she was with him. The fear that he'd lose her. It was a conscious decision, allowing those fissures to spread and then crack and burst free. A rush of hope crashed through him.

They'd find a way.

He brushed his lips over the shell of her ear, the softness of her cheek, her jaw, her slender, elegant neck, the firm mounds of her breasts. He showed her his feelings for her in each tender kiss, in each reverent touch.

"You've given me such a gift, Élise," he told her between kisses.

"What's that, my Sam?" she whispered, arching her body into his, her hands stroking up and down his back.

"Life," he said. Because she had. Before Élise, he'd been an automaton, existing on food and drink but not living. There had been no enjoyment, no vitality, only his duty, and even that had been chipping away at his barren existence.

She'd given him hope and love and a reason to continue to exist. *Life.*

Sam moved between her legs. His fingers curled over the hem of her nightgown, pulling it up over her legs, then her hips. He swiped his fingers over her hip, then over her mound and between her legs. She was already slick with desire for him. He stroked her for long minutes, until she was gasping and complaining that she needed him now.

Smiling, he withdrew his hand and settled his body over her. He pushed his cock into her in one firm, heavy stroke, bending down at the same time to draw her sweet gasp into his mouth. He kissed her deeply, his tongue claiming her mouth as they became one, joining in the most basic yet most meaningful of ways.

This woman—this beautiful, vivacious woman—had become part of him. Integral to his existence. Fundamental to his next breath.

She kissed him back, and when he moved slightly to nibble the edges of her lips, she wrapped her arms around him, arched her hips to meet his next thrust, and murmured, "I love you, Sam. I'm never letting you go."

Thank God, he wanted to say. But his eyes sank shut, and sensation overwhelmed him. Pleasure coursed under his skin, through his veins, and infused his heart.

She was his. She wouldn't let him go. And he'd never let her go, either. *Never.*

Élise moaned into his mouth, her body tightening below him. Around him. Clasping him tight, a vise of pleasure. Her body shook and then squeezed him in deep, rhythmic pulses.

"I love you," he gasped out. Then the pleasure overtook him, a crashing tidal wave. He tumbled through it, his body, racked by spasms, releasing into hers.

It seemed to go on forever. He couldn't think, couldn't even breathe. He was totally lost to ecstasy.

Finally, awareness edged in. He hovered over the woman he adored, his weight resting on shaking forearms, his body shuddering, his cock still pulsing. Élise's arms and legs were wrapped around him, her body clutching him tightly everywhere. But she was looking up at him, her eyes a silvery blue in the starlight. Her expression was pure love.

He dipped his head and kissed her deeply. Seconds passed. Minutes. Hours, maybe. Finally, he pulled back. Just an inch or so, so the warmth of her exhalations still tickled his lips.

"Marry me," he said gruffly.

"Of course."

He laughed out loud as joy rushed through him, joining company with the love and hope that now resided within him. Falling to his side, he pulled her against him, holding her tight, pressing his lips into her silky blond hair.

"Élise," he murmured, his voice breaking on her name.

She wrapped her arms around him and held him as tightly as he held her, her face buried in his chest.

"*My* Sam," she whispered, and her voice shook with emotion.

It was true. He was irrevocably, permanently, uncompromisingly, forever . . . *hers*.

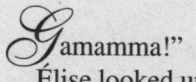

Epilogue

Ironwood Park
Eighteen months later

"Gamamma!"

Élise looked up from her hundredth botched attempt at embroidery to see little towheaded Lukas Samson burst into the room on chubby, wobbling legs. The precocious almost-two-year-old's harried nurse followed him carrying little Marie.

Sarah and Esme had been doing their best to teach Élise how to embroider, but she really was hopeless. Still, she kept trying, mainly because she liked the company. She'd grown to love her two sisters-in-law as if they were her sisters in truth.

"Is your grandmamma already here?" Sarah asked her son in surprise. She rose, wobbling a little, since she was in her sixth month carrying her second child.

"And Ganpapa!" Lukas loved to watch his "grandpapa" Steven Lowell juggle.

Sarah said that Lukas Samson had been just like his

uncle Sam as a babe, serious and contemplative. But when he'd learned to walk, he'd seemed to develop a surplus of energy, and now people were more apt to compare him to his wild uncle Luke.

Élise rose, too. She took Marie from the nurse and gazed down into her perfect little face. The babe gave her a one-toothed smile, and Élise's heart twisted. Her nine-month-old daughter was dark-eyed, dark-haired, and beautiful, just like her father.

It seemed *Dunthorpe* had been the one who was barren, not her.

Élise had told Sam she was with child two months after they'd found the dowager. That very day, Sam had received a letter from Adams requesting his presence in London.

At first Sam had refused, not wanting to go near Adams and not wanting to leave Élise. But Laurent was the one who'd delivered the missive, and he vowed on his life that only good would come of this meeting. So Sam had grudgingly gone.

A week later, he returned with the news that for the first time in his career, Adams had rescinded an order. Due to her service to England in saving the Duke of Trent from a traitor to the Crown, Élise was now a bona-fide heroine, and the Agency was no longer demanding her head on a platter.

While he was in London, Sam had also formally submitted his resignation to the Agency. It was accepted, though by all accounts the Agency never allowed its agents to retire. Élise wasn't positive, but she'd wager that the Duke of Trent had a hand in that decision.

With that heavy burden removed from their shoulders,

Sam and Élise began the happiest days of their lives. They'd married that November and set up a household at the lake cottage, dividing their time between the lake and Ironwood Park. Their marriage caused quite a stir in London, but word had also leaked that the Viscounts Dunthorpe had never been quite what they seemed, and the scandal died down quickly, eclipsed by other more significant scandals.

In any case, neither Élise nor Sam cared much about what went on in society, because they had made the decision to no longer be a part of it. They lived far enough away from it now to hear only fringes of it when they went into Kendal on market days.

Murmurs of scandal bothered them only when it upset the rest of their family, and not one of the Hawkins siblings had cared whether Élise had married too soon after her first husband had died. In fact, they'd all encouraged Sam and Élise to wed as soon as possible.

In January, little Marie was born. Sam had been petrified with worry, but although she'd never experienced such hellish pain in her entire life, the doctor told Élise it was one of the easiest births he'd ever attended.

Sam adored his daughter. Élise loved to watch him with her, how his face crumpled into a hundred lines of joy when he gazed at her.

Élise was so happy she'd been able to give him this gift, that she'd proved to him that looking toward the future with hope usually *didn't* result in horrible things happening.

She hitched Marie on her hip and followed the others out the door. "We're going to see your grandmamma and grandpapa," she murmured to her daughter in French.

Marie grinned wider. She loved it when her *maman* spoke French to her.

Élise trailed behind, watching and smiling as embraces were exchanged between family members. The dowager and Steven Lowell both looked hearty and hale. Élise and Sam had seen the older couple a few months ago, but they hadn't tarried at the cottage for long, leaving after a few days to return to their troupe of traveling players.

The dowager and Steven weren't content in one place for any length of time, and although it was difficult at times for the rest of the family to accept that, it was just one of their many odd traits. Sam had told Élise he had decided just to be happy when he did see his parents, grateful that his mother was alive, that his father existed, and that they were happy together.

Though the dowager had feared that Trent would wish her dead rather than word getting out that she'd chosen to be a gypsy over a duchess, Trent had given her his blessing to visit Ironwood Park whenever she wished.

Of course, the news that the Dowager Duchess of Trent was alive had spread through England like wildfire. When it came out that she'd married a gypsy, the gossip grew shrill and harsh, but the House of Trent fortified its walls and stood tall within them. With solidarity and sheer force of will, they'd built a fortress that would not be breached.

Loving Sarah had changed the Duke of Trent more than anyone had expected, and though he'd borne the brunt of the rumors, he'd done so with good humor, saying he'd rather have his children know their grandmother than have them think her dead just to avoid scandal.

Gossip regarding the dowager and her "unacceptable" love match still rang in Sam's and Élise's ears, even a year and a half later, even though they tried their best to ignore it. Sam had turned his primary focus to protecting his younger siblings and ensuring their futures. Indeed, Mark, Theo, and Esme had flourished over the past year and a half.

Luke and Emma appeared, looking rather flustered, from upstairs. Wryly, Élise wondered what the two of them had been doing. Luke and Emma were like two halves of a whole. They were perfect together, and perfectly happy. Thinking about how inseparable they were, she watched them embrace Luke's mother and Steven Lowell in turn.

"Ah, there is my little granddaughter!" the dowager cried, taking Marie from Élise's arms.

Marie stared at her *grandmère* with big brown eyes that filled with tears, but the moment she opened her mouth to wail, Esme snatched her away.

"Oh, stop," she chided the babe gently. "That is your grandmamma."

"She does not know me," the duchess murmured sadly.

"It's the age," Sarah said. "They all are frightened of anyone new."

"In two days, you will adore her, I promise!" Esme told Marie, who was already giggling as her aunt peppered tickling kisses across her nose.

"I hope so," the duchess said. And then she turned to Élise. She took both of her hands in her own. "You look lovely, my dear."

"Thank you."

"And darling Marie is the most beautiful creature I have ever seen."

"Her papa would agree," Luke said with a grin.

And everyone laughed, because it was true.

* * *

After dinner that night, they all gathered in the drawing room. Just the adults, since Sarah and Élise had put the children to bed before they'd sat down to eat dinner. Marie, Élise's oldest friend and their daughter's godmother, had come from the village, where they'd bought her a cottage of her own. Laurent and Carter were here, too. Both of them had been reinstated into the Agency, and though they were as busy as Sam had once been, they visited Sam and Élise often between missions.

Sam gazed at his wife, contentment washing over him. He'd almost dropped dead with surprise when she'd told him she was with child. And then he'd spent the next seven months in a state of near-constant panic, knowing that by getting her with child, he might've made the biggest mistake of his life. Terrified that he'd lose her as he'd lost Charlotte . . . and that this time he wouldn't be able to bear the pain of it.

But it hadn't happened that way. His long history of being deprived of the things he'd thought were his seemed to have ended. Because Élise and little Marie were safe, they were happy, and they were *his*. His to stay. His forever.

Élise squeezed into the seat beside him—he often found himself relaxing in chairs these days rather than standing guard near windows and doors—and he huffed, lifting her and settling her squarely on his lap. She laughed, then blushed, glancing around at his family.

His mother was gazing at them, giving them a fond smile, while Steven Lowell gazed down at her with adoration in his dark eyes.

Trent ignored them and sat beside his wife like the proper gentleman he was, keeping a discreet distance between them, though clearly that was not always the case, given her expanding belly.

Luke glanced at Sam and Élise, then chuckled and swallowed a big gulp of tea—he had maintained his pledge of abstinence from spirits for more than a year and a half. Then he wrapped a firm arm around Emma and leaned down to smack a kiss to her cheek. She laughed delightedly and looked up at him with a twinkle in her eyes.

Marie watched Élise with a look of motherly satisfaction on her face. Marie had always loved Élise, and she'd told Sam that nothing gave her such contentment as seeing her charge finally happy after all these years.

Laurent, Carter, Mark, Theo, and Esme were engaged in a lively discussion about Napoleon, who'd been exiled to Elba six months ago. They weren't paying any attention at all to Sam cuddling with his wife on the chair.

Against all odds, his younger siblings were doing well. This past summer, the whole family had attended Theo's commencement from Trinity College. Now he and Mark were pursuing the lives of gentlemen of leisure, but they were doing so in responsible ways. Mark had immersed himself in politics and was hoping to be elected to the House of Commons someday, while

Theo was talking about traveling—perhaps to India, perhaps beyond.

Esme's secret writings were still just that—a secret. Sam and Élise were the only ones who knew about her stories, and this knowledge they had about her had caused her to open up to them more than she'd ever opened up to anyone else. Élise and his sister had grown very close. For that matter, and very surprisingly to him, he and his sister had grown very close, too.

He'd trusted her enough to tell her about his position at the Agency, and Esme had told him that his life gave her about a thousand ideas for different stories. That had made him smile. Parts of him wished his life wasn't so suitable for fictional tales. But other parts of him were content that it was. If he hadn't lived the life he had, he'd never have met Élise. He'd never have found happiness or ecstasy in her arms.

He gripped her tight, and she slipped her slender arms around his neck, turning toward him with a soft smile on her face. "What are you thinking about?"

"About us," he said. "All of us."

"Ah, I have been thinking about very similar things, too. Now that your mother is back, it feels..." She trailed off.

"It feels right," he murmured, bending forward a bit so he could nuzzle her ear with his lips.

She gave a little sound of pleasure. "It is always right with you, my Sam. Always."

He closed his eyes, letting her words flow through him. "You have made me such a happy man."

"Of course I have," she said. "It is because I am very perfect for you, you know."

He chuckled, because he couldn't argue with that.

He leaned back into his chair, bringing her with him and fitting her against him. He thought of his sweet baby girl upstairs and his family chattering happily around him.

And everything was perfect.

See how Jennifer Haymore's sizzling
House of Trent series began!

❦

Please see the next page
for an excerpt from

The Duchess Hunt.

Prologue

❧

*S*arah Osborne had only lived at Ironwood Park for a few days, but she already loved it. Birds serenaded her every morning, their trilling songs greeting her through the little window in the cottage she shared with her father. Each afternoon, the sun shone brightly over the Park, spreading gentle warmth to her shoulders through the muslin of her dress as she ran across the grounds. And in the evenings, lanterns spilled golden light over the façade of the great house, which sat on a low, gentle-sloped hill and reigned like a king over the vast lands of the Duke of Trent.

If Sarah looked out the diamond-paned window of the cottage she shared with her father, she could see the house in the distance, framed by the graceful, curving white branches of two birch trees outside the cottage. She gazed at the house often throughout the day, always giving it an extra glance at night before Papa tucked her in. It stared back at her, a somber, massive sentry, and she felt safe with it watching over her. Someday, she dreamed, she might be able to draw close to it. To weave through those tall, elegant columns that lined its front. Someday, she might even be able to go inside.

But Sarah wasn't thinking of Ironwood Park right now—she was thinking about a butterfly. She dashed down the path in pursuit of the beautiful black-and-white speckled creature flitting from leaf to leaf of the box hedge that marked the outer boundary of the garden. She hiked up her skirt and chased it through the wrought-iron gate that divided the garden from the outer grounds.

Finally, the butterfly landed, seemingly spent, on a spindly branch. Sarah slowed and approached it cautiously, reaching her hand out. She let out a long breath as her finger brushed over one of the wings. The butterfly stared at her. So delicate and gentle. It seemed to nod at her, then in a soft flutter of wings, it flew away again, leaving Sarah gazing at the bush.

"Oooh," she murmured in delight. It wasn't just any bush—it was a blackberry bush. Last summer, when Mama had been so ill, Sarah had picked blackberries nearly every day. Blackberry root tea had soothed Mama's cough-weary stomach, but Sarah loved the berries' bumpy texture and burst of sweetness when she bit into one.

It was early in the season for blackberries, but among the ripening berries that loaded the bush, Sarah found a small handful that were ripe enough to eat. She gazed at her surroundings as she ate them one at a time, savoring the sweet taste edged with the slightest tinge of sour.

Not only one blackberry bush grew here—there were

many. They sprawled from the ground in no orderly fashion along the bank of a trickling stream.

Sarah turned to glance in the direction she'd come from to make sure she wasn't lost. The domes of the roof of the great house peeked through the elms, a reassuring beacon.

Her handful finished, she went back to searching for ripe berries, picking through the thorn-covered branches. She searched and picked and ate until her belly was full, light scratches from the thorns crisscrossed her arms, and the dark juice stained her hands. Looking dolefully down at her skirt, she realized blackberry juice had stained her dress as well. Papa would be displeased if he saw, but she'd scrub out the stains before he came home.

Her braid was being unruly again—strands had fallen out of it, and her dark hair wisped across her cheeks. She blew upward, trying to get them out of the way, but that didn't work, so she pushed them away and tucked them behind her ears with her dirty hands.

And then she saw the butterfly again.

At least, it looked like the same butterfly. Beautiful and enormous, its wings speckled like a sparrow's egg, it had settled on a twig deep and high inside one of the blackberry bushes.

Sarah stepped onto a fallen branch. On her tiptoes, she leaned forward, peering at it. "Don't fly away," she murmured. "Don't be afraid."

She reached out—this time not to touch it, but to catch it. She wanted to hold it, feel its delicate, spindly legs on her palm.

Just a little farther... *Crack*! The branch snapped under her feet, and she lurched forward, her hands wheeling against the air as she tried to regain her balance. But it was no use. With a crash, she tumbled headfirst into the blackberry bush, gasping as thorns grabbed at her dress and tore at her skin.

She came to a stop on her knees inside the bush, her hands clutching the thorny undergrowth.

Panting against the smart of pain, she squeezed her eyes shut as she freed one hand and used her fingers to pick the thorns from the other. Blood welled on her arms, a hot stream of it sliding down around her forearm. Each breath she released came out in a little moan of pain. Her knees hurt horribly, but she couldn't regain her balance without something to hold onto, and there was nothing to grab except painfully thorny branches.

"Can I help you, miss?"

She tried to look over her shoulder toward the voice, but a thorn scraped over her cheek, and she sucked in a breath.

It was a man's voice, she thought. A kind voice. "Yes, please, sir."

"All right. Stay still."

It seemed to take forever, but slowly, using a small dagger, he cut away the thorny branches that twisted around her. Holding her by the waist, he gently extracted her, pausing to cut away any branch that might scrape her on the way out.

Finally, he settled her onto her feet on solid, thorn-free earth. Taking a deep breath, she turned around and looked up at him.

He was a boy. A big boy—far older than she was. Freckles splashed across his nose, and dark blond hair touched his shoulders. He gazed at her, concern denting his forehead between his crystal-green eyes.

"Are you all right?"

Sarah wasn't accustomed to talking to boys. Especially handsome boys wearing breeches and fine dark wool coats. And boys whose voices were deepening with the imminent arrival of manhood.

Speechless and wide-eyed, she nodded up at him. His expression softened.

"Here." He crouched down and withdrew a handkerchief from his coat pocket. Ever so gently, he swiped the cloth over her cheek, dabbing up the blood that had welled when she'd tried to turn to him. Then he folded it and tried to clean her hands. Then he looked at her knees. Following his frowning gaze, she looked down, too.

"Oh no," she whispered.

Her skirt was rent from her knees to her feet, and her stockings, also ruined, showed through. Worse, caked blood stuck her dress to her torn stockings.

Papa would be furious.

She must have made a sound, because the boy's brow furrowed. "Does it hurt terribly?" he asked, his voice grave.

Sarah swallowed hard. "N-n-no."

The edges of his lips tilted up in a smile. "You're very brave, aren't you?"

At those words, her fear melted away. She squared her shoulders, and, standing tall, she looked directly into his green eyes. "Yes, I am."

"Where do you live?" he asked.

She pointed toward the grand domes of the roof of Ironwood Park. "There."

"Well, isn't that something? I live there, too. Can you walk?"

"Of course I can."

Side by side, they walked down the path that led toward the house. Sarah's knees hurt, and she couldn't help it—she hobbled just a little. Without a word, the boy put a firm arm around her waist, steadying her.

They passed the gardener's cottage where Sarah lived with her father and headed toward the back side of the great house itself. Sarah didn't speak, and neither did the boy. She bit her lower lip and glanced at him from the corner of her eye, watching him walk. He was tall and strong, and she liked the way the sun glinted on his hair.

But as they drew closer to the house, and it looked more and more like he actually intended to enter it, her body grew stiff. She didn't know where Papa was, but he'd be very angry if he discovered she'd ventured too close to the house. Above all, he'd stressed the importance of her staying out of the family's way. If she bothered anyone, he might lose his position.

The boy slowed as they walked beneath the shadow of the enormous house, and then he looked down at her. "Are you all right?"

"Mm hm." Her voice wasn't much more than a squeak.

He stopped altogether and pulled away from her, watching her carefully to make sure she was steady.

"What's your name?" he asked.

"Sarah."

"I'm Simon." He glanced at the back of the house, which now loomed over them, so massive and heavy she could hardly breathe, and then back to her. "Come inside and I'll make sure you're taken care of."

She licked her lips, unsure. Then she whispered, "My papa said I mustn't disturb the family."

"You won't be disturbing the family." He said it like a promise.

She gazed up at him. She didn't know why, but she trusted him completely. He could have told her he took daily walks on the surface of the moon, and she would have believed him.

He continued, "I've been a rather poor doctor, so I'd like Mrs. Hope to take a look at those cuts. She has a salve that cures scratches like those in a trice."

Sarah had no idea who Mrs. Hope was, but the scratches still hurt—they stung and ached and itched. A salve that could cure them fast worked as sure as a lure into the forbidden.

She gave a little nod.

He took her least-affected hand, gentle with her scratches. "Come, then."

He led her up the stairs and into a vast room that made her hesitant steps grind to a halt. It was the largest room she'd ever seen. Open and cold and vast, lacking furniture except for a few benches and tables lining the walls. But those were too ornate to even be called benches. Metal legs shaped into vines held enormous slabs of marble. The tables held beautiful vases and busts of important-looking men. The room was almost overwhelmingly pale—the giant stones that made the walls were of an off-white color, and the plasterwork that adorned the walls and ceiling pure white. The only color was provided by the black checks on the tiled floor, the metalwork of the benches, and the enormous gilded chandelier that hung down in the center of the room.

Sarah tilted her head up, looking past the chandelier and gallery rails at the elaborately carved ceiling—it seemed as high as heaven itself.

Simon stood beside her, and he looked up as well. She stole a glance at him, watched the considering look passing over his face—as if he were seeing the room for the first time, too.

She gripped his hand tighter. "Are you sure it's all right?" Her whisper seemed to echo in the cavernous space.

Simon shook off whatever he'd been thinking and smiled down at her. "Of course. This is the Stone Room. We don't spend much time in here. Come."

Holding her hand, he tugged her along. It seemed to take forever just to cross the vast area and reach one of the two doors that flanked a magnificent metal sculpture of a bearded, naked man and two naked boys. An enormous snake twined around their bodies. From the expressions of agony on their faces, she was sure the snake was crushing them.

He paused just in front of the door, no doubt seeing that her jaw had dropped as she stared at the statues. "Do you know the story of the Laocoön?"

She shook her head, unable to speak. She'd never heard of "Laocoön." She'd never seen a naked man or naked boys before. She'd never seen anything quite so *vicious*, either.

"Have you heard of the Trojan War?" He hesitated while she shook her head again. "Well, there was a war between Troy and the Greeks. Laocoön was the son of the Trojan King. When the Greeks tried to trick the Trojans by bringing them a gift of a giant wooden horse, Laocoön didn't trust them at all. He warned them to 'beware of Greeks bearing gifts.' But the gods were on the side of the Greeks, and Laocoön's warning made them angry. Poseidon, the god of the sea—"

"I've heard of him!" Sarah exclaimed, seizing on the one element of the story that was familiar to her. Mama had told her nighttime stories of Poseidon and the other gods.

"Well, Poseidon sent a giant serpent from the sea to kill Laocoön and his two sons. And that's what this statue represents."

Sarah stared at the statue. She had seen real death. Recently. Real death was bad enough, so why on earth would people choose to remind themselves of it on a daily basis?

Simon turned from her to gaze at the statue again. "I don't like it either," he said in a low voice.

After another minute during which they both frowned at the gruesome thing, Simon opened the door and led her into another room, this one smaller but equally magnificent. In contrast to the echoing cavernous feel of the previous room, this one was warm and colorful and full of laughter. Children's toys covered a carpet containing a design of reds and golds and browns, and a large fire crackled heartily in the enormous hearth.

The room seemed to be brimming with people, and Sarah came to a dead stop at the threshold, her heart surging to her chest. For as soon as she and Simon entered, all eyes turned to them.

Oh no, she thought with a sinking heart. Except for the woman standing in the middle of the room and the toddler she held in her arms, the room was filled with children ranging from about her age to one who looked older than Simon—all of them boys.

This was the family. It must be. Servants didn't wear satin frocks or the fine wools and linens that these boys wore. Servants never played in spaces with silk hangings and Persian carpets. Servants' toys weren't carved of ivory and adorned with gilt.

Papa was going to be so angry.

Sickness welled in Sarah's gut. Simon had led her right where her father had told her never to go. And nothing weighed on her more heavily than the idea of disappointing her father. Now that Mama was gone, he was all she had.

She tried to tug her hand from Simon's grip, but he held firm, keeping her standing beside him.

The woman who stood in the center of the room had mahogany hair speckled with gray coiled elaborately on her head, but a few curls bounced down at the sides of her face. All that lovely blue satin she wore accentuated her voluminous bosom and narrow waist. The toddler was darker-haired than his—or her, Sarah couldn't be sure—mother, with soft ringlets brushing his—or her—nape and a round, pink-cheeked face.

Sarah blinked hard. The lady of the house was a duchess. One day, she'd dreamed about meeting a duchess.

There was no doubt in Sarah's mind. Though children surrounded this woman, and she even carried one on her hip, she was no nursemaid. She was far too elegant, far too regal. She had to be the Duchess of Trent.

And here Sarah was, finally face to face with a real duchess. But Sarah was bleeding and dirty, with torn stockings and a ripped dress, and her traitorous fingers itched to stroke that blue satin that clung to this beautiful lady's body.

If it were possible to die of mortification, Sarah would have dropped dead right then and there.

The duchess looked at her hand holding Simon's— her grip had tightened as she'd realized exactly who she was facing—then smiled. "What sort of creature have you brought us this time, darling? A forest nymph?"

Sarah's brows crept toward her hairline. *Darling?*

Simon shrugged, a little chagrin seeping into his expression. "Not sure. I found her under attack from a blackberry bush by the stream."

"Come closer, child." Hitching the toddler higher on her hip, the duchess approached them. What a contradiction—such a fine lady doing something so common as adjusting a babe on her hip. Weren't such actions reserved for more lowly people, like Sarah herself?

Simon stepped forward to meet the duchess, pulling Sarah along with him.

"What's your name? Where do you come from?"

Sarah opened her mouth but no words would emerge.

"She said her name is Sarah, and she's from here," Simon supplied.

The duchess cocked a dark brow. "Is that so?"

"Down, Mama!" the toddler complained, squirming. "Down, down, down."

With a sigh, the duchess lowered the child, never taking her gaze from Sarah. The toddler stared at Sarah curiously for a moment, then ran toward the cluster of boys, but Sarah couldn't drag her eyes away from the duchess long enough to see what was happening on the other side of the room.

"I don't recall having any little girls in residence at Ironwood House," the duchess mused. "Do you, Trent?"

"No, ma'am. But I've not been home. There have been no new arrivals this summer?"

"No, only the..." The duchess's brown eyes brightened. "The new gardener. Fredericks hired him. I had naught to do with it. I'd wager she belongs to him."

Simon looked down at Sarah. "Are you the gardener's daughter?"

Biting her lip and looking down at the beautiful carpet her dirty feet had trod upon, Sarah knew she'd made a horrible mistake. She should have stopped Simon when they'd passed the gardener's cottage. She should never have come into the house. What on earth had she been thinking?

She hadn't been thinking.

"Yes," she whispered.

Firm fingers grasped her chin, forcing her to look up into the stern face of the duchess. Tears sprang to Sarah's eyes. Now was her only chance.

"Please," she whispered. Her throat opened just enough for her to speak in a croaking voice. "Please don't dismiss my papa."

The woman's eyes narrowed, and Sarah's heart sank so low, she could feel it beating in her toes.

"What has your Papa done?"

Sarah stiffened. "Nothing!"

"Then why should I dismiss him?"

Sarah's eyes darted toward Simon, pleading for help.

"Mother," he said quietly, "you're scaring her."

The duchess dropped her chin, leaving Sarah with blazing cheeks. *Mother?* Simon was one of the family, too, then. Oh, she was a royal idiot.

"I brought her here because she needs medical attention." A touch of irritability had seeped into Simon's smooth voice. "Where is Mrs. Hope?"

"I've no idea." The duchess turned away toward the group of boys. "Mark, my love, will you go find Mrs. Hope? Tell her to bring some of the salve she uses on you ragamuffins when you get a cut. Sam—run and fetch the new gardener, will you? Explain that his daughter has been injured, but do let him know it's not serious. Bring him back to the house if he wishes it."

Sarah flinched. Her father had never beaten her before, but she had committed a severe enough infraction that she was entirely deserving of a whipping. Hopefully he would wait until they had some privacy. Nothing would be more disgraceful than being beaten in front of Simon.

"Can I go with Sam, Mama?"

"Yes, Luke, but stay with him and come straight back here. Understand?"

"Yes, ma'am."

"Me too?" said the smallest of the boys. "I want to go with Sam, too, Mama."

"All right, Theo, but do stay with your brothers."

As the door swung silently shut behind the four boys, the toddler wandered back to the duchess—a girl, Sarah thought, deducing from the child's features rather than her dress. Taking her plump little hand, the duchess turned back to Sarah. "Really, child, there's no reason to be afraid. You've done nothing wrong." A hint of a smile touched her lips. "The duke said the bush attacked *you*, after all. You probably didn't even encourage it."

Slowly, as if through a bucket of thick syrup, Sarah turned to Simon. "The *duke*?" she whispered.

Not quite meeting her eyes, Simon gave a one-shouldered shrug, and Sarah's heart began to kick its way back up her body.

"I see he didn't introduce himself properly." The duchess turned on her son. "Really, darling, must you always ignore the fact that you're the duke now? It has been almost three years."

"We didn't exactly have a proper introduction. Trust me, Mother," he added dryly, "whenever I am involved in a proper introduction, the title is *never* forgotten."

The duchess stared at her son for a moment, then smiled. "Of course it is not." She held her free hand out to Sarah. "Now, come, child, and sit down. Your leg is still bleeding. It must pain you to stand upon it."

Sarah glanced at the pristine silk sofa that the duchess was gesturing to and shook her head. It was so beautiful, the deepest color of purple she had ever seen, and shining in the sunlight streaming in from the window. "Oh, no, ma'am. I can't. I'm too dirty."

"If I was afraid of a bit of dirt and blood, I'd have never been able to countenance raising one child. But I am raising six, and I assure you, you are *not* too dirty to sit upon my sofa."

Simon gave her an encouraging look. "I think you should sit."

So she took the duchess's hand and allowed the great lady to guide her to the sofa. Simon helped Sarah to settle on the sleek silk upholstery before he sat beside her, and the duchess took an elegant armchair across from them while the toddler wandered toward a pile of shiny toys in the corner of the room. Sarah studied the duchess. She looked like a beautiful fairy tale ice queen regally sitting upon her throne. That was, until she gave Sarah a smile that rivaled her son's in its kindness. "Do you like tea, Sarah? I'll ring for some."

"Um...?" She glanced at Simon for guidance.

He nodded, then winked, making her feel like she'd just exchanged some communication with him that she hadn't yet deciphered, before turning to his mother. "Some warm milk?"

Sarah looked into her lap, smiling. That did sound nice.

"Of course." The duchess rang a bell, and a dainty maid came in to take the order for a bit of warm milk from the kitchen. The maid didn't even slide a disparaging look toward Sarah, just hurried to do the duchess's bidding without comment.

When the door closed behind her, the duke and his mother looked at Sarah expectantly, and the absurdity of the situation washed over her.

She was lounging in the parlor of a duke. She'd just been offered tea, and now a duke and a duchess were gazing at her as if expecting her to begin some sort of important conversation. And here she sat, torn and bleeding, her legs dangling from the adult-sized sofa, smearing dirt and blood onto the fine silk.

Feeling a little desperate for a completely different kind of saving, Sarah glanced at the door.

"She's charming, isn't she, Simon? And lovely, too, I imagine, underneath all that grime. The best thing that's happened to us all day." The duchess made a face as if reconsidering. "Well, aside from those wretched abrasions."

Just then, the door opened, and an older woman with

fluffy white hair bustled in. Simon rose to his feet. "Mrs. Hope. Thank you for coming so quickly."

The woman curtsied. "Your Grace."

Sarah should have curtsied and said, "Your Grace," too, to both the duke and duchess, but it was too late now. She would have at least risen from the sofa, but the older lady came bustling toward her brandishing a bottle, and she shrank back against the cushions.

"Here now, little one, let's have a look at all those cuts." Mrs. Hope crouched in front of the sofa, first taking each of Sarah's arms in her gentle hands, then carefully peeling her stocking away from the worst of the scratches on her knees. "We'll have to wash them first. Binnie, hand me a towel."

Sarah hadn't noticed the young, dark-haired maid who had entered with Mrs. Hope before now. She stood at attention near the sofa holding a basin and several small white towels, one of which she handed to Mrs. Hope. Mrs. Hope finished removing Sarah's stockings and cleaned her knee, muttering about how the injuries looked horrible, but they were really quite minor, and once she'd cleaned them and applied a bit of salve, Sarah would feel as good as new. At one point, when Mrs. Hope had pulled Sarah's dress up over both her knees, she glanced up at Simon. "If she were any older, Your Grace, I'd have you leave the room."

Simon's expression didn't falter. "I found her, so I am responsible for her. I'll stay until I'm certain she'll be all right."

She gave him a shy smile. She was already all right, thanks to him. She wouldn't have ever imagined that a duke could be so kind. Or a duchess, for that matter.

Ever since she'd come to Ironwood Park with Papa and lived under the shadow of the enormous house and his dire warnings should she go anywhere near the family, she'd formed an image of the House of Trent as a group of cold, unkind aristocrats who would brush her aside like an annoying fly—if they'd even bother to look down their noses at her. But they were nothing like that. Beneath the great gabled roofs and beyond the marble and silk and gilt, they were a shockingly regular family.

One of the boys—Mark, Sarah remembered—stepped forward, cradling a steaming cup in his hands, which the duchess took and handed to Sarah after blowing a bit upon its surface. It was sweet and warm and soothing, and Sarah sipped at it and held her body as rigid as the statue of the Laocoön while Mrs. Hope applied the woodsy-smelling salve. If the Laocoön could be so still while being strangled by a gigantic serpent, then she could be still while her cuts stung and burned.

And if Simon had thought her brave, then she would be.

Just then, the door opened, and yet another servant stepped in, followed by her father. He rushed inside, then halted suddenly, drawing himself up and fumbling to remove his wide-brimmed gardener's hat as the boys tumbled in behind him.

"Your Graces." He bowed low toward Simon and his mother. "Please forgive me. My daughter—"

"Ah, you must be Mr. Osborne." The duchess rose from her chair to greet him. "Welcome to Ironwood Park. I do hope you have found its landscape to your liking."

Papa's gaze flitted to Sarah, who gave him a fearful look, but she was still trapped behind Mrs. Hope's ministrations, her leg being held down, and she couldn't move to his side despite the fact that his expression summoned her.

"Ironwood Park is an idyllic setting, Your Grace. I am honored to be employed here. The landscape is nothing less than an artistic masterpiece, and I will do my best to maintain its glory."

Sarah swallowed hard. She knew what Papa was doing. Trying to convince the duchess that despite his daughter's wayward behavior, he was determined to perform his duties well.

He was trying to keep his position. And it was Sarah's fault he had to do this.

"It *is* quite lovely, isn't it? Boys"—the duchess waved her hand toward the door as she addressed her sons— "you are excused. You may remain outdoors until dinner. Keep an eye on each other, and please try not to ruin your clothes today."

"Yes, Mama!" The four boys tumbled back out of the room, but Simon didn't move from his mother's side. He stood quietly, his shoulders straight and hands clasped behind his back. He gazed at her father with solemn green eyes, his face a mask of politeness.

The duchess smiled at Sarah's father. "The duke rescued your daughter from the throes of a blackberry bush attack." Her dark brows rose into perfect arches. "No one informed me when we took you on that you were in possession of a family, Mr. Osborne. Fredericks has been remiss. I have told him time and again that he must tell me everything about everyone who makes their home at Ironwood Park."

Papa bowed his head. "It is only Sarah and I, Your

Grace. My wife, she—died last year." Papa still couldn't talk about Mama without a catch in his voice. "I gave my assurances to Mr. Fredericks that I would keep the child out of the family's way."

The duchess waved her hand. "The more children frolicking happily about this cold and desolate place, the warmer and friendlier it becomes. And your daughter, despite her ruffian appearance, is quite the epitome of sweetness. Not to mention that this house lacks in female blood."

Simon turned to his mother. "We do have Esme," he pointed out.

The duchess laughed. "I tend to forget that my youngest is female sometimes. But that poor child—with five older brothers, she's more likely to turn into a ruffian like the rest of them than into a proper young lady."

Papa gazed at the little girl, then looked back to the duchess, clearly unsure how to respond.

"Now," the duchess said, "back to the problem of Sarah. As I told you, she suffered a brutal attack from a thorned assailant. However, the housekeeper has assured me that the damage is minor. I am relieved to report to you that the scratches are not deep and, thanks to Mrs. Hope's miraculous salve, will not scar, save the one on the knee, perhaps."

Papa gave a short nod, then cleared his throat. "My daughter has a tendency to wander. However, I can assure you that it will not happen again. She will remain in our cottage from now on." There was a note in his voice that promised future discipline, and Sarah cringed inwardly at the sound of it.

"Oh, but Mr. Osborne, it is natural for children to wander, to explore their surroundings and to discover. Especially in an unfamiliar place. I have always encouraged my children to explore to the extent of their curiosity."

Papa gaped a little at that, but then he gathered his wits and bowed his head, clutching his hat to his chest. "Nevertheless, ma'am, my daughter should not be gallivanting about the grounds as if she owned them. She will refrain from doing so henceforth."

The duchess's expression softened. "Can you truly expect a child of her age and disposition to sit in that tiny cottage of yours every day while you go about your duties? No child should be constrained so, Mr. Osborne."

Papa glanced toward Sarah again but didn't answer. Clearly he wanted to be out of this great house and back to tending his beloved bushes.

The duchess's gaze moved from Sarah to her father, an odd glint in her brown eyes. "Tell me, does Sarah know her letters?"

Papa's body jolted at the change of topic, then he straightened a little. "Why, yes, ma'am. Her mother was quite learned—she was the schoolmistress at the parish's charity school before we were married. She taught the girl to read and to write."

The duchess clasped her long-nailed hands together in front of her. "Ah! I thought there was something about the way both of you speak..." Musingly, she turned toward Sarah, who was holding out her arm to Mrs. Hope while the older woman dabbed salve over a cut on her forearm. "Would you like to continue your studies, dear?"

Unsure how to respond, Sarah glanced at Papa. The answer was yes, of course she'd love to learn more. About everything. Especially the Trojan War Simon had mentioned earlier. If Mama were still alive, Sarah would run home and beg her to tell her the story right away.

But how would Papa want her to answer?

The duchess followed her gaze. "I see she turns to you, Mr. Osborne. Well, then, did your daughter enjoy her mother's teachings?"

"She did," Papa admitted reluctantly. "Very much."

"Good!" the duchess exclaimed, clapping her hands. "It's settled, then."

Everyone stared at her, including Simon. "What's settled, Mother?" he asked.

"Starting tomorrow, Miss Sarah Osborne will join your brothers in their studies with Miss Farnshaw."

No one said a word. Sarah watched as her father's jaw slowly fell open.

And that was how a gardener's daughter ended up being educated with the offspring of a duke.

THE DISH

Where Authors Give You the Inside Scoop

♥ ♥ ♥ ♥ ♥ ♥ ♥ ♥ ♥ ♥ ♥ ♥ ♥ ♥ ♥ ♥ ♥

From the desk of Jennifer Haymore

Dear Reader,

When Lady Dunthorpe, the heroine of THE SCOUN-DREL'S SEDUCTION, came to my office, she filled the tiny room with her presence, making me look up from my computer the moment she walked in. The first thing I noticed was that she was gorgeous. Very petite, with lovely features perfectly arranged on her face. She could probably be a movie star.

"How can I help—?" I began, but she interrupted me.

"I *need* you," she declared. I could hear the smooth cadence of a French accent in her voice. "My husband has been murdered, and I've been kidnapped by a very bad blackguard…a…a *scoundrel*."

I straightened in my chair. "What? How…why?" I had about a million questions, but I couldn't seem to get them all out. "Please, my lady, sit down."

She slid into the chair opposite me.

"Now," I said, "please tell me what exactly is going on and how I can help you."

She leaned forward, her blue eyes luminous and large. "My husband—Lord Dunthorpe. He was killed. And his murderer…his murderer has captured me. I don't know what he's going to do…" She swallowed hard, looking terrified.

"Do you know who the murderer is?

She shook her head. "*Non*. But his friends call him 'Hawk.'"

Every muscle in my body went rigid. I knew only one man called Hawk. His real name was Samson Hawkins, he was the oldest brother of the House of Trent, and I'd just finished writing books about two of his brothers.

Yet maybe she wasn't talking about "my" Hawk. Sam was a hero, not a murderer. Still, I had to know.

"Is he tall and broad?" I asked her. "Very muscular?"

"*Oui* . . . yes."

"Handsome features?"

"Very."

"Dark eyes and dark hair that curls at his shoulders?"

"Yes."

"Does he have a certain . . . *intensity* about him?"

"Oh, yes, very much."

Yep, she was definitely talking about Sam Hawkins.

I sat back in my chair, stunned, mulling over all she had told me. Sam had killed her husband. He'd kidnapped her . . . and was holding her hostage . . . *Wow*.

"I need your help," she whispered urgently. "I need to be free . . ."

"Of course," I soothed.

Her desire to be free sparked an idea in my mind. Because if she truly knew Sam—knew the man inside that hard shell—perhaps she *wouldn't* want to be free of him. She was beautiful and vivacious—she'd lit up my little office when she'd walked inside. Sam had certainly already noticed this about her. Now . . . all I had to do was work a little magic—okay, I admitted to myself, a *lot* of magic, considering the fact that Sam had killed her husband—and I could bring these two together.

Sam hadn't lived a very easy life. He *so* deserved his very own happily ever after.

This would be a love match born in adversity. *Very* tricky. But if I could make it work—if I could give Lady Dunthorpe to Sam as his heroine—it would probably be the most fulfilling love story I'd ever written.

With determination to make it work, I turned my computer screen toward me and started typing away. "Tell me what happened," I told Lady Dunthorpe, "from the beginning…"

And that was how I began the story of THE SCOUNDREL'S SEDUCTION—and now that I've finished it, I'm so excited to share it with readers, because I definitely believe it's my most romantic story yet.

Please come visit me at my website, www.jennifer haymore.com, where you can share your thoughts about my books and read more about THE SCOUNDREL'S SEDUCTION and the House of Trent Series. I'd also love to see you on Twitter (@jenniferhaymore) or on Facebook (www.facebook.com/jenniferhaymore-author).

Sincerely,

Jennifer Haymore

♥   ♥

From the desk of Kristen Ashley

Dear Reader,

As a romance reader from a very young age, and a girl who never got to sleep easily so I told myself stories to get that way (all romances, of course), I had a bevy of "starts" to stories I never really finished.

Not until I finally started to tap away on my keyboard.

One of them that popped up often was of a woman alone, heading to a remote location, not feeling well, and meeting the man of her dreams who would nurse her back to health. Except, obviously (this *is* a romance), at first meeting him, she doesn't know he's the man of her dreams and decides instantly (for good reason) she doesn't like him all that much.

Therefore, I was delighted finally to get stuck in Nina and Max's story in THE GAMBLE. I'd so long wanted to start a story that way and I was thrilled I finally got to do it. I got such a kick out of seeing that first chapter unfold, their less-than-auspicious beginning, the crackling dialogue, Max's A-frame (inside and out) forming in my head.

But I had absolutely no clue about the epic journey I was about to take—murder, assault, kidnapping, suicide and rape, trust earned and tested—and amongst all this, a man and a woman falling in love.

The focus of the book is on Nina's story—oft-bitten, very shy, to the point where she's hardly living her life anymore, feels it, and knows she needs to do something about it even as she's terrified.

But whenever I read THE GAMBLE, it's Max's story that touches me. How he had so much from such a young age and lost it so tragically. How he took care of everyone around him in his mountain man way, but also was living half a life. And last, how Nina lit up his world and revived that protective, loving part of him he thought long dead.

The struggle with this, however, was Anna, the love Max lost. See, I knew her well and she was an amazing person who made Max happy. They were very much in love and neither Max (in my head) nor I wanted to give her short-shrift or make any less of the love they shared even as Max fell deeply in love with Nina.

I didn't know if this was working very well, for Nina was so very much *not* like Anna, but, at least to me, I found her quite lovable. This was good; you shouldn't try to find what you lost but simply find something that makes you happy. But still, it was important for me that the love Max shared with Anna wasn't entirely overshadowed by the love he had for Nina because Anna was in his life, she was important, and being so was part of what made him the man he turned out to be.

In a book that has a good deal of raw emotion, one line always jumps out at me and there's a reason for that. I was relieved when a friend of mine told me it was her favorite in this whole, very long book. So simple but also, by it being her favorite, it told me that I'd won that struggle.

It was Max saying to Nina, *"I see what I had with Anna*

for the gift it was but now that's gone. With this act, are you sayin', in this life that's all I get?"

In a book where grave tragedy had consistently struck many of the characters (as life often hands us our trials), I love the hope in this line. I love that Max finally comes to realize that the beauty he had and lost was not all he should expect. That he should reach out for more.

And he *does* reach out for more.

And in the end, he finds that it isn't all he would get. Being a good man and taking a gamble on a feisty woman who shows up in a snowstorm with attitude (and her sinuses hurting), he gets much, *much* more.

So I was absolutely delighted to take his journey.

Because he deserves it.

Kristen Ashley

♥ ♥ ♥ ♥ ♥ ♥ ♥ ♥ ♥ ♥ ♥ ♥ ♥ ♥

From the desk of Nina Rowan

Dear Reader,

What is the worst part of writing a historical romance? Once upon a time, I might have thought it was most difficult to unravel the plot and character motivations, but the more I write, the more I realize the truth. It's the research! And I don't mean that in a moan-and-groan-it's-homework way. I mean that the more I research for the sake of a book, the more I get flat-out distracted by all the little golden nuggets I find.

When I start researching, I tend to trawl the London Times archives, which has a searchable database that is so beautiful and easy to use that it almost makes me cry. For A DREAM OF DESIRE, I started by looking up articles about prisons and juvenile delinquency, but got quickly distracted by other things like the classified advertisements. The Times was full of ads for polka and mazurka lessons, "paper hanging" sales, tea companies, and job openings for schoolmistresses and butlers. The "prisons" search term appeared in the classifieds in an advertisement for "prisons supply of coal, meat, bread, oatmeal, barley, candles, and stockings." The ad requested that suppliers submit an application to the keeper of the prisons to be considered for the position.

I also get distracted by other articles about criminal court proceedings (a goldmine of story ideas), new laws, intelligence from overseas, and details about royal court life, like the state ball of 1845 at Buckingham Palace, which was attended by over one thousand members of the nobility and gentry and where Her Majesty and the Hereditary Grand Duke of Mecklenburgh Strelitz danced the quadrille in the ballroom, which was festooned with crimson and gold draperies and lit by a huge, cut-glass lustre.

I find that fascinating. But distractions aside, it really is within the pages of the newspapers and magazines published in the nineteenth century that the most vivid details of a story can come to life. When I first started writing A DREAM OF DESIRE, I thought surely the term "juvenile delinquent" was a historical anachronism, but it was used often in Victorian-era *Times* articles about "juvenile destitution and crime."

I've come to accept the fact that rather than being a dedicated, focused researcher, I'm more like a magpie whose attention is caught by shiny objects. But I've also learned to appreciate how much all those little tidbits of information come in handy when crafting a story—what might happen if the hero and heroine were in attendance at Her Majesty's state ball? What if the heroine was having a clumsy moment (or better yet, was distracted by the hero's rakish good looks) and tripped over the Grand Duke in the middle of the quadrille? What if she found herself face-to-face with a rather irate Queen Victoria?

Must go. I have some writing to do!

Nina Rowan

♥ ♥ ♥ ♥ ♥ ♥ ♥ ♥ ♥ ♥ ♥ ♥ ♥ ♥ ♥

From the desk of Jane Graves

Dear Reader,

I like wine. Any kind of wine. I've learned a lot about it over the years, but only because if you use any product enough, you'll end up pretty educated about it. (If I ate

147 different kinds of Little Debbie snack cakes, I'd know a lot about them, too.) I can swirl, sniff, and sip with the best of them. But the fourth S: spit? Seriously? The theory is that one should merely taste the wine without getting tipsy, but come on. Who in his right mind tastes good wine and then spits it out?

My husband and I once went to a wine tasting/competition where we took our glasses around to the various vintners' booths and received tiny tasting pours, which we were to sip, savor, and judge. By the time we sampled the offerings of about two dozen vineyards, those tiny pours added up. At first we discussed acidity, mouth feel, and finish, then thoughtfully marked our scorecards. By the end of the event, we'd lost our scorecards and were wondering if there was a frat party nearby we could crash. Okay, so maybe that spitting thing has some merit.

In BABY, IT'S YOU, the hero, Marc Cordero, runs an estate vineyard in the Texas Hill Country that has been in his family for generations. As I researched winemaking for the book, I discovered it's both a science and an art, requiring intelligence, intuition, willpower, and above all, heart. The heroine, Kari Worthington, feels Marc's pride as he looks out over the grapevine-covered hills, and she's in awe of his determination to protect his family legacy. For a flighty, free-spirited, runaway bride who's never had a place to truly call home, Cordero Vineyards and the passionate man who runs it are the things of which her dreams are made.

So next time I go to a wine tasting, I'm going to think about the myriad challenges that winemakers faced in order to present that bottle for me to enjoy. But I'm still not gonna spit.

I hope you enjoy BABY, IT'S YOU!

Jane Graves

JaneGraves.com
Twitter @JaneGraves
Facebook.com/AuthorJaneGraves

♥ ♥ ♥ ♥ ♥ ♥ ♥ ♥ ♥ ♥ ♥ ♥ ♥ ♥ ♥

From the desk of Adrianne Lee

Dear Reader,

I have a secret to confess: I'm not creative with my hands.

My mother and sister inherited an artistic gene that I did not. My mother drew a Christmas scene on the mirror over the fireplace every year. Drawings I create look as though they were done by a toddler.

My sister can wrap a present that is too pretty to open. Gifts I wrap look as though I've hired a chimpanzee and given it ten rolls of Scotch tape, though that is probably insulting to chimpanzees.

I have zero skills at flower arranging. People think I'm joking when I say that, but it's actually true. If I set out to arrange a bouquet of my favorite blooms, by the time I'm done, I end up with two-inch stems. And if a food item needs to look as appealing as it tastes, I'm in trouble.

Therefore, when I set out to write the Big Sky Pie series, I had to imagine pastry chefs with the skills of sculptors, who create masterpieces, not with clay, but with pie dough. Molly McCoy is at loose ends after the sudden death of her husband. She has always dreamed of opening her own shop, a venue to sell her blue-ribbon pies, and she decides life is too short to not act now. But just as her dream is about to become a reality, Molly suffers a life-threatening health crisis. Worrying about the pie shop might be the end of her—if her son and his about-to-be-ex-wife don't step up and take over.

When my mother passed away unexpectedly, I was thrown off kilter so badly I lost forty pounds in six weeks. So I really understood how Quint McCoy could lose himself after his beloved dad died suddenly. Up to that point, Quint had always had a sense of who he was and what he wanted. He just didn't understand that work wasn't as important as family until after his grief caused him to push away everyone he loved.

Callee had grown up unable to trust that anyone would ever love her. Quint's rejection proved her right. She didn't fight for their marriage; she just went along with his request for a divorce. And that divorce is almost final when Molly collapses. She tricks Callee into agreeing to work with Quint to open her pie shop, but can this sizzling hot couple work together without their emotions setting flame to the Big Sky Pie kitchen?

I hope you'll enjoy DELECTABLE, the first book in my Big Sky Pie series. All of the stories are set in northwest Montana near Glacier Park, an area where I vacationed every summer for over thirty years. Each of the books is about someone connected with the pie shop in one way or another. So come meet the couples whose relationships grow from half-baked into a love that will melt your heart. Also, each book offers a different delectable pie recipe. What more could you want?

Adrianne Lee